I0772319

PARADISE

A Zombie Apocalypse Saga, Volume 1

Matthew Stracco

FOREWORD

I FEEL AN IMPENDING finality as I write these words. Knowing that at some point another review and revision of these pages will not be possible weighs heavily on me. There are feelings of relief for the conclusion of a very long and emotionally taxing journey. Equally so is the mixture of hope and fear for every word to be as perfect and meaningful as possible. I have come to the end of many adventures only to look back and struggle to understand how I had the resilience to complete the journey. Writing this book has been no different. In many ways it has been my most difficult and significant undertaking.

I am reminded of a discussion some years ago with Ric Wynn and the distinction he made between getting what you want and getting what you want the way you want it. As the sun sets on this endeavor and I prepare to check writing this novel off my bucket list, I can honestly say I not only got what I wanted...I got what I wanted the way I wanted it. If there is a more complete feeling in this life I have yet to experience it.

The world you are about to enter as you read these pages; was not informed by politics or a pro or anti-war sentiment. In truth, at its core it was not intended as a survival horror story. What you are about to read was always to be a story about loyalty, love and the bonds of friendship and brotherhood. The genesis of this story came in the form of an extremely vivid dream in the spring of 1989, which is recounted at the beginning of Chapter 50. As the greater story took shape around these themes, my intention was to depict how the bonds shared by the characters could be tested and withstand even the most severe of conditions.

Many of the main characters and locations depicted within this world were inspired by real people and places. I chose the concept of a zombie apocalypse as the mechanism best suited to create this world around because that was an area of considerable interest for both my brother Christian and I. From watching the films of George A. Romero to reading, I Am Legend by Richard Matheson, our fascination with the concept of the undead grew until I felt it was the perfect vehicle with which to tell this story.

The creation of this world in the pages that follow has been a long strange journey, but a labor of love none the less. The original outline was developed to overcome stagnation and writer's block while on a plane to Alaska in July 2006. As the characters developed and story took shape, that initial 15-chapter outline evolved into what you now have before you.

So, I thank you dear reader for opening this book. My hope is that you will find within its pages a story whose themes in some way speak to you. I hope that you enjoy the world of 'PARADISE' as much as I enjoyed creating it!

DEDICATION

THIS STORY IS DEDICATED to the life and memory of my brother Christian. He was taken from us far too soon. His passing left a void that will never be filled, a sadness that is struggled with daily and a wonderment about all that should have been. It was impossible during his eulogy as it is now to do justice to the man he was, to all that his life meant and how positively he impacted so many. A better friend, fiercer ally, more talented artist, kinder soul, and speaker of truth, I may never know. Those who knew him loved him and those who loved him miss him more than words can ever say. I have faith that what follows this life will find us together again. Until that day dear brother, rest easy and know that...we'll take care of it.

Loss is a difficult thing to fully appreciate until you go through it. Even those who experience the same tragedy may view, process, and grieve it differently. Loss can cripple you. Loss can make you question the world and your place in it. Loss can rip happiness and joy from you like nothing else.

Even after all the sorrow, anger and hurt, loss can somehow motivate. Loss can drive you to create and achieve what had otherwise seemed impossible. Loss can push you beyond what you believed your limits to be. The journey may be lonelier and the perils of the world may appear scarier, but there is solace to be garnered in completing a goal your loved one would have been with you for. The creation of this book has been that kind of journey. A promise made in another time...and with its completion now kept.

The author would also like to thank:

Michael W. Stracco and William E. Lindaberry for being my heroes.

Wagner, Lucia & Rockwell, who make me remember what I miss about being young.

Jeff, Aaron, Matt Chico, Kevin, Rob & Paul, who stood with me through good times and carried me through bad. Thank you for your friendship and the unforgettable adventures.

Tim, Kathleen, Patrick, Beth, Robyn & Christie, who Christian, Giovanni and I were so fortunate to share so many wonderful memories.

Kelly Battersby for her honesty, integrity, and willingness to edit and improve the overall story.

Jesse Glass – for the most beautiful cover photo and her exceptional talents.

Special thanks to the late George A. Romero for being a masterful story teller and Godfather of the modern Zombie horror genre.

CONTENTS

CHAPTER 1

where will you be when the end begins?

L ATE MAY WAS A visually stunning period in the Garden State. Trees and flowers were in full bloom and the air had a sweetness about it as spring prepared to surrender to summer. The heavy winds and torrential rain which hammered the east coast for almost a week had finally subsided. The dark ominous cloud cover had given way to sparse whitish gray clouds spread across an otherwise pastel blue sky. Mist rose from the saturated ground through soft beams of sunlight which escaped from breaks in the clouds. The month started very cool and rainy, but with the first of June less than a week away it seemed as if the weather was finally on its way to warming up.

It was barely 6:30 a.m. as the vehicles on the north bound side of Route 25 rolled slowly along. A multi-car accident less than a mile north slowed the morning commute to a crawl. The highway was a montage of New Jersey radio stations. From vehicle to vehicle, talk radio hosts provided social commentary on politics and reported breaking news. While on other stations DJs announced the artist of the next song on their play list and shock jocks commented on the latest celebrity scandals.

The cars, what few of them there were, moved quickly along the south bound side of the highway. While across the median emergency services dispatched to the scene of the accident halted traffic in the two north bound lanes. Vehicles stopped behind the mile marker 18 placard were in view of the large green metal sign which read "Omega Arsenal U.S. Army Main Entrance."

"Copy that," Sergeant Slocum called into the handset of the Motorola radio clipped to his dark blue uniform shirt. "Look alive boys!" He called to the three young officers stationed at the main gate with him.

Traffic through the two inbound lanes at the main gate was minimal at that time of the morning. The vehicles that had navigated their way through the maze of Jersey barriers all bore Department of Defense decals. Bleary eyed personnel more concerned with drinking coffee waited indifferently to show their I.D. and have their vehicle searched before passing through the checkpoint and onto the arsenal.

"What's going on Sarge?" Officer Evans asked as he yawned and rubbed his eyes. Short in stature with lean features, he was the newest of the three young officers. He had been out of the academy less than a month and not accustomed to the shift which began several hours earlier. "Everything ok?"

"Get it together Evans!" Sgt. Slocum ordered. Silver hair protruded from the edges of his dark blue hat with the Omega Arsenal Police Department logo on it. He had been a career infantryman in the Army, before joining the federal police force. Sgt. Slocum was nearing the end of a long career but didn't see that as an excuse to cut the officers under his command any slack. "You're a professional now. Act like it!"

"Easy Sarge," Officer Gonzalez encouraged. The olive-skinned Columbian officer smiled as the attractive red-haired woman behind the wheel of the white Jeep wrangler handed him her ID card.

"There's an accident just north of here," Sgt. Slocum announced. "Emergency services have been deployed. We'll be operating with minimal support until they're finished."

"We're always operating with minimal support," Officer Collins said with a shrug. He clasped his hands around the back of his neck and pulled his head forward before pressing his palms against his round face. "What does it matter anyway? Nothing ever happens here."

Officer Gonzalez looked at the front and back of the ID card before handing it back to the woman. "Thank you," he said with a nod as he waved her through the checkpoint. "Evans is a good kid, Sarge. He's just getting adjusted to the early shift, that's all."

"Get out Evans...get out before you get adjusted and it's too late," Officer Collins warned. "I'm up before dawn, standing for hours wondering why my back is sore and questioning the life decisions that brought me here." He continued as his eyes opened wide. "It's a cautionary tale my friend. I suggest you heed the warning and run while you can."

"Don't listen to him Evans," Officer Gonzalez said as he swiped his hand across the air. "You've got everything you could ever want right here. Plenty of fresh air, all manner of wildlife to enjoy and hard-fought life lessons you didn't know you needed from the Sarge."

"In my day..." Sgt. Slocum began before being interrupted by laughter from Officer Gonzalez and Officer Collins.

"Come on Sarge," Officer Gonzalez said as he shook his head. "Just because you crossed the Delaware with General Washington..."

"That's enough!" Sgt. Slocum barked as he tugged at the brim of his hat. He was no stranger to being ribbed but during duty hours with civilians present was completely off limits as far as he was concerned. "Cut the bullshit! We have a job to do."

A car horn blared just beyond the main gate checkpoint which drew Officer Evans attention, "What's going on?" He asked as he placed the silver travel mug on the concrete barrier next to him and turned to look back. "Hey Sarge..."

"Probably just deer running across the road again," Officer Collins offered without looking back. "That or oversized turkeys...ugly prehistoric looking things...yeah, probably just oversized turkeys."

"Hey Sarge!" Officer Evans repeated more forcefully. "I think you need to take a look at this."

"What is it Evans?" Sgt. Slocum asked as he held up his hand to stop the next car in line.

"Sarge," Officer Evans repeated with apprehension in his voice.

"Easy Evans," Sgt. Slocum said as he turned to see what had the young officer spooked, "What the?" He questioned as he squinted his eyes. "Officer Gonzalez, Officer Collins, hold the line. No more cars through." He ordered as he turned and moved towards the edge of the checkpoint.

Some of the personnel stopped in and amongst the Jersey barriers awaiting their turn tapped nervously on their steering wheels and glanced at their watches. Others cursed the delay and the time they would have to make up at the end of their tour. Some sang along with their radios. While others sipped hot coffee and tried to eat breakfast, careful not to get to much of what they were eating on themselves. A few even managed to enjoy the gentle breeze which had picked up.

"What kind of bullshit is this?" Sgt. Slocum asked. He stood at the end of the check point with his hands on his hips and watched as four soldiers staggered down the center of the road. They were less than 100 yards from the front gate and dressed for PT. "Officer Evans!"

"Yes, Sergeant," Officer Evans answered as he hurried to where Sgt. Slocum stood.

"Hustle out there and tell those jokers to get out of the road," Sgt. Slocum ordered. "I don't know what their shirts are covered in but from here they look like they've been up all-night partying. The Army still has standards. The last thing these lazy civilians need to see is green suiters not holding themselves to a proper standard."

"What's going on back there?" Officer Gonzalez called as the line of cars at the front gate increased.

"Gonzalez, you just hold your position," Sgt. Slocum instructed. He turned his attention back to Officer Evans. "They know better than to be this close to the main gate and in the middle of the road no less. Tell them to report back to their C.O. or I'll contact the Garrison Commander myself."

"Roger that Sarge," Officer Evans answered with a nod. He took off in a sprint towards the four soldiers.

"Everything ok back there Sarge?" Officer Collins asked as he glanced back.

"Just fine, Collins," Sgt. Slocum answered. He turned back and looked at his officers. "Control your lane and do your job. I've got this under control."

It was not unusual to see soldiers running around designated sections of the arsenal as part of their daily physical training requirements. The front gate was off limits due to how remote it was in relation to the rest of the arsenal, unless approved by the Garrison

Commander. With no notification through the chain of command and a group of four instead of the required twelve soldiers, Sgt. Slocum was intent to find out what was going on and retake control of his sector.

As the soldiers neared their disheveled appearance gave Officer Evans pause, "Sarge." He called. "Sarge, something's going on."

"What?" Sgt. Slocum called back. From his remove, he was unable to discern what had the young officer so concerned. "Get those idiots out of the road!"

Officer Evans turned and looked over the gaunt faces as they approached him, "I need you four off the road." He called as he held his hands over his head. The soldiers didn't acknowledge his instruction but instead continued towards him. "I need you off the road now!"

"Sarge, what are we doing here?" Officer Collins asked. "These lines are getting long." He said as he motioned to the line of cars that stretched almost back to the highway.

"Hold your position!" Sgt. Slocum barked. His face reddened as a car horn blared. "Officer Collins, control your lane until we get this situation resolved."

"Roger that Sergeant," Officer Collins answered. He moved swiftly along the row of cars to address the impatient young man behind the wheel of the red sports car who continued to press the horn. Officer Collins placed his right hand on his holster and raised his left hand. "That's enough! We're dealing with a situation and that isn't helping."

The young driver smirked as he let go of the wheel and held both hands up. He waited for Officer Collins to turn and walk away before he ran his hands through his thick blond hair and mumbled, "Asshole."

Officer Evans shuddered as he came within several yards of the soldiers, "What the fuck is going on?" He said to himself. He felt his chest tighten and hands tremble as he realized the burgundy stains on their gray shirts appeared bright red against their neon yellow PT belts. "You guys realize Halloween is still a few months away...right?" He said nervously as he glanced back towards Sgt. Slocum.

The soldiers didn't answer. They just continued to move awkwardly towards the young officer. Their skin was pale and faces drawn. Dark circles encompassed their blood shot eyes. Each had at least one open wound visible. It looked as though the flesh had been torn from their bodies.

"Evans, Goddammit!" Sgt. Slocum shouted. "Get them off the road. We've got cars backed up to the highway!"

Panicked, Officer Evans turned around, "Sarge, I think you need to see this!"

Sgt. Slocum cupped his hands around the brim of his hat, "Evans, what's the problem?"

"Sarge!" Officer Gonzalez called as several impatient drivers blew their horns simultaneously. "We've got a problem here."

"Gonzalez, Goddammit!" Sgt. Slocum shouted frustratedly as he turned around. "Control your lane!"

"Sarge!" Officer Evans called in a high-pitched panicked voice. "Sarge, I think we need an ambulance..."

"What?" Sgt. Slocum snarled as he turned back to face Officer Evans. "What the fuck are you talking about?"

"Sarge, these guys are in bad..." Officer Evans began just as the soldiers descended on him. They grabbed hold of his shirt and arms. "What are you..." He screamed as he tried to pull away from them. "NO! Get off me...get off me!"

"LET HIM GO!" Sgt. Slocum ordered as his right hand moved instinctively to the grip of the M17 pistol.

"HELP!" Officer Evans screamed as he struggled to pull free. "Help me..." He cried as teeth sunk into either side of his neck.

"Sarge, what the fuck?" Officer Gonzalez shouted when he heard Officer Evans cries.

"Oh, my God!" Sgt. Slocum uttered to himself. He watched in shock and horror as two of the soldiers ripped flesh from either side of Officer Evans throat.

Dark red blood jettisoned from the severed carotid arteries as Officer Evans let out a gurgled scream. His eyes opened wide as he fully realized what was happening. Two of the soldiers followed him to the ground as his legs buckled. They continued to ravage his limp body as the last remnants of life slipped painfully away.

"SARGE?" Officer Gonzalez called.

"Stay where you are!" Sgt. Slocum shouted to his officers without looking back.

"What the fuck is going on back there?" Officer Collins called.

"I don't know," Officer Gonzalez answered. "If this is a prank, I'm not laughing." He added as he turned back to Sgt. Slocum. "Sarge, what's going on?"

"Hold the line!" Sgt. Slocum ordered as he drew the M17 pistol from the polymer holster on his belt. He brought the pistol up to the ready position and moved hastily towards the two soldiers who were still upright and moving towards him.

Officer Evans body gave a final twitch and became still. The two soldiers who had cannibalized him appeared to lose interest. Their faces dripped with blood as they awkwardly got to their feet and set out to join their cohorts who were less than ten yards away from Sgt. Slocum.

"On the ground!" Sgt. Slocum ordered as he neared the soldiers. His heart raced as the ashen gray discoloration of their skin became evident. Their mouths hung open and exposed broken blood-stained teeth and for the first time he heard their haunting moans. "I said...I said on the ground now!"

The soldiers ignored the order. Their hollow lifeless eyes fixated on the Sergeant as their outstretched arms reached unforgivingly for him.

Sgt. Slocum issued a desperate second order, "Get on the fucking ground...NOW!" That order also went ignored. Less than five yards separated them. Sgt. Slocum gritted his teeth in frustration. Horrified at his hesitation that cost Officer Evans his life, the wide-eyed Sergeant exhaled and opened fire on the soldiers.

The distinct pop of 9mm rounds shattered any remnants of morning calm. Hot led tore through the torsos and chests of the soldiers. The impact of the rounds failed to stop them. They slowed only momentarily before continuing their advance toward the fear-stricken Sergeant.

"What the fuck is going on?" Officer Collins shouted. The gunfire startled people awaiting entrance to the arsenal to attention. Car horns blared and tires screeched. "Call somebody...call somebody!"

"Call who?" Officer Gonzalez shouted as he looked around panicked. "Emergency services are off post responding to that fucking accident!"

"Gonzalez...Collins!" Sgt. Slocum screamed as he ejected the empty magazine from his pistol. He quickly retrieved a loaded magazine from the pouch on his belt, slammed it into the mag well depressed the slide stop lever and continued firing. "Gonzalez...Collins!"

"Hang on Sarge! We're coming!" Officer Gonzalez called as he drew his pistol. "Come on Collins!"

The squeal of car tires was quickly followed by the unmistakable sound of metal as it impacted against metal. Vehicles collied with one another as desperate drivers attempted to flee the maze of Jersey barriers. Punctured radiators sent a foul-smelling cloud of white smoke into the air as antifreeze poured out over racing engines.

"Fuck that!" Officer Collins replied as he pointed to a larger group of soldiers who staggered down the long stretch of road towards the main gate. Their appearance was more ghoulish than the first four. "We're outnumbered! We need to get to out of here!"

"No...not like this!" Sgt. Slocum pleaded. He watched in desperate horror as his blood sprayed across the face of his attacker.

"But the Sarge!" Officer Gonzalez called. "We've got to help the Sarge!"

Unable to stop their advance, Sgt. Slocum was quickly overtaken, "AHHHHH!" He screamed as the flesh was ripped from his face and neck. The pistol dropped from his hand and slapped against the asphalt before his flailing body followed.

"Fuck the Sarge!" Officer Collins said coldly as he took off running. "It's every man for himself!"

A panicked middle age man with a white beard and gray suit stumbled out of his disabled vehicle. He stood trembling as he fumbled with his cell phone, "Oh, God please." He pleaded as he tried to enter the code and unlock the phone. "PLEASE!" He screamed as he frantically dialed 911 and brought the phone to his ear.

"9-1-1, what is your emergency?" The operator asked calmly.

"WE NEED HELP!" The bearded man cried just as a fleeing sedan slammed into his legs. "AHHHH!" He cried as the phone was ejected from his hand and his body was thrown several feet. His head bounced off the asphalt before his body slid to a stop. A bright red puddle pooled under what was left of his face.

Like a biblical plague, the soldiers descended on the people trapped within the confines of the checkpoint. They forced their way into vehicles and pulled terrified commuters to an agonizing end.

"You fucking coward!" Officer Gonzalez shouted as Officer Collins ran for the visitor's center. The old brick building had thick steel doors and roll down gate that could be deployed in an emergency. Panicked, he drew his pistol and struggled to steady himself. "There are people here who need our help...you fucking coward!"

A young brown-haired woman in a cream-colored blouse and black skirt was pulled from the broken driver side window of her green Toyota Corolla; shards of broken window shredded her hamstrings and calves. Her legs flailed as she screeched, "Help me please!"

Officer Gonzalez's ears rang as he moved the pistol's front site post from target to target and fired, "What the fuck?" He shrieked to himself as the center mass hits had no discernable effect. "They're not going down...they're not going down!"

The young woman's cries were reduced to a screeching gasp as her attacker tore flesh and muscle from her throat with his teeth, "No...Ahhh!" There was an eruption of crimson which soaked the woman's face and blouse. Her hazel eyes rolled back as her body shuttered and went limp.

The sound of gun shots continued, so too did that of screeching tires and agony filled screams. The vehicles caught within the Jersey barriers were easy prey for the unrelenting soldiers.

"Please!" The middle-aged woman in the blue BMW screamed as she clamped her hand tightly over the gaping wound on her neck. She struggled to free herself from her attacker who still had hold of her blood-soaked blonde hair as her corroded artery jettisoned blood across the car's tan interior. "Help, God please!" She cried as she clung desperately to the steering wheel. With a final deliberate action, she slammed her foot on the gas, the engine raced and the car lunged forward and slammed loudly against the concrete barrier.

"Fuck!" Officer Gonzalez shouted as the slide of his M17 locked opened. He grabbed for the magazine pouches on his belt only to find them empty. "Oh, God no!"

Many of the people trapped within the Jersey barrier maze exited their vehicles and took their chances on foot. Several followed Officer Collins as he raced towards the visitor's center. Others ran frantically back towards the highway.

Those too scared to leave their vehicles locked the doors and began to pray. Several desperately tried to hide beneath their dashboards in an effort not to be seen.

"Fuck you!" Officer Gonzalez shouted as desperation overtook him and he threw his empty pistol at the advancing horde. He pulled the stainless steel Spyderco Police knife from where it was clipped to the pocket of his uniform pants. Officer Gonzalez let out a deep guttural battle cry as he lunged at his assailants, "UHHHHH!" The serrated blade sliced easily through the ashen flesh of his attackers. His cry was reduced to an excruciating whimper as he was quickly overtaken.

It took only moments for things at the main gate to devolve into chaos. Terrified people ran. Despondent cries of the dying and low ominous moans of the soldiers echoed across open ground and decimated the illusion of serenity which had existed only minutes earlier. Wrecked vehicles and bodies littered the check point and created a nightmarish scene. The bright crimson of pooled blood glistened in the morning sunlight.

Motorists on the north bound side of the highway, unaware of what was coming, went about their morning routine, and waited for the accident ahead to be cleared. Carnage spilled from the entrance of the arsenal, and quickly looked as if the gates of hell opened.

CHAPTER 2

small town america revisited

HOME WAS A SLEEPY little town tucked away in the hills of northern New Jersey. It had all the hallmarks of the greatest generation and a bygone era. The town resembled something borrowed from a Norman Rockwell painting or the pages of the Saturday Evening Post. It was the kind of town where everyone knew each other and people didn't feel the need to lock their doors, even at night. It was a place people returned to after college to start a family and homes were passed down from generation to generation.

Several streets from the town square with its white gazebo, wrought iron benches topped with dark cherry stained wood and four-sided pewter clock which kept perfect time, two brothers occupied the oldest house on their street. Constructed after the first world war the steep peaked roof was covered with green shingles. The sides and rear of the house were covered with a thick sturdy aluminum siding which was no longer manufactured. The brilliant white of its original coloring long since faded to a dull flat white that showed every scratch and dent. The front of the home was covered in rustic stone which had been excavated from the hill behind the house and set carefully in place by their great uncle decades earlier.

"You sure you don't want anything?" Matt asked as he entered the living room. His socks made a soft rubbing sound against the thick faded blue carpet as he walked. "Juice or water or something?"

"No," Christian answered from where he lay. His large frame was stretched out on the brown couch which had the look of distressed leather against the wall. His left hand was partially tucked into the waist band of his gray sweat pants as he kept it pressed against his stomach. "I'm good."

"You sure?" Matt asked as he twisted his head from side to side until it released an audible crack. He set the black ceramic coffee mug down on the coaster next to the lamp on the small end table near the front door. "I can whip you up some scrambled eggs and toast."

"I said, no," Christian repeated firmly without moving. He covered his eyes with his right hand and used his middle finger and thumb to apply pressure to his temples. "I don't want anything."

"Alright," Matt acknowledged with a nod. "If you change your mind," he offered. The old tan recliner creaked as he took a seat across from his younger brother.

Christian didn't respond. His body stiffened as he twisted from side to side to get the pain in his abdomen to subside.

The room was quiet except for the faint sound of the antique clock as the gears ticked away in the other room. Sunlight streamed through the living room as a gentle breeze carried warm morning air through the open windows.

"Did they call you back?" Matt asked as he watched steam rise from the hot coffee in the mug.

"They called," Christian answered as he motioned to the iPhone on the coffee table next to him.

"What'd the doctor say?" Matt asked as he held the mug in front of his face and inhaled deeply. He closed his eyes and anticipated how good the first sip of morning coffee would taste.

"I don't know," Christian said as he tugged at the collar of his white t-shirt. "Nothing really."

"What do you mean nothing really?" Matt asked before taking his first sip from the steaming mug. "What did he say?"

"What doctors say I guess," Christian answered as his body twisted against the cushions of the couch again.

"Well, what was that?" Matt inquired as he tried not to sound pushy.

Christian's right hand dropped away from his face. He opened his eyes and blinked several times as he stared at the ceiling, "Blood work, test results, more meds, different meds. That kind of bullshit." He said before letting out a deep exhale.

"Ok," Matt said as he bit down on his bottom lip. He tugged at the collar of his black t-shirt. "What's the prognosis? He expects things to improve...right?"

Christian didn't speak immediately. He clenched his jaw as he tucked his bare feet under the throw pillow at the other end of the couch, "Things could improve, or they could get worse. It could go into remission never to return or it could come screaming back at some point."

"That's it?" Matt asked as he tapped his fingers frustratedly against the top of the end table next to the recliner. He tried to slow his breathing as he felt his face redden. "What kind of fucking doctor is this? That isn't a prognosis...that's spaghetti against the wall."

"Modern fucking medicine for you," Christian said through clenched teeth. He rubbed his forehead before running his hand through his thick red hair. "Modern fucking medicine."

"What about the medication?" Matt asked. "I thought they were trying you on some new stuff."

"Yeah," Christian answered. "That's still the plan. We're going to try some different meds and dosages and see if that makes more of a difference."

"Did he have anything else for you?" Matt asked as he ran his index finger around the rim of the mug. "Different medication, is that the only course of action he suggested?"

"I don't want to talk about this right now. I just want to rest," Christian said as he turned his head to look at his brother. "What are you doing?"

"What do you mean?" Matt asked as he took another sip of coffee.

"I mean blue jeans and a black t-shirt isn't exactly college attire," Christian said as his eyes narrowed. "Don't you have a class to teach?"

"No," Matt said with a slight shake of his head. "Not today."

"What do you mean not today?" Christian asked in a firmer tone.

"They've got someone to cover my course load," Matt explained as his gaze dropped to the floor. He pursed his lips and used his foot to push the pair of black Asics sneakers further under the end table.

"What do you mean?" Christian asked as he propped himself up on his right elbow and glared at his older brother. "For how long?"

"For the rest of the semester," Matt answered as matter-of-fact as possible.

"Rest of the semester?" Christian questioned. "What precipitated this?"

"I took a leave of absence," Matt explained before taking another sip. "No big deal. Nothing to worry about."

"You realize, counting the summer semester that's almost twelve weeks?" Christian asked rhetorically as he forced himself to sit up. He took the bottle of orange Gatorade from where it sat on the coffee table unscrewed the cap and took a long drink.

"Yes, I know how much time it is."

"Final exams for this semester?" Christian asked as he tightened the cap on the top of the bottle and returned it to the table in front of him. "What about those?"

"Submitted already," Matt said as he ran his left hand over his clean-shaven face. "Like I said, it's just a leave of absence."

"What about the fall?" Christian asked. "Are you still going to have a job?"

"Yes," Matt answered. He ran his hands anxiously through his short blondish brown hair. "I will still have a job in the fall."

"Why?" Christian asked with considerable concern in his voice. "This is going to affect you getting tenure. Why take a leave of absence? It's only your second-year teaching."

Matt paused for a moment. He finished what was left of the coffee and returned the mug to the coaster on the end table, "To keep an eye on you." He admitted. "At least until you start getting better. The doc said it could go into remission. That's got to be just around the corner."

"Remission, hmmm," Christian said as he shook his head. "Fucking doctors..."

Matt didn't say anything. He just gave a slight nod and waited to see what his brother's reaction was going to be.

Christian was quiet for a moment as he rubbed his eyes, "What about going back in the fall?"

"What about it?" Matt questioned.

"Are you actually going to go back in the fall?" Christian pressed.

"We'll play it by ear," Matt said. "Let's not worry about that right now. Let's just focus on getting you well."

"No job means no pay check," Christian said as he leveled his gaze at his brother.

"I know," Matt acknowledged. "Let me worry about that."

"What about your place?" Christian asked.

"I've got the rent covered," Matt assured him. "I plan to be here most days but I can bounce back over there if I need to. It's just the other end of town."

Christian shook his head and tried to understand his brother's thinking, "You worked so hard to get where you are."

"Yes, I did," Matt said with a nod. "But some things are worth more than career aspirations."

Christian's body straightened and his head cocked to one side as his brother's comment caught him off guard, "Yes, some things are."

Things went quiet again as the brothers grinned and nodded at each other. They had long since lost count of how many conversations had taken place between them over the years in this very room. The breeze subsided for the moment and the only sound was the ticking clock as it marked the passage of time.

Finally, Matt conceded and changed the subject, "Did she call to check up on you?"

"Who?" Christian asked as he returned his left hand to the front of his stomach.

"Mother of the year," Matt said with a bitter smirk.

"You could refer to her as mom if you wanted," Christian offered.

"Sure, I could," Matt said as he wrapped his fingers around the handle. He tipped the mug towards him in hopes of finding more coffee. "When she starts acting like a mother instead of an entitled teenager, maybe I will. Until then..."

"I wouldn't hold my breath on that one," Christian said as he tipped his head back against the couch. "Then again...hell could freeze over."

"That it could," Matt scoffed. "That it could."

"She did not," Christian said as he reached again for the bottle of Gatorade. "She'll be gone for another two weeks. I don't expect to hear from her until she gets back."

Matt shook his head, "What about Giovanni?"

"Baby brother?" Christian questioned as his face contorted in pain. "Yesterday. Haven't heard from him today yet. He's probably in class right about now. I'm sure he'll call later." He added

"Is he still with..." Matt began.

"Heather?" Christian questioned as he finished his brother's question. "Yes, he is."

"Love birds," Matt cooed jokingly.

Christian smiled, "Don't be surprised if they end up married."

"Married?" Matt questioned.

"He's a smitten kitten, our baby brother," Christian said as he ran his hands over his face and rubbed his eyes. "I could see the two of them settling down after college, maybe starting their own P.T. practice. Three or four kids."

Matt laughed, "Baby brother a dad...yeah, I can picture that."

"I think he'd be a good dad," Christian said as his body stiffened against the back of the couch. He closed his eyes and pressed the palm of his hand against his stomach. "Oh...fuck."

"You'll feel better tomorrow," Matt offered.

"You keep saying that," Christian reminded his brother. His face reddened as he tipped his back.

"I know I do," Matt said as he rubbed his eyes. He hated to see his younger brother in pain. The worst part by far was his inability to help. "That's because I believe it."

"And why's that?" Christian asked as he pressed his palms against his temples.

Matt let his gaze wander around the room for a moment, "Tomorrow may be the best day either of us has ever lived…all we have to do is get to it."

"Forget teaching," Christian teased as he got slowly to his feet. "You should write greeting cards."

Matt laughed, "I'll keep that in mind if I'm ever in the market for a career change."

"Yeah, you do that," Christian said as he moved towards the doorway. "I'm going to take a shower."

Matt looked at the Garmin watch around his left wrist, "Why now?"

"Because I've been laying on this couch for two days," Christian said as he turned back to look at his brother. "And I stink."

"Can't argue with that."

"Did you call her yet?" Christian asked as he paused in the doorway. He used his left hand to steady himself.

It was not lost on Matt that his brother just used his own tactic against him, "No, not yet." He answered as he brought his gaze up to the ceiling.

"What are you waiting for?" Christian demanded. "She's all you've been talking about and I've been trapped on the couch forced to listen to you lament."

"You haven't been trapped on the couch," Matt insisted.

"Never mind that," Christian said playfully. "Just answer the question. Why haven't you called her?"

"I don't know," Matt said with a shrug, "I messed things up...overreacted. She's not going to want to talk to me."

"You don't know that," Christian said sternly. "You've got needs and insecurities...congratulations you're human."

Matt chuckled uncomfortably as he tugged at the sleeves of his black t-shirt, "Is that supposed to make me feel better?"

Christian stepped back into the living room and leered at his older brother, "You want to put this to rest?"

Matt nodded, "Sure."

"Fine," Christian said as he brought his right arm up and extended his index finger at his brother. "One answer, yes or no...do you love her?"

"Yes, I love her," Matt said without hesitation.

"Then no more excuses," Christian ordered as his eyes narrowed. "Call her and tell her...never leave anything unsaid."

"I can do that," Matt assured him.

"Did you run today?" Christian asked as he exited the living room.

"Yes," Matt answered looking towards the empty doorway that his brother had just passed through.

"How far?" Christian's voice questioned from down the hallway.

"Almost made two miles today," Matt said with a level of pride in his voice.

"Almost two miles?" Christian's tone echoed. "What's the hold up?"

"I'm trying," Matt assured. "I hit the wall after a mile and a half."

"Cut back on the weight training," Christian suggested. "You don't need heavy squats and the rest of it."

"Old habits," Matt said as he looked at his muscular arms. "But I'll try."

"Stop trying and just do it," Christian ordered, "You want to improve your conditioning, knock it off with the heavy weights. You hear me?"

"Yeah, I hear you," Matt assured his brother.

"Good. Leave me in peace to decontaminate," Christian instructed. "I expect you to call her before I return." He added as the bathroom door closed behind him and the shower turned on.

Matt nodded and retrieved his cell phone from the front pocket of his jeans. Nervously he dialed before putting the phone against his left ear. A moment of panic washed over him as the phone rang and he struggled with what to say if she answered. He felt strangely relieved when the call went to voicemail after the third ring. Relief quickly turned to regret as he listened to her sweet voice.

"Hi, it's Lauren, please leave me a message and I'll call you back...bye."

"Hi Lauren...it's Matt. I just wanted to call...and," Matt began as he fumbled with the words. He took a deep breath and continued. "Lauren, I'm sorry. I know I overreacted and I know it's my fault. I know I don't deserve another chance at bringing you happiness, but I want you to know that I love you and at the very least I hope that we can talk. I'll be home all day if you want to give me a call...ok...bye."

Matt pressed the call end button and slid the phone across the end table towards the lamp. He sat back in the recliner, starred up at the ceiling and exhaled deeply. He appreciated the way Christian pushed him to be better even when it was uncomfortable.

The water stopped and bathroom door eventually creaked open. Christian looked refreshed when he returned to the living room with a clean shirt and pair of sweat pants, "Did you call?" He asked as he adjusted the throw pillow and took a seat on the couch.

Matt nodded, "Left a voicemail."

"Good," Christian said as he finished the rest of the Gatorade. "It's on her now to call you back."

"Fingers crossed for that," Matt said with a grin. He picked up the television remote control from the end table. "Do you want to play a little Resident Evil on the Game Cube?"

"I don't feel well enough to drive," Christian said as he slumped against the arm of the couch.

"I can drive," Matt offered. "You can navigate."

Christian chuckled, "I'm not up for watching you run our character in circles while you try and figure out the controls."

"Yeah, I guess my driving does leave something to be desired," Matt admitted. "How about an episode of Deadwood? We're almost finished with the first season."

"Not right now," Christian said as he closed his eyes. "Too much swearing. Just put something on in the background. I'm going to lay back down for a bit."

The television hummed quietly in the background as Matt enjoyed a second cup of coffee. He kept a careful watch over his brother who lay quietly on the couch with his eyes closed. When the pain got severe, Christian would twist and grimace.

"You alright," Matt asked as he tapped nervously on the ceramic mug.

"I'm fine," Christian said a hint of frustration in his voice. "Better if you'd stop tapping on that mug."

"Ok," Matt said with a nod. "Is there anything I can get you?"

"We've been over this already," Christian grumbled. "I'm fine. Just let me lay here."

Matt slumped back against the recliner. He glanced over at his brother occasionally as he clicked through the channels. He enjoyed the breeze as it picked up when the words "Omega Arsenal" caught his eye at the bottom of the screen, "Hey." He called to Christian as he sat straight up in the chair. "Somethings going on at the arsenal. You need to see this."

"What is it?" Christian asked as he struggled to open his eyes and sit up.

"I don't know," Matt said as he moved to the edge of the recliner. He leaned forward, rested his elbows on his thighs and turned to look at his brother, "It looks serious." He said as images of carnage and mayhem flashed across the screen.

"Turn the volume up," Christian ordered as the mask of exhaustion and pain on his face was replaced by alertness and concern. The two of them watched the live feed from the local news helicopter. The highway and main entrance to the arsenal was littered with burning vehicles, mangled bodies, and all manner of emergency services. "What the fuck happened out there?"

"I have no idea," Matt said in disbelief. An abrupt change in camera angle redirected their focus. The news helicopter pulled up and to the left, which sent the view from the camera panning across the south side of the highway, then to the tree tops before the feed cut back to the studio news room.

Trent Ashworth, the daytime news host, sat alone in the studio behind a large desk. He shuffled papers from left to right in front of him before he cleared his throat and looked directly at the camera,

"We at News 21 apologize for the disruption. We just received word from our helicopter news crew that they had to clear the air space. Emergency Heli-vac units have arrived and are preparing to evacuate survivors to at least three local area hospitals. Our hearts and prayers go out to the survivors of this tragic incident." He said calmly as he furrowed his brow. His teeth were an unnatural shade of white and his demeanor was inappropriately energetic for the grim news he conveyed. "Saint Mary's hospital in Stone Land Park has their new state of the art trauma center standing by to receive the most severely wounded." He said as he paused and placed his index finger against the ear piece in his right ear. "I am being told now that we need to go to commercial break. Stay with local News 21 as we bring you the latest on the massacre at the arsenal. We will be right back."

"What the fuck was that?" Matt asked as a blue heron soaring over a lake replaced the news report as the image on the screen.

Christian shook his head as he pressed his left hand against his stomach. His insides hurt and pain seared through his temples, "Police, fire and Hazmat crews...I have no fucking idea."

"You were supposed to have been there today?" Matt asked. "Weren't you?"

"If I was well enough, yes," Christian answered with a nod. "We were scheduled to brief the General on our program today. When I spoke to my Chief, he said he would do it, because I couldn't."

"What do you think?" Matt asked as he tried to reconcile what they had just seen.

"I don't know," Christian said as he motioned with his hands. "Throw me your phone."

"What about Tyler and Patrick?" Matt asked. "Do you think they were on the arsenal this morning?"

"Not sure, but I have to think so," Christian said as he hastily dialed. "They always travel in early together. We can check with Aunt Athena and Uncle Tony."

"Anything?" Matt asked impatiently as Christian held the phone to his ear.

"Not yet...it's ringing," Christian said as he raised his left hand. He paused and shook his head. "No, nothing. It just forwarded to the arsenal's emergency recording." He took the phone from his ear and dialed quickly with his thumb. "Stone Land Park is the next town over; even with a new state of the art trauma center I can't imagine that their facility would be able handle a mass casualty incident from the arsenal...Dammit, right to voicemail." He said as he tossed the phone onto the coffee table.

The news room returned to the television screen and recaptured their focus.

"We are back live with you now," Trent Ashworth announced as the camera pulled in tight on his face. His yellow and silver paisley neck tie stood out against his white shirt and charcoal gray suit jacket as he organized the small stack of papers on the desk in front of him. "I have been informed that our News 21 helicopter will not be able to return to the air space, but we do have an on-scene reporter Cara Manning who is standing by to give us an up to the minute account of what is unfolding. Cara, can you hear me?"

"I'm here Trent," Cara answered as the feed cut to an attractive young woman with shoulder length wavy blonde hair. Her navy-blue blazer had the News 21 logo displayed over the left breast pocket. Even with both gold-colored buttons fastened, the blazer did little to cover her low-cut white blouse. She gazed into the camera lens almost seductively. Her piercing green eyes were accentuated by dark eye liner.

Her pursed lips were covered in a shade of lipstick too dark for her fair complexion. Cara struggled to keep her hand gestures to a minimum. She glanced down periodically at her note pad as she spoke excitedly into the black microphone in her right hand. "At this time Trent, we still do not have a motive for what has been happening here. These attacks began almost two hours ago."

"Holy fuck!" Matt said as he slid off the recliner onto the floor. He moved closer to the television to try and get better look at what was going on as images bounced across the screen.

"Police officers from four townships have responded to the scene as well as more than two dozen officers from the State Police Emergency Response Task Force," Cara Manning explained as she reported from scene. The camera man tried unsuccessfully to hold the camera steady as they moved closer to the action. As they neared, she had to shout to be heard over the noise of gunfire, and sirens. "Several fire departments have dispatched trucks, and there are a number of EMT squads here now also. As you can see behind me, emergency services are still struggling to get the scene under control!"

"What is she doing?" Christian asked as slid to the end of the couch. "She shouldn't be in front of the barricade?"

"We have moved closer to the scene in an effort to show you just how serious the situation is," Cara Manning said as her eyes sparkled. "Despite what appears to be excessive blood loss the assailants continue to get back up and appear to be moving west towards the approaching emergency services."

"Cara, did I hear you correctly?" Trent Ashworth asked off camera. "Did you say the assailants continue to get up despite excessive blood loss?"

"Yes, Trent. That's correct," Cara Manning answered. "Officers from multiple departments have used an assortment of lethal and non-lethal small arms to subdue the assailants."

"Could this be due to the use of methamphetamine or bath salts or a narcotic stimulant of that nature?" Trent Ashworth asked.

"Trent, we may very well find that these individuals are under the influence of some type of powerful narcotic or stimulant which would explain what is keeping their bodies going," Cara Manning explained as she and the camera man continued to move towards the chaos. "But at this time, we just don't know."

"She's walking right into the middle of a war zone!" Matt blurted.

"Things seem to be unfolding right behind you Cara," Trent Ashworth called from off camera. "Do you have a sense of how the first responders are doing with this situation?"

"Somebody, get her to get out of there," Christian shouted as he pointed to the television screen.

The camera captured the gruesome scene, before it was knocked from the camera man's hands and struck the ground. The live feed flickered in and out, and left only the audio feed intact.

"Oh, God help me!" Cara Manning shouted as the picture flashed on and off the screen. She struggled to pull free from two assailants that had hold of her arms and head. "GET OFF ME!" She cried as she was pulled to the ground. The flesh made an audible ripping sound as it was torn from her face and neck. Blood sprayed across the asphalt in the foreground of the frame as the camera caught the anguished final moments of her life.

The images of the attack lasted only a few haunting seconds. The gut-wrenching cries of Cara Manning and her camera man were the last sounds to be broadcast live before the screen went black.

The living room was still, neither brother spoke. Seconds ticked by and finally Matt pulled himself away from the television and stood up. He took a few steps towards Christian and put his hand on his brother's shoulder. Blinking, Christian turned his head and looked at his brother.

"Did she say they were headed west?" Matt asked as he struggled to regain his composure. He breathed heavily as his eyes narrowed. "That's less than thirty minutes away...isn't it?"

Christian nodded as a renewed look of determination overt took his face, "We have work to do."

"You think they could make it out this far?" Matt questioned with concern in his voice.

"You just saw what I saw," Christian replied as his body stiffened.

"We both did," Matt admitted uncomfortably. "But the media sensationalizes anything even remotely tragic. If it bleeds it leads. Think about the recent past...lockdowns, riots, civil unrest, assassination attempts. Except for the lockdowns none of it made it out this far."

"We just watched a woman get torn apart on live television," Christian reminded. "You really want to take a chance that whatever's going on isn't going to find its way here?"

CHAPTER 3

new dawn fades

"Do we have a plan?" Matt asked as he descended the steep narrow staircase.

"We always have a plan," Christian answered confidently as he joined his brother. The weathered boards creaked as they made their way to the basement.

"Alright," Matt said. "Let's hear it."

"What'd you do with the left-over lumber?" Christian asked as he took a quick puff from his inhaler. His asthma made it difficult for him to be in the basement for any length of time.

"From the renovation?" Matt inquired as he glanced back at this brother.

"Yes," Christian confirmed. The boards felt smooth against his bare feet. "Did you get rid of it?"

"Didn't have a chance," Matt answered as he stepped into the cool dark room. "It's all still down here."

"Good," Christian said as he stepped out of the stairwell and joined his brother. "We're going to need it."

When the house was built, the basement had been a wide-open room which ran the entire length. Almost two years earlier the brothers set out to transform it from white washed cinder block walls, open ceiling with exposed beams and concrete floor covered with battle ship gray paint into a livable space. They framed rooms, added recess lighting, and tiled the bathroom and foyer. It took longer than expected but they were both satisfied with the result.

"Where's everything?" Christian asked as he took another puff from his inhaler.

"Most of the lumber is on the far wall in front of the storeroom," Matt said. "The left-over tile and some of the scrap plywood is in the garage."

"Power tools?" Christian asked as he surveyed the basement.

"Laundry room," Matt answered. "We'll need to throw the spare batteries on the quick charger but everything else should be good to go."

"We did a fucking good job down here," Christian said with a grin.

"Yes, we did," Matt agreed as he looked around the room.

Sunlight streamed through the two rectangular windows on the south wall and illuminated dust particles as they floated through the otherwise darkened room. The basement was affectionately referred to as the war room. With the low ceiling and majority of it being underground it had a bunker-like feel.

"Alright," Christian said as he looked at his cell phone. He set the timer for thirty minutes. "We're on a clock now. Where do you want to start?"

"We ought to start by walking down the sidewalk and checking with Aunt Athena and Uncle Tony," Matt suggested. "Maybe they've heard from Tyler and Patrick."

"We will," Christian assured him. "I'm just as worried about them as you are, but time's ticking. If things go south, we're not going to be able to help anybody if we don't have this place ready."

"Alright," Matt said with a nod of agreement, "We start in the laundry room."

The laundry room occupied the north wall along with a half bath. The door in between them allowed access to a single car garage which had been a coal cellar when the house was originally constructed.

"Hand me the spare drill batteries please," Matt said as he gave the chain attached to the old porcelain light fixture nailed between the open beams of the ceiling a tug. The single bulb crackled to life and illuminated the small laundry room. "We'll get them charged in case we need them later."

"Uh, huh," Christian groaned.

"Let me have those batteries." Matt repeated as he placed the cases for the power tool on top of the washing machine.

"Yeah," Christian answered in a gravely tone. He stood with his eyes closed and back against the door frame. His hands were clamped over his stomach. "Just give me a second."

"What?" Matt questioned as he turned around. "What the fuck?"

"I'm fine," Christian said through clenched teeth as he struggled to right himself. "I just need a minute."

"You're not fine," Matt insisted as he reached for his brother. "You need to sit down. Let me help you."

"I said I'm fine," Christian snapped as he waved his brother's hand away. "It's been a while since I've been upright this long."

"Why don't you go back upstairs and lay down," Matt suggested. "I can get everything together down here."

"No," Christian said with a smirk. He took the spare batteries from where they sat on the shelf next to where he stood and handed them to his brother. "We're on a clock and you work too slow."

"Yeah, there is that," Matt said as he shook his head. He grabbed an empty cardboard box form the stack next to the refrigerator and filled it with two 18-volt drills, two 20-ounce hammers, a box of corrugated three-inch screws and a box of masonry nails. "Come on, let's take a look at the lumber."

Most of the scrap lumber was stacked along the far end of the south wall in front of the storeroom. The room was tucked away at the very back of the basement. It was separated by a thick wood door with an archaic latch lock fastened just above a rusted metal handle. The foreboding odor of mildew permeated throughout the confined space. A single rectangular window in the back corner of the room looked out from beneath the back porch of the house.

"What do we need?" Matt asked as he looked at the pile of plywood and 2x4's.

"All of it," Christian said with a groan. He grimaced as he tipped his head back and his body tensed. "We need all of it."

"Hey!" Matt called as he turned back to his brother. "You alright?"

"Stop asking me that," Christian said sharply. "I said I'm fine."

"Alright," Matt begrudgingly agreed. "What if you sat down for a couple minutes?"

"There isn't time for either of us to be sitting down," Christian said through gritted teeth. He shook his head from side to side and forced his eyes open. "We need all the lumber." He repeated. "Come on, we've got work to do."

The larger pieces of plywood leaned against the wall next to the stairs. The rest of the wood was stacked neatly in the middle of the floor where it could be easily retrieved. With the last piece moved, they paused for a moment to catch their breath. Matt brushed wood shavings from the front of his shirt. Christian took another puff from his inhaler and worked to steadied his breathing.

"Where are we on time?" Matt asked as he used his forearm to wipe the sweat from his forehead.

Christian looked down at his phone, "Less than 10-minutes. We're in good shape."

Matt twisted his head from side to side until his neck released an audible crack, "That's good."

"You ought to knock that off before you paralyze yourself," Christian chided.

"I need to see Dr. Larry," Matt said as he used his hands to stretch his neck. "I missed my last two appointments. At least we made good time."

That's why I didn't let you do this on your own," Christian said.

"Yeah, I work slow. I got it," Matt said with a smirk.

Christian placed his left hand on his chest and took several deep breaths. He looked over at Matt and motioned with his head to the large gun safe and ammo closet in the corner of the room opposite the bed, "After we lock this place down, we're coming back to finish getting ready."

"Fuck yeah," Matt replied. "Where do you want to start?"

"Upstairs," Christian said as he retrieved the box of tools from the bed against the east wall. "There's a lot more up there that needs securing."

"Front door?" Matt asked.

"Yes, that's a good place to start," Christian answered as he headed upstairs. "I can't be down here anymore."

Matt reached for the wood against the wall, "I'll grab a couple of bigger sheets of plywood."

"We can double up on the plywood if needed."

The front door had been cut from a large heavy piece of Oak. Its only failing as a security measure was the fifteen small panes of glass evenly spaced in rows of three from top to bottom.

"I never liked this door," Matt said as he held a large piece of plywood over the top half of it. "Molding or door?"

"Center it on the door," Christian instructed. "We don't want to leave a gap."

"That'll cover the glass," Matt said. "How are we going to keep it from being breached?"

Christian adjusted his grip on the drill, "I'll punch screws through the door and into the frame on either side."

"Sounds good," Matt said as he centered the piece of plywood.

"I never liked it either," Christian said. The DeWalt drill hummed as he secured the thick piece of plywood to the top half of the door. "Good for letting light in, but too accessible otherwise."

"Here?" Matt asked as he placed a second piece of plywood over the bottom half of the door.

"Lower," Christian said as he retrieved a handful of screws from the box on the coffee table. "Can you leave a three-inch gap between them?"

"Gun port?" Matt asked as he lowered the piece of plywood.

"Gun port," Christian answered with a nod as he secured it in place with several screws. "Just in case."

Matt got up and took a step back to view their work. "We'll have a good view of the front yard and street from this vantage."

"And if we have to take it down, a little wood putty and stain and it'll look good as new," Christian said before he drove screws through either side of the door and into the frame.

"What about the rest?" Matt asked.

Christian looked around the room as he thought about it for a moment, "We've got 8 windows including the ones in my bedroom that are accessible without a ladder from outside. I want to cover those with plywood and reinforce them with 2x4's."

"We can do that," Matt said as he wiped sweat from his forehead and face. "That's going to use most of our larger pieces of plywood. What do want to do about the other 4 windows?"

"Double up on the 2x4's. Space them several inches apart. We'll be able to see between them and shoot between them if we need to," Christian said. He opened a bottle of orange Gatorade and took a long drink. "Nobody's going to be able to breach them without giving us plenty of warning. What do you think?"

Matt nodded, "That'll work."

With the windows and doors boarded up, the house was uncharacteristically dark. As the temperature increased the air inside became sultry and added to the already claustrophobic feel. The only sound was the antique clock as it ticked rhythmically in the distance.

"What now?" Matt asked as he pulled at the collar of his sweat-soaked t-shirt.

"Get something to drink," Christian instructed. "Then we'll work on the kitchen."

The kitchen was at the rear of the home. There was a south facing window above an ancient cast iron radiator. The window above the sink faced west and overlooked the steep grassy hill behind the house. The back door faced north and was next to the door to the basement. It opened onto a narrow wooden porch finished in a dark cherry stain and faced what had been their grandparents house. A white wood railing ran the length of the porch. Three concrete steps with a wrought iron railing led to the sidewalk, patio and stone wall which preceded the hill behind the house.

"What do you want to do with the back door?" Matt asked as they finished barricading the windows.

"We lock it for now," Christian answered as he turned the deadbolt clockwise. "We don't want to trap ourselves in here without a way out."

"There's always the garage, if we need a way out," Matt said as he poured himself another glass of water.

Christian nodded, "Sure, but there's always the chance we'll lose power. Besides the garage door is wide. There's a lot of space to cover if we're trying to get out or keep something from getting in."

"Makes sense," Matt said before he finished drinking. He placed the glass on the counter next to the sink. "I miss that breeze...it's hot in here."

"It is," Christian said as sweat dripped from the ends of his short red hair. He tightened a threaded drill bit into the bit clip of the drill. "We can drill pilot holes through the 2x4's and molding in case we need to secure the door quickly."

"It's a shame what we did to all that old molding," Matt said as he and Christian descended the stairs back into the basement. "I can't imagine Uncle Frank would have approved."

"Under the circumstances, I'm sure he would have understood," Christian said. "Besides...nothing lasts forever."

"Where are we on time?" Matt asked as he collected several smaller pieces of plywood and moved to the pair of narrow rectangular windows on the south wall.

"Few minutes to spare," Christian answered as he readied the screws and drill. "We'll make it."

The beam of sunlight lessened and disappeared as they fastened plywood over the first window. They hastily repeated the process with the second. Moments later both were covered and the room was without sunlight.

"Garage," Christian said as he moved towards the screen door on the north wall. "Let's finish this."

"Right behind you," Matt said as he collected two more small pieces of plywood and followed his brother.

Despite the pair of windows on the far north wall of the garage it was the darkest room in the house. The dim light gave it more the appearance of a cave. A faulty drainage line installed when the sidewalk had been replaced caused the back corner of the foundation to flood.

"I should have put fucking shoes on," Christian said as the two of them waded through the stagnant water that covered the garage floor.

"So should I," Matt said as the water soaked immediately through his socks. "Oh well, fuck it." He said as he closed the first window and slid plywood over the frame. "Ready."

"So much for being prepared," Christian joked as he sunk a screw into each corner of the plywood. "Done, next one."

The water sloshed around their feet as they took the ten steps to the final window. Layers of green paint and the passage of time had so warped the wood Matt could barely get it half way closed, "Mother fucker!" He hissed.

"Just leave it," Christian instructed. "The window is almost too small to climb through anyway."

"Fuck that," Matt snarled. "We've come this far. We're not leaving this unfinished."

"Leave it!" Christian ordered.

Sweat soaked and red-faced Matt gave a hard thrust. The rotting wood cracked under the force and sent his left hand through the center pane of glass. "GODDAMMIT!" He yelled as he pulled his hand back. Shard of glass protruded from his palm. Blood trickled from the laceration and splashed against the water on the floor.

"You alright?" Christian asked with urgency in his voice.

"Fine," Matt grumbled. He held the final piece of plywood in place as blood dripped down his arm. "Finish it."

"Gladly," Christian said as the alarm on his phone sounded. He drove a screw in each corner of the board. "Done."

"What's next?" Matt asked as they moved back into the basement. He depressed the switch on the wall and turned off the power to the garage door. The green light on the wall mounted opener dimmed for a second before going out. "Just in case."

"Get you hand cleaned up," Christian instructed. "Hundred years of dust and dirt out there. You don't want it to get infected."

"That's for fucking sure," Matt said as he turned on the faucet and held his hand over the bathroom sink. He pulled two large shards of glass out of his palm. "Take a look in the cabinet please and see if we've got Band-Aids and Neosporin."

"Both and white medical tape," Christian said as he opened the narrow metal cabinet.

"What about the window in the storeroom?" Matt asked as he scrubbed his still bleeding hand.

"We don't need to secure that one," Christian said as he shook his head. "That window is hidden under the back porch. Nobody's going to know to look for it."

"Makes sense," Matt said. He gently dried his hand before he applied Neosporin. "Fucking thing is still bleeding."

"Did you get all the glass?"

"Yeah," Matt said as he shoved his hand back under the running faucet. "One of those shards left a decent size hole."

"Get it clean and bandaged," Christian instructed. "Is your gear still here?"

"Go bag in the car," Matt said as he scrubbed the wound again. "But all the tactical gear is still down here."

"Good," Christian said. "I'll be right back."

"Where are you going?" Matt asked.

"Upstairs," Christian said. His voice quieted as he ascended the staircase. "Not dressed for this. Sweat pants and bare feet aren't going to cut it."

With his hand cleaned and bandaged, Matt made his way to the dresser next to the bed. He collected a pair of khaki 5.11 tactical cargo pants, socks, a black t-shirt, and a pair of Blackhawk Black Ops boots, "That ought to do it," he said. He finished tightening the laces of his boots just as his hand began to throb.

"The news is still talking about the arsenal," Christian called as he descended the stairs. The gray coveralls stretched across his broad shoulders. His pant legs were tucked into a pair of black light assault boots. "Sounds like they've called up more resources. I don't think they've got anything under control."

"At least we're ready," Matt said as he typed the seven-digit code into the key pad on their titanium-colored Heritage safe. The safe was positioned on the south wall next to a closet they constructed to house their stock pile of ammunition. When the locking mechanism sounded, he turned the five-pronged handle clockwise and retracted the internal bolts. "Pick your poison."

"Pistols and shotguns to start," Christian said as he joined his brother. The recess light had been well placed. The powerful LED bulb was more than enough to illuminate the front of the safe and surrounding area in the otherwise dark basement. "I never get tired of that view." Christian continued as he looked over the rows of long guns.

"God bless America," Matt said with a grin. He opened several boxes of Speer Lawman 230-grain .45 caliber bullets and began loading magazines for his Sig Sauer P220.

Christian fastened a black web belt with Serpa drop leg holster around his waist. He used the quick-disconnect swivel buckles to clip the rubberized leg straps around his right leg. "FMJ?" He asked as he retrieved magazines for his H&K USP .45 caliber pistol.

"Yes," Matt answered as he used the cobra buckle to fasten a G-Code low viz scorpion belt with Kydex drop leg holster around his waist. He placed loaded magazines in the Tuff mag pouch fastened to the back of the belt.

"Good," Christian said as he pressed his left hand against his stomach.

"Medication helping?" Matt asked as he continued to load magazines.

"Barely," Christian said with a frustrated shrug. When the last magazine was loaded, he slammed it into the mag well of the USP. He racked the slide and chambered the first round. Christian depressed the decocking lever with his right thumb, slid the pistol into his holster and snapped the retention band into place. He placed the additional magazines in mag pouches fasted to the web belt. "It takes the edge off enough to get by."

Matt placed a loaded magazine in the mag well of the P220 and racked the slide. He depressed the decocking lever and slid the pistol into the Kydex holster. The retention canopy clicked as it locked in place. "Shotguns?"

"Shotguns," Christian answered. He attached two CCW tactical shotshell strippers to the front of his web belt. Each shotshell stripper held six 2 ¾ inch Hornady Critical Defense 12-gauge shotgun shells. He retrieved his parkerized Mossberg 590 pump shotgun from the safe and loaded two shells into either side of the speed feed stock. He placed six shells in the side saddle opposite the ejection port and loaded seven Critical Defense shells into the magazine. "How's your hand?"

"Throbbing," Matt answered as he looked at the white medical tape and gauze that covered his left hand. He fastened a brown leather shell pouch around his scorpion belt and maneuvered it to rest over his left hip. He filled the pouch with thirty 2 ¾ inch Hornady Critical Defense 12-gauge shotgun shells. He retrieved his Mossberg Mariner 590 pump shotgun from the safe. He placed six shells into the side saddle and loaded another seven in the magazine.

"What are you thinking?" Christian asked as he cradled the shotgun with his left arm. The single bulb cast long shadows over the rest of the room.

"I'm thinking, if this turns out to be nothing. We can never tell anyone we did this," Matt said with a grin. "Because we will never live it down."

"I pity the fool who doesn't appreciate our commitment to preparedness," Christian said as he managed a slight smile. "So, what are you really thinking?"

Matt grinned and appreciated the reference, "I'm going take some Advil and check the news again. Let's see if there's an update."

"If things get worse," Christian began as he furrowed his brow. "We may get to a point where we're not be able to stay here."

"I was thinking about that," Matt said with a nod. "The farm."

"Exactly," Christian replied. "Bill must have seen the news. He's got to know what's going on."

"I hope so," Matt said with a nod. He used his thumb to disengage the retention canopy on his holster. He wrapped his right hand around the Hogue grip, drew the pistol and checked the holsters retention. Satisfied, he reengaged the canopy and looked over at Christian. "Too many unknowns. Too many unanswered questions."

"Yes, there are," Christian agreed. "Let's see if we can't get some answers."

CHAPTER 4

crusaders

"WAIT," MATT SAID AS he reached the top of the stairs. He placed his shotgun in the corner between the end of the cabinet and back door. "I'm not going to get much further if I don't eat something. Do you want anything?"

Christian nodded, "Pastina, lightly butter, please."

"Like when we were kids," Matt said as he took a bowl from the cabinet.

"It's the only thing I can handle right now," Christian said as he placed his shotgun next to his brother's. His cheeks were flushed as he eased his body onto the chair at the end of the small rectangular kitchen table. He didn't think twice about having his back to the door. He was just relieved to be off his feet. Christian placed his left elbow on the table and pressed his forehead against his palm. "My fucking stomach."

"I'll have it ready in a couple minutes," Matt assured him.

"Lightly buttered," Christian repeated.

"I got it," Matt acknowledged with a nod as he opened the refrigerator. He motioned to the cabinet. "You want to grab a pair of glasses?"

"No," Christian said without looking up. "I don't want to get up. Just grab me a Gatorade from the fridge please."

"Gatorade it is," Matt said as he placed a bottle on the table in front of his brother. He returned to the refrigerator and collected a loaf of rye bread, lunch meat and cheese. "Water's almost boiling. It'll just be a couple more minutes."

Christian nodded and kept his palm pressed against his forehead, "Uh, huh."

There was a thin layer of steam that coated the window above the sink as the water boiled. Somewhere in the distance the brass gears of the antique clock ticked rhythmically and marked the passage of time. The kitchen was warm and quiet as they sat across from each other and ate.

"How is it?" Matt asked as he chewed. He glanced past his brother to the 9 panes of evenly spaced glass that comprised the top half of the back door.

"It's fine," Christian answered. "You see anything?"

"Not from here," Matt said as he took another bite of his sandwich. "You?"

"No, not from here either," Christian said as he glanced up at the south facing window above the old cast iron radiator and shook his head. He moved his spoon around the bowl of pastina. "Maybe emergency services have the situation under control."

"Hmm," Matt replied with a shrug. "I guess that's always a possibility."

"Then again," Christian said with a smirk. He finished the last of his pastina and placed the spoon in the empty bowl. "That may be too much to ask."

"You want any more?" Matt asked as he got up.

Christian shook his head, "No, I'm good." He answered as he pushed the empty bowl across the table. "Is that going to be enough?"

"No," Matt said as he collected the plate, bowl, and silverware. He placed them on the counter next to the sink. "Hour, maybe two before I'll have to eat again."

Christian's eyes looked tired as he looked up at his brother, "Uh...mother fucker," He groaned as he tried to get to his feet.

"Don't," Matt instructed. "We can sit for a minute."

"Yeah, ok," Christian said with a nod as he slumped against the back of the chair. "You going to call him."

"Yeah, I'll call him," Matt answered as he scrolled through his contacts. He pressed the call button and held the phone against his ear.

"Anything?" Christian asked impatiently.

"It's ringing," Matt answered.

"Hello," Bill's voice called from the other end of the phone as the sound of machinery idled in the background.

"Hi Bill," Matt called.

"How are you doing?" Bill asked. The sound of the machinery quieted as Bill pulled back on the throttle lever.

"Good, thanks," Matt began. "What's going on over there? It sounds like you've got the tractor running."

"Oh, yeah," Bill answered. "I'm in the field across the street. I need to get this hay cut but with all the rain...it's just not dry enough."

"Christian and I..." Matt began.

"How is Christian feeling?" Bill interjected.

"He's ok," Matt answered before he quickly changed the subject. "Christian and I wanted to know if you watched the news today?"

"No," Bill said as he turned the tractor off. "Not since early this morning. I got down to barn to feed the animals just as the sun was rising and haven't been back up to the house yet. This field is just still too wet."

"Three days?" Matt asked. "Don't you need three days of dry weather."

"Typically, yes," Bill answered. "You need three good days of dry weather. The problem is the first cutting should have been down two weeks ago...but with all the rain. You can't let the hay go to seed because it affects the quality and doesn't store well."

"Come on," Christian insisted from across the table as he pressed his palms against his temples. "Tell him."

Matt nodded, "Bill, something big happened at the arsenal this morning. Christian and I caught the tail end of it on the local news station. We just wanted to see if you'd heard anything about it."

"Not yet," Bill answered. "I'll have to check with Marge when I get back to the house. I wouldn't worry too much though...the way the media sensationalizes things."

"I don't know, Bill," Matt said. The chair creaked as he shifted his weight and stood up. "It looked bad...the part we saw anyway. They had first responders and emergency services out there."

"What about your cousins?" Bill asked. "Were they on the arsenal today?"

"We think so," Matt said as he paced along the linoleum floor of the small kitchen. "But we haven't been able to track them down yet."

"Have you talked to your aunt and uncle?" Bill asked.

"Not yet. They're still out. Uncle Tony had chemo today," Matt answered as he rubbed his eyes. "We've been...we've been busy that last 30 minutes or so."

"At that point, you may want to check in with them first," Bill suggested. "I've got some things to finish at the barn. When I get back to the house, I'll see what the news has to say."

"We'll check in with our aunt and uncle," Matt said. "Please send Marge our best."

"Will do," Bill said as his voice quieted. "You're both welcome here anytime."

"Thanks Bill, we really appreciate that," Matt said before the call ended.

"He didn't see it, did he?" Christian questioned.

"No," Matt answered as he placed the phone on the kitchen table. "No, he didn't."

"Did he seem concerned at all?"

Matt shook his head, "No, but you know Bill. He always plays his cards close to his chest."

"Did he say anything?" Christian asked.

"Just that he was trying to cut hay...and that we were welcome there anytime."

"Did you tell him we may need to take him up on that?" Christian inquired as he pulled himself up from the chair.

"No," Matt answered as he twisted his head from side to side. "We ought to check the news before we go calling anyone else."

Christian nodded, "Yeah, let's do that."

They collected their shotguns from where they leaned next to the back door and headed to the living room. The television hummed with the sounds of the local news room as Trent Ashworth continued his broadcast.

"We want to assure our viewers that what was reported this morning about Omega Arsenal was a tragic, but isolated incident of workplace violence," Trent Ashworth stated unconvincingly from behind the large news room desk.

"What the fuck did he just say?" Christian questioned. "Workplace violence?"

"New reports from the scene confirm that the act was carried out by a lone perpetrator," Trent Ashworth continued. "The still unnamed perpetrator was an Army Private who suffered from severe PTSD."

"One man...one man did all that damage?" Matt snarled. "Fucking revisionist history."

"Reports also indicate that the alleged suspect had just returned home from an eighteen-month overseas deployment," Trent Ashworth stated as his face reddened. "We here at News 21 have learned that upon his return he suffered several personal setbacks which included a divorce. These contributed to the downward spiral of his behavior and drove him to assault a co-worker and resist arrest by the arsenal's federal police officers. Again, for our viewers, this was a tragic but isolated incident of workplace violence."

"This is such bullshit," Christian said as he adjusted his grip on the shotgun. "How can anyone who saw the report from earlier buy this crap?"

Trent Ashworth looked uncomfortable as he shuffled papers from left to right in front of him, "Thankfully there were no fatalities this morning and I am pleased to report that the alleged suspect is currently in police custody."

"People buy this crap, because nobody wants to believe what we saw earlier could really happen," Matt said as he ran his bandaged hand over the short-cropped hair on the back of his head.

"Again, we want to let you our viewers know that there were no fatalities this morning," Trent Ashworth said as beads of sweat became visible on his forehead. His eyes wandered and his voice had an audible rasp as if the moisture in his mouth had dried up, "Several individuals experienced minor injuries and are being treated at local area hospitals."

"I don't know who he's trying to convince with this fucking nonsense," Christian growled. "But he looks like someone off camera is holding him at gun point."

"We at News 21 would like to assure all of you watching at home that the incident has been contained," Trent Ashworth added as he wiped sweat from his forehead. "The situation is under control and there is absolutely nothing for anyone in the surrounding townships to worry about."

"Well, I'm fucking convinced," Matt announced sarcastically as he sat down on the recliner. "Let's unbarricade the house."

"Our News 21 family would also like to wish Cara Manning our correspondent in the field a speedy recovery," Trent Ashworth stammered with an unconvincing smile. "Also, our thoughts and prayers go out to Sterling St. James, Cara's cameraman...um as he recovers also. We here at the studio knew him as Grover...and...um...he was a tremendous person."

"This fucking guy," Matt said as he motioned to the screen.

"What?" Christian asked as he placed his shotgun on the coffee table and took a seat on the couch.

"What he just said," Matt said with a look of disgust. "They wished him a speedy recovery and then referred to him in the past tense."

As Trent Ashworth's voice began to crack and trail off the live newsroom feed quickly cut away to a commercial that urged the adoption of rescue dogs and cats. Still photos of neglected and abandoned animals danced across the screen accompanied by somber music intended to illicit an emotional response.

Matt and Christian sat in front of the television in disbelief. As one commercial morphed into another, they struggled to rectify what they had just witnessed. In less than an hour they watched two news reports with staggering discrepancies and each claimed to be the official version.

"I know what we saw this morning," Matt said as his eyes narrowed. "That wasn't it...that wasn't it at all!"

"Does it surprise you?" Christian asked with a shrug. "We've seen enough over the years to know that if it looks bad, it's going to look bad for the government. They'll down play what happened at the arsenal and redirect focus to an alleged lone perpetrator. That'll be the headline and he'll be their scapegoat."

"Yeah, if *he* really exists," Matt said as he motioned angrily at the television, "He could be a fairytale like the rest of the bullshit that reporter was spouting."

"Easy," Christian said as he held up his hand. "Think about it. This is how the government handles a mess. They did this in Iraq in 2005 with the private security contractors. They did this in 2012 in Benghazi. They did this with COVID...the war in Ukraine...gas prices...inflation. How many more examples do you need?"

"Fine," Matt said. "But that doesn't make it any less wrong."

"It's all about optics," Christian explained. "That's nothing new."

"Maybe not," Matt said as he rubbed his forehead. "But having it so close...that's new for us."

"You're right," Christian continued. "Local news jumps on a hot story. Blood and carnage not only on U.S. soil but outside a military installation whose primary mission is research and development. That has bad press and conspiracy written all over it."

Matt exhaled and shook his head, "The live report we saw this morning didn't look censored. That means there's a good chance somebody uploaded it."

"If it's out there, I'm sure we can find it," Christian said with a nod. "Not to mention any time someone goes out of their way to tell you how isolated something is...it probably isn't."

"Alright," Matt said as he got to his feet. "Let's get after it. We've got people to call."

The air was stagnant as the temperature in the house increased. The television hummed in the background as the brothers collected their phones and returned to the living room.

"Giovanni," Christian said as he held his phone to his ear. "Where are you?"

"Hey! I'm running in between classes. I've only got a minute," Giovanni replied. "What's up?"

"Paul!" Matt blurted when his friend answered the phone. "Paul, can you hear me?"

"Brother Matthew, how the hell are you?" Paul's voice boomed from the other end of the phone.

"Good...I'm good," Matt replied. "Listen, have you seen the news this morning?"

"Just the sports scores," Giovanni answered. "The Phillies won again..."

"Listen!" Christian interrupted. "You need to get off campus and come home...now!"

"Negative," Paul answered. "Ralph and I are on our way back from the cabin. We were up there for a few days doing some hiking and some shooting. You should have come with us!"

"Tell him I said hi," Ralph called in the background.

"Ralph says hi," Paul repeated.

"Have you seen the news this morning?" Christian asked as he paced back and forth across the living room.

"Yeah, tell him I said hi. Listen, there's some stuff going on," Matt explained as he paced back and forth between the dining room and living room. "Where are you?"

"I can't leave," Giovanni argued. "I've got classes and then Heather and I are meeting at the library later to study for our labs."

"Are you listening to me, Giovanni?" Christian called into the phone. "You need to come home. Forget your classes. Find Heather, get off campus and get back here!"

"We're not too far from you. I'd say we're less than an hour out," Paul answered. "What's going on? Oh, before I forget, we've got something new to show you."

"You need to get over here!" Matt insisted. He listened as Paul and Ralph discussed.

"Somethings going on," Paul said.

"How serious?" Ralph asked.

"He wants us to come over," Paul answered.

"Fuck it, let's go," Ralph said.

"What?" Giovanni questioned. "Listen, there's no cell reception in the building I'm going to lose you. I'll find Heather after class and call you back."

"Hang tight brother," Paul said. "Ralph and I are on our way."

"Great...that's great!" Matt said in a manic tone. "See you both soon!"

"Goddammit!" Christian snarled as he hung up the phone.

"Is he coming home?" Matt asked.

"Not sure," Christian answered. He scrolled through his contact list and placed the phone against his ear. "He, said he'd call back after class. Chico should be in Jersey by now. I'm going to call his parents' house."

"Sounds good," Matt mumbled as he dialed the next number. "Kevin!"

"What's going on?" Kevin asked. He was not used to hearing from Matt so early on a weekday. "Everything alright?"

"Hi, Mrs....Kerri. Sorry, still not used to calling you and Josh by your first names," Christian began. "It's Christian, is Matt Chico there?"

"Oh, hi Christian. Not to worry, you'll get used to it," Kerri answered. "He's here, but I think he's still asleep."

"Kevin, have you seen the news this morning?" Matt asked.

"No," Kevin answered. "I caught the early bus to Jersey City this morning. I barely had a chance to drink my coffee."

"Asleep?" Christian questioned.

"Yes," Kerri replied. "He arrived late last night."

"Last night?" Christian repeated.

"Yes," Kerri answered. "He came up early to help Josh and I do some things around the house. His brother is bringing the rest of the family up from North Carolina tomorrow. Can I have him call you when he wakes up?"

"The news reported some things this morning that I think are more serious than they are letting on," Matt explained.

"What kind of things?" Kevin asked.

"No," Christian said bluntly. "I don't want him to call me back. Please just wake him up and tell him I'm on the phone and it's important."

"What's going on?" Kerri asked. "Is everything ok? You sound agitated."

"I can't get into it right now," Matt said as he continued to pace back and forth. "It has to do with the arsenal. I think you should get Jackie and get over here."

"What?" Kevin asked with considerable concern. "What's going on at the arsenal that I need to leave work and collect my wife?"

"I'm fine," Christian assured her. "Please just get him."

"Ok, just hang on a minute," Kerri said. "I'll go get him."

"Kevin, please..." Matt began. "Just trust me on this...please just trust me on this."

"Um," Kevin stammered. "My boss is not going to be good with this. Listen...I'll see what I can do...but right now I've got to go."

"Ok, Kevin call me back," Matt said as he hung up. Beads of sweat ran down his temples as he turned and looked at Christian. "Anything?"

"Chico's asleep," Christian said as he shook his head. "His mom is going to wake him up."

"I don't get it," Matt said as he scrolled through his contact list.

"What's not to get?" Christian said as he rubbed his forehead. "It's early on a weekday. Nobody's around."

"I guess," Matt said as he held up his hand. "Melissa? Hey, Melissa, it's Matt. Is Rob there?"

"No, sorry Matt," Melissa answered. "He's on days this week. You might be able to catch him on his cell. How's everything going?"

"I'll try and catch him on his cell," Matt replied as if in a daze. "Thanks."

"Hello," Matt Chico said. His dry mouth added to gravely sound of his voice. "Christian?"

"Matt Chico!" Christian ordered. "Shake out the cobwebs and listen. You need to pack a bag get some things together and get over here. There isn't time to go into all the details. Listen to the seriousness of my voice. Listen to what I am telling you. Don't think about it, don't play devil's advocate with me, just get yourself together and get over here!"

"You want me to cover over?" Matt Chico asked.

"Yes," Christian said forcefully. "That's what I just said."

"This sounds serious," Matt Chico said with a yawn. "Should I bring my parents?"

"Yes!" Christian shouted. "Bring your parents. Call me when you're on your way."

"But my brother is coming up tomorrow," Matt Chico said. "He's bringing his family and my son."

"We'll figure it," Christian said sharply. "Right now, you need to get some things, get your parents and get over here."

"I'll get back to you," Matt Chico replied before he hung up.

"Rob!" Matt called into the phone.

"Hey, I can't talk right now," Rob said. "My department is being mobilized."

Christian shook his head as he dialed the next number, "Jeff, where are you?" He asked.

"Work," Jeff answered. "How are you feeling?"

"Mobilized?" Matt repeated. "Because of what happened at the arsenal?"

"Not sure," Rob answered. "Maybe. Listen, I have to go."

"Never mind, how I'm feeling," Christian said. "You need to get home. Gather some supplies. Get your parents and get over here."

"What?" Jeff asked. "What are you talking about?"

"Wait, Rob," Matt called. "Don't go to the arsenal. Fake an injury or something."

"I can't do that," Rob said with an uncomfortable chuckle. "I need to go. I'll call you later if I can."

"I'm serious Jeff," Christian blurted. "I'm serious! Parents, supplies, get over here...and for the love of God bring your guns!"

"Is this a joke?" Jeff asked. "Is this like the time I wouldn't go to Qdoba with you guys?"

"This is not a joke!" Christian insisted. "Collect your parents. Pack some supplies, your guns and ammo. Don't think about it, just do it....do it now!"

"Kurt!" Matt blurted as the call went to voicemail. "Kurt...it's Matt. Call me back when you get this." He scrolled to the next contact and dialed.

"Anthony," Christian said.

"Hey," Anthony answered. "I was going to call you and Matt. Did you see the news this morning?"

"We did," Christian replied. "That's what I'm calling about. Where are you? Can you get some things and get over here?"

"Katherine," Matt said as his cousin answered the phone. "Have you seen the news this morning?"

"What's going on, Matt," Katherine answered. "I'm at work. I haven't seen the news. What's the ringing in the background?"

"It's Christian's phone," Matt said. "Have you seen the ..."

"How's he feeling?" Katherine asked.

"Giovanni!" Christian called. "Where are you?"

"On campus," Giovanni answered. "I'm still on campus. I told you I have class."

"Fine...ok," Matt blurted almost incoherently. "Katherine, I think he's a little better today."

"Tell him I hope he feels better soon," Katherine said. "I've got to get back to work."

"I don't give a shit about your classes," Christian snarled. "Pack a bag and get home."

"I can't really leave right now," Giovanni insisted. "Besides, I'm supposed to meet up with Heather and I can't just no show."

"Katherine, stop!" Matt insisted. "Just listen. You need to come home. I don't have time to explain. Do you know when your parents will be back?"

"I don't," Katherine stammered. "I assume my parents will be home when my father finished with his treatment. What...what's going on?"

"Then bring her with you, Giovanni," Christian insisted. "Pack a bag, collect your woman and get on the road."

"Yeah, I don't know," Giovanni quipped. "She's in class...we can't leave."

"Katherine, what about Tyler and Patrick? Do you know if they were on the arsenal today?" Matt asked. "Have you heard from them?"

"I don't know. I guess they went to work today...Matthew what's going on?" Katherine asked as her tone intensified. "Did something happen?"

"I don't have time right now," Matt said. "You need to stop what you're doing and get over here."

"Listen to me baby brother," Christian barked. "If this escalates, there may come a point when you're not able to get back here. You better think about that."

Over the next twenty minutes they called everyone in their contact lists. Most everyone was at work and had not seen the news. Those who had, dismissed the discrepancies between reports as nothing more than an error by an overly ambitious young reporter.

"Fuck!" Matt shouted as he dropped his cell phone on the end table next to the front door. The old recliner creaked as he collapsed his body onto the chair. "Do you think we're overreacting?"

"You have to ask?" Christian questioned. "If I thought we were overreacting I would have told you before we started boarding up doors and windows. You don't see the report we did and do nothing."

"So, what now?" Matt asked.

"Did Katherine say if Tyler and Patrick went to work today?" Christian asked as he took a seat on the couch across from his brother.

"She thought so, but she wasn't sure," Matt answered. "Why?"

"Call Patrick," Christian instructed. "I'll call Tyler."

Matt dialed quickly and placed the phone to his ear. After the third ring the call was sent to voicemail, "Voicemail." He said as he hung up.

Christian shook his head, "Same here."

"Do you know their office extensions?" Matt asked.

"No," Christian answered bluntly. "It wouldn't matter anyway."

"Why's that?"

"Any incident serious enough to lock the arsenal down or enlist the help of outside agencies, the Ops Chief assumes tactical command. The FPCON level is increased and the police and security offices execute steps outlined in the EAP."

"FPCON? EAP?" Matt questioned. "What does all that mean?"

"Force Protection Condition, is the level of protection a military installation operates under. It's based on the threat level," Christian explained. "The EAP is the Emergency Action Plan. It's the Operations Center's document that outlines the protocols to follow in the event of a catastrophic incident."

"Phone calls are part of the protocol?"

"Yes," Christian said with a nod. "All calls are automatically rerouted to the arsenals recorded message center and all outgoing calls are blocked."

"To what end?"

"To maintain maximum control over the flow of information until the situation can be assessed and dealt with," Christian explained.

"So how do you think it all ended up on the news this morning?" Matt asked as he tugged at the gauze and medical tape that covered his left hand.

"Simple," Christian said bluntly. "It spilled outside the gates. The revision we just watched is their attempt to regain control of the flow of information. It's been over an hour since we watched the original broadcast. The leadership has had time to initiate containment protocols and manufacture a story."

"They would do that?"

"I told you it's all about optics."

Matt rubbed his eyes, "What a fucking mess."

"It is," Christian said with a nod. "I want to know if this is happening any place else."

With an anxious sigh, Matt shifted his attention back to his contact list. He scrolled through the 'S's' until he got to '*Spahl, Aaron*' and clicked the call button. He held the phone to his left ear. He tapped anxiously on the grip of his pistol as the phone rang. "Aaron's stationed at Ft. Hood. Do you think this could be happening there?"

"If the call goes straight to voicemail..." Christian said without looking up.

"Voicemail," Matt announced a moment later. "Aaron, it's Matt, call me please when you get this. Alright, stay safe my friend."

The air in the house felt heavy. The quiet still of the living room was uncomfortable. They were startled when both of their cell phones rang simultaneously.

"It's Paul," Matt announced.

"Baby brother," Christian said.

"Paul, what's going on?" Matt asked. "Are you guys on your way?"

"Not yet," Paul said stoically from the other end.

"Giovanni, where are you?" Christian asked.

"Still at school," Giovanni answered. "I have to wait for Heather, but I don't think she's going to want to leave."

"What's the hold up?" Matt asked.

"Danny, just got the call. His SWAT team has been activated," Paul explained. "I'm not sure if Ralph and I going to make it to you. We may need to head home."

"Danny needs to think twice about going in," Matt urged. "I think there's more going on than is being reported."

"You either leave her there or convince her to come with you," Christian said bluntly. "Call me back and let me know as soon as you and Heather are on the road."

"Yeah," Paul's deep voice rumbled from the other end of the phone. "I'm sure you're right about that."

"We're standing by," Matt said. "When you figure out what you're doing call me back."

Christian no sooner hung up, than his phone rang again, "It's Chico." He said as he answered. "Matt Chico, where are you?"

"At my parents place," Matt Chico answered.

"What are you still doing there?" Christian asked. "Matt and I are in the living room with shotguns and pistols, why aren't you here with us?"

"We turned on the news," Matt Chico explained. "It didn't sound that bad. They're reporting that it was an isolated incident and it's under control."

"You wouldn't think it was isolated if you saw the live feed from this morning," Christian insisted. "Emergency evac helicopters from multiple hospitals. You can't stay at your parent's house. There are too many ground-level windows and you have no way to defend yourselves."

"You guys think maybe you're making too much of this?" Matt Chico asked.

Christian didn't answer the question. He just shook his head and growled, "Call me back when you make up your mind."

"Nobody wants to process something like this. It's just easier to believe the news when they tell you not to worry and to go on with your day," Matt said with a frustrated shrug.

"The important thing is we're ready," Christian said. He traded his phone for his shotgun. "We've got food, water, guns, ammo, medicine, first aid. We've got a plan to shelter in place and if that becomes untenable, we've got a plan to bug out. That's all we can do right now. If the time comes and everybody shows up, we'll have a numbers advantage if things get worse. Until then...it's just you and I."

"Yeah," Matt agreed. "But there's something we've got to check."

"What's that?"

"Come on," Matt said as he collected his shotgun and stood up. "We need to see if anything's been posted on-line about that initial report."

Christian had a small office set up in his bedroom. It gave them good visibility of their aunt and uncles house. The old wooden chair creaked loudly as Matt took a seat behind the monitor. His fingers pounded the keyboard as he opened multiple browsers. His eyes scanned the digital pages quickly for any information about the arsenal.

"Anything?" Christian asked. He kept a careful watch over the steep hill behind the house. He shifted his gaze every few seconds to the east facing window where he hoped to see his aunt and uncle arrive home.

"Yes," Matt answered. "I found both broadcasts on a couple of web-sites. Come here, you need to look at this one."

"What is it?" Christian asked.

"Look at this," Matt insisted. The chair creaked as he turned to look at Christian. "Whoever posted this used the original broadcast. They looped the footage, inserted still frames and running commentary."

They quickly traded places. Christian moved the mouse back and forth as Matt kept watch between the two windows. He cradled the shotgun in his left arm while his right hand rested on the grip of his pistol.

Christian's eyes fixated on the images that flashed across the screen. He listened intently to the narrator's monotone voice, who with each still frame explained away the notion of an isolated incident of *workplace violence.* The narrator insisted that what had taken place was something far more insidious and far reaching.

"Did you get all this?" Christian asked without turning away from the computer screen. "This guy's claiming the outbreak is a fast-acting virus that kills the infected."

"I heard that," Matt answered without looking back. "I thought the intent of a virus was not to kill the host. If the host dies, the virus dies."

"He goes further though," Christian said. "He claims the virus kills the host before reanimation occurs."

"Yes," Matt said. "I heard that also. He believes the virus is spread through bites, the transmission of infected saliva into the blood stream, but that it can also be spread through scratches or if your skin is broken or compromised in any way by someone who is infected."

"Makes sense," Christian said. "That's how most illnesses are transmitted."

"But then he goes on to claim that after reanimation, the infected stalk the living to feed on them."

"They did rip that reporter apart with their teeth," Christian reminded him.

"That's true," Matt acknowledged. "He's got a host of theories on incubation and reanimation times. Not to mention theories about transmission from the newly infected through sexual intercourse with the non-infected."

"The one I took note of was his prediction that we'll start seeing similar reports from military installations across the country and eventually the world."

"I heard that too," Matt said. "Not sure how to feel about that."

"Me neither," Christian said as he got to his feet. "I need to know our cousins are alright. The guy who posted this video has some interesting points. There's something going on, but I'm not sure I'm ready to believe there's a virus that reanimates the dead."

"Aunt Athena and Uncle Tony just got home," Matt observed.

Christian picked up his shotgun, "We need to talk to them...now!"

CHAPTER 5

static

"A UNT ATHENA," MATT SAID almost in a whisper as he attempted not to startle his aunt. He and Christian stood in front of the white aluminum screen door at the back of his aunt and uncle's house. The small enclosed porch that led to the kitchen was littered with fishing gear and tools. The back door to the house with all its layers of egg shell white paint was open and they could see their aunt standing at the sink washing dishes. "Aunt Athena."

"She can't hear you," Christian stated impatiently as he adjusted his grip on the shotgun.

"I'm trying not to scare her," Matt explained as he pressed his palm against the screen.

"Stop whispering," Christian ordered. "We need to talk to them."

"Aunt Athena!" Matt called again, this time with a significant increase in the volume of his voice.

"Oh, my!" Aunt Athena yelped as she dropped the pan back into the sink. A splash of soapy water followed as she grabbed her chest with her right hand. "Ah! Who's there?" She called as she used her left hand to hold onto the counter top and steady herself.

"Great," Christian said with a smirk. He shook his head and rolled his eyes. "We're off to a great start."

"I'm sorry...I'm sorry," Matt exclaimed as held up his hand. "It's just us. We didn't mean to scare you."

"What do you mean we?" Christian chided. "You're the one who scared her."

"I wasn't trying to," Matt replied as he shot Christian a glance. "But she didn't hear me."

"Next time don't whisper," Christian said as he opened the screen door and stepped into the porch.

"Oh, Matthew, you scared me," Aunt Athena proclaimed as stepped out onto the porch to greet her nephews. She moved her hand from her chest to her forehead and tried to catch her breath. "I wasn't expecting any visitors."

"He didn't mean to scare you Aunt Athena," Christian assured his aunt as he gave her a hug. "We just didn't want to walk in and surprise you."

"When I dropped the pan, I got dish water all over myself," Aunt Athena explained as she pulled at the front of her white blouse. "It's silk. I think I ruined it."

"I'm really sorry Aunt Athena," Matt said. He gave Christian a nod before he quickly changed the subject. "Can we come in for a minute. Christian and I need to talk to you and Uncle Tony."

"Come in, come in," Aunt Athena insisted. She stepped into the kitchen and motioned for them to take a seat at the small round table which sat opposite the stove. "It's not your fault. I should have changed. We just got home. Uncle Tony is resting on the couch and I thought I'd get some of the dishes washed. I don't know what I was thinking. You know how the house work can get away from you if you don't keep up with it."

"That it can," Christian agreed. No sooner had he taken a seat at the table than his body tensed in pain. He rested the shotgun across his lap and used his hands to press on his temples.

"Oh," Aunt Athena gasped as she covered her mouth. "Christian, are you ok? How are you feeling?"

Christian nodded without looking up, "Yeah, it'll pass."

"Is Uncle Tony available?" Matt asked as he took a seat next to his brother. He placed his right hand gingerly on his brother's shoulder. "We were hoping to talk with you both...it's important."

"He's laying down Matthew," Aunt Athena repeated as she motioned to the living room. "He's not feeling very well. We just got back from his treatment and you know how it makes him sick afterwards."

"It's really important," Christian insisted as he opened his eyes and looked up at his aunt. "It's really important and I promise we'll be brief."

"Well..." Aunt Athena began as she placed her hands on her hips. "Ok, let me see if he feels well enough to join us in the kitchen. You boys wait here."

The house had changed significantly since they were kids. They had enjoyed more Sunday afternoons with their grandparents in that very same kitchen than they could count. Holidays were especially memorable, with the entire family gathered in the dining room around the large table with intricate designs carved into the wood.

Uncle Tony was a skilled craftsman. He had made many upgrades to the old house when he and aunt Athena took it over. The kitchen was the first room to be renovated. The old worn cabinets with their layers of dark stain were replaced. Cherry color cabinets matched the crown molding. The wood complemented the dark granite counter tops with gold pattern and matching back splash.

"He did a nice job in here," Matt said as he adjusted his grip on the shotgun.

"He did," Christian agreed. "I miss the way nana and poppy had it though."

"Yeah, me too," Matt said with a nod. "A lot of good memories in this house."

Christian nodded and dropped his head into his hands, "Yeah, lot of good memories." He said almost to himself as his body twisted with pain.

The ceiling fan directly above the table hummed as it kept the air moving in the small room. With the sun almost directly overhead, the kitchen was warm and bright. Aside from the firearms the brothers carried no one who observed the two of them sitting at the table would have reason to believe they were there for anything other than a friendly visit.

"You alright?" Matt asked.

"No, I'm not," Christian said bluntly as he shook his head. "Stop asking me. We don't have time to sit here."

"It sounds like she's trying to get him moving," Matt said as he glanced back through the doorway. "We're here...there's no sense in leaving."

It took almost 20-minutes before Uncle Tony finally shuffled into the kitchen. Aunt Athena followed close behind. She watched over him and made certain he didn't fall. His feet were covered in thick gray wool socks which made it easier for him to move across the hardwood floors throughout the house. Most of the gray sweat pants and white t-shirt he wore were covered by the heavy green fleece robe which hung on his now narrow shoulders.

"Jesus," Christian whispered to himself as he got a good look at how emaciated their uncle was. "That really is an unforgiving illness."

"Fucking unfair," Matt muttered to himself.

Uncle Tony's stocky build had withered under the toll of cancer and chemotherapy. His head of thick black hair had not survived the months of treatment. He often wore a wool hat even during the warmer months to keep his head warm. His round face had narrowed. His cheeks were drawn and the color of his skin now carried with it a hint of gray. His eyes looked more sunken behind his wire rimmed glasses than they had been the previous week. He slowly slid a chair from beneath the table and carefully sat down.

"How are you boys?" Uncle Tony asked. His voice was gravely but somehow there was still a glimmer of hope about him as he managed a slight smile.

"Good Uncle Tony," Matt answered. "We're good."

"That's good," Uncle Tony said quietly. "Christian, how are you feeling?"

Christian nodded, "I'm ok, Uncle Tony. Good days and bad...but I'm ok."

"Good," Uncle Tony replied with a nod of his own. "That's good. You've got to keep a positive mental attitude." He continued as he tapped his index finger against his temple. "That makes a big difference."

"The body follows the mind's lead," Christian said with a grin.

Uncle Tony smiled, "That's right. What'd I tell you Athena somebody listened to my words of wisdom."

"Yes, Tony. Somebody always listens to your words of wisdom," Aunt Athena acknowledged as she collected the coffee pot and moved to the sink. "Matthew and Christian were on their way to play paintball and they wanted to stop by and see how you were feeling. "Why don't I make some coffee." Aunt Athena offered as she held the glass pot under the running water. "Uncle Tony can only have decaf, is that ok with you two?"

Uncle Tony adjusted his glasses and slowly scanned the shotguns his nephews carried. He turned back to his wife, "Athena, these aren't paintball guns."

Aunt Athena turned back from the sink with her hand on her chest, "What do you mean those aren't paintball guns?" She shrieked.

It was common knowledge within the family that it didn't take a lot to get Aunt Athena panicked. The concern was always whether medical intervention would be required.

"Here we go," Matt whispered under his breath.

"If she has a stroke, it's your fault," Christian said with a dead pan expression.

"Are those real guns?" Aunt Athena asked as her eyes widened. "Oh, my lord, what are you two doing carrying real guns? You could get into trouble."

Uncle Tony shook his head, "Athena, please." He insisted as he reached under his glasses and rubbed his eyes. "Just calm down and make the coffee."

"Tony..." Aunt Athena began as her hands trembled. "I don't want guns in my kitchen."

Uncle Tony let out a deep sigh, "Athena, the coffee please." He insisted as he turned back to his nephews. "Alright boys, what's going on? Why did you two get all dressed up and come over here carrying guns?"

Matt held his hand up to calm his aunt before he spoke, "Aunt Athena, I talked with Katherine this morning. Has she tried to call you?"

"Oh, I don't know," Aunt Athena replied flustered. "I had my cell phone off while Uncle Tony was going through his treatment. Let me check." She continued almost skittishly as she turned the coffee pot on. The coffee pot began to hiss as Aunt Athena rummaged through her purse and tried to locate her cell phone. "Oh yes, I have seven missed calls from her." She announced as she held her phone up. "You know that Katherine, I'm going to get an ear full from her about not answering my phone."

Christian glanced over at Matt before he rested his elbows on the table and folded his hands under his chin, "Before you call her back, we have some things we need to discuss with you both. Aunt Athena, I think you should sit down first."

"Wh...what?" Aunt Athena stammered as she took a seat next to Uncle Tony. "What's going on? You boys are worrying me."

"There was an incident at the arsenal this morning," Christian began. His voice was calm and deliberate. His tone was even and the pace at which he recounted the details of the day was intentionally methodical. He never looked away and maintained eye contact with either his aunt or uncle as he spoke.

Aunt Athena's face went flush as Christian recounted the mornings events. She took hold of Uncle Tony's right hand with both of hers. He gave her hand a gentle squeeze to reassure her. In stark contrast of their aunt, Uncle Tony sat stone faced. His eyes narrowed as his focus locked onto Christian's every word.

By the time Christian finished speaking, Aunt Athena was in tears and visibly shaken, "What about Tyler and Patrick?" She managed in between sobs.

Uncle Tony's hand trembled as he used his thumb to wipe the tears from his wife's cheeks. His voice was raspy as he spoke, "Athena, go in the other room and call Katherine please."

"But...Tony," she questioned.

"Please...Athena," Uncle Tony insisted. "Go in the other room and call our daughter."

Aunt Athena reluctantly nodded, got up from the table and left the kitchen.

"Matthew, go down into the basement and bring up both my rifles and the green ammo can."

"On it," Matt said as he got up from the table and headed to the basement.

Uncle Tony rubbed his temples and glanced over at Christian, "I hope you both are wrong about this."

Once their aunt and uncle were situated, Matt and Christian somberly returned home. Despite the chatter from the television, the house was eerily quiet. With the doors and windows barricaded the mid-day sun left the air inside the house stifling and uncomfortably still.

Christian returned to the couch as a flare up of abdominal pain doubled him over. Anxious and hungry, Matt retrieved a frozen meal from the freezer. He heated it in the microwave and returned to the old recliner where he waited for it to cool enough to eat.

"I had hoped that would have gone better," Christian said quietly as he stretched out on the couch. He clamped his left hand over his abdomen and his right hand over his eyes.

"Agreed," Matt said as he blew the steam from what was supposed to pass for Salisbury steak, mashed potatoes, and green beans. "They should have just come over here. They could have waited for Katherine with us and we could have worked on getting a hold of Tyler and Patrick so they wouldn't have to."

Frustrated Christian just shook his head, "Nobody's going listen until things get worse and by that time..."

"Let's not go there right now," Matt insisted as he sat back in the recliner. He filled his mouth with a fork full of food from the microwavable tray and refocused his attention on the television.

The local news station had started the morning with live coverage from the incident at the arsenal. A revised version by noon reported on an isolated incident of workplace violence. By the early part of the afternoon the arsenal and whatever had gone on wasn't even being mentioned.

"Are you hearing this?" Matt asked as he placed the empty plastic tray on the end table.

"I'm ignoring it," Christian said as his body contorted. "I need a break from it."

"Yeah, I get that," Matt acknowledged. "Whatever I just ate was pretty awful."

"What did you expect?" Christian asked almost rhetorically. His right hand still covered his eyes. "They're garbage. I told you not to buy those frozen meals."

"They're not bad in a pinch," Matt insisted as he tipped his head back and filled his mouth with water. He swished the water around and tried to wash the aftertaste from his mouth.

"They're garbage," Christian repeated. "Shut the T.V. off for a while."

The distinct sound of a car door as it slammed pulled Matt's attention from the television. He got up and peered between the boards that covered the front door. Parked in front of the house was a silver four door Honda Civic.

"Hey!" Matt called as he turned back towards Christian. "Anthony's coming up the driveway!"

Christian opened his eyes and sat up quickly, "Is he alone?"

Matt turned back and peered out from between the boards that covered most of the front door, "Looks like it. He's got a backpack and sleeping bag and he's headed up the walk towards the back door."

"I guess we better let him in," Christian said as he pulled himself up from the couch.

They collected their shotguns and moved quickly through the house to the kitchen. Anthony was already standing at the back door. The straps of his backpack pulled the gray t-shirt tucked into his blue jeans tight across his chest. He had a burgundy sleeping bag tucked under his left arm. His favorite dark blue Yankees ball cap sat just above his eye brows and covered his head of jet-black hair.

The three of them had met in high school, where Anthony had been a varsity athlete in multiple sports. Stocky and quick, he had considerable success on the wrestling mat and had won two consecutive state championships. He was being scouted for a scholarship by several Universities until a dislocated hip during a semifinal match his junior year ended his wrestling career. After high school he studied finance at the county college before being hired on at Sweet Tooth Inc. as a staff accountant. Sedentary employment with New Jersey's largest candy manufacturer had all but decimated his years of eating 6 balanced meals and split routine workouts.

"What are you guys all dressed up for?" Anthony asked uncomfortably. "Are we at war and somebody forgot to tell me?"

"It's good to see you Anthony," Christian said as he shook Anthony's hand and welcomed his friend inside.

"Glad you made it over," Matt added as he slapped Anthony on the shoulder. "Why don't you put your stuff down in the dining room."

"Yeah," Anthony said as he moved through the kitchen and surveyed what Matt and Christian had done to the house. "Thanks for inviting me over."

"Over there next to the hutch," Christian instructed as he pointed to the empty dining room chair.

Anthony nodded and placed his backpack and sleeping bag on the chair, "Do I get a shotgun?" He asked with an awkward chuckle.

"I'm sure we can find you something," Matt said as he motioned for Anthony to join them in the living room.

"What did you guys do in here?" Anthony asked as he took a seat on the couch. He dropped his ball cap on the coffee table and ran his hands through his thick black hair as he scanned the fortifications that covered the front door and windows.

"Too much?" Chrisitan asked sarcastically.

Anthony cocked his head to one side, "It's a lot."

Matt returned to the recliner, "What did you bring?" He asked as he changed the subject.

"Not enough by the looks of things," Anthony replied as his face contorted and eyes narrowed. "Granola bars, candy bars, a couple bottles of water, some extra cloths and my sleeping bag."

"Just the essentials," Matt said with a laugh.

"You know I can't get very far without my candy bars," Anthony admitted as he slumped back against the couch.

Christian placed the shotgun on the coffee table and took a seat next to Anthony.

"So, what now?" Anthony asked almost confused.

Matt glanced over at Christian, who returned the look and gave a nod.

Christian turned and looked at Anthony, "We need to discuss some things."

Much in the same way that Christian had laid the situation out to their aunt and uncle, he now shared with Anthony everything that he and Matt had seen beginning with the original broadcast that morning. It wasn't until Anthony viewed the original broadcast from in front of the computer screen that the color began to drain from his face.

The last frames flickered across the screen and then were gone. As the screen faded to black, Anthony pushed the chair from beneath the desk. Anthony flinched as the old chair made a loud cracking sound, "I just don't know." He said as he rested his elbows on his knees.

"You're not convinced?" Matt asked.

"Don't get me wrong," Anthony said as he motioned with his hands. "It's compelling and it sounds legit."

"But?" Matt inquired.

"The thought there could be any truth to it makes me feel like I need a garbage can to throw up in, but the internet is full of professional trolls who create stuff like this every day. What is it about the recently deceased reanimating?" Anthony laughed. "God, even to say it out loud sounds crazy. What makes this anymore legit than the other bullshit out there?"

"It could be bullshit," Christian acknowledged. "But we've got two cousins still unaccounted for that were on the arsenal today."

"Not to mention," Matt interjected. "If any of this is even close to being accurate it's practically happening in our back yard. For that reason alone, we need to be prepared."

"I know better than to argue with either of you about being prepared," Anthony said with a nod. "But what can an accountant, a college professor and a mad scientist..."

"Mechanical engineer," Christian corrected.

"Right...mechanical engineer," Anthony said with an uncomfortable chuckle. "What can we do?"

Christian motioned towards the bedroom door, "Downstairs."

Unlike the main floor of the house the mid-day sun had not had the same effect on the basement. The change in temperature was noticeable as they descended the stairs. The air was dry and considerably cooler.

"You guys did a great job done here," Anthony commented as he stepped into the main portion of the basement. "When do you think you'll finish it?"

"Probably after the apocalypse," Christian said stoically as he punched the code into the keypad and opened the safe. "Come on over. Let's see about getting you a shotgun."

Anthony stood for a moment with his mouth open and a vacant look in his eyes, "Wow." He managed to utter. "That's more than I remember. I guess it would be stupid for me to ask if you two think you've got too many."

"Yeah, don't ask that," Matt said as a sinister grin stretched across his face. "The collection has grown since we took you shooting last."

"Do you remember what shotgun you used the last time we took you skeet shooting?" Christian asked as he motioned towards the safe and quizzed his friend.

Anthony rubbed his forehead as he thought about it for a moment, "You told me it was...you told me it was your Mossberg 500, and you told me not to forget."

"Very nice," Christian said with a smile. He removed the shotgun from the safe and retracted the pump to make sure it was empty. "Since you're already familiar with that one, that's what we'll give you. I put the short barrel back on it and installed a six-shot side saddle to carry extra shells. Do you remember the safety rules?"

Anthony nodded, "Treat it as if it's loaded until I check it myself. Keep my finger off the trigger until I'm ready to fire and don't point it at anything I don't want to destroy."

"And after you follow those safety rules?" Matt asked as he folded his arms.

"Continue to follow all three until I'm ready to shoot," Anthony answered.

"Excellent!" Christian proclaimed as a much-needed smile stretched across his face. "How about the function?"

"Shells feed into the tubular magazine below the barrel," Anthony stated confidently. "The pump needs to be retracted then pulled forward to charge it. The safety is on top of the receiver. It needs to be pushed forward to be disengaged."

"Damn," Matt said with a smirk. "When did we take you shooting...last fall? Good memory."

"Well..." Anthony began. "You guys taught me well."

"This is how I want you to keep the shotgun," Christian instructed as he handed the firearm to Anthony. "I want it unloaded with the breach open until I tell you otherwise. Do you understand me?"

Christian had a soft side that was greatly appreciated by those who knew him. He was fair and expected the same high standard from the people he called his friends as he held for himself, especially when it came to the safe handling of firearms.

Anthony nodded and maintained eye contact, "I understand. I will keep it unloaded with the breach open, until you say otherwise."

"Good," Christian said with a nod. "I'm loading the side saddle with six 2 ¾ inch slugs. If we get to that point...and I hope we don't, you know how to load, fire and what to expect from the recoil."

They stood for a moment around the open safe and enjoyed the cool of the basement. It was a quiet calm moment and left each to wonder if what they were preparing for would come to fruition. The silence of the moment was shattered by a loud knock at the back door.

It was a relief to have Jeff and his parents in the kitchen. They had grown up with Jeff and his three siblings. Aaron and Matt had become friends in second grade and because of their older brother's friendship, Christian and Jeff quickly followed suite. Mr. and Mrs. Spahl had watched Matt and Christian grow up and were thought of by them as surrogate parents. They exchanged handshakes and hugs before the group moved into the living room.

"As you can see Christian and I have been doing some light remodeling," Matt joked as he gestured to the plywood and 2x4s which covered the doors and windows.

"You guys think you may have gone a bit overboard in here?" Jeff asked as he furrowed his brow.

Jeff was a gifted athlete in high school and had earned varsity letters in both track and football. In his mid-twenties he picked up a pack a day smoking habit, which had only now almost a decade later begun to affect his stamina. His head of bushy blond hair was all but a memory and the older he got the more he resembled his father. Despite a sporadic training regime his lean muscular arms protruded from the short sleeves of his plain white t-shirt. A thick brown belt kept the waist of his badly frayed jeans sinched around his narrow waist. The red, black, and silver Nike sneakers Christian had given him were laced tightly to his feet.

"Matthew...you boys," Mrs. Spahl said as she waved a scolding finger. "I just don't know about all of this. I think this whole thing has been blown way out of proportion."

Mrs. Spahl had grown up as an Army brat. Her father had retired a full Colonel and had seen combat in every conflict from World War Two to Vietnam. She was a wonderfully proper southern belle and though several decades removed still spoke with a southern twang. Despite the strands of gray that stood out against her auburn hair she was still very lovely. She was known for being very outspoken and had no compunction about voicing her opinions.

"You're going to need some wood putty," Mr. Spahl commented dryly as he looked around the room. "Wood putty and a fine grit sandpaper. That's the only way you're going to be able to fix all the holes in the molding after you take all this down."

Mr. Spahl was tall and lean. He was soft spoken and very observant. The little bit of hair he had left was cropped short and had long since gone gray. In his youth, he had enlisted in the Army and served 2 tours in Vietnam during some of the fiercest years of the war. Having lived through the conspiracies of the 60s and 70s, he was not quick to believe the discrepancy in the news reports as a government cover up in the making.

"Alright Jeff, let's see what you brought," Christian said as he pointed to the black Pelican case.

Jeff knelt and unfastened the cable locks. His white t-shirt had visible sweat stains in the underarms, "I brought my Remington 870,

Ruger Mini-14 and Bushmaster AR." He said proudly as he opened the top of the case.

"What about your P90?" Christian asked.

"In my duffle bag," Jeff answered as he motioned to the black bag that leaned against the living room wall.

"Nice. How much ammo did you bring?" Christian asked as he took a knee next to Jeff.

"Six hundred rounds of .45 ACP," Jeff responded.

"230-grain?" Christian asked.

Jeff nodded and smiled, "It would be wrong to run a lesser grain round through my pistol."

Christian gave a slight chuckle before he clamped his hand over his abdomen, "What else?"

"A thousand rounds of 62-grain 5.56mm...green tip. Fifty 2 ¾ inch 00 buck shotgun shells," Jeff answered as he opened his duffle bag and olive drab ammo can.

Christian nodded and patted Jeff on the shoulder, "That'll work."

Mrs. Spahl folded her arms and shook her head, "You boys..."

"I think this is an overreaction Matt," Mr. Spahl said as he took a seat on the couch. "I really do. Think about how often the weather man is wrong. There is no greater conspiracy at work the man is just an idiot."

"Mr. Spahl," Matt began.

"I can appreciate your level of preparation and concern," Mr. Spahl interrupted as he held up his hand. "The news made an incorrect report. That's all. It's not a reason to sound the alarm and take shelter."

"Mr. Spahl," Matt began as he leaned his shotgun against the coffee table and took a seat at the other end of the couch. "I promise you the news station could not have gotten the story this wrong."

"I think this is just silly," Mrs. Spahl said as she stood in the archway which separated the living room from the dining room. "It's always nice to see you boys but I really don't think we should be entertaining this and I don't think Jeff should have brought his guns with him."

Anthony was watching the conversation from some remove. He scratched his head uncomfortably as the debate continued.

"We're here and nothing has happened," Mrs. Spahl continued. "No monsters have jumped out, nothing lurking in the shadows. The news report says everything's okay and we need not worry. I really think it's time to go home."

"I don't think that's a good idea," Christian said as he slowly got to his feet. "Just give us a few hours...just to be on the safe side."

"Christian," Mrs. Spahl began in a very calm and reassuring tone. "You know that Mr. Spahl and I love you both but the two of you are not being realistic...and look what you've done to your home."

"We're staying!" Jeff said defiantly. He slammed a loaded magazine into the mag well of his Ruger P90 and racked the slide. He decocted the hammer and slid the pistol into the waist band of his jeans. "At least for a few hours."

Mrs. Spahl shook her head disapprovingly and looked over at her husband, "Would you like to weigh in on this?"

"We're going to stay for a little while," Mr. Spahl said as diplomatically as he could. "At least until we're certain that everything is really ok."

Time felt as if it slowed in the quiet still of the old house. With the doors and windows barricaded the air was oppressively hot and stagnant. The mid-afternoon brought with it the unrelenting felling of lethargy.

Mr. and Mrs. Spahl had moved to the love seat where they each now napped. The Mossberg 500 lay on the coffee table close to where Anthony was slumped over the arm of the couch. A quiet rhythmic snore emanated from his still body.

Matt sat alone in the kitchen. His blood sugar was low and his hands trembled as he hastily ate a breaded chicken breast and sautéed spinach. In between bites, he tried unsuccessfully again to call his cousins. Christian and Jeff retired to the basement where they took a final inventory of weapons, ammunition, and other essential supplies.

"You guys ever think maybe you have too much ammo?" Jeff asked as he opened the last of the olive drab ammo cans that lined the bottom shelf of the book case on the far wall outside of the store room.

"Never," Christian said bluntly as he finished counting the ammunition in the closet next to the safe. "You can't leave. You need to convince your parents to stay. I'm telling you…"

"You don't have to convince me," Jeff interrupted as he got to his feet. "I'm all about being here. It's my mother who is the hard sell."

"I'm counting on your father to help with that."

"You'll get a little more leeway from him, but his patience isn't inexhaustible," Jeff said with a nod. "Hey, how many ARs did you guys build?"

In the hours since everyone arrived there had been no new internet conspiracy videos and the local news station no longer mentioned Omega Arsenal. As the day wore on it seemed the initial reports may have been wrong.

"Fucking bullshit," Matt muttered to himself as another call to his cousins went to voicemail. He placed the cell phone on the table next to his water bottle as he angrily chewed the last of the chicken. "Where are they?" He said frustratedly as he ran his bandaged left hand through his hair. He looked up just as Matt Chico and his parents appeared from around the corner of the house as they made their way to the back porch. "Chico's here!" Matt called down the basement stairs as he unlocked the back door.

Jeff handed the rifle back to Christian and repeated, "Chico's here."

"We better get upstairs and greet him," Christian said as he returned the rifle to the safe and headed for the stairs.

"Matt Chico!" Matt said excitedly as he welcomed his friend into the kitchen. "Get you and your parents in here!"

"Good to see you Matt," Matt Chico said with a firm hand shake. His khaki polo shirt and blue jeans hung loosely on his slender frame. "Where's Christian?"

Much in the same way Matt and Christian had grown up with Jeff and Aaron they had too with Matt Chico and his older brother. Matt Chico was tall and lanky with dark brown hair and piercing blue eyes. A thick beard covered the lean features of his face. A pronounced scar covered most of the back of his head and neck. A decade prior he was almost killed in a work place accident, which left him with a traumatic brain injury. Despite a miraculous recovery he suffered the occasional memory lapse and never regained full use of his left arm.

"In the basement with Jeff," Matt answered. "I hear them coming up now."

"Matt Chico," Christian said sternly as he reached the top of the stairs. "I was afraid you weren't going to show."

Matt Chico shook his head, "You, said it was important. I collected my parents and here we are."

"It's good to see you Mr...." Christian began.

"First names," Josh said as he extended his right hand. "You boys are old enough now. You can drop the Mr. and Mrs. and just call us by our first names."

The last few years had not been kind to Josh. A stroke had derailed most of his post-retirement plans. Despite putting up a brave front it had left him obvious cognitive impairments. His blond bushy head of hair and beard had turned stark white. He moved more slowly now and his posture had a visible hunch. He seemed disorientated often and there was a noticeable tremor which came and went in his hands.

Christian nodded as he shook Josh's hand, "It's good to see you and Kerri."

"It's so good to see you both," Kerri said as she hugged Christian. "How are you feeling?"

Kerri was tall and slender with an olive complexion. Her short raven black hair didn't quite reach her shoulders. She had spent the better part of the last four decades teaching special education, but with Josh's failing health she had decided to retire at the end of the school year. She was also an exceptional cook and in their younger years the brothers had always welcomed an opportunity to visit their friend's home for dinner.

"I'm ok," Christian said with a nod. "Come on into the living room. Jeff's parents were asleep on the love seat and I think Anthony is sacked out on the couch."

The living room was alive with chatter as Josh and Kerri caught up with Mr. and Mrs. Spahl. No one noticed as Matt and Christian collected Jeff, Anthony and Matt Chico and disappeared to the basement to discuss strategy.

"So, you're saying you watched the reporter get torn apart on live television?" Matt Chico asked as if he had not understood the events as the brothers had just recounted them.

"That's exactly what we're saying," Christian answered.

"So, where's the footage of that?" Matt Chico asked. He had a reputation for playing devil's advocate. "I heard that was reporting on the incident of work place violence and may have been injured..."

"For the love of God," Matt blurted. "Do you have to do this every Goddamn time. We told you what we saw."

"No, I totally believe you," Matt Chico said unconvincingly. "I'm just saying that if it did happen that way why haven't we heard about it...that's all."

Matt shook his head and looked over to Christian, "I got nothing. You want to weigh in on this."

Christian nodded, "Jeff, in or out?"

"Fuck!" Jeff snapped as if offended. "You have to ask? Of course, I'm in."

"Anthony?" Christian questioned.

"Nothing else to do today," Anthony answered with an uncomfortable chuckle. "I'm in."

"Chico?" Christian questioned as he furrowed his brow.

"I'm not disagreeing with you," Matt Chico insisted as he shrugged his shoulders and held his hands up. "All I'm saying is we should try and contact emergency services again..."

"In or out?" Christian insisted.

"Hey," Matt Chico said with an awkward grin. "I'm here, aren't I?"

"Good," Christian said. "Then cut the opposing viewpoint bullshit. We've got things to do."

"Look, Christian," Matt Chico began with quick animated hand gestures. "I'm not saying I don't believe you both but look at it out. It's a beautiful day. The sun is shining and you're barricaded in your house."

"We're being cautious," Christian insisted.

"Paranoid is more like it," Matt Chico chided as he cocked his head to one side.

"Hey!" Matt snapped angrily as he gritted his teeth. "Knock that shit off."

"I've always appreciated your ability to be the voice of reason," Christian interrupted. "But that's not what we need right now."

"Sorry," Matt Chico said sincerely as he held up his hands. "Look, my brother and his family left North Carolina a few hours ago. Their bringing my son up and we're all going to enjoy some time with my folks. We've only got a couple of days here and I don't think this is the best way to spend it."

"We're not trying keep you from spending time with your family," Christian assured him. "Quite the opposite. We're trying to keep all of you safe. Even if you question the validity of what we're saying all I'm asking is that you and your parents stay here until we're sure everything's ok."

"Well..." Matt Chico began. "I just don't..."

"I don't want to hear it!" Christian snapped impatiently. "You're here. You're staying. Now that that's settled, if you want to try and contact emergency services again, have at it. In the meantime, we have things to do!"

CHAPTER 6

who goes there?

A S DAY FADED INTO evening, hope the phone would ring with word from loved ones dissipated further with each hour that passed. There was no mention of the arsenal or the events of the morning anywhere to be found on the news. The temperature in the house had cooled as the sun slowly lowered in the distance, but the mood was tense and uncertain.

Matt and Christian tried again unsuccessfully to convince their aunt and uncle to join them. Aunt Athena and Uncle Tony insisted they had to wait for Katherine and her husband Marcus, whose arrival they claimed was imminent. When the issue was pushed, Aunt Athena was steadfast that Tyler and Patrick would most certainly arrive soon after their sister and she would have all her children under one roof with her where they belonged.

"What do you want to do?" Matt asked quietly as he hung up the phone.

"They won't even consider it?" Christian asked as he pressed his palms against his temples.

"No," Matt answered. "At least not until Tyler, Katherine and Patrick are all home."

Christian shook his head, "In the meantime everybody upstairs is getting antsy. I was sure of what we saw. We couldn't have gotten it that wrong, could we?"

"Regardless of the media blackout, getting everybody here was the right move," Matt insisted. "We just need a way to convince them to stay."

"Dinner," Christian said as he clasped his hands behind his head and closed his eyes. The pain in his stomach had returned with a vengeance and it was everything he could do just to stay on his feet.

"Dinner?" Matt repeated. "Are you hungry?"

Christian shook his head without opening his eyes, "That's how we convince everyone to stay. At least for a little while longer. If nothing's changed after that we can't expect them to stick around."

"Ok," Matt said with a nod. "What's the plan?"

"See what you can whip up in the kitchen," Christian instructed. "I'll gather everyone in the dining room."

"Alright, let's go," Matt said as he ushered his brother up the stairs. "I know just what to make."

As they reached the top of the stairs, they immediately found Matt Chico as he paced back and forth in the small kitchen. He muttered to himself as he stared blankly at the screen of his cell phone.

"Chico, we're going to meet in the dining room," Christian said as he placed his hand on his friend's shoulder.

Startled Matt Chico flinched and turned, "Christian? What's going on?"

"We're going to meet in the dining room," Christian repeated as he motioned towards the doorway. "Come on."

"In a minute," Matt Chico insisted. "I need to make another phone call."

"Who are you calling?" Matt asked as he took the large skillet from the cabinet.

"Huh?" Matt Chico responded. He sounded confused as he looked around the kitchen. "Calling? Um...I'm going to try the local police department again."

"How many times have you called them?" Matt asked as he opened the refrigerator.

Undeterred, despite being in pain, Christian made his way to the living room. There he found the faces of his friends long and chatter minimal.

"Matt's going to make dinner," Christian announced. "Would you all join me in the dining room please. I know everybody's tired but we'd like to get everybody fed and then see where we are."

"Where we are," Mrs. Spahl began. "Is that it has been very nice to visit but we need to get going and it looks like the two of you are going to have a lot of dismantling to do."

"What are we having for dinner?" Jeff asked as he pulled himself away from the break in the boards that covered the front door."

"Matt's making potatoes and hotdogs the way our grandfather used to."

"Potatoes and hotdogs?" Jeff questioned with an undeniable lack of enthusiasm.

"Trust me Jeff," Christian insisted. "It's our grandfather's recipe. You won't be sorry you stayed."

"I am getting hungry," Mr. Spahl said as he got to his feet. "You've got my vote. Let's eat."

Kerri and Mrs. Spahl helped Christian set the table as everyone gathered. Despite the lack of decorations, the dining room almost had the feel of the holidays with everyone together around the table.

"Where's Chico?" Jeff asked.

"In the kitchen on the phone," Christian answered. "We've got water, juice, milk, what would everybody like to drink?"

The mood had improved some and the conversation around the table was more jovial. It was aided in no small part by the mouthwatering aroma that wafted in from the kitchen.

"I'm impressed," Mrs. Spahl said. "Whatever he's making out there really smells good."

"Wait til you taste it," Christian assured her with a nod as Matt Chico entered the dining room. "Chico, anything?"

Matt Chico shook his head. His shoulders were slumped forward and the look on his face was one of defeat. "No. The local police department had no information. I'm not sure the dispatcher even knew what I was talking about."

"Doesn't surprise me," Christian said. "Local law enforcement is under staffed, underfunded and under trained. If things get serious don't count on them to be able to do anything about it."

"He, told me not to call back. How can a police department tell you not to call back?" Matt Chico questioned as he took a seat at the dining room table. The look on his face was a mixture of confusion and fatigue. "Somebody's got to know what's going on."

"How many times have you called?" Jeff asked before he raised the bottle of water to his lips and took a long drink.

Matt Chico shrugged as he stared off into the distance, "Don't know...six...seven times maybe."

"That could have something to do with it," Jeff said as he cleared his throat. "You might want to leave them alone for the rest of the night."

"I don't know," Matt Chico muttered as he shook his head. "I just figured, if anyone would know what was happening the police department would."

"I don't know Chico," Christian began. "I get the feeling these local departments are probably the last to know."

Matt Chico just shook his head, "I guess maybe...I don't know. We should probably get going after we eat."

"How about we just eat," Christian suggested as he calmly changed the subject. "We can discuss the rest after dinner."

The talk around the dining room table was sparce and mostly innocuous. It was 20-minutes before Matt placed the large skillet on top of the trivet in the center of the table.

"Let's eat!" Matt announced as he began to fill everyone's bowl with the delicious mixture of potatoes, hotdogs, and diced onion. "There's ketchup which I highly recommend and salt and pepper if anyone would like to add a little extra."

"Smells delicious," Kerri said with a smile as she offered up her bowl. She glanced over at her husband. "Josh, would you like me to give him your bowl?"

"I can do it," Josh said with a scowl. His hands trembled as he held the bowl out in front of him.

Matt nodded and took hold of the bowl, "Say when."

"I can hold onto it myself," Josh insisted as he pulled the bowl back. Some of the contents spilled out onto the table in front of him.

"Oh Josh, let me help you," Kerri offered as she placed a hand on his shoulder.

"Stop treating me like a damn invalid!" Josh shouted. He slammed his hands down on the table, stood up and stormed out of the dining room. "I want to go home!"

"Dad," Matt Chico called as he started to get up.

"Don't," Kerri insisted as she collected the spilled food from the table. She placed her finger tips against her forehead and shook her head. "Just let him be. He'll calm down and come back when he's ready."

"Is there anything we can do?" Mrs. Spahl asked. Her expression was a mixture of compassion and concern.

Kerri shook her head, "No. It's been like this ever since the stroke...these bursts of anger. He just needs some time to cool down. It's difficult for him...losing so much of his independence." She paused and shook her head again as she held back tears, "Come on...let's just eat."

As the conversation continued, Josh returned to the table. He took a seat next to his wife and slowly began to eat. Matt excused himself and moved quickly through the second floor of the house. He closed the curtains and blinds and made sure the windows were covered.

"What are you doing?" Jeff questioned.

"Street lights are on," Matt answered. "The sky is clear. Tonight's the new moon."

"Was wondering when you were going to mention that," Jeff said sarcastically. "So, you're worried about werewolves now?"

"Knock it off," Matt ordered as he returned to the table. "We keep it dark in here, it makes it easier for us to watch the street and surrounding property for movement and it makes it more difficult for anyone to see in."

"Anyone?" Anthony questioned. "Who's trying to look in?"

"It's just a precaution," Christian assured him. "We're not taking any chances, especially when we're all gathered in the same room."

"You boys," Mrs. Spahl began as she placed her fork on the napkin next to the empty bowl. "I think what you boys saw was reported incorrectly and you've taking it as fact and ran with it."

"Ockham's razor," Mr. Spahl added.

"Who's razor?" Anthony questioned.

"Ockham's razor," Christian repeated. "Sometimes known as Occam's razor."

"I don't get it," Anthony said before he shoveled the last of his potatoes and hotdogs into his mouth. "What does a razor have to do with this?"

"It's not a razor," Christian explained as he ran his right hand through his hair. "It's a theory that basically says the simplest explanation is the correct one."

"The news reported the incident at the arsenal incorrectly?" Anthony questioned.

Christian nodded, "If we believe the theory of Ockham's razor...than yes."

"All due respect to Ockham and his razor," Matt quipped sarcastically. "He wasn't there. He didn't see what we saw and he can fuck all the way off."

"Very intelligent rendering," Mrs. Spahl chided. "I can see all that schooling has really paid off for you."

"So, what's..." Anthony began as he shook his head.

"Wait," Christian instructed as he held up his right hand, "The problem as I see it is that you can't get what we saw that wrong."

"Christian, I don't..." Mrs. Spahl began.

"I've seen the news get things wrong, but nothing like what we saw," Matt interjected. "We saw a woman get torn apart on live television. Add to that the fact that we still haven't heard from our cousins."

"What about a simulation?" Mr. Spahl asked.

"Like dark winter?" Matt questioned. "The bio-terror simulation from June of '01?"

"Sure, why not?" Mr. Spahl answered. "A simulation that the media mistakenly announced as real."

"That's a level of irresponsibility and ineptness usually reserved for Washington politicians," Christian interjected.

"True," Mr. Spahl acknowledged. "But it's still a viable explanation."

"Maybe," Matt begrudgingly admitted. "But keep in mind the event dark winter simulated went live several months later."

"Oh, please," Mrs. Spahl said as she shook her head, "This is too conspiracy heavy for my liking."

"What about the local police?" Matt Chico asked in an effort to change the subject.

"What about them?" Matt asked rhetorically. He motioned with his hands to emphasize his feelings of indifference. "You called them. What great revelation did they have for you?"

Matt Chico paused for a moment, "I...I don't...well they couldn't really tell me anything."

"Exactly," Matt said with a shrug. "They couldn't tell you anything. I wouldn't count on them to go the mailbox and get the mail. Let alone provide an explanation for what's going on outside this little town...especially something so serious."

"You're talking about this as if it's inevitable," Mr. Spahl commented as his eyes narrowed. "The fact of the matter is we don't have any new information and the information we do have is far from definitive."

"So that's it?" Matt snarled angrily. "When did everybody stop erring on the side of caution? Huh? Something happened today and just because it hasn't affected us yet doesn't mean we shouldn't be ready..."

"Alright!" Christian said as he slid his bowl towards the center of the table. The tone of his voice was a demanding calm.

The conversation around the table quieted as everyone gave Christian their full attention.

"First off, we're glad you're all here," Christian began as he looked around the table. "I know this has been a strange day and the situation hasn't been ideal for any of us. We've all got questions that need answers and we're trying to get in touch with loved ones."

"Amen to that," Matt added as he put another scoop of potatoes and hotdogs in his bowl.

"With the exception of what Matt and I saw this morning, I don't believe the media is being truthful about what's going on," Christian continued as the intensity in his voice increased. "We're being deceived about how it started, what it is and how long it's going to last."

"Based on what?" Mrs. Spahl asked. "It's going to take more than a meal...good as it was and your gut feeling to convince us to stay."

"Fair enough," Christian said as he looked down at his watch. "It's almost 6:30. Give us until 8. If nothing has happened and no new information is available, we'll chalk it up to a nice dinner with friends and call it a night."

The brothers were not known for playful pranks, or overreacting. They were fiercely loyal to each other and to their small group of tightly knit friends. Everyone at the dining room table, even the most skeptical knew that if the brothers were asking them to stay, it was for a good reason.

Christian's talk had been effective. After dinner everyone settled in and waited for the 8 o'clock hour to arrive. The television hummed with the local news station in hopes that an update of any kind about the arsenal would be forthcoming. Aside from the glow of the television, the only other light source throughout the house was sporadic rays of moonlight which crept in past the blinds and illuminated most of the interior.

Matt crouched at the front door. He peered out from between the plywood boards. His shotgun leaned against the end table, less than an arm's length away. His focus was fixed on the front lawn and street just beyond. The street light on the opposite side of the road was bright and afforded him excellent visibility into the next yard.

Jeff knelt next to the love seat. He held fast to his Ruger Mini-14 as he kept watch from the windows on the west facing wall of the house. The empty lot next to the house was bathed in pale blue moonlight which gave Jeff a clear line of sight to the adjoining street and houses.

Christian pulled one of the chairs away from the kitchen table and placed it next to the back door. He could almost see the hill behind his aunt and uncle's house from where he sat. Aunt Athena and Uncle Tony still had their living room lights on. Even though he didn't agree with keeping the house lit up for all to see Christian understood their motivations.

Anthony stood at the kitchen sink and kept watch out over the back hill of the house. With the moonlight he could easily make out the chain link fence at the top of the hill.

Matt Chico excused himself and headed to the basement. He placed his hand on his chest and tried to steady his breathing in the cool dark of the room. With tear filled eyes, he dropped to his knees at the foot of the bed, clasped his hands together and prayed aloud, "Dear lord God, please keep my family safe. Please guide my brother as he travels with his family and my son to New Jersey. Please keep us safe and whatever happened at the arsenal today, please help everyone to be alright with no further incidents. In Jesus's name we pray...amen."

After the meal Josh complained about being tired. Kerri took him to one of the bedrooms to lay down. Mr. and Mrs. Spahl kept a close watch on the news from where they sat on the couch. During the commercial breaks, Mr. Spahl would yawn and rub his eyes.

"Just a little longer," Mrs. Spahl chided as she pushed her elbow playfully into his ribs. "Don't you go falling asleep. I don't want to have to drive home."

"I'm fine," Mr. Spahl insisted. "I think I just ate too much and you're not driving my Tahoe so banish the thought."

"You and that car. He did do a nice with job dinner," Mrs. Spahl said as she motioned towards Matt.

"Thanks," Matt said without turning around. "It turned out good. That was our grandfather's recipe. I haven't put that together in quite a while." He added as he continued to peer out from between the plywood. As he scanned the yard across the street, movement just beyond the area illuminated by the street light caught his eye. "Jeff..." He called just as the phone rang and startled him.

Jeff turned quickly, "Are you going to answer it?" He asked as the phone rang a second time.

Almost confused, Matt looked at Jeff and then down at the phone which rang again, "Yes...yes, I'm going to answer it." He responded as he picked up the phone and pressed the call button. "Hello..."

The muffled voice in the background was almost indistinguishable. It sounded like a mixture of crying and shouting.

"Hello," Matt repeated. "Aunt Athena is that you?"

"Who is it?" Christian demanded as he entered the living room.

"Not sure," Matt said with a shrug as he looked up at his brother. "Aunt Athena is that you?"

The muffled voices continued for a second, then the line went silent for a moment before his aunt spoke, "Matthew, oh my God it's a miracle!" Aunt Athena shouted.

Matt covered the receiver and nodded, "It's Aunt Athena."

"Is she ok?" Christian asked impatiently. "What's going on?"

"Not sure," Matt said as his eyes widened. "She sounds hysterical."

"Well, fucking ask her," Christian ordered as his voice intensified.

"Aunt Athena," Matt interjected. "Aunt Athena, is everything ok?"

"Better than ok," Aunt Athena shrieked. "It's a miracle!"

"What's a miracle?" Matt asked.

"Katherine and Marcus," Aunt Athena shouted. "They're here! They made it home safe!"

"That's great, Aunt Athena," Matt said to reassure her. "That's really great!" He covered the receiver and motioned to Christian. "Katherine and Marcus made it home safe."

"Great!" Christian said with a nod. "Has she heard from Tyler and Patrick?"

Matt shook his head, "I don't know. She didn't say."

"Matthew, would you and Christian come over and talk to Katherine and Marcus about what you told Uncle Tony and I earlier?" Aunt Athena asked.

"Right now?" Matt asked.

"Yes, right now," Aunt Athena answered. "Please, it would really mean a lot."

"Sure, Aunt Athena. Christian and I will be right over," Matt said as he hung up the phone. "She wants us to go over and talk to Katherine and Marcus."

"Now?" Christian asked as he looked at everyone in the living room.

"That's what she said," Matt answered as he collected his shotgun.

"Alright then," Christian said. "Let's not keep her waiting."

"Hey," Matt called as Christian turned to leave. "Before we go, look out at the Santini's property. I could have sworn I saw something move just beyond the lighted part of the yard."

"Could have been an animal," Christian said as he quickly squatted and looked out from between the plywood. "I don't see anything."

"You guys go," Jeff instructed. "I'll keep an eye on the Santini's yard."

"Sounds good," Christian said as he got to his feet. They moved quickly through the kitchen. "Anthony, keep an eye on the back hill. Matt and I will be right back."

Christian was the first to exit the house through the back door. His Mossberg 590 shotgun was pressed firmly against his shoulder as he moved quickly onto the small porch. He raised the shotgun and scanned the hill behind the house as he navigated the three concrete stairs that led to the sidewalk, "Clear."

Matt followed close behind. As he stepped onto sidewalk he turned left, raised his Mossberg 590 shotgun, and checked the narrow path that ran between the house and stone wall, "Clear." He called quietly. He lowered the shotgun as he turned to follow Christian.

"Moving," Christian answered as he started down the sidewalk towards their aunt and uncle's house.

Matt followed several yards behind. He continually scanned the hill behind the houses across to the steep grassy yard that led to the road.

The night air had cooled considerably since the sun slipped out of sight behind the mountains to the west. The gentle breeze which had felt so good in the early morning hours had begun to gust through the trees. They were less than half way down the sidewalk when the wind carried with it the hauntingly distinct sound of a low moan. Immediately they froze.

Christian glanced back at Matt, "Did you hear that?"

"I did," Matt answered with a nod. "What do you want to do?"

Christian shook his head, "Watch for movement and keep going. I'll cover the hill. You watch the front yard."

Matt nodded, "Move."

When they reached their aunt and uncle's they charged in, this time without knocking. Their aunt stood in the living room. Tears streamed down her face as she refused to let go of her only daughter.

"Mom, that's enough," Katherine insisted as she struggled to free herself from her mother's grasp. She looked up to see her cousins coming through the dining room. "Enough mom, we have company."

"Oh, Katherine," Aunt Athena sobbed. "I was afraid I was never going to see you again."

"Are the two of you happy?" Katherine asked angrily. "I don't what you told my parents but my mother is acting like it's the end of the world."

Katherine was two years younger than her brother Tyler and three years older than her brother Patrick. Her long curly blonde hair reached the middle of her back. She was short in stature at just over 5 feet tall, with hazel brown eyes and a face full of freckles. The cuffs of her red fleece jacket were rolled up past her wrists. The short sleeve white t-shirt she wore beneath was tucked into a pair of tight blue jeans. She was infamous within the family for her fiery hair trigger temper.

"Well?" Katherine demanded. "Would one of you like to fucking explain yourselves?"

"We're glad you're home safe," Matt said as he hugged his cousin.

"STOP!" Katherine ordered. "And why are you carrying shotguns? What's wrong with you two?"

"Marcus," Christian acknowledged stoically as he turned to face his aunt. "Has there been any word yet from Tyler or Patrick?"

"Hey," Marcus replied from the recliner where he sat with his hands folded.

Marcus was tall and lean with a head full of messy black hair. His powder blue button-down shirt and khaki slacks looked too big for his narrow frame. The pair of black dress shoes he wore looked out of proportion to how tall he was. His pale complexion made him look sickly. When he was around Katherine's family, he rarely spoke.

"Aunt Athena," Christian said firmly to secure her attention. "Has there been any word from Tyler and Patrick?"

"Oh, my boys," Aunt Athena wailed.

"I'm sure their fine," Christian tried to assure her. "The arsenal has rooms designated for personnel to shelter-in-place and lock down if necessary. I'm sure they're safe and have food and water. Katherine made it home and they will too."

"Athena, please," Uncle Tony pleaded from the couch. "Just come and sit down."

"Oh, Tony...our boys," Aunt Athena continued as she began to sob again. "Where are our boys?"

"I'm sure it's like Christian said," Uncle Tony assured her. "Just come and sit down."

"Uncle Tony," Matt began.

Uncle Tony held his hand up, "Easy boys. Your aunt is very fragile right now. Do me a favor and take a seat. The local news said after the commercial break the Governor is going to make an announcement."

They waited as patiently as they were able. Finally, the last commercial ended and the picture on the screen transitioned back to the news room. Trent Ashworth still occupied the seat behind the large news desk. He had been on the air for more than a dozen hours and the makeup was no longer concealing the deep bags under his eyes.

"Ladies and gentlemen," Trent Ashworth began as he fidgeted with the stack of papers in front of him. "We are taking you live now to the Governor's Mansion where New Jersey Governor Mitchell Garrison is holding a press conference."

Trent Ashworth offered no further explanation. He sat stoically behind the large desk until the broadcast from the newsroom ended. The video feed from the Governor's mansion was a wide shot. Personnel hurried from one side of the riser where the podium stood to the other until finally the Governor emerged from off camera. His administration had been embroiled in multiple high-profile scandals over the last 2-years. The stress was beginning to take a visible toll. He moved slowly to the microphone. His dark blue suit looked as if it had been slept in. His sparce gray hair was matted down and beads of sweat were visible on his forehead.

"My fellow citizens," Governor Garrison began. His voice was shaky. His eyes appeared glassy and his hand trembled slightly as he wiped sweat from his forehead with a white handkerchief. "There has been an outbreak that we are working to contain. I have declared a state of emergency beginning at 10 p.m. tonight. It will continue for the next 48-hours. During this time, you will be asked not to leave your homes and to keep your movements to an absolute minimum. My office is working to coordinate support from both FEMA and the CDC. I have placed the National Guard on high alert and they will be activated if necessary. We are not able to provide any additional details currently. May God continue to bless us and these United States of America."

"What was that?" Christian asked as the picture cut back to the newsroom. Trent Ashworth looked unprepared to be back on the air so quickly. "What the fuck was that? That's it? State of emergency, outbreak, no other information available?"

"Oh, my boys," Aunt Athena wailed.

"It's ok, Athena," Uncle Tony urged. His voice was weak and his breathing labored. "Katherine, help me please."

"Come on mom," Katherine insisted as she helped her mother to her feet. "You need to lay down."

"Why don't you come back with us?" Matt asked.

Uncle Tony shook his head, "I can't boys. I'm just not up for it. Besides, your aunt needs to be here for when Tyler and Patrick get home."

"We'll be just down the sidewalk if you need us," Christian assured him.

Uncle Tony nodded, "Before you go, I was doing some digging on what you told us earlier."

"Find anything?" Christian asked.

"Unfortunately, yes," Uncle Tony answered as he pulled his robe tight around his frail body. "Just before you got here, two of the lesser-known news stations were running stories about outbreaks of violence at six different military installations across the country. There haven't been many other details yet, but the footage has been extremely graphic."

Christian nodded as he tried to process what he was hearing, "Lock the doors and windows and close the blinds. We'll be back in the morning to check on you. In the meantime, don't go outside."

Not even the cool night air could take the edge off what they just heard. Neither said it aloud, but they were both worried about what was coming. They moved quickly along the sidewalk. Another wind gust carried a low ominous moan that caused the hair on the backs of their necks to stand up. They stopped abruptly and looked out towards the road.

"Did you hear that?" Matt asked as he squinted into the dark.

"Yes. It sounded like it came from..." Christian stopped mid-sentence as a second moan was followed by a faint visceral scream somewhere in the distance.

"What the fuck was that?" Matt asked as his heart pounded in his chest. He adjusted his grip on the shotgun. "That sounded like it came from the other side of Mr. Santini's property."

"We need to be ready. Nobody's leaving!" Christian growled through clenched teeth, "Come on let's get inside."

CHAPTER 7

wide awake in america

NIGHT PASSED WITHOUT INCIDENT. The five of them kept watch in rotating shifts with two in the living room, two in the kitchen and the fifth with some time to rest. No one really slept though. Even Jeff and Matt Chico's parents who retired to the two upstairs bedrooms shortly after the Governor's address tossed and turned throughout most of the night.

Matt dozed off in the recliner for an hour or so. Christian briefly returned to the couch. Anthony unrolled his sleeping bag in the narrow hallway, but just starred at the ceiling. Jeff used one of the throw pillows from the couch and found a quiet corner of the dining room to curl up in for a few hours. Matt Chico just sat on the edge of the coffee table, placed his elbows on his thighs and rested his head in his hands.

"Chico, why don't you go downstairs and close your eyes for a bit," Matt suggested from where he crouched at the front door. "You're burning up all your down time sitting on the coffee table."

"Can't," Chico said as he rubbed his eyes. "I just can't...not until I know my son is safe."

"Why don't we shut the T.V. off for a while," Jeff offered as he rested his rifle against the love seat and turned away from the window. "It's just more of the same at this point. Reports of atrocities and graphic images."

"Shut it off," Matt said as he motioned to the remote control. "We probably should have shut it off a few hours ago...but..."

Jeff gave Matt Chico's shoulder a reassuring pat as he reached passed him and picked up the remote control, "I'm sure this isn't helping any of us."

"It's everywhere," Matt Chico muttered hopelessly to himself as graphic images of cannibalistic violence flashed across the screen. What spilled from the gates of Omega Arsenal so many hours earlier now appeared to be everywhere. The media reported attacks from across the country. Similar reports trickled in from Canada, parts of Europe and the middle east. No amount of spin could put a positive slant on what was being broadcast, nor could it keep the conspiracy theorists from having their day on the internet. "Dear God, it's everywhere."

"At least we know the media blackout is over," Jeff said as he pressed the off button. The picture disappeared and the screen went dark. For a moment the room was silent. "We'll pick it back up in a few hours."

"Sounds good," Matt said as he yawned and redirected his focus back to the front yard and street. "Chico, why don't you get some water and at least go lay down for a little bit. We've got it covered up here."

Reluctantly Matt Chico nodded and got to his feet, "Yeah, maybe I'll do that." He said as he shuffled out of the room.

"I hate seeing him this way," Jeff said as he rubbed his temples.

"Yeah, me too," Matt agreed. "Too many loved ones still unaccounted for."

"Nothing happening over here," Jeff said. "I'm going to the kitchen to see how Christian and Anthony are. You want anything?"

"Bottle of water, please," Matt answered.

In the early hours, darkness reluctantly gave way to the dim light of morning. The sun was not yet visible in the sky which left the landscape shrouded in shades of gray.

Christian rubbed his eyes and watched fine whisps of mist rise from the hill behind the house. He leaned his shotgun against the cabinets, grabbed a green apple from the fruit bowl on the counter and took a bite.

Anthony retired to the kitchen table. He intended to sit for a minute but his head slowly lowered as if he were melting. Finally, his eyes closed and his head came to rest on his folded arms.

Jeff placed the open pack of cigarettes under his nose and inhaled deeply. He closed his eyes and shook his head before he removed one of them. He broke the filter off and placed the wrapped tobacco in his mouth between his cheek and gum.

Matt yawned, shook his head, and tried to maintain his focus. He finished the last of his water, placed the empty bottle on the end table and adjusted the holster attached to his right leg. He tried to blink the tiredness from his eyes.

The front yard was steep and in the low light of morning the vibrant green of the grass was significantly muted. Even the asphalt on the street appeared to be washed in a gray hue.

On the other side of the street was the home of the Santini's. They were an elderly couple who had been friends with Matt and Christian's grandparents. With their own children out of state, the brothers made sure to help them year-round with all manner of tasks. Because the brothers would accept no money, the Santini's always made sure to send them home with food, which was always appreciated.

Decades earlier Mr. Santini converted the back yard into a picturesque Italian landscape for his wife. He constructed a wooden frame in the center of the yard that hosted a grape vine. They used the large purple grapes to make wine. Throughout the rest of the property stood replica marble statues surrounded by beautifully robust rose bushes. Mrs. Santini was known locally for her roses which had been featured in several publications over the years.

While the rest of the landscape was shrouded in shades of gray the vibrant red of the roses didn't appear diminished in the least. Matt allowed himself a moment as he appreciated the beauty of the rose bushes. He exhaled as a feeling of calm washed over him until movement and another shade of crimson caught his eye.

"Movement...I've got movement!" Matt shouted.

"Where?" Christian called as he hurried from the kitchen.

"What?" Anthony asked as he was startled awake. He rubbed his eyes and struggled to pull his stiffened body up off the chair. "What's happening?"

"Santini's yard!" Matt answered as he pointed between the gap in the plywood. "There's somebody moving around by the grape vine."

Amidst the softened light of the early morning a gangly figure lumbered across the Santini's back yard. His movements were awkward and clumsy. Much of his light blue polo shirt was in tatters. A large section of the back of the shirt was missing completely. There was a large open wound visible at the middle of his back. The exposed skin was covered in dark red which continued down and stained much of the back of his khaki shorts.

"I see him," Christian said in near disbelief. "Look at his back. He looks mangled."

"Yeah, like he stepped right out of yesterday's news broadcast," Matt said with a shaky voice.

"I've got movement on this side!" Jeff called from where he knelt.

"Jesus," Matt said as he turned to look at Christian. "It got here. It took less than 24-hours, but it got here."

Chrisitan nodded, "Yeah…looks like it did."

"What is it?" Anthony asked as he hurried to the living room. "What's going on?"

"Somebody's in the Santini's yard," Christian said as he turned.

"Do we know who it is?" Anthony asked.

"I need you to watch the back of the house," Christian answered as he shook his head. "If you see anybody, call it out."

"Will do," Anthony said with a nod. He turned and hurried back to the kitchen as Matt Chico made his way up from the basement.

"What's going on up here?" Matt Chico asked as he rubbed his eyes.

"Two of them on this side!" Jeff called with noticeable alarm in his voice. "Looks like a man and a woman."

"Anthony!" Christian called. "Load that shotgun!"

"Hey!" Matt Chico blurted. "What's going on?"

"We've got movement on two sides," Matt answered. "Three people so far."

Anthony dropped to one knee and pulled the first shell from the side saddle. He placed it in the open breach and pulled the pump forward. He made sure the safety was engaged before he loaded the next five shells into the magazine, "Loaded!" He called as he got to his feet.

"And for that we're loading shotguns?" Matt Chico asked with concern in his voice.

"As a precaution," Christian assured him. "Take a look at the guy across the street and tell me if he should be up and moving."

"What the?" Matt Chico muttered as he peered out at the figure across the street. "Is that blood?"

"Good," Christian called to Anthony as he moved to where Jeff knelt. "Keep the safety on."

"It's on," Anthony called from the kitchen. He breathed heavily as he tapped his index finger nervously against the receiver just above the trigger guard.

"Matt!" Christian called as he looked out at the two figures who staggered across the empty lot. "I think we know these two!"

"What?" Matt asked as he moved quickly across the room to where Christian and Jeff were positioned. "Oh, my God." He blurted. "That's Costanza the butcher and his wife Marie...but what happened to them?"

Costanzo and Marie owned *Taste of Italy Butcher Shop and Delicatessen*. The family business was a town staple and had been started by Costanzo's grandfather upon his arrival to America at the turn of the century. The couple was revered for their delectable food dishes and exceptional service.

However, to see them now, they appeared to have stepped straight out of a nightmare. Their skin was abnormally pail with dark discolored veins visible. The skin around their open wounds had an almost unnatural yellowish gray discoloration.

Marie was missing a large patch of hair from the right side of her head. Dried blood covered the side of her face where her ear had been. Nerve endings and tissue hung from the empty socket that had been home to her right eye. Most of her right cheek was torn away. The wound left her back teeth exposed. Dried blood covered the pastel-colored floral patterned spring dress she wore and her bare feet left bloodied prints along the green grass as she walked.

There was a gaping wound to the left side of Costanzo's neck. With so much flesh missing his head cocked awkwardly to one side. His white polo shirt and apron were saturated with the deep red of dried blood. His mouth hung open and a mangled stump where his right hand used to be left a trail of blood as he walked.

"You know them?" Jeff asked. "Should we go out and help them?"

"No," Christian answered bluntly.

"What do you mean, no?" Matt Chico asked. "I thought you knew them?"

"What if this is part of the outbreak the Governor talked about in his address?" Matt questioned. "We don't know what they have, how contagious it is or how to treat it."

"So, what then?" Matt Chico asked. "What about calling 911?"

"Do you have your phone?" Christian asked.

Matt Chico nodded, "I do." He said as he took his cell phone from his pocket.

"Call them," Christian instructed.

Matt Chico looked down at the screen on his phone and back at Christian, "It says, no service."

"Try the land line," Matt offered as he continued to watch Costanzo and Marie.

Matt Chico took the portable phone from the cradle and quickly dialed. He held the phone to his hear as it rang, "Nothing. No one's picking up!" He blurted. "How can 911 just ring?"

"What the fuck?" Jeff questioned. As Costanzo and Marie neared. He was better able to make out the extent of their wounds. "Neither of them should be upright and walking."

"I've got movement at the top of the hill!" Anthony called from the kitchen.

"This can't be happening," Matt Chico mumbled to himself as he dropped the phone on the coffee table. He turned back and continued to watch in disbelief as the figure across the street shambled awkwardly through the Santini's yard. "This can't be happening."

"What's going on out here?" Mr. Spahl asked as he pulled a white t-shirt over his torso and entered the living room.

"How many?" Christian called.

"Four...maybe five," Anthony replied. "At the top of the hill."

"Go," Jeff urged as he gave Christian a nod. He reached under the Mini-14 with his left hand and retracted the charging handle. "Make sure Anthony's alright. Matt and I will keep an eye on things from here."

"If they make it onto our property or if you see anyone else, call it out," Christian instructed as he hurried to the kitchen to check on Anthony.

"Jeff!" Mr. Spahl said sternly to secure his son's attention. "What is going on out here?"

"Dad..." Jeff began. He was about to turn around and answer his father when a rescue green Jeep Wrangler Unlimited raced down the steep road directly behind Costanzo and Marie. The large tires of the Jeep screeched and brake lights lit up as the driver tried to slow the vehicle enough to make the left turn onto the street. "Who the fuck is this?" He asked as he motioned towards the vehicle as it began to slide on the loose gravel.

"That's Paul's Jeep!" Matt shouted. "He's coming in too fast. He's not going make the turn...not with those tires."

The back end of the Jeep slid wide and almost turned the entire vehicle over. Paul was somehow able to maintain control and complete the turn. The four of them watched from the front windows as the Jeep slid to a stop just before it collided with Josh's dark blue Buick Roadmaster which was parked in the street across from the house.

"Fucking Paul," Jeff said as he shook his head. "The guy really knows how to make a fucking entrance."

The driver's side door of the Jeep swung open as Paul's large frame hurried from behind the wheel. His well-worn brown leather cowboy boots made an audible thud against the asphalt. He pulled the back door open and retrieved his Springfield Armory M1A Scout rifle and large black duffle bag.

Ralph jumped from the passenger side door. He had a coyote tan backpack slung over his right shoulder and a Kimber 1911 in his left hand. He scanned the area before moving quickly to the driver's side of the Jeep.

"Who is it?" Christian questioned as he hurried back to the living room.

"Paul and Ralph," Matt answered as he got to his feet and motioned from the window for them to come around the side of the house.

"Do you see him?" Ralph asked as he adjusted the backpack strap over his right shoulder. "There, in the window!"

Ralph was the elder statesman of the group or so he liked to refer to himself. His thick dark hair and beard were streaked with silver which made him look older than he was. He was soft spoken and usually the voice of reason for the group. He wore a short sleeve brown plaid button-down shirt, blue jeans, and dark colored sneakers.

"I see him," Paul answered with a nod. "Come on, let's go." He growled as the two of them crossed the street and ascended the steep driveway.

Paul was large and formidable. He looked like a lumberjack with thick forearms and a wide back. He kept his brown hair short and let his beard now speckled with gray grow down to his chest. He wore his favorite pale blue t-shirt with the Gem Saloon logo on the back and khaki cargo pants.

"Jeff, stay here," Matt instructed.

"Where are you going?" Jeff asked.

"We need to bring them in safe," Matt said as he charged from the living room.

"Anthony, get ready," Christian ordered as he followed Matt through the house.

"I don't like this," Matt Chico said as he stepped away from the window. "I don't like this at all."

"I'll watch the front Jeff," Mr. Spahl said as he moved to the front door. "You keep watch where you are."

"Thanks, dad," Jeff said with a nod. "Do you want my pistol?"

Mr. Spahl shook his head uncomfortably, "No. No...I don't."

Beads of sweat ran down the sides of Matt's face as he moved cautiously to the end of the small porch. He could hear the unnerving moans from the top of the hill as he glanced around the corner of the house to his left, "Clear." He called as he moved down the stairs and onto the sidewalk.

"Move," Christian said as he followed closely behind.

"Where do you want me?" Anthony asked as he stepped on to back the porch.

"Anthony, you stay here," Christian instructed without looking back. "Anybody comes down the walkway call it out. I don't want any surprises on the way back in."

"Got it," Anthony said. His gaze panned across the top of the hill. To his horror he could see a half dozen badly wounded people pressed up against the chain link fence. The most gruesome of them drug the bloody tattered stump of what had been his right arm back and forth across the metal fence as if he were trying to climb over. His eyes were sunken into their sockets and a portion of his jaw was missing. Anthony gasped and pressed his left hand against his chest as he tried not hyperventilate. "Keep it together." He whispered to himself as his hands trembled and stomach churned.

Christian covered their aunt and uncle's property as Matt came around the north east corner of the house with his shotgun raised.

"Easy, brother Matthew," Paul said in a gruff voice as he and Ralph hurried up the sidewalk that ran along the side of the house.

"Got them," Matt called as he lowered the shotgun.

"Good," Christian answered. "Let's get inside. It's getting crowded out here."

"Goddamn good to see you both," Matt said with a smile.

"Likewise," Ralph said as he engaged the thumb safety on his 1911. He used his right hand to wipe the beads of sweat that trickled down his forehead. "It was a hell of time trying to get here."

"You should have called," Matt said half-jokingly. "We could have given you a warmer welcome."

"We tried," Ralph explained. "Cell service has been sporadic at best."

"What?" Matt asked.

"Not out here!" Christian shouted as he saw several more bodies moving towards them from the property adjacent to their aunt and uncle's. "We need to get inside!"

"Didn't you notice there was no cell service?" Paul asked as he tried to catch his breath.

"There was so much going on," Matt said as he shook his head. "Some calls went through, some didn't. We were on and off the land line. I guess I didn't catch it."

"Did you see the Governor's address?" Paul asked. "What the hell's going on?"

"Inside!" Christian ordered. "We need to continue this conversation inside!"

The five of them were single file on the narrow porch as they tried to crowd through the back door and get into the house.

"Faster would be better," Matt said as the intensity of the moans amplified behind them.

"We're moving," Ralph assured him as the front of his sneaker caught the edge of the porch. As he tripped, he grabbed for the faded white siding to steady himself.

"I got you," Paul said as he turned to help Ralph.

"Anthony, get up here ahead of me," Christian ordered. "I'll pull up the rear."

"You go ahead," Anthony said with a nod. "I got this."

"Alright, keep your eyes open," Christian instructed.

"I am," Anthony assured him without turning around. "I'm watching the back hill."

Christian's head whipped around, "Not the fucking hill!" He blurted angrily. "I told you to watch the..."

"AHHHH!" Anthony screamed as a pair of teeth ripped through the flesh on his left forearm. He dropped the shotgun as Marie's cold pale hands took hold of his wrist and shirt. Anthony tried desperately to pull away from her. His flesh made an audible tearing sound as blood spilled from the wound and splashed across the ground.

"NO!" Christian shouted. He stepped to the edge of the porch, leveled the barrel of the shotgun at Marie's chest and fired. The near point-blank blast tore through her sternum and threw her body backwards. Blood and tissue trickled down the stone wall as what was left of her lay contorted on the ground.

Pain pulsated through Anthony's body. His ears rang and spots began to cloud his vision. He clamped his right hand over the wound and tried to remain conscious. His legs gave way and he crumpled in a heap to the ground. His agony filled scream quieted to a hollow whimper.

The shotgun blast was deafening. Christian blinked and tried to regain his bearings. Unsure of what happened, Matt and Paul threw themselves on top of Ralph to protect him.

"Get off me!" Ralph demanded. "Get the fuck off me!"

"Get inside!" Christian hollered. He could see Anthony writhing on the ground in pain. His mouth was open but what little of Anthony's voice he could make out sounded miles away. "Matt, I need you!"

"Come on!" Matt shouted as he grabbed Anthony under the knees. "I'll get his legs!"

"Hang on Anthony," Christian shouted as his ears continued to ring. He grabbed Anthony under the right shoulder. "You're going to be ok!"

"No! It fucking hurts!" Anthony cried. His blood curdling screams echoed off the stone wall and aluminum siding as the brothers lifted him on to the porch. "Oh, God it fucking hurts!"

"Take him!" Christian shouted. "Come on Goddammit, we're not alone out here!"

"Let him go!" Paul said as he grabbed Anthony around the torso, "Ralph, get his legs."

"I've got him," Ralph said as they hoisted Anthony's limp body up and carried him towards the back door.

"I killed Marie," Christian said horrified as his ears rang and he looked at Matt.

"What happened?" Matt asked as if in a daze.

Christian was about to answer when his face dropped, "Oh, my God..."

Matt turned quickly as Marie's mangled and bloodied body began to move, "What the fuck?"

Pieces of bone protruded from the gaping wound in her sternum as Marie climbed to her feet. Her mouth hung open and exposed broken blood-stained teeth. The sound from her mouth intensified as her lifeless eye fixated on the brothers.

"Impossible!" Christian blurted as he retracted the pump of the shotgun. "Fucking impossible!" He continued as he pulled the pump forward and chambered the next shell. He raised the shotgun to his shoulder pulled the trigger. The sound of the blast was deafening. Buckshot ripped through Marie's right shoulder. The impact spun her around and tore her arm from her body. It tumbled through the air and landed a few feet from her.

"What the fuck?" Matt called as Marie's mangled body began to move again. He raised the shotgun and lined the bead at the end of the barrel up with Marie's forehead. The blast of buckshot jettisoned blood, bone, and flesh against the stone wall. Her head was instantly reduced to a cloud of red mist. What was left of her contorted carcass fell again and this time did not get up.

Christian picked up Anthony's shotgun from the ground just as Costanzo's blood-soaked apron became visible, "Hold this." He said as he handed the shotgun to Matt.

"Come on," Matt urged as he took the shotgun. "Let's just get inside."

Christian shook his head, "Not leaving him like that." He said as he cycled the action and chambered the next shell. "I don't know what this is...but he was always good to us and I'm not leaving him like that."

"What if there's a cure," Matt argued as he scanned the property nervously.

"Take a look at his face," Christian instructed.

Reluctantly, Matt's gaze found the old butcher. The agony seared onto the pale flesh of Costanzo's lifeless face was haunting. His sunken hollow eyes were devoid of any hint of humanity or reason. Dried blood covered his gaping neck wound and cloths.

"What do you see?" Christian asked as he raised the shotgun to his shoulder. "Anything look curable to you?"

"No," Matt said stoically as he shook his head. "Finish it."

Christian zeroed the ghost ring sites on the blood-stained teeth that hung in Costanzo's open mouth. He exhaled and squeezed the trigger. Buckshot ripped through Costanzo's twisted face and sent the top half of his head bouncing across the lower portion of the grassy hill. The impact threw the rest of his body back against the stone wall.

"Now!" Matt insisted. "Let's get inside."

"Fine," Christian agreed. He pulled the pump of the shotgun back and watched as the spent shell ejected from the breach. It tumbled through the air before it landed on the blood-soaked ground. "Now, we can go inside."

CHAPTER 8

the long bright dark

I T WAS BEDLAM IN the house as everyone crowded into the small kitchen. Frantically they shouted over one another about what to do and how to help. Anthony screamed and writhed on the kitchen floor as blood pooled on the linoleum around him.

"DEAR GOD IT FUCKING HURTS!" Anthony cried. His torso was saturated in the deep red that poured from his arm. The pain was so excruciating he threw up. Remnants of vomit covered his face as his body convulsed. "FUCK...PLEASE GOD IT HURTS SO BAD!"

"I've got towels!" Mrs. Spahl announced as she hurried into the kitchen with an arm full of clean linens.

"Don't touch him!" Christian hollered as he hurried inside from one nightmare to another. He could barely hear his own voice over the ringing in his ears. "Don't fucking touch him!"

"HELP ME!" Anthony wailed from the floor. "PLEASE GOD!"

"What?" Mrs. Spahl asked startled. She stopped abruptly and almost dropped the arm full of sand stone colored towels she carried. "But he's hurt!"

"He's been bit!" Christian shouted. "He may be contagious. Don't touch him without gloves on."

"Where are the fucking gloves?" Matt Chico hollered from the doorway.

"We carried him inside!" Paul blurted as he motioned angrily with his hands. "Where does that leave us?"

"Bathroom closet!" Matt shouted as he slammed the back door shut. He turned the deadbolt clockwise. "Nitrile gloves...bathroom closet, second shelf!"

"I'll get them!" Matt Chico said as he turned and hurried out of the kitchen.

"We need to call an ambulance!" Kerri cried. She and Josh watched in horror from where they stood next to the refrigerator.

"My arm won't stop bleeding," Anthony whimpered as mucus ran from his nose and blood seeped between his fingers. "AM I GOING TO DIE? PLEASE GOD I DON'T WANT TO DIE!"

"Somebody, do something!" Kerri demanded. "PLEASE...HELP HIM!"

"Kerri, I don't want to be here anymore," Josh said as his cheeks went flush. A blank distant stare covered his face as he helplessly watched the chaos.

"Did you get any of his blood on you?" Christian asked red faced as he tried to catch his breath.

"We need to get a tourniquet on that arm!" Mr. Spahl insisted.

"What?" Paul stammered as he turned and looked at Ralph. "I...I don't know. I don't think so."

Josh's left hand clung tightly to the refrigerator door, while his right hand hung at his side with a noticeable tremor. "I want to go home." He managed to utter as he stared at Anthony with tear filled eyes.

"Well check!" Christian ordered. "Both of you!"

"TOURNIQUET, GODDAMMIT!" Mr. Spahl shouted. "We need to get a tourniquet on that arm and stop the bleeding!"

"Josh, it's ok," Kerri tried to reassure him as her focus shifted. She collected his right hand in both of hers. "It's ok. We'll go home very soon."

"Basement!" Matt shouted as he pressed his body against the back door and motioned to the stairs. "CAT tourniquets and first aid supplies in the black backpacks lined against the laundry room wall."

"I don't think I've got any blood on me," Ralph said as he frantically checked his arms and cloths. "I need to wash just in case!"

"I found them!" Matt Chico called as he hurried back to the kitchen with a white and green box of black nitrile gloves. He and Ralph almost collided in the doorway. "I found the gloves!"

"Laundry room," Mr. Spahl repeated as he stepped over Anthony and headed for the door to the basement. "I'll get them."

"Sorry!" Ralph said as he lurched back and held his hands up. "Careful, I don't know if I've got any of his blood on me."

"Chico, give me a pair of gloves," Christian ordered.

"I'll take a pair too," Matt called as he leaned his shotgun in the corner between the cabinet and back door and wiped the sweat from his face.

"I think you're good," Matt Chico said as he gave Ralph a quick look. He looked at Matt and shook his head. "We've got this. You need to keep watch on what's going on out there."

"Not taking any chances," Ralph said. "Gotta get cleaned up and change...come on Paul."

"If anybody's got any blood on their person or their cloths," Christian began as he pulled a pair of gloves over his hands. "You need to strip down and shower immediately!"

"Right behind you," Paul said as he followed Ralph out of the kitchen.

"What about bleach?" Mrs. Spahl asked as she set the towels down on the kitchen table.

"Please, help him!" Kerri begged as she held fast to Josh's hand. "Anthony needs a doctor!"

"The phone's on the wall!" Christian snarled angrily as he pointed.

"Container of bleach, under the kitchen sink," Matt answered as he peered from the back door. "Another on the floor of the bathroom closet and more in the basement."

"I found them!" Mr. Spahl announced as he emerged from the basement with a black 5.11 All Hazards backpack slung over his right shoulder. "I've got the med supplies...give me a pair of gloves!"

"Somebody, do something!" Kerri insisted as she waved her right arm frantically.

"You want something done?" Christian hollered rhetorically. He dropped a towel next to Anthony and used it to kneel on as he tried to hold him still. "Dial 911 if you think somebody'll actually answer this time!"

Mr. Spahl placed several towels over the blood pooled around Anthony, "Hold him still." He instructed as he knelt and readied the tourniquet. "Hang on Anthony, we're going to get you patched up."

"It hurts," Anthony whimpered. "It won't stop bleeding and it hurts so bad."

"What can I do?" Mrs. Spahl asked as she moved to the doorway of the kitchen.

"Pain meds!" Mr. Spahl said as he pulled the tourniquet tight around Anthony's upper arm.

"AHHH!" Anthony screamed as his body convulsed.

"Hold him still!" Mr. Spahl ordered.

"I'm trying!" Christian wheezed as he pushed Anthony's body against the floor. "What about pain meds?"

"Do you have any?" Mr. Spahl asked.

"Top shelf, bathroom closet!" Matt called as he kept watch from the door. "There should be Percocet and Oxy."

"I'll get them," Mrs. Spahl said as she hurried from the kitchen.

"Hold him!" Mr. Spahl ordered as he fed the red tip through the buckle and pulled the band back on itself. He twisted the tourniquet rod several times and secured the rod inside one of the plastic clips.

"AHHHHH...NOOOO!" Anthony shrieked before he passed out.

Mr. Spahl pealed the gloves off his hands and sat back against the cabinet under the sink. He used his forearm to wipe the sweat from his forehead, "Jesus, even with the tourniquet on his wound is still seeping blood."

"What the fuck?" Christian uttered. His face was red and beads of sweat ran down his cheeks. Carefully he removed the gloves and dropped them next to the towel as he retrieved his inhaler and took a several puffs. "What now?"

Mr. Spahl shook his head, "Pack the wound with gauze."

"And if that doesn't work?" Christian asked as he wiped his face.

"Cauterize it," Mr. Spahl answered. "But, let's hope it doesn't come to that."

"JEFF!" Matt called from the kitchen as reloaded his shotgun. "Jeff...what do you see?"

"I only found Percocet," Mrs. Spahl said as she hurried back to the kitchen. "The Oxy bottle was empty."

"Fuck!" Christian said as he shook his head.

"Tyler?" Matt asked as he turned around.

"Who else?" Christian asked rhetorically as he glanced back at his brother.

"When was Tyler here?" Matt asked.

"Last week," Christian answered. "Said he wanted to see how I was feeling…"

"What the fuck," Matt snarled. "I thought he was over that."

"Over that?" Christian questioned. "He's got a pain killer addiction no one wants to acknowledge. You don't just get over that."

"Fucking Tyler," Matt muttered as he turned back. "JEFF! What do you see?"

"The street's filling up!" Jeff shouted from where he crouched at the front door. "Movement at both ends."

"Fucking great," Matt grumbled to himself.

"What about the back?" Jeff called from the living room.

"Two that I can see!" Matt answered. "Headed this way but moving slow."

"What are we going to do with Anthony?" Matt Chico asked. "We can't leave him on the kitchen floor."

Christian nodded without looking up, "See if Paul and Ralph can give us a hand moving him."

"Yeah," Matt Chico answered with a nod as he turned and left the kitchen.

"Christian, please we need to get him some help," Kerri pleaded. "If he is infected with something he needs to be treated at a hospital."

"I'm sorry Kerri, I don't think there's anyone for us to call," Christian said as calmly as he could.

"We have to try," Kerri insisted. "Anthony needs a doctor."

"Phones on the wall," Christian said as he raised his head and looked at her. "If you want to try...by all means."

Kerri nodded, took the cordless phone from its base, and dialed. She held the phone to her ear and listened as it rang. She was certain at any moment the 911 operator would answer, "It just keeps ringing." She whispered quietly to herself.

"On their way in," Matt Chico announced as he reentered the kitchen. "They were getting cleaned up."

After the fourth ring an automated message picked up. The inflection in the woman's voice had an unnatural metallic sound about it, "*By order of the Governor, a state of emergency is in effect. Citizens should remain in their homes until further notice.*"

"There isn't any help coming," Kerri said as tears streamed down her cheeks. She turned the phone off and placed it back on the charger. "We're on our own."

"We'll be alright mom," Matt Chico said as he placed a comforting hand on his mother's back. "Why don't you take dad in the other room and sit down. We've got everything covered in here."

Kerri nodded without looking up at her son. She turned back towards Josh and took his hand, "Come on honey, let's go in the living room and sit down."

Josh shook his head as his mouth hung open, "I don't want to go in there. I just want to go home."

"We will," Kerri said as she led him out of the kitchen. "I promise, we will soon."

"Christian," Matt said as he glanced back at his brother. "Reload your shotgun."

"What do you need me to do?" Matt Chico asked.

"Chico, watch the back," Matt said. "I'm going downstairs for a minute."

Matt Chico nodded, "I can do that." He said as he moved to the back door.

"Hey," Matt called to Chrisitan as he moved towards the stairs.

"What?" Christian answered as he glanced at his brother. "I heard you...what?"

"Reload your shotgun," Matt repeated as he descended the stairs.

"Yeah, I will," Christian assured him as he rubbed his eyes. "I will...don't take too long."

The basement was quiet and dark. Matt took a moment at the bottom of the stairs to draw the cool air into his lungs. He felt dizzy, rubbed his eyes, and tried to steady himself, "Keep it together." He whispered. He leaned the shotgun against the corner of the wall and headed to the bathroom opposite the laundry room. The chain made a metallic sound as he pulled it away from the light fixture. The single bulb above the sink crackled to life. It hummed just above Matt's head as he tried to figure out who looked back at him from the mirror.

"Whatever's going on out there..." Christian said as he got to his feet. He pulled several shells from one of the CCW tactical shotshell strippers attached to his web belt and reloaded his shotgun. "It seems to be spreading quickly."

"Regardless," Mr. Spahl said. "That tourniquet should have stopped the bleeding...and it hasn't."

Matt let the faucet fill his cupped hands with cold water as he stared at his reflection and tried to make sense of what just happened, "What the fuck?" He muttered to himself. His body trembled as if overloaded with caffeine. Slowly he lowered his head to the sink and ran handfuls of cold water over his face.

"Is he breathing?" Paul asked. He motioned towards Anthony as he and Ralph returned to the kitchen.

"Unconscious," Christian answered.

A night without sleep, left dark circles under Matt's eyes. Water dripped from his face as he closed his eyes and tried to steady his breathing. He rubbed his bandaged left hand through his short hair as his chin quivered and mouth filled with warm saliva, "Come on!" He hissed through gritted teeth as a sick feeling began to twist in the pit of his stomach. He breathed slowly through his nose until he could no longer hold it back. His face lowered again to the sink and he threw up.

"How can we help?" Ralph asked as he pulled a white t-shirt over his torso.

"We need to carry Anthony to the bedroom over the garage," Christian answered.

"You want to put him on the bed?" Mr. Spahl asked. "He'll bleed through the sheets."

"What if we put the comforter on the floor?" Ralph asked as he ran his hands through his still damp hair.

"We're not taking him anywhere like this," Paul said firmly.

"We're not leaving him in the fucking kitchen," Christian snapped.

"He's covered in blood, Goddammit!" Paul barked as he pointed and took a step towards Christian. "Wasn't it you who said not to get any his blood on us? Now you want us to carry him through the fucking house?"

"Get him off the fucking floor!" Christian ordered as he unsnapped the retention band on his holster. "Pick him up and take him to the bedroom...NOW!"

"STOP!" Mr. Spahl shouted as he got in between the two of them. He held up his hands as his gaze traveled back and forth between Christian and Paul. "STOP! The enemy isn't in here. Do you fucking hear me?"

Christian nodded, "Yeah, I hear you."

"You?" Mr. Spahl asked as he looked at Paul.

"The enemy isn't in here," Paul said as he lowered his arm and took a step back. "Yes...I hear you."

"You want to save your friend?" Mr. Spahl asked rhetorically. "Work with each other, not against."

"Alright," Christian said with a nod. "What do you have in mind?"

"I want you to go to the basement and find your brother," Mr. Spahl instructed. "Tell him to get himself together and get back up here. We've got things to do."

"What about us?" Ralph asked.

"Ralph, I want you and Paul to collect the comforter from the bed," Mr. Spahl began. "Get the shower curtain liner also. We're going to improvise a stretcher to move him without spreading any blood in case it is infected."

"What about the floor?" Ralph asked. "There's a lot of blood in here."

Mr. Spahl looked over the dark red pools that surrounded Anthony's motionless body, "We'll see if my beautiful bride found the bleach...then we'll get to scrubbing."

"Careful on how much you use," Christian cautioned as he moved towards the basement stairs. "There's no air circulating in here and we can't open a window."

The mouthwash numbed his tongue and gums as Matt swished it around his mouth. Satisfied, he turned the faucet on and spit aqua colored fluid into the sink. He sipped cold water from his cupped hands until the feeling returned to the inside of his mouth, "How do we come back from this?" He asked himself before he used the small blue towel to dry his face. He hung the towel on the wire rack next to the sink, turned off the light and exited the bathroom.

"You throw up in there?" Christian asked from where he sat at the bottom of the stairs.

"Christ!" Matt blurted as his brother's voice startled him. "What are you doing sitting there in the fucking dark?"

"The part I can't get out of my head…" Christian said without acknowledging his brother's question. He pulled the zipper of his coveralls down to the bottom of his chest as he got to his feet. "It took three shots to finally put her down."

"Who?" Matt asked confused.

"Marie," Christian answered. "It took three shots…"

"Yeah," Matt acknowledged with a nod. "Three shots."

"That first shot," Christian said as his breathing quickened. "00 Buck, from that range…"

"Did you see the bone fragments protruding from her chest?" Matt asked.

"That's my point," Christian said as he shook his head. "Nobody could have survived that."

"When the second shot took her arm off," Matt began. "It didn't seem to faze her."

Christian rubbed his eyes and ran his hand through his sweat-soaked red hair, "What are we really up against here?"

Anthony remained unconscious. His body was still except for the slight expansion of his chest as he breathed. The blood on the floor around him darkened to an almost brown color.

"Where do you want this stuff?" Ralph asked as he and Paul returned to the kitchen.

Mr. Spahl motioned to the floor in front of the refrigerator, "Shower curtain liner first and the comforter on top of it. Keep it away from the blood."

"Roger," Paul said as he carefully unfolded the shower curtain liner on the floor.

"Good," Mr. Spahl said. "Now the comforter."

"How is he?" Ralph asked. He motioned towards Anthony as he handed Paul the comforter.

"Breathing," Mr. Spahl answered. "Get you gloves on. Let's be careful how we move him."

"About before," Paul began. "I..."

"It's over," Mr. Spahl said. He shook his head. "We're not supposed to know how to act in a situation like this...all we can do is make sure we don't turn on each other. Come on...let's get him off the floor."

Anthony whimpered slightly as they carried him through the doorway of the bedroom and lowered him to the dark stained wood that covered the floor.

"Is he sweating?" Ralph asked.

"That bite is still fucking bleeding," Mr. Spahl said frustratedly. "Sweating...what?"

"He looks like he's sweating," Ralph observed as he motioned to the beads of moisture on Anthony's forehead.

"It seems too soon for a fever," Paul said as he peeled the gloves off his hands.

"It is," Mr. Spahl said firmly. "We need gauze and white medical tape. If he regains consciousness, we'll get some Percocet in him.

"What do you mean if?" Ralph asked with a look of deep concern. "It's just a bite."

Thick strips of deep red dripped from the end of the mop as Mrs. Spahl lowered into the bucket of hot water and bleach. She swished it around the edges of the bucket before she pushed it back and forth against the linoleum again.

"Where is everybody?" Christian asked as he and Matt emerged from the basement.

"Living room I think," Mrs. Spahl said without looking up.

"What about Anthony?" Matt asked.

"Mr. Spahl is with him," Mrs. Spahl answered.

"Any word on how he is?" Christian asked.

"Not sure," Mrs. Spahl said as she returned the blood-soaked mop to the bucket. "You should go check on him."

Matt and Christian made their way through the house. Even with the hum of the television from the living room the house was eerily quiet. They found Mr. Spahl kneeling next to where Anthony lay on the floor of the bedroom.

"How is he?" Christian asked.

Mr. Spahl carefully collected several soiled towels and placed them in a black plastic garbage bag. He glanced back at the brothers as they stood in the doorway, "Not great. He's running a fever and I can't get the wound to stop bleeding."

"What about the tourniquet?" Matt asked.

"If I tighten it anymore," Mr. Spahl began as he got to his feet. He carefully removed his gloves and placed them in the bag with the towels. "I'm afraid he'll lose the arm."

"Is he conscious?" Christian asked.

"Hasn't been," Mr. Spahl answered as put on a new pair of nitrile gloves. "He's lost a lot of blood."

"What can we do?" Matt asked as he stepped further into the room. The color had drained from Anthony's face. It left his skin unnaturally pale.

"Not sure," Mr. Spahl answered. "We're burning through rubbing alcohol, gauze, and towels. If his fever worsens, we'll need to get him in an ice bath."

"Should he be that color?" Matt asked with a look of horror on his face.

Mr. Spahl's eyes lowered as he shook his head, "No...no he should not."

"We want to meet downstairs," Christian interjected. "Can you come down?"

"I need to stay with him," Mr. Spahl said. "You can bring me up to speed when you're done."

"Alright," Matt said as he and Christian stepped out of the bedroom. "Open or closed?"

"Closed," Mr. Spahl answered as he turned back to tend to Anthony.

The old hinges creaked as Matt pulled the door shut.

"Get everybody," Christian instructed as the two of them headed down the narrow hallway. "Meet me in the basement."

"Kerri and Josh?" Matt asked.

"Best to leave them be," Christian said.

"We'll be down in a minute," Matt said with a nod as the two parted ways at the dining room.

The recessed lights hummed in the ceiling as they gathered in the basement. Despite the windows being covered, the Aspen Summit white paint made the room appear exceptionally bright. With the six of them in proximity, the air in the basement quickly warmed.

Christian stood with his back to the safe and ammo closet. He had taken the top of his coveralls down and tied the arms around his waist just above his Serpa belt, "There are some difficult things we need to discuss."

"Did you kill those two?" Jeff asked. "Marie and…"

"Costanzo," Matt answered somberly. "Marie and Costanzo…yes we did."

"They weren't Marie and Costanzo anymore," Christian offered stone faced.

"Not sure if that will hold up in court," Ralph said uncomfortably.

"If this keeps up," Matt said as he rubbed his eyes. "Those rules won't apply."

"Look I'm…" Ralph began.

"We need to get Anthony some help!" Matt Chico blurted as his face reddened. "I've been trying to reach emergency services and I keep getting the same recording about the state of emergency."

"There may not be help coming," Christian said as he folded his arms.

"Then we need to get him to a hospital," Matt Chico insisted.

"It may not be that simple," Matt offered as he cradled his shotgun in his left arm.

"What do you mean?" Jeff asked.

"If we can't get help to come here," Matt Chico said loudly. "We need to bring him to a hospital!"

"Chico…" Christian began as he unfolded his arms.

"NO!" Matt Chico shouted. "Anthony needs medical attention. My father won't stop talking about how he wants to leave and my mother is a wreck. We can't stay here!"

"Have you taken a look outside?" Paul asked. "It's getting crowded out there."

"You may be right," Christian offered as he gave Matt Chico a nod.

"What do you mean?" Ralph asked. "During his address, the Governor said citizens should remain in their homes until the state of emergency is over."

"Yes, he did," Matt said. "But you know we can't trust the fucking politicians."

"What are we going to do?" Matt Chico asked frantically as he began to pace. "I can't get a hold of my brother. They are probably on the road already. What's going to happen if they get to my parents' house and we're not there?"

"We need to deal with what's happening here first..." Christian began before Matt Chico interrupted.

"Do you understand that I can't get in touch with my son!" Matt Chico shouted as his eyes filled with tears. "Anthony is upstairs unconscious! We can't get in touch with the police or emergency services! You guys are carrying guns like you're in some kind of fucking militia!"

"Chico!" Christian snapped. "Calm down. We're here. We're together and for the moment we're safe."

"For the moment?" Ralph questioned.

"We will do what we can for Anthony," Christian continued. "As for the rest of it, Matt and I talked through some options."

"What kind of options?" Jeff asked.

"Whatever this is," Matt began. "I think we can agree it's gone beyond any state of emergency we've ever seen."

"I'd say that's the understatement of the year," Paul acknowledged as he gave his beard a tug. "So, what do we do?"

"For the time being, we harden our defenses," Matt said. "We continue to keep watch. We monitor the news and internet. Try to determine where the outbreak is concentrated..."

"Outbreak?" Ralph questioned. "You sure you're not jumping to conclusions."

"No, not entirely," Matt acknowledged. "But considering what we know...I think outbreak is an accurate depiction. We need to try and determine the areas hit hardest and direction it's moving in case we do need to bug out."

"What if we lose power?" Paul asked.

"That's a possibility," Matt acknowledged. "The stove is gas, so we'll still have that. The refrigerators will last for a short period, so we should plan to eat that food first.

"What if we do have to leave?" Ralph asked as he ran his hands through his thick hair.

"If it comes to that," Christian said. "At the very least we'll need to have food, water, cloths, weapons, and ammo ready. We'll have to take multiple vehicles so we'll have to plan the primary and alternate routes in advance."

"This doesn't sound like a plan!" Matt Chico said angrily. "This sounds like an excuse to dig around in your gun safe then go upstairs and sit in front of the television."

"We'll find a way to get Anthony help," Christian assured Matt Chico. "You're not the only one with loved ones out there."

"I never said..." Matt Chico began.

"Giovanni and Heather are out there...hours away," Christian interrupted as he took a step towards his old friend. He put his hand on Matt Chico's shoulder. "We've all got people we're worried about. They should be here with us now...but they're not."

Matt Chico nodded and wiped the tears from his eyes. For a moment the basement was silent. They each looked at each other, unsure of how to react to their surreal new reality.

"We need to do an immediate inventory of our weapons, ammunition, food, water, antibiotics," Matt said as his words broke the silence. "Anything we may need to use or take with us if we have to leave."

"About that," Ralph began. "When you say leave...I haven't seen any mention of safe zones or camps."

"I wouldn't trust them if we did," Christian interjected. "Not after what Matt and I saw with Costanzo and Marie. Too many people trapped together. We're better off on our own."

"What the fuck?" Matt Chico blurted as he shook his head. "You two and your fucking paranoia..."

"So where would we go?" Ralph asked as he glanced over at Paul.

Matt nodded, "Christian and I believe the best place to go is the farm."

An uncomfortable mixture of fear and skepticism covered their faces. For a moment it was as if the air had been sucked out of the room.

The sound of metal against metal broke the silence as Paul retracted the charging handle of his M1A Scout, "We could have stayed home. We could have gone someplace else...but we didn't." Paul's deep voice rumbled like thunder as he spoke. "We knew our best chance of getting through this was to be here together. As sure as I'm standing here, whatever this is will get worse before it gets better. Whether we like it or not, this is the real thing gentlemen. We are in harm's way..."

The creak of the basement door interrupted them as it opened. They stopped and looked towards the stairwell.

Mrs. Spahl called from the top of the stairs, "Anthony's awake!"

CHAPTER 9

the sound and the fury

A S THE SUN CREPT across the sky the temperature in the house warmed considerably. The old wood creaked as the six of them ascended the narrow staircase. The air in the kitchen was thick with the odor of bleach.

"Dear God," Matt winced as he covered his nose. "That's fucking pungent."

"I told them not to use too much," Christian said as he pulled his coveralls over his shoulders and closed the zipper. "Matt Chico, can you watch the front?"

"I...I need to check on my parents," Matt Chico said frantically as he hurried from the basement and moved past the group.

"I'll watch the front," Jeff offered.

"Thanks Jeff," Matt said. "Ralph, can you stay here and cover the back?"

Ralph nodded, "I can do that."

"I'll keep watch here with Ralph," Paul added.

"Come on," Christian insisted as he hurried Matt out of the kitchen. "Let's go before I have an asthma attack."

"We need to get Aunt Athena and Uncle Tony over here," Matt said they made their way through the dining room.

"One thing at a time," Christian said. "Let's see how Anthony is first."

"Fine," Matt reluctantly agreed. "We never should have left them. They should be over here with us."

"They're not alone," Chrisitan reminded his brother. "And, it was their decision to wait for Tyler and Patrick. It's not our place to force anybody over here."

Matt was about to offer a counter argument when the two of them found Mr. Spahl at the end of the long hallway. He stood with his back pressed against the wall and his hands braced against his knees. His eyes were closed. He took several deep breaths in through his nose and exhaled through his mouth.

"Mr. Spahl, are you ok?" Matt asked.

Mr. Spahl raised his right hand and pointed towards the bedroom. His hand trembled as he spoke, "He's awake. My wife is with him."

Matt Chico found his parents huddled together on the couch. Unable to ingest any more news, Kerri turned the television off. She stroked Josh's hair as he rested with his eyes closed.

"Mom, dad, are you two, ok?" Matt Chico asked as he took a seat on the coffee table across from his parents.

Kerri nodded, "Shhh, your father is sleeping. What's going on?"

"Not sure," Matt Chico answered. "Mrs. Spahl said Anthony's awake."

"That's good news," Kerri said as she managed a slight smile. "I hope he's ok."

"Me too," Matt Chico agreed. "How is dad?"

Kerri's eyes narrowed, "Not good. It was everything I could do to calm him down enough so he could sleep. I'm not sure what we're going to do when he wakes up."

"I don't know," Matt Chico said as he rubbed his eyes. He twisted his neck from side to side until his neck cracked several times. "I really don't know."

Anthony lay motionless on the blood-soaked comforter. Beads of sweat soaked the pillow beneath his head. His breathing was shallow and labored. His forearm was wrapped tightly with gauze and white medical tape. Despite the tourniquet secured around his upper arm, blood continued to seep from the wound.

"How is he?" Christian asked as he and Matt stepped into the bedroom.

"His fever is worse," Mrs. Spahl said as she pulled a clean pair of nitrile gloves over her hands. She took a dark colored washcloth from the red plastic bucket filled with ice water next to her and placed it on Anthony's forehead. "I gave him two of the Percocet."

"Two?" Christian questioned.

"There aren't that many left in the bottle," Mrs. Spahl said as she looked up from where she knelt next to Anthony. "I wasn't sure how long we were going to be here, so I thought it best to use them sparingly."

Despite the oppressive odor of bleach, the kitchen floor gleamed. No evidence remained of the earlier carnage suffered within the confines of the room.

Ralph rubbed his eyes and adjusted his grip on the Mossberg shotgun. His Kimber 1911 was tucked into the waist band of his blue jeans behind his left hip, "What do you think?"

"I think if we don't open a fucking window one of us is going to pass out," Paul grumbled. He rested his rifle against the refrigerator and stared out at the top of the hill. He turned the sink faucet on and used his cupped hands to splash water over his face.

"Yeah, there's that," Ralph acknowledged. "But I meant with everything going on."

Paul shook his head as water dripped from his long beard, "Not sure. Not sure what to make of all of it. Not sure coming here was the best decision."

"What do you mean?" Ralph asked as he glanced from the door to Paul and back. "What about what you said downstairs...about the best way through this was here together?"

"I know what I said," Paul acknowledged as he rubbed his eyes. "And, I meant it in the moment."

"So, what then?" Ralph pressed.

"I don't want to get trapped in this house if things escalate," Paul said bluntly as he ripped several paper towels from the roll and dried his face. "It may be safer to be on the road.""You really think so?" Ralph asked with surprise at Paul's revelation. "We could end up stranded out there...Jeep could break down...we could get a flat tire, run out of gas. Any of those leave us exposed and on foot. I don't know about you but my running days are behind me."

"Hmmm, I don't remember you ever running anywhere," Paul jabbed.

"Is that so?" Ralph questioned with a grin. His focus shifted to the back of the house. "Either way, I'd rather not start now."

"You're right, I guess," Paul begrudgingly admitted. He swished some cold water around in his mouth and spit into the sink. "Danny's out there somewhere and we're here."

"That's true," Ralph agreed. "But he's not alone. He's got his brothers in blue with him."

"Yeah," Paul muttered. "For whatever that's worth."

"See anything on the hill?" Ralph asked as he changed the subject.

"No," Paul answered. "You?"

Ralph shook his head, "Quiet out the back."

Jeff tried to ignore the conversation between Matt Chico and his mother as it continued behind him. He rubbed his eyes and adjusted his grip on the Mini-14. He peered from between the boards on the front door. Despite the commotion earlier, the street in front of the house now seemed eerily still. Even the figure spotted across the street in the Santini's yard was gone, "That's fucking odd." Jeff muttered to himself.

Anthony shuddered and gave a slight whimper as Mrs. Spahl replaced the washcloth with another from the bucket of ice water. His skin was unnaturally pale and there was a yellowish discoloration on either side of the bandage on his forearm.

"What can we do?" Christian asked.

Mrs. Spahl shook her head, "I don't know."

"Is Mr. Spahl, ok?" Matt asked quietly as he motioned behind him.

"No," Mrs. Spahl said bluntly. "The gunfire and blood...none of its good for him."

"Is there anything you need?" Christian asked.

"I know you've got reservations about leaving," Mrs. Spahl began as she got to her feet. "I know we're all waiting to hear from people, but you boys have got to come to grips with the fact that Anthony needs real medical attention."

"We know," Matt assured her.

Mrs. Spahl looked at him skeptically, "Saying it and meaning it are two different things. The longer he lays here and suffers and the worse his condition gets..."

"We know Mrs. Spahl," Christian assured her. "We know."

Mrs. Spahl used her forearm to brush a tear from her cheek. She removed the gloves and placed them in the black garbage bag. She moved to the doorway, paused, and turned back to the brothers, "If we don't get him to a hospital...he's not going to make it."

Mr. Spahl stepped into the bathroom to compose himself. He gently pushed the door closed until he heard the metal latch catch the frame. He stood in front of the sink as water poured from the faucet. He gripped the edges of the porcelain fixture to keep his hands from shaking as he stared at his reflection in the mirror, "No...please God no." He whispered as everything went dark. For a moment he was back in the jungle with the roar of helicopter rotors and distinct crack of rifle fire. The anguished cries of the wounded and dying echoed in his ears as he slowly dropped to his knees.

"Jeff, how are you making out?" Christian asked as he entered the living room.

"I need a cigarette," Jeff said as he got to his feet.

"Shhh, my dad is sleeping," Matt Chico said as he motioned for them to lower their voices.

Christian nodded and motioned to Matt as he came around the corner, "Josh is asleep."

"Come on," Matt said with a nod, "Let's talk in the other room."

The four of them moved into the dining room as Paul and Ralph joined them from the kitchen.

"We need to crack a window," Paul said as he rubbed his eyes. "Nobody should be in there for too long."

"I've got a fucking headache," Ralph said as she shook his head.

"Advil in the medicine cabinet in the bathroom," Matt said as he motioned with his head. "The smell notwithstanding, we could all benefit from a good night's sleep."

"I'll second that," Paul said as he tried to blink the tiredness from his eyes.

"Not sure the next time that's going to happen," Jeff said as he held the open pack of cigarettes under his nose.

"Yeah," Paul said as he looked at Jeff. "I need one of those too."

"How is Anthony?" Ralph asked as he used his thumbs to rub his temples.

"Not good," Christian said as he shook his head.

"What are we going to do?" Jeff asked.

"I don't know if we can stay..." Matt Chico interjected. "My father's asleep, but when he wakes up, I'm not sure how we're going to keep him calm enough to stay."

"Hold up," Christian said as he raised his right hand. "We can address that when he wakes up. In the meantime, let's get back to what we were discussing in the basement."

"Which was?" Matt Chico asked.

"An inventory," Matt said. "Of our weapons, ammo, food, water, medicine and anything else we may need."

"I don't like the idea of bugging out," Jeff said as he folded his arms.

"Why's that?" Ralph asked.

"Because if we have to leave," Jeff began. "We'll be nothing more than glorified refugees."

"Refugees?" Paul questioned. "Sounds a little dramatic."

"He's right," Christian insisted. "But we may not have a choice."

"What do you mean?" Matt Chico asked.

"Anthony needs a doctor," Christian answered.

"From a bite?" Matt Chico questioned as he shook his head. "I told you he needed a doctor. How could a bite do that...and so fast?"

"I don't know," Christian answered. "Maybe it's viral. Either way, his fever is worse. His skin is badly discolored and Mrs. Spahl thinks that if we don't get him to a hospital soon, he may not make it."

"What?" Matt Chico questioned in disbelief. "How can that..."

"This is what we're going to do," Matt interjected. "Jeff and Paul, you two go downstairs. You can smoke in the garage. When you're done, inventory the weapons and ammunition."

"Where do you want me?" Ralph asked.

"Take a break from kitchen," Matt offered. "Watch the front of the house."

"Gladly," Ralph said with a grin. "I can do that."

"What about me?" Matt Chico asked.

"Chico, we'll keep you close in case your father wakes up," Matt began. "Back bedroom. See if the internet's working and see what else you can find out about what's going on. Also, see if there's information on hospitals in proximity and see if you can contact any of them."

Matt Chico nodded, "I can do that."

"What about you two?" Paul asked.

"Christian's going to keep an eye on the news," Matt explained as he motioned towards his brother. "I'll keep watch from the kitchen...meet back here in an hour."

The mood in the dining room was somber as they each went their separate ways. The house wasn't that large but it didn't prevent a feeling of finality to their parting.

Stagnant water sloshed around their feet as Jeff and Paul stepped from the basement to the garage. The single car garage remained cool, despite the suns position directly overhead. The small room was dark except for the light that crept in from the basement.

"Do you have a lighter?" Jeff asked as he slid a cigarette from his pack.

Paul nodded, "Yeah." He touched the flame from the Bic lighter to the tip of his cigarette. The tip glowed a bright orange red color as he inhaled deeply. "Here."

"Thanks," Jeff said as he took the lighter and lit his cigarette.

"That's got a unique smell," Paul commented as he motioned to the pack Jeff held in his left hand. "What are those."

"It's just an old pack, I reuse," Jeff said as he looked down at the worn box. "I hand load the papers with pipe tobacco."

"Pipe tobacco," Paul said as he took another drag from his cigarette. "Bold choice."

Matt Chico sat at the computer. He listened intently in case his father woke up. The old chair creaked as he scrolled through multiple web-sites. He read posts, looked for articles and watched videos to try and make sense of what was happening, "Come on." He whispered to himself. "Somebody's got to know what's really going on out there."

Ralph took a knee on the old worn blue carpet at the front door. He rested the shotgun against the small end table as he peered out from between the boards, "Quiet...almost too quiet." He said to himself. He glanced back at Kerri and Josh who were now both asleep on the couch and thought longingly about his own parents. He was certain his older brother was with them. With the three of them out of state and unable to be reached, Ralph couldn't help but worry.

Christian gently placed himself in the old recliner not far from where Ralph knelt. He closed his eyes and tipped his head back as the pain in his stomach returned with a vengeance. When he was finally able to reopen his eyes, he turned the television on and lowered the volume so as not to wake Kerri and Josh, "What the fuck?" He muttered to himself. His focus was glued to the report that chronicled the outbreak of violence at the hospitals where the victims from Omega Arsenal were taken. "Are you hearing this?"

"I'm trying not to," Ralph confessed. "I need a break from it."

Matt stood at the sink and tried to contend with the overbearing smell of bleach that hung in the kitchen. He rested his shotgun against the refrigerator, closed his eyes and splashed cold water on his face. He flinched when Mr. Spahl's voice startled him.

"Where's Jeff?" Mr. Spahl asked as he stepped into the kitchen. His palms were damp and his face flush. The underarms of his polo shirt were sweat soaked.

"Jeff...uh...basement," Matt fumbled to say. "He and Paul are having a smoke and then doing inventory."

Mr. Spahl nodded, "I could use a smoke too. I'll see if they need any help."

"Any change with Anthony?" Matt asked.

Mr. Spahl shook his head, "No." He answered before he disappeared down the stairs.

The house went quiet again as everyone carried out their tasks. The air was stagnant and temperature inside continued to increase as the mid-day sun radiated down.

"I hear you two might need some help down here," Mr. Spahl offered as he stepped into the garage.

"Why don't you take a break," Paul said as he gave Mr. Spahl's arm a smack. "You've earned it."

"Thanks," Mr. Spahl said with a nod. "But if it's all the same to you, I like to keep busy."

"Fair enough," Paul said as he flicked ash from the tip of his cigarette. It sizzled as it hit the water that covered the garage floor.

"You have another one of those?" Mr. Spahl asked as he motioned to Paul's cigarette.

"When did you start smoking again?" Jeff asked.

Mr. Spahl shook his head, "Doesn't matter."

"Does mom know?" Jeff chided.

"Knock it off," Mr. Spahl insisted as he glared at his youngest son. "We've got bigger things to worry about, don't you think?"

"You're right," Jeff said with a nod. He held the pack of cigarettes out to his father. "You can have one of mine."

"Jesus, God no," Mr. Spahl said as he shook his head. "That pipe tobacco is too strong for me."

"Here," Paul said as he handed the pack of Winston Select 100s to Mr. Spahl. "It'll take the edge off."

"Thanks," Mr. Spahl said with a nod. He removed one of the cigarettes from the pack, brought to his mouth and lit it. He closed his eyes as he drew the smoke deep into his lungs. He held it for a moment before he exhaled. "God, I needed that."

Matt rested his elbows on the counter and dropped his head into his hands. His stomach growled and head throbbed as he realized they had not stopped for lunch, "What the fuck." He muttered to himself. "One more thing to do."

"The news is going off the air," Christian said as he slid his body to the edge of the recliner.

"What?" Ralph asked as he reluctantly turned around. "How can the news be going off the air?"

"That's what they just said," Christian explained. "The news is going off the air and the emergency broadcast system is taking over."

"Shit," Ralph muttered. "That's not a good sign."

"No," Christian agreed. "Not at all."

"When's that happening?" Ralph said.

Christian motioned to the television screen, "Looks like it's happening right now."

Mr. Spahl crumpled the smoldering cigarette butt between his fingers and dropped what was left of it in the water, "Alright, what's next?"

"Everything," Jeff said half-jokingly as he discarded a second cigarette butt. "Let's start with the ammo. They keep a running tally so we only need to add what we brought to it."

"That's better," Matt said to himself as he finished a hastily made salami and cheese sandwich. The shake in his hands subsided as the food leveled off his blood sugar. As he sat at the small kitchen table, he felt his body relax until the distinct crack of a large caliber rifle startled him to his feet. "What the fuck?" He hollered as he bolted to the back door.

Uncle Tony stood on the sidewalk just outside his back-porch door. He wore a heavy fleece robe over dark blue denim overalls that covered his frail body. A lit cigarette dangled from his mouth. The recoil staggered him backwards as he fired several rounds from his 30-06 lever action rifle, towards the top of the hill.

"Where the fuck did that come from?" Christian called as he hurried to the kitchen.

"Uncle Tony's shooting at something!" Matt shouted.

"What was that?" Josh shrieked as he was startled awake.

"Everything's ok," Ralph assured him. "Just stay calm."

"No, I want to leave!" Josh shouted.

"JEFF!" Christian called from the top of the stairs. "Get up here! We've got gunfire next door."

"On our way!" Jeff called as he and Paul dropped the OD green ammo cans next to the safe and hurried upstairs. "Come on dad!"

"Don't wait for me!" Mr. Spahl shouted as he hurried out of the storeroom. "Just go!"

"Can you see what he's shooting at?" Christian asked.

"No!" Matt called. "My view's obstructed. We need to get out there!"

"We will," Christian assured him. "We need to be smart about it."

"We can't leave him out there alone," Matt insisted. "He's in no shape to defend himself."

"We're not!" Christian said firmly. "Ralph, we need you in here...NOW!"

Uncle Tony fired several more shots as Jeff and Paul reached the top of the stairs.

"Who's shooting?" Jeff called as he readied his rifle.

"What's going on?" Ralph asked as he hurried to the kitchen.

"Uncle Tony's shooting!" Matt answered without turning around. "I can't see at who though."

"We're going out to back him up!" Christian declared. "Ralph, stay here and cover us."

"Roger," Ralph said with a nod.

"Where's Chico?" Christian asked.

"With his parents," Ralph answered. He felt his palms dampen as he adjusted his grip on the shotgun. "His dad's in a bad way."

"Where's my wife?" Mr. Spahl asked as he reached the top of the stairs.

"With Anthony, I think," Ralph answered.

"We're wasting time here!" Paul growled as he adjusted his grip on the M1A Scout. "We going or not?"

Matt and Christian were the first two out of the house. Jeff and Paul followed quickly behind. Uncle Tony bit down on the filter of the cigarette and cursed with every shot as he continued to fire towards the top of the steep hill.

"Your shotgun!" Christian called as Matt hurried down the concrete stairs to the sidewalk.

"No time!" Matt called as he drew the pistol from his holster. He turned and covered the path between the house and stone wall. "Clear!" He called. Matt shuddered as his eyes scanned what was left of Costanzo and Marie. "GO!"

Christian charged down the sidewalk, "Uncle Tony!" He called. "What are you doing?"

Matt turned and quickly followed his brother as Jeff and Paul reached the sidewalk.

"Go!" Paul shouted. "I'll take rear guard."

Jeff bolted down the sidewalk after Matt and Christian.

"Uncle Tony!" Christian shouted as he closed the distance between them.

A brass shell casing ejected from the breach as Uncle Tony cycled the action of the rifle, "Fuck!" He growled as he struggled in his weakened state to hold the rifle up.

Ralph watched from the back door as Paul cleared the narrow path. He swung the rifle as he scanned the hill behind the house before he hurried after Jeff.

"What is he shooting at?" Matt called as his boots pounded against the sidewalk. The thick tree cover at the top of the hill made it impossible to discern what Uncle Tony's intended target was.

"Uncle Tony!" Christian called again. "What are you shooting at?"

"My boys!" Uncle Tony growled.

"WHAT?" Christian shouted in disbelief.

"My boys!" Uncle Tony wheezed. "They're after my boys!"

"Oh, fuck," Christian muttered to himself. "MATT...GET OVER HERE!"

Uncle Tony continued to fire as Matt and Christian reached him. When they did, they saw their cousins, Tyler and Patick, stumble as they cleared the tree line at the top of the hill. Tyler limped badly. His right arm was wrapped around his younger brother's shoulders. Patrick had his left arm around Tyler's waist and held onto his belt to take the weight off his brother's injured right leg.

"Those things are after my boys!" Uncle Tony hollered as he fired again.

Matt and Christian watched as a group of partially mangled figures shambled from the tree line. Jeff and Paul reached the stone wall at the base of the hill as Uncle Tony discharged his last round. Out of breath and exhausted, Uncle Tony struggled to pull the lever open and eject the spent shell casing.

"My God, there must be twenty of them!" Matt shouted as the figures continued to move awkwardly across the top of the hill.

"We're in position!" Jeff called as he raised his rifle.

"This fucking rifle!" Uncle Tony hollered. The cigarette tumbled from his mouth to the grass below as he tried to retrieve bullets from the front pocket of his overalls. "Out of bullets? How the fuck can I be out of bullets already?"

"Head shots!" Christian shouted over the ominous moans that emanated from the gaping mouths of the creatures. "Take head shots!"

"We can do that," Paul hissed as he brought the rifle up to his shoulder. He trained the Eotech's reticle on the head of the closest ghoul and fired. A stream of dark red burst from the skull as the body was thrown back several yards before it hit the ground.

"Get Aunt Athena, Katherine and Marcus!" Matt instructed. "I'll collect Uncle Tony, Tyler and Patrick and meet you back at the house."

"FUCK!" Jeff shouted as he cupped his hand over his left ear and turned his head away from Paul. "Don't fire that thing next to my head!"

"Hurry!" Christian ordered as he left Matt and ran to the back porch. "We don't have enough ammo to be out here long."

Shell casings spit from the ejection port of the Mini-14 as Jeff opened fire on the hoard.

"Uncle Tony!" Matt shouted as he grabbed his uncle's arm. "We don't have time to reload. We need to go!"

"Aunt Athena!" Christian shouted. He pulled the back porch door open and hurried inside. He found the kitchen empty and moved quickly through the dining room. "Katherine! Aunt Athena! We need to go now!"

"NO!" Uncle Tony gasped as he struggled to pull his arm away from Matt. "Not without my sons!"

Brass shell casings tumbled through the air as Jeff and Paul continued to fire. Tyler and Patrick neared the concrete stairs that led to the back yard as well-placed rounds stopped their pursuers and jettisoned blood and skull fragments across the top of the hill.

"Aunt Athena!" Christian called as he charged through the house. "Aunt Athena!"

"Christian!" Katherine called from the bedroom at the far end of the house. "We're back here!"

"I'll get them!" Matt shouted as he wrestled the rifle away from his uncle. "I'll get them! Down the sidewalk...GO!"

"Loading!" Jeff called as the bolt on the Mini-14 locked open. He snapped a loaded magazine into the mag well, released the charging handle and continued to fire.

The crack of the rifles was deafening as Matt bolted up the concrete stairs to collect his cousins.

"What are you doing back here?" Christian called as his broad shoulders appeared in the bedroom doorway.

"My mother's terrified!" Katherine barked as she motioned to her mother huddled between the large oak dresser and side of the bed. "Where should we have gone?"

"We need to go!" Christian insisted as he adjusted his grip on the shotgun. "NOW!"

"Wait..." Katherine pleaded.

"NO!" Christian snapped as he lunged into the room and grabbed his aunt under the arm. "We're going...NOW!"

"OUT!" Paul called as the bolt of the M1A locked open. He placed the rifle on the concrete ledge in front of him and pulled the Sig 1911 Spartan from his waist band. He depressed the thumb safety and continued to fire.

"Careful!" Tyler whined as beads of sweat poured from the golden blond curls that covered his head. "I think my ankle's broken."

"Hang on!" Matt instructed as bullets hissed and snapped around them. He hoisted his cousin across his shoulders in a fireman's carry.

"Matty?" Patrick asked disoriented. The exhaustion was seared onto his face.

"No time Pat," Matt insisted. "Come on, we're getting off this hill!"

"I need something for the pain!" Tyler wailed.

"I'd love to give you some Oxy," Matt chided angrily as he bounded back towards the stairs. "But we're all out. Somebody took it all."

"HURRY UP!" Ralph shouted from the other end of the sidewalk. He stepped off the small porch and pointed to the top of the hill as mangled bodies pressed themselves against the chain link fence. "THEY'RE EVERYWHERE!"

"OUT!" Jeff shouted. He slung the rifle across his back, pulled the P90 from his waist band and continued to fire.

"I'm in a lot of pain!" Tyler hissed as he tried to ignore his cousins' taunts.

"Fuck you!" Matt shouted as he and Patrick hurried down the stairs.

Ralph ran to the corner of the house and looked out towards the street, "COMING UP FROM THIS WAY TOO!"

The smell of gun powder hung in the air as Christian hastily pulled his aunt, cousin, and Marcus from the house.

"Nooo!" Aunt Athena cried as she covered her ears. "TONY!"

"MOVING!" Christian shouted as they started back down the sidewalk.

"Finally," Ralph muttered to himself. He ran back to the narrow porch. To his terror he found himself face to face with two figures who moved along the path between the house and stone wall. From where he stood, Ralph could see that their skin had a grayish yellow discoloration. Pieces of clothing were torn away from their bodies and exposed ghastly wounds. Their movements were awkward and their open mouths emitted an unsettling sound. "Oh, fuck!" He blurted.

"OUT!" Paul called as the slide of the 1911 locked open.

"ME TOO!" Jeff answered.

"CONTACT!" Ralph shouted. The ghoulish figures reached for him as he raised the shotgun and fired. Buckshot separated the head from the body of the first pursuer. Ralph cycled the action. Another well-placed blast ripped the jaw and most of the left side of the contorted face from the second being.

"We can't be out here! We need to move!" Matt hollered. "NOW!"

"TONY!" Aunt Athena shrieked as she reached back for her husband. "I CAN'T GO WITHOUT HIM!"

"I'll get him!" Christian assured her. "Katherine, get your mother out of here!"

"Athena, I'll be right behind you," Uncle Tony assured her as he retrieved his rifle. His hands trembled as he shoved bullets into the magazine.

"What about my boys?" Aunt Athena wailed.

"We don't have time for this!" Christian snarled as he turned back to collect his uncle. "Katherine, Marcus, get her out of here!"

"COME ON! THEY'RE EVERYWHERE!" Ralph shouted from the other end of the sidewalk as he pulled two shells from the side saddle and fed them into the magazine. "HURRY UP!"

"TONY!" Aunt Athena screamed. She reached desperately for her husband as Katherine and Marcus pulled her down the sidewalk. "TONY COME WITH US!"

"I'll be right behind you," Uncle Tony called as he struggled to catch his breath. The words barely left his mouth as cold lifeless fingers grabbed hold of his robe and blood-stained teeth closed around the side of his neck. He shrieked as a chunk of flesh was torn away and blood sprayed from the wound.

"TONY, NOOO!" Aunt Athena screeched.

Uncle Tony let out a shrill cry as he fell to his knees. Blood spurted through his fingers as he tried to cup his hands over the deep bite.

"NO!" Christian shouted as he leveled the barrel of the shotgun and fired. Buckshot decimated the ghoul's sunken blood-soaked face. Streaks of red saturated the green grass as its body was thrown back several yards.

"DAD!" Patrick cried as he lunged towards his father.

"NO!" Christian shouted as he pulled his cousin back. "GET TO THE HOUSE!"

"GET INSIDE!" Ralph shouted. He moved to the end of the sidewalk and provided cover fire. The shotgun thundered as Jeff and Paul hurried past him to the house. Ralph dispatched several ghouls as they made their way up the front lawn towards him.

"OH MY GOD, TONY!" Aunt Athena screamed. She tried to get to him but Katherine and Marcus pulled her away.

"NO, MOM!" Katherine cried. "WE HAVE TO GO!"

"HURRY!" Ralph ordered. He fed the last four shells from the sidesaddle into the magazine as Patrick ran by followed by Matt with Tyler on his back.

"Athena..." Uncle Tony gasped. "Go!"

"TONY!" Aunt Athena shrieked. She writhed as she tried to pull free from her daughter and son-in-law. "TONY...NO!"

"I watched the news reports...I know what happens now," Uncle Tony said as sadness replaced the look of anguish seared across his face. Blood jettisoned from the wound as he took his hands away from his neck. He reached down and collected his rifle. He placed the barrel under his chin as his eyes filled with tears. "I'm sorry Athena...I love you!"

"NOOOOO!" Aunt Athena screamed as she collapsed to her knees.

There was a loud pop as Uncle Tony depressed the trigger. An eruption of crimson glistened against the brilliant sunlight. His head snapped back before his lifeless body fell to the ground.

CHAPTER 10

of helplessness

"COME ON!" Ralph called as everyone hurried past him. Sweat ran down his face as he trained the bead at the end of barrel on the head of an approaching ghoul and fired. A cloud of red mist followed the body to the ground. "GET INSIDE!"

"TONY!" Aunt Athena shrieked as Katherine and Marcus pulled her down the sidewalk towards the back porch. "NO...TONY...NO!"

"GET HER IN THE FUCKING HOUSE!" Christian ordered.

"WE'RE TRYING!" Katherine snapped. She flinched as Ralph fired two more blasts from the shotgun in quick succession.

The kitchen was a bottleneck of confusion and screaming. Tempers flared as rational thought gave way to fear and exhaustion.

"Get the fuck out of my way!" Matt shouted as he charged towards the dining room. "Mr. Spahl!"

"Ahhh!" Tyler cried as his head smacked against the door frame.

"Bring him back here!" Mr. Spahl called as he hurried Matt with Tyler on his back to the bedroom at the back of the house.

"My fucking head!" Tyler wailed. "Watch my ankle!"

"Shut the fuck up!" Matt snarled. His chest heaved as he hurried down the narrow hallway. "Patrick! Where are you?"

"Right behind you Matty," Patrick called as he struggled to catch his breath.

Christian watched as Katherine and Marcus forced Aunt Athena into the house. As the ringing in his ears deadened, everything sounded as if he were underwater. He was unphased by the deafening sound of the shotgun as Ralph continued to fire. The ghastly images appeared to move in slow motion as he scanned the hill and narrow path. Christian glanced back at his uncle's body and shook his head. "How are we going to come back from this?" He muttered rhetorically to himself as he moved towards the back porch.

"THEY'RE EVERYWHERE!" Ralph called desperately. "WE HAVE TO GET INSIDE!"

"LAST ONE!" Christian shouted as he regained his focus. He slapped Ralph's shoulder as he hurried past him. "LET'S GO!"

Ralph's ears rang as he cycled the action and ejected the last shell, "RIGHT BEHIND YOU!" He called as he turned and followed Christian into the house.

Panic spread through the group like a highly contagious illness. Raised voices levied accusations and blame like a lit fuse on its way to detonating an explosive. At the far end of the house Mrs. Spahl did what she could for Anthony, while Mr. Spahl tried to get Tyler situated.

"Lay him on the floor," Mr. Spahl instructed.

"The floor?" Matt questioned as he maneuvered his cousin across his shoulders.

"We need to get his leg elevated," Mr. Spahl said as he motioned to the bed. "I have to get his boot off and see what we're dealing with."

"It's broken," Tyler whined. "I'm sure it's broken."

"Shut the fuck up!" Matt ordered. "Patrick, help me get him off my shoulders."

Patrick and Matt carefully lowered Tyler's lanky body onto the small red and gray area rug next to the bed. His head of thick curly blond hair left a puddle of sweat against the dark stained hardwood floor. Deep sweat stains protruded from the under arms of Tyler's light blue, short sleeve button down shirt. The white t-shirt beneath was also visibly soiled. His blue jeans were caked with dried mud and dirt. He winced as he reached under his wire rim glasses and rubbed his eyes, "Please...I need something for the pain."

"Then maybe you shouldn't have taken all the fucking Oxy!" Matt scolded angrily. "What kind of fucking degenerate comes over to check on my brother and takes all his pain meds?"

"Please..." Tyler whimpered in a high pitched nasally voice. "Please."

"Matty," Patrick urged as he took hold of his cousin's arm. His cheeks were flushed as he struggled to slow his breathing. "Please cut him some slack." He pleaded as tears filled his eyes. "My father...and now...please just let him be."

Patrick was the youngest of his siblings. He was seven years younger than Katherine and nine years younger than Tyler. He had a stocky muscular build and was fair skinned with a head of long wavy reddish blond hair that reached almost to the top of his trapezius muscles. He was known in the family for his abundance of energy and distinct laugh that emerged when he was nervous or anxious. His red polo shirt with the arsenal logo on the left breast was so saturated with sweat it looked as if it had been run under a faucet. His navy-blue Dockers slacks and gray shoes were in tatters and covered with dirt and debris.

Matt ran his bandaged left hand over his face, "Yeah, Pat. I'm sorry. I just...it just got away from me."

"I know Matty," Patrick said with a reassuring nod. "I know."

"I'm going to elevate your right leg," Mr. Spahl explained as he took hold of Tyler's tan work boot. He extended Tyler's leg, rested it against the mattress and undid the laces. "Just try and hang on."

"Wait!" Tyler shrieked. "I really need something for the pain."

Mr. Spahl glanced up at Matt and Partick, "Hold him."

"Wait...what?" Tyler yelped as Matt and Patrick pinned his arms and torso to the floor. "No..."

"Do it," Matt instructed.

"AHHHH!" Tyler screamed. His face turned a deep red as Mr. Spahl pulled the boot off his swollen foot. "NO...FUCK YOU...GET OFF ME..." His voice trailed off, eyes rolled back in his head and body went limp.

"Hang on kid," Mr. Spahl encouraged. "The worst of it's over. Your sock is the easy part."

"What happened?" Patrick asked with considerable alarm in his voice. He placed his index and middle finger on the side of his brother's neck. "He's got a pulse!" Patrick announced with some relief in his voice.

"He's breathing," Mr. Spahl said as he motioned to Tyler's chest. "Just unconscious. He'll come out of it."

Christian appeared in the doorway. His face was a mixture of anger and frustration as he breathed heavily, "How is he?"

"What are you doing?" Matt asked as he glanced up at his brother.

"Looking for you," Christian replied. "How is he?"

"Not sure yet," Mr. Spahl answered. "His ankle and foot are very swollen."

"We're meeting in the basement," Chrisitan explained. "Can you join us?"

"Not immediately," Mr. Spahl said. "I've got to get Tyler situated here and see how my beautiful bride is doing with Anthony."

"After?" Christian asked.

"Yes," Mr. Spahl answered. "I'll be down after."

"Pat, what about you?" Christian inquired. "Can you join us in the basement?"

Patrick's cheeks went flush, "Um...probably not. I've got to make sure Tyler's alright, then I need to check on my mother."

"I understand," Christian said. "Matt?"

"Right behind you," Matt answered as he got to his feet. He turned back to Mr. Spahl. "Anything else you need me for?"

Mr. Spahl shook his head, "No, not right now."

"I'm really sorry Pat...about your dad," Christian said somberly. "He was a good man and a good uncle."

"I'm sorry too Pat," Matt added. "Your dad loved all of you so much. He was a good man."

Patrick gave a slight nod. He cupped his hands over his eyes as tears ran down his cheeks, "Thanks." He managed to say just above a whisper.

It was noticeably cooler in the basement. The change in air temperature did little to alleviate everyone's tension. The room was eerily quiet except for the hum of recessed lights and sound of bullets being loaded into pistol and rifle magazines.

"What are we doing down here?" Paul asked impatiently. His voice was gravely as he used his thick forearms to wipe the sweat from his face. His cheeks were a deep shade of red as he struggled to catch his breath.

"Drink some water," Ralph encouraged from where he sat just under one of the lights at the bottom of the basement stairs. His hands trembled and his white t-shirt was so saturated with sweat it was almost transparent. The shotgun lay across his lap with the breach open. The spring made a distinct sound as he fed shells into the magazine tube. "You don't want to dehydrate."

"Yeah, some water would be good," Paul grumbled. He looked around almost disoriented. "What are we doing down here?"

"We're getting ready," Christian answered with noticeable agitation in his voice. He made no effort to turn around from where he stood. His broad shoulders obscured the view of the open safe as he pressed 5.56mm rounds into a black Magpul PMAG. His ears rang so badly he could barely make out the low buzz of the light just above his head.

Jeff placed the duffle bag on the bed, opened the main compartment and retrieved his ranger green 5.11 Maverick battle belt, "I can't hear anything out of my right ear." He said as he looped the inner belt through his jeans and affixed his Blackhawk special operations holster to the outer belt.

"It'll get better," Matt tried to assure him as he took a seat on the bed next to Jeff's duffle bag. His legs felt weak and hands trembled as the image of his uncle's suicide raced through his mind. "Yeah, I'm sure it'll get better..." He continued as his voice trailed off.

"I hope so," Jeff said as he slammed a loaded magazine into the P90's magwell. He used his right thumb to depress the slide stop lever. He decocked the hammer and slid the pistol into the holster. "Everything sounding like it's underwater is getting fucking annoying."

"Come on," Matt Chico whispered to himself. He stood at the sink in the small half bath and stared at his reflection in the mirror. Cold water poured from the faucet over the light gray washcloth he collected from the narrow linen closet next to the door. His heart raced as he feared for his son's safety. The adrenaline left him feeling weak and he had to use both hands to turn the faucet off. He took several deep breaths, swallowed hard and fought back the tears at the edges of his eyes as he pressed the cold washcloth against his face. "Please God, let my son be ok."

"Keep going," Ralph insisted as Paul took a long drink from the plastic bottle of spring water. "Finish it."

Jeff took several boxes of ammunition from the duffle bag and placed them on the bed next to the rows of magazines. With a sense of urgency, he pressed 5.56mm rounds into the rifle magazines. The brass shell casings made a distinct clicking sound as he snapped them in place beneath the metal feed lips. When each was loaded, he held it by the floor plate with his left hand and smacked the back of the magazine against his right palm to ensure each round seated properly. He rubbed his eyes and picked up the first of the pistol magazines, "I should have stockpiled more .45 caliber ammo."

Paul finished the last of the water. He crumpled the plastic bottle and deposited it in the garbage can in the laundry room, "I'm stepping into the garage for a smoke." He announced from the foyer.

"There's things to do!" Christian said sharply as he turned around. "How about you take a break from killing yourself slowly in the garage and help us get ready."

"What's your fucking problem?" Paul asked angrily as he stormed back through the doorway.

"Easy!" Matt hollered as he jumped to his feet.

"Fights not down here," Ralph added. His tone was even and he held his hands out just above his waist as he got up. "Let's just take a breath."

"NO!" Paul barked. "I want to know what the fucking problem is!"

"I'll tell you what the fucking problem is," Christian said as he stepped around his brother. "Our uncle is laying out there dead. Our friend is upstairs dying. We...each of us has people out there we can't get in touch with."

"I'm sorry," Paul's deep voice rumbled. "I'm sorry about your uncle..."

Christian shook his head, "Did you like what happened out there?"

"What?" Paul questioned as his eyes narrowed.

"You think our first full on engagement with those things went well?" Christian hissed.

"Don't refer to them as those things," Jeff muttered to himself as he continued to load pistol magazines.

"What kind of fucking question is that?" Paul asked angrily.

"We go on a rescue mission and leave a man behind," Christian snarled. "And run out of ammunition on top of it! What kind of fucking bullshit is that?"

"We'll be ready next time," Ralph offered as he stepped in between Christian and Paul.

"Next time?" Christian blurted. "We should have been ready this fucking time!"

Paul motioned to himself, "Are you trying to say it's my fault?" He demanded.

"WE weren't prepared!" Christian shouted as his face reddened. He was about to say more when he was interrupted.

"This isn't productive." Matt Chico said as he rejoined the group. He was as diplomatic as he was able to be under the circumstances. "Everybody needs to take a breath. A second encounter isn't going to go any better if we're at each other."

"He's right," Ralph agreed with a nod. "What can I do to help? Give me some magazines to load."

"Why don't you sit down for a minute," Matt suggested as he gently put his hand on Christian's arm. "Just sit down. You can help Jeff load some of his mags."

Christian took 2 quick puffs from his inhaler. "Yeah...yeah, let me sit down and help Jeff." He said as he took a seat on the bed.

Jeff slid half a dozen pistol mags and 2 boxes of ammo towards Christian, "Here, to get you started."

"Ralph, would you give me a hand?" Matt asked as he motioned behind him to the safe.

Ralph nodded, "Yeah, I can do that." He gave Christian's shoulder a reassuring pat as he moved past him.

"Paul," Matt said as he motioned with his head. "Go have your smoke. We'll get this going. When you're finished, you come back and give us a hand."

Paul nodded as his chest heaved, "Yeah...I'll go have that smoke."

The metal latch echoed off the concrete block walls as the door to the garage closed behind Paul. The room was dark except for the slivers of light that escaped around the edges of the boards that covered the two windows on the north wall. Stagnant water sloshed around his boots as he moved to the middle of the room and retrieved the pack of cigarettes from his pocket. The flame from the lighter shone brightly as he touched it to the end of the cigarette. The tip glowed a vibrant reddish orange as he inhaled deeply. He felt the tension subside as the nicotine quickly took effect.

"I wish Aaron was here," Jeff said as he snapped a loaded magazine into the Mini-14's magwell. He released the charging handle, engaged the safety, and placed the rifle on the bed.

"Yeah, me too," Christian said as he loaded the last of Jeff's pistol mags. The pain returned to his stomach and with it a feeling of helplessness that the worst was yet to come.

"I called him earlier," Matt added as he turned back from the safe. He pressed the last 3 rounds into an OD green PMAG as he spoke. "There was no answer, but I did leave him a message."

"My mother called him too...a couple of times," Jeff said as he rummaged through the duffle bag. "She couldn't get in touch with him either. It was all she talked about on the way over here. You would have never known she had 3 other kids with the way she went on."

"Don't take it personal Jeff," Matt urged. "Aaron's the only one who's got to worry about being deployed."

"I guess there is that," Jeff said as he stacked the empty ammo boxes next to the duffle bag.

"I wouldn't worry about Aaron," Christian said as he slowly got to his feet. "He made it through Ranger School, Jump Master School, Pathfinder School, survived how many combat deployments...whatever this is won't stop him. He'll figure a way through...and hopefully get back here."

"Texas is a ways away," Jeff said as he adjusted the holster over his right hip.

"Yes, it is," Christian agreed as he moved to the safe. He tapped Matt on the shoulder. "Let me have some of those rifle mags and ammo."

"Don't count him out Jeff," Matt said as he handed Christian a stack of PMAGs and several boxes of 55-grain 5.56mm FMJ ammunition.

Jeff smirked, "I know better than to count my brother out."

"Where do you want this stuff?" Matt Chico asked as he emerged from the foyer. His arms were full with cases of MRE's.

"Opposite side of the stairs," Christian instructed. He motioned to an area along the wall. "Stack them over there out of the way."

Matt Chico nodded, "You have any idea how much of this stuff you have down here?"

"Right down to every last book of matches and roll of toilet paper," Christian answered. He finished loading the last PMAG and tapped the back of the magazine against his palm. "These are loaded. Hand me a few more."

"I think we're just about finished with rifle mags," Ralph said as he lined the loaded magazines up along the top shelf of the safe.

"Pistol mags are next," Matt said as he reached for a box of Speer Lawman 230-grain .45 caliber ammunition.

"Give me some magazines and some ammo," Christian instructed. The pain was such that he couldn't help but grit his teeth. "It'll be a different outcome the next time we go up against those things."

"We need to stop calling them those things," Jeff said as his body stiffened. He was visibly agitated as he spoke. "We know exactly what they are..."

The old hinges creaked loudly as the door at the top of the stair opened. The shrill high-pitched sound startled them. Their collective gaze shot towards the stairwell as pistols were drawn hastily from their holsters.

"Coming down," Mr. Spahl announced as he quickly descended the stairs.

"Good thing he announced himself," Matt muttered. He shook his head as he slid the P220 into his holster.

"We've got to work on that," Christian said as he rubbed his eyes. "That could have gone bad, real quick."

"We're all out of our element," Ralph said as he stepped away from the safe and took a few deep breaths. "We've never faced a situation like this."

"Isn't that the truth," Matt Chico added.

"We're not supposed to know how to act," Ralph continued. "For all the shooting we've done over the years it's never been at anyone."

"That's very true," Paul agreed as he stepped in from the garage. His demeanor was calmer as he rejoined the group. He walked over to Christian and extended his hand. "It'll be something we work on together."

"Yes, we will," Christian said as he nodded and shook Paul's hand. "We'll work on it together."

"You guys alright down here?" Mr. Spahl asked as he reached the bottom of the stairs.

"Better now," Jeff said as he holstered his pistol. "Glad you announced yourself."

"Yeah, me too," Mr. Spahl said as he looked around the room. "You boys gearing up for war?"

"Just trying to be prepared," Matt said as he tried to manage a grin.

"That's quite a number of long guns," Mr. Spahl observed as he motioned towards the open safe. "All AR15's?"

"Not all," Christian answered. "Just the first six."

"Just the first six," Mr. Spahl repeated. "They look a lot different than the M16A1 I was issued when I served."

"Same basic function," Matt explained. "Without full auto or 3-round burst capability of course."

"Why so many?" Mr. Spahl asked. "If it's all the same basic function."

"Different configurations," Matt answered. "Barrel length, optics, triggers. The two older ones are stock Bushmaster rifles. We reoutfitted them with upgraded bolt carrier groups, charging handles, new pins and springs and different furniture. The other four we built with specific intent."

"You boys really put a lot of effort into being prepared," Mr. Spahl acknowledged.

"We felt the need," Christian said as he took one of the black rifles from the safe. "This is my primary." He explained. "Aero Precision M4E1 lower. Two stage Geissele trigger and lower parts kit. MK2 enhanced lightweight Bravo Company upper. 14.5-inch barrel with a mid-length gas system and M-LOK 13-inch rail. Troy battle sights, Raptor charging handle and Hogue furniture."

"And on the top?" Mr. Spahl asked as he motioned to the optic mounted on the Picatinny rail.

"Aimpoint PRO," Christian answered. "Sturdy, reliable...holds zero."

"All important features," Mr. Spahl said as he motioned to Matt. "What about you?"

"Similar," Matt said with a nod as he took a rifle from the safe, "Spikes Tactical lower receiver. Geissele single stage trigger and parts kit. Troy battle sights, Raptor charging handle and Bravo Company furniture. I've got a Eotech EXPS2 holographic site with G33 magnifier behind it on a Geissele URGI upper receiver."

"Single stage trigger," Mr. Spahl said. "What kind of pull?"

"Three pounds," Matt answered.

"Impressive," Mr. Spahl commented with a nod. "I guess we did come to the right place." He added with a slight grin. "You boys really know your stuff."

"What's going on upstairs?" Matt asked as he changed the subject. He placed the rifle on the bed and slid three loaded PMAGs into the magazine pouches along the left side of his belt.

"That's what I came down here to talk about," Mr. Spahl began. "I'm sorry about your uncle."

"Thank you," Matt said. "I don't think it's fully sunken in yet."

"That's understandable," Mr. Spahl assured them. "Things upstairs aren't great."

"Why? What's going on?" Christian asked. "How is our aunt?"

"She was hysterical," Mr. Spahl answered. "Your cousin Katherine gave her some Xanex. That calmed her down a bit. She's quiet now at least."

"That's something anyway," Matt offered. "Is Patrick coming down?"

Mr. Spahl shook his head, "I doubt it. He's in a state of shock. He's on the love seat with your aunt. I wouldn't expect a lot out of him right now."

"How are my parents?" Matt Chico asked.

"Your mother is holding her own," Mr. Spahl answered.

"And my father?" Matt Chico inquired cautiously.

"Your mother gave him some of Katherine's Xanex too," Mr. Spahl answered. "He's asleep on the couch."

"What about Tyler?" Christian asked as he continued to load magazines.

"He's not in great shape," Mr. Spahl explained. "I think your cousin broke the lower part of the tibia bone in his right leg. His ankle is very swollen and discolored. It may be dislocated."

"He wasn't bitten or scratched, was he?" Christian asked.

Mr. Spahl shook his head, "No, nothing like that...but he's in a lot of pain."

"Are there any Percocet left?" Matt asked.

"No," Mr. Spahl answered somberly. "My wife gave the last 2 to Anthony about an hour ago."

"Is there anything you can do for Tyler?" Matt inquired.

"Right now, just Advil and a splint," Mr. Spahl answered. "He's on the bed in the back bedroom with his leg elevated. If the bone is broken and I'm pretty sure it is, Tyler needs to go to a hospital."

"How is Anthony?" Christian asked with a sense of urgency in his voice.

"I wish I had better news," Mr. Spahl said as his eyes narrowed and voice got raspy. "Honestly, I don't see him living through the night."

Their faces dropped as if someone let the air out of the room.

"What?" Matt Chico asked visibly emotional. "What do you mean; he might not make it through the night?"

"We're trying everything to bring his fever down, but nothings working. He's burning up," Mr. Spahl explained. "He's been in and out of consciousness. We had him in an ice bath but..."

"What are our options?" Christian interrupted.

"We can't get the fever to break," Mr. Spahl said stoically. His face reddened and he became agitated as he explained. "The veins around the bite are more discolored. The wound won't stop bleeding. I've changed the dressing on it half a dozen times. It doesn't matter how much gauze and tape I wrap his arm in, it just keeps bleeding through. He needs a hospital, but honestly at this point I don't know what they could even do for him."

"Where is he now?" Matt asked.

"Back on the floor in the bedroom over the garage," Mr. Spahl answered.

"You didn't come into contact with any of his blood, did you?" Matt Chico asked as he folded his arms nervously.

Mr. Spahl shook his head, "No." He said bluntly. "We were careful."

"It's settled then," Matt Chico insisted. "We need to leave. We need to get Anthony and Tyler to a hospital."

"Nothing's settled," Jeff blurted as he held his hands out to his sides. "What makes you think anything is settled?"

"Easy," Ralph insisted as he tugged nervously at his beard. "What do we know?"

"What do you mean, what do we know?" Jeff asked impatiently.

"I mean, what's our increase in knowledge?" Ralph clarified.

"Situational awareness," Paul said calmly as he folded his arms.

"Exactly," Ralph agreed. "Christian, you were monitoring the television before. Did you see if they announced anything since the Governor declared a state of emergency?"

Christian stood for a moment and collected his thoughts, "Regular news is off the air. The emergency broadcast system has taken over."

"DHS, FEMA and the CDC," Jeff said. He folded his arms and shook his head. "Fucking government bureaucrats. They probably had a hand in causing this, like all those train derailments a few years back."

"Easy," Ralph encouraged as he motioned towards Jeff. "Let's just figure out where we are in all this."

"He's right," Paul offered. "If we have to leave, we'd be better to know what we're walking out to."

"What do you mean, IF we have to leave?" Matt Chico questioned. "We can't stay here. There are too many of us and Tyler and Anthony need actual medical care, not whatever you can pull out of a first aid kit."

"Easy, Chico. The monologue isn't helping," Matt insisted. "Let Christian finish."

"It's spreading," Christian said bluntly. "At least from what I saw on the television. Things are getting worse. FEMA is trying to establish safe zones and evacuation points."

"I doubt they have the resources for that," Jeff added.

"Jeff," Mr. Spahl said as he shot his son a look. "Enough with the commentary."

"What?" Jeff quipped angrily. "This is what happens when government prioritizes social programs over public safety and things that actually matter!"

"Alright," Mr. Spahl insisted. "That's not helping. What about the hospitals?"

"That's the thing," Christian began. "We know based on earlier reports that survivors from the arsenal were taken to all 3 area hospitals."

"Yeah," Matt agreed. "I remember hearing that."

"With the latest revelation about the involvement of FEMA and the CDC," Christian explained. "There hasn't been any mention about utilizing the hospitals as a safe zone, evacuation point or anything else."

"You think those locations have been compromised?" Mr. Spahl asked.

"I don't see how they couldn't be," Christian answered. "Look at the symptoms Anthony is suffering from one bite. Can you imagine the chaos those hospitals must be experiencing?"

"We should still try for one of them," Matt Chico insisted. "Anthony and Tyler..."

"The Governor called for residents to stay in their homes," Christian interrupted. "He's promised to deploy search and rescue teams from the National Guard to collect people."

"Well, if the Governor promised, I guess we don't have anything to worry about," Jeff said sarcastically.

"Jeff!" Mr. Spahl said sternly.

"What?" Jeff insisted.

"Knock it off!" Mr. Spahl ordered.

"You believe anything Mitchell Garrison says?" Jeff asked with in a raised voice. "The guy's a fucking scumbag. You see his teeth? Nobody's teeth should be that shade of white."

"Jeff always has the best arguments," Matt said as he let out an unexpected chuckle. He clasped his hands behind his head and took several deep breaths. "I'm not waiting around for the National Guard to evacuate us and I'm sure as shit not going to a fucking FEMA camp."

"Agreed," Christian said sternly. "Chico, what did you see online?"

"The internet kept going down," Matt Chico began. "But I did see that the press secretary for the CDC held a briefing. The CDC doesn't know exactly what this is. They're calling it a pandemic outbreak and say they've got they're top people are working on it."

"Not reassuring," Paul said as he rubbed his eyes.

"They think it's a virus," Matt Chico continued. "Problem is they don't have a way to treat it. They don't think it's airborne. They think it's transmitted through saliva and blood...if those things bite or scratch you...they infect you..."

"Internet sources had that information yesterday," Christian said angrily.

"That's the fucking government," Jeff chided. "A day late and pandemic outbreak short."

"That's a good point," Matt said as he motioned to Jeff. "How is it the official story is a day behind the internet trolls?"

"It's all speculation," Mr. Spahl offered. "It's a good question, but probably one we're not going to get an answer to anytime soon."

"Chico, anything else?" Christian asked.

"Most of what else I saw was conspiracy theories and end time prophecies," Matt Chico explained as his voice tensed. "If what I read was correct, it's only a matter of time before Anthony succumbs to it. The high-grade fever will kill him and at some point, he'll...reanimate and try and kill us."

"That's reassuring," Jeff said as he took a seat on the bed. "Smoke 'em if you got 'em I guess."

"Hey!" Matt Chico snapped. "You asked me what information I had and I'm telling you."

"Easy, Chico," Christian insisted. "Everybody's tense. Was there anything else?"

Matt Chico shook his head, "Just that no one knows if the intent of the reanimated is to feed, spread the virus or both."

"I'm just going to chalk it up to getting bit or scratched is a bad thing," Jeff said. He rubbed his eyes and head. "Christ, I need a drink."

"If the internet connection was spotty," Paul began. "What's happening with cell service and the land line?"

"Mr. Spahl, you want to weigh in on that?" Christian asked.

"There's no cell service, at least none upstairs," Mr. Spahl explained. "The only thing I was able to get from the land line was the emergency message, but I couldn't dial out."

"That being the case," Paul began. "Losing power completely can't be far off."

"You're probably right," Christian said as he rubbed his forehead.

"I don't see staying here as being an option," Paul said bluntly. He took the pack of cigarettes out of his pocket.

"I would have to agree," Mr. Spahl said with a nod. "You going to smoke?"

Paul nodded, "I am."

"Do you have an extra one?" Mr. Spahl asked. The look on his face was a mixture of eagerness and desperation.

"Always," Paul said as he motioned towards the garage.

"Jeff, you smoking?" Mr. Spahl asked as he and Paul headed through the foyer.

"Be there in a minute," Jeff answered. "Don't feel like getting up just now."

"Wait," Christian insisted before Mr. Spahl and Paul exited the basement.

"What is it?" Mr. Spahl asked as they turned back.

"We leave here at dawn," Christian declared.

"You just decided this now?" Paul questioned as he and Mr. Spahl reentered the main room of the basement.

"It's too dangerous to try to stay here beyond that," Christian said. "We'll leave through the garage, which means everything we intend to take needs to be down here prior to that door opening."

"Wait, I don't..." Ralph began.

"When that door opens," Matt said. His voice was low and eyes widened as he spoke. "We're going to be very exposed and need to move quickly. Three, maybe four trips back and forth from the house to the cars at most."

"Shouldn't we discuss this?" Matt Chico asked with a look of deep concern on this face.

"I want weapons and ammo split between my Forester and Paul's Jeep," Christian instructed. "I'll drive the lead vehicle. Paul, you bring up the rear. We'll put the other three vehicles in between us. Sound like a plan?"

"Fuck yes it does," Paul said with a nod. "Sounds like an excellent plan."

"Good," Christian said. "Matt's going to drive his Grand Marquis. Matt Chico, you're going to drive your father's roadmaster. Mr. Spahl, I'm guessing you're going to want to drive your Tahoe."

"Yes," Mr. Spahl answered. "How long have the two of you been cooking this plan up?"

"It's been discussed," Matt answered. "Given everything we've just talked about, Christian and I feel it best to leave at dawn."

"Discussed?" Mr. Spahl questioned with a hint of sarcasm in his voice. "Alright, let's hear the rest of your plan so we're all clear with what needs to happen."

"I want the supplies split between the three middle vehicles," Christian instructed. "I'll take Patrick and my aunt. Paul you and Ralph take Katherine and Marcus."

"Roger," Paul responded.

"Jeff, you're with your parents. Matt Chico, you're with yours. Tyler is going in the back of Matt's car," Chrisitan explained. "Everyone clear so far?"

"No, not exactly," Matt Chico said sternly. "What...what about Anthony? You didn't mention Anthony. We need to deal with him."

"I'll do it quickly," Matt offered. His voice was uncharacteristically stoic. "He won't suffer."

"WHAT?" Matt Chico blurted. "What the fuck did you just say?"

"You said we needed to deal with him," Matt reminded as he pointed at his friend. "And, I just told you that I would take care of it, so none of the rest of you had to."

"Are you fucking nuts?" Matt Chico asked rhetorically as his face turned a deep shade of red. "I said deal with him as in get him help, not euthanize him."

"It's mercy!" Matt insisted.

"It's fucking murder, that's what it is!" Matt Chico retorted.

"This isn't up for discussion!" Christian interjected sharply. "It's sucks Chico, but Anthony's suffering and we won't put everyone else in danger by taking him with us."

"I can't...I can't believe we're even talking this way," Matt Chico stammered. "Anthony is our friend. He's been our friend for years."

"No one's debating that!" Christian insisted. "But it's been decided."

"What about the hospital?" Matt Chico demanded. "If we're leaving anyway, why can't we take him to one of the hospitals?"

"There's a reason the government isn't telling people to go to the hospitals," Matt said firmly.

"More conspiracy bullshit!" Matt Chico snapped. "He's our fucking friend."

"No," Mr. Spahl interjected. "There may be something to staying away from the hospitals."

"It's been decided Chico," Christian repeated coldly. "We don't have to like it, but this is how it is."

Matt Chico's gaze dropped to the floor. He shook his head in disgust, "I don't even know who you two are anymore."

The decision to kill one of their own shifted the mood in the basement from tense to somber. With the adrenaline high long worn off the gravity of the situation hung over them like a dark storm cloud. For a few brief moments they just stood in silence.

"Alright, listen up!" Matt began. "We leave at dawn."

"What if we lose power before then?" Ralph asked. "How are we getting out?"

"Even if we lose power," Christian explained. "We'll still be able open the garage door. The problem is we won't be able to secure it...at least not in a reasonable timeframe and not without putting anyone of us at risk."

"Why would we need to secure the door if we're leaving?" Ralph inquired.

"Depending on how things go in P.A., there's a chance baby brother may try and get back here. We need to leave this place intact for him in case that happens," Matt explained. "When the garage door opens, Christian and Paul will be the first two out. They'll provide cover so we can move everybody to the vehicles. Ralph, you, and I will carry Tyler and get him in the back of my car. Once we've got everybody situated, we need to move the weapons, ammo, food, and other supplies as quickly as we can...whatever happens try not to panic. Remember your jobs and keep moving."

"What do we do until dawn?" Jeff asked.

"Same as we have been," Christian said. "Stay low, sleep in shifts, and keep watch. Questions?"

"This isn't fucking right," Matt Chico said as he shook his head in disgust. "Nothing about this is fucking right."

The heat from the sun dissipated as the day wore on. It was aided by the breeze as it picked up and made the budding branches appear to dance playfully back and forth. In the distance, the shrill sound of sirens and distinct pop of gunfire preceded long shadows as the sun crept lower and lower behind the mountains. Pillars of black smoke littered the sky to the north and west and stood out against the deep red and orange of the setting sun.

"You all, right?" Jeff asked as he and Christian kept watch from the kitchen.

Christian closed his eyes and shook his head and clamped his right hand over his abdomen, "Been better." He answered.

"Lot of movement out there," Jeff commented as he filled a glass with water.

"Yeah," Christian answered without opening his eyes.

Day prepared to surrender to dusk. Matt looked out over Mrs. Santini's rose bushes from where he knelt at the front door. It was a much-needed moment of serenity until it was abruptly shattered by screeching car tires.

"CAR!" Matt hollered as his eyes opened wide.

The tires smoked as the back end of the small white sports car fishtailed around the turn and onto the street. Black stripes covered the faded gray asphalt as the car slid to a stop in front of the house.

"WHO?" Christian called as he and Jeff hurried in from the kitchen.

"DON'T KNOW!" Matt shouted as he jumped to his feet. "We need to get out there. They may need our help!"

CHAPTER 11

cry havoc

MOST OF THE GROUP found themselves again huddled in the small kitchen. Tear filled eyes and hidden faces served to intensify feelings of tension and dread. The smell of gun powder and sweat permeated the stagnant air. It somehow managed to temper the oppressive odor of bleach that clung to the linoleum floor.

"I thought that was your car," Matt panted as his chest heaved. He stood with his body pressed tightly against the narrow corner between the back door and cabinets. Beads of sweat ran down his face. They sizzled as they fell against the hot barrel of his AR15.

"Matty," Kurt said red faced as he held Kim tight against his body. His expression was a mixture of panic and confusion. "What was that? What's happening out there?"

Kurt was strong and agile, with thick round shoulders and muscular arms. His narrow waist gave his back an impressive V-shape. His hazel eyes and spiky black hair complimented the lean features of his face. Kurt was personable and respectful and there was an ease about the way he could carry on a conversation.

"It's the end of the world. Didn't anyone tell you?" Jeff asked. He snapped a loaded magazine into the Mini-14's magwell.

"Jeff!" Christian chided as he took two ceramic mugs from the cabinet above the stove.

Kim flinched as Jeff released the charging handle, "Please." She whimpered into Kurt's chest. "No more loud noise."

Kim was fair skinned with delicate features. She had light blue eyes and golden blonde hair that reached the middle of her back when she wore it down. She had a smile that could light up a room and the personality to match.

Jeff rubbed his temples and twisted his neck from side to side, "I'll go check the front." He said as he navigated his way out of the crowded room.

"A better showing..." Paul declared. His broad shoulder and thick frame almost eclipsed the doorway to the basement. His cheeks were red and he breathed heavily as he leaned against the door frame. He used his left hand to wipe sweat and remnants of gun powder from his face and beard. His M1A Scout leaned next to him against the wall. The bolt was locked open and exposed the follower of the empty magazine. "But still too close for my liking."

"At least we didn't run out of ammo this time," Ralph added. His hands trembled slightly as he leaned against the refrigerator. His face and forearms were speckled with black gun powder residue.

"Yeah, there is that," Matt agreed with a nod. "I have a shell pouch downstairs you can use and I'm sure we can find you a Serpa belt and holster..." He offered as his voice trailed off.

Ralph nodded and used his forearm to wipe the sweat from his face, "Yeah, that'll work."

Jeff was visibly frustrated as he made his way to the front door. He engaged the safety on his rifle and checked his pistol. He looked back at Josh who was still asleep on the couch. Then over to aunt Athena who was slumped against the arm of the love seat, "This is turning into such a fucking shit show." He muttered to himself as he knelt and peered in between the boards.

Matt's gaze wandered around the room before it found Kurt again. "What's going on? We're not entirely sure. The news reported it as some type of virus...but whatever it is, I think it's safe to say it's getting worse out there."

Kurt's shoulders slumped forward as he let out a deep exhale, "I agree with you on that."

"Here," Christian offered as he motioned to the kitchen table. He placed the mugs on the counter, stepped around Kurt and Kim and pulled out two of the chairs. "You should both sit down."

Kim's body trembled as Kurt guided her gently to one of the chairs, "It's alright." He assured her as he buried his face in her soft blonde hair. "I'm not going anywhere."

She did her best to wipe the tears from her eyes as she took a seat at the table, "Thank you." Kim whispered.

"I'll make you both some tea," Christian offered as he turned the sink faucet on and took the kettle from the stove.

"Yes, please," Kim answered without turning around. Tears streamed down her cheeks as she reached across the small table and took several napkins from the rustic bamboo napkin holder.

"Honey, don't use those," Mrs. Spahl insisted. "They're too coarse. I'll get you some tissues."

"Thank you," Kim managed as she looked up at Mrs. Spahl.

Mrs. Spahl nodded and put a comforting hand on Kim's shoulder, "I'll be right back honey, you just hang in there." She said as she turned and ushered Kerri and Mr. Spahl out of the kitchen, "Come on, we've all got people to check on."

"On that note," Paul said. He motioned to Ralph as the three of them left the kitchen. "I'm going downstairs to smoke. You coming?"

Ralph nodded as he followed Paul to the basement, "Yeah, sure. What's a little second-hand smoke at this point?"

The kettle on the stove whistled just as Mrs. Spahl returned. She placed a blue and white box of Kleenex in front of Kim, "Here honey. Use these." She instructed. She gave Kim a hopeful smile before she turned and left.

"Thank you," Kim managed. Her eyes were red with dark circles beneath them. Streaks of black mascara and tears covered her cheeks. She used several tissues to wipe her face as Kurt gently rubbed her back.

"You're safe now," Matt assured them as he took a seat next to Kim. "Let's just take a moment to catch our breath."

Christian filled the two mugs with boiling water from the kettle, "Here, this should help." He said as he placed them in front of Kurt and Kim. "Let it cool a little." He added as he took a seat next to Kurt.

"Smells good," Kim said quietly. Steam rose from the top as she wrapped her hands around the white mug with the faded sun flower design on the side. The heat from the ceramic felt good against her palms. She felt the tremble in her hands begin to subside as she brought the mug to her mouth and let the steam rise into her nostrils. "What is it?"

"Chamomile and raw honey," Christian answered. "It should help take the edge off."

"I didn't realize how weak my legs were until I sat down," Kurt said as he reached for the black mug in front of him. His hands shook as he wrapped his fingers around the handle. "They feel almost numb."

"That's the adrenaline," Christian said. "The sugar in the honey will help."

"Now you know why I was always on you to train legs," Matt offered in a fleeting attempt at levity.

"We're a long way from those great days at Powerhouse Gym, aren't we?" Kurt asked as he tried to manage a smile.

"Yes, we are," Matt answered. "Those were great days."

"Yeah, what I wouldn't give to have you busting my balls about training legs," Kurt said as he brought the mug up to his lips.

"Well," Matt began. "Maybe after all this we can get back to it."

"Ladies aren't interested in quads," Kurt jabbed. "They're interested in abs..."

"Did you have to kill those people?" Kim interjected. Her voice trembled as she spoke. "Please...what's going on out there? What's happening?"

Christian got up from the table. His boots made an audible squeak against the linoleum as he walked to the sink. He took a faded yellow washcloth from the drawer and ran it under cold water, "Take this." He insisted as he handed it to Kim.

She looked up at him with uncertainty in her eyes.

"Put it on the back of your neck," Christian said softly.

Kim nodded, "Thank you." She said as she took the wash cloth. She breathed slowly as she lifted her long blonde hair and placed the cold damp cloth against the back of her neck.

"The truth of it is," Matt began. "We don't know much more than what we've seen on television and been able to piece together from the internet."

"Which is what?" Kim asked as she took a sip from the mug.

"Reports indicate this started yesterday," Christian said as he rejoined them at the table. "Patrick and Tyler were actually on the arsenal when the outbreak began..."

"What did they say about it?" Kim asked.

"Not up for talking about it," Christian explained. "I can tell you the government is treating this as a highly contagious virus..."

"But not airborne," Matt interjected.

"Not airborne," Christian repeated. "But spreading fast."

"What about the people you guys shot?" Kurt asked as he twisted the mug nervously between his hands. "Getting us from the car to the house..."

"Not people anymore," Christian answered. "At least not the way they were. Infected...dangerous."

"We lost our uncle trying to get our aunt and cousins over here," Matt added as he motioned behind him.

Kim shuttered, "That's terrible." She said as she brought the mug to her pursed lips and sipped the contents. "I'm so sorry."

"Thank you," Christian said as he rubbed his temples. "It's been a difficult two days."

For a moment the kitchen was still. The chair creaked slightly as Christian got up. He moved to the sink, tipped his head back and closed his eyes. His head throbbed and pain seared through his abdomen. As his eyes opened, his gaze almost unconsciously drifted to the hill behind the house. Despite his calm demeanor, the sound of gunfire echoed in his ears. Visceral images of the earlier slaughter flashed before his eyes. Fresh corpses littered the ground around the house. It was the toll they paid to get Kim and Kurt safely inside.

"The tea is very good," Kim offered as her words broke the uncomfortable silence. "Thank you."

Matt managed a grin, "Sure." He replied with a nod.

"Chamomile and raw honey," Christian said as he rubbed his eyes. "It's supposed to have a calming effect."

"It's helping," Kim said as she managed a meek smile.

"Good...glad to hear it," Christian said. To his surprise when he turned back, he found Matt Chico standing in the doorway.

"Everybody ok in here?" Matt Chico asked.

"Yeah," Matt answered. "We're ok."

"Chico, do you know Kim and Kurt?" Christian asked.

Matt Chico nodded and extended his hand, "I'm sure our paths have crossed before."

"You look familiar," Kurt said as he shook Matt Chico's hand.

"How is everybody in the other room?" Matt asked.

"Hanging in there," Matt Chico answered as he folded his arms.

"Anthony?" Christian asked as he returned to the table.

Matt Chico shook his head, "Unconscious right now. Fever seems to be holding at 106."

"Degrees?" Kurt blurted in disbelief. "Jesus, that's serious."

"I know," Matt Chico said as his eyes widened. "That's why I keep saying we need to get him to a hospital."

"Let's not revisit that right now," Matt said sternly from where he sat.

Matt Chico opened his mouth to speak as Paul and Ralph emerged from the basement.

"Everything alright up here?" Paul asked.

"Getting there," Matt answered.

"Good," Paul said as he made his way to the sink and filled a glass from the faucet. "Ralph, thirsty?"

"Yeah," Ralph replied. "I could use some water."

Paul filled a second glass and handed it to Ralph, "Here."

"Kurt," Christian began calmly. "What happened?"

Kurt finished the last of his tea and placed the mug on the table in front of him. He rubbed his forehead and ran his hands through his hair. He bit down nervously on his bottom lip before he cleared his throat and spoke, "I just finished a class with my middle school kids. I was headed over to the high school to teach a sophomore health class..."

"That's got to be uncomfortable," Paul chuckled as he refilled his glass.

"More for them I think," Kurt replied. "Anyway...I was about to call Kim on the drive over when I saw the missed call and voicemail from Matty. I heard the message and just left...I just left and drove to Kim's office as quick as I could. I told her we couldn't wait...what Matty's message said...and that we had to leave to come here immediately."

"Why didn't you bring the 4-Runner?" Matt asked curiously.

"It's in the shop," Kim answered as she maneuvered her hands around the still warm mug. "It's getting a new clutch."

"Well...you did the right thing," Matt assured them. "Coming here I mean."

"Did we?" Kurt asked as tears filled the corners of his eyes. "My parents...Kim's parents...we couldn't get in touch with them."

Paul put the glass on the counter and placed a comforting hand on Kurt's shoulder, "We've all got loved ones out there. Once we get situated, we can see about organizing search parties to collect them."

"We're not going to take Anthony to a hospital but we're going to organize search parties? You guys are out of your fucking minds," Matt Chico snapped as he stormed out of the kitchen doorway.

"There's no way for us to get to them," Kim said as she took Kurt's hand in hers. "The four of them left last Friday for a Caribbean cruise."

"We couldn't get in touch with them...even trying to go through the cruise line," Kurt continued. "I was afraid to wait...we just packed a bag and came here."

"You did the right thing," Ralph offered as he handed Kurt a glass of water. "There's safety in numbers."

"In all seriousness," Matt said. "With all that's going on, it may be safer for your parents to be on a ship in the ocean."

"Do you really think so?" Kim asked as her cheeks reddened.

"I do," Christian answered confidently. "It may be the safest place right now. Those ships are built and stocked to sustain a full crew and passengers for 6-weeks beyond the scheduled trip. The cruise lines do that in the event of a catastrophic event where they're not able to return to port."

"I had no idea," Kurt admitted as he brushed tears from his cheeks. He placed the glass on the table in front of him and rubbed his eyes. "6-weeks...a month and a half?"

"Exactly," Paul said as he gave Kurt's shoulder a squeeze. "This will all be sorted by then."

"I hope you're right," Kurt said with obvious desperation in his voice.

"I love you, Kurt," Kim reassured him as she squeezed his hand. "Please try not to worry, it's going to be ok."

Kurt nodded and pulled her chair close to his. He wrapped his arms around her, "I know it will." He said unable to hold back the tears which rolled down his face and dampened her silken hair. "I love you, Kim. I won't let anything happen to you...no matter what."

"We need to know what's happening out there." Christian interrupted. "How was it trying to get here?"

"Chaos," Kurt said as he composed himself. Slowly he turned the empty glass counter clockwise with his left hand as he continued. "It was as if half the people knew something was going on and were trying to get away and the other half had no clue about any of it."

"Why is that no surprise?" Ralph asked as he shook his head. "This fucking state."

"Were you on any highways, main roads?" Christian asked as he leaned forward in his chair.

"80, 287. Traffic patterns seemed heavier than usual...but then I'm never on the road during that time of day. Things really slowed down when I got onto route 10. East bound traffic was dead stop as far as I could see. The west bound was slow, but still moving. Luckily, I used back roads and managed to get around most of it."

"What was that, two towns away?" Christian asked.

"Yes," Kim answered with a nod. "Two towns away. We're on the far side though. Maybe eight miles from here."

"It was a rough 8-miles," Kurt said. He tapped his fingers nervously against the glass. "The local police were nowhere to be found. There were a couple road blocks set up but no officers manning them. We ran through a couple on our way here."

"Anything else?" Christian asked. The intensity in his voice increased as his eyes narrowed. "Anything we may have to anticipate on our way out of here."

"Wait, what?" Kim stammered. "Are we leaving?"

"I don't know," Kurt began as he squirmed uncomfortably in his chair. "It was like nothing we've ever seen before. The only way to describe it was anarchy. There were gun shots, car tires squealing, sirens...plenty of sirens. Everything seemed to be happening all at once. There were people everywhere...in cars...out of cars...everywhere..."

They listened intently as Kurt spoke. So much so that no one noticed when Mr. Spahl emerged in the doorway.

As Kurt continued his speech slowed and voice carried with it the unmistakable sound of exhaustion, "Some of the people looked mangled...open wounds...bloody...pulling other people out of cars...just chaos."

Mr. Spahl startled everyone when he asked, "Where does that leave us for getting out of here?"

"We leave at dawn as planned," Christian said firmly. "Before things escalate and we end up trapped here."

"Do we have to?" Kim asked anxiously. "Why can't we just stay here?"

"We don't have the resources," Christian said bluntly. "Not with the amount of people here now. There's a good chance we'll lose power. That'll compromise food storage and sanitation. Beyond that it would only be a matter of time before we ran out of food, potable water and found ourselves up against looters or were overrun by those things..."

Matt interjected as he saw the expression on Kim and Kurt's faces revert to a look of horror, "We don't need to get into this now. There's a bathroom in the basement, fresh towels in the cabinet. Why don't the two of you go downstairs, get cleaned up and try and relax for a bit. The sheets and comforter on the bed are clean if you want to lay down. We're going to have an early dinner and we'll bring everybody up to speed on the plan."

The basement was cool and dark, except for the light that poured from the open door of the bathroom. Kurt stood statuesque in front of the sink as cold water ran from the faucet. He tried to make sense of the day as he starred at his reflection in the mirror. Gradually he peeled off his sweat-soaked black t-shirt with the orange Hasbrouck Heights district logo on the back and draped it over the towel rack.

Kim sat on the corner of the bed as her mind raced. The tea and cold washcloth helped to momentarily take the edge off. She rubbed her palms against her jeans to warm them. The denim felt strangely coarse against her skin.

Kurt closed his eyes and pictured the Rosary beads wrapped around the praying hands tattooed on his back. He clasped his hands together and prayed quietly, "Hail Mary full of grace the Lord is with you…"

As Kim's eyes adjusted to the dark, she could see everything stacked next to the safe. Curious she leaned forward and removed the pair of faded brown leather boots that adorned her feet. They were her favorite, from the gold buckles over each ankle to the way they hugged her calves. Most of all she loved that they had been a gift from Kurt. He surprised her with them before taking her horseback riding for her birthday some years prior. It was on that day when he proposed.

Kurt lifted his head from the sink. He watched as water ran down the face of his reflection. He straightened his body and tipped his head back as water trickled down his shoulders and chest. For a brief quiet moment, he felt rejuvenated.

Kim slipped her boots off and placed them in front of the dresser next to the bed. The dark blue denim loosened away from her calves and she felt the cool air of the basement creep up her lower legs. She gave a slight shiver, unbuttoned the second button on her white blouse and slid back onto the bed until her head found the pillow. Exhaustion quickly overtook her and she slipped away to sleep.

Kurt pressed the light blue towel against his face and dried the last remnants of water. Satisfied he folded the towel in half and ran it over his chest and arms. He hung it on the rack next to his t-shirt and shut off the light on his way out of the bathroom.

His eyes adjusted slowly to the darkness. He found the corner of the bed and quietly slipped off his black Asics sneakers and socks. He removed his dark gray Under-Armor warm up pants with the black pinstripe down each leg. Kurt stood for a moment in his black boxer briefs and watched his wife sleep. Exhausted he moved slowly onto the bed. The box spring gave an audible creek as he sat down.

Kim stirred, her eyes fluttered and she reached up and placed her left hand on his back, "Kurt?"

"It's just me," Kurt reassured her. "I didn't mean to wake you."

"Are we going to be, ok?" Kim asked without opening her eyes.

"Everything's going to be ok," Kurt answered. He pulled his legs onto the bed and rolled on his right side next to her. She pressed her back against his chest and curled her body against his. He slid his right arm under her neck, wrapped his left arm around her waist and kissed her just behind the ear. "I'm not going to let anything happen to you. Matty and Christian won't let anything happen to us...and Paul...nobody's going to mess with him...that guy's a monster."

"What are all the boxes against the wall?" Kim asked.

"Matty and Christian are ready," Kurt said as he glanced over towards the safe. "You've heard them talk about their grandparents and the store room when they were kids."

"Hmm Mmm," Kim acknowledged as her body relaxed. She loved to be close to Kurt, to have his muscular arms around her. It gave her a feeling of safety that nothing else did.

"Matty talking about how their grandparents taught them to be prepared. How their grandparents were part of the greatest generation and lived through the depression and World War Two." Kurt continued just above a whisper. "That's what all that stuff over there is. Don't worry, we're with the right people."

"Promise?" Kim asked softly.

"I promise," Kurt said tenderly. "Let's get some rest." He encouraged and kissed her softly on the neck before he closed his eyes and lay his head on the pillow next to her.

The second floor was uncomfortably warm as day turned to evening. It was eerily quiet without the television on. Exhaustion replaced angst as everyone searched for a place to rest.

Mrs. Spahl commandeered the kitchen. She riffled through the cabinets and tried to find something easy to prepare that would make enough to feed everyone. She settled on Dinty Moore beef stew over egg noodles and potato rolls.

Paul stood guard at the back door. He cradled his M1A Scout in his left arm. There was a half full bottle of water on the counter next to him. He tugged at his long beard as he watched gaunt figures shamble across the hill behind the house, "There really is no way we can stay here." He muttered to himself.

"Did you say something?" Mrs. Spahl asked as she poured the second large can of beef stew into the Dutch oven.

"Just that it's getting crowded out there," Paul answered as he glanced back at her. "And that I'm getting hungry."

"We'll eat shortly," Mrs. Spahl assured him. "In the meantime." She continued as she motioned to the door. "Back to it."

"Yes, ma'am," Paul said with a grin. He adjusted his grip on his rifle and turned his attention back to what was happening outside.

Christian and Mr. Spahl checked on Anthony. He lay shivering on the comforter. The discoloration of the veins around the bite were more pronounced.

"He's getting worse, isn't he?" Christian asked.

"I'm afraid so," Mr. Spahl answered.

"What's our recourse?" Christian inquired.

"At the moment...nothing," Mr. Spahl said as he got to his feet. "Come on, let's go across the hallway and check on your cousin."

They found Katherine and Marcus tending to Tyler. His face was a deep shade of red as he squirmed. They almost had to restrain him so he didn't fall off the bed.

"How is he?" Mr. Spahl asked.

"How the fuck do you think I am?" Tyler hissed. "I'm in fucking agony! I need something for the pain! Please!"

"Are you sure we can't give him anything?" Katherine asked as she turned back to Christian and Mr. Spahl.

"We don't have anything to give him," Mr. Spahl answered. "The Percocet is all gone."

"No...no!" Tyler wailed. "You have pills...I know you do!"

"Please," Katherine pleaded. "Can't you give him something? Christian, you must have something. I know the doctor gave you something stronger than Advil."

"There was Oxy," Christian admitted. He motioned to Tyler. "But someone took it all."

"Oh, come on!" Katherine shouted. "You and Matt are always blaming my brother..."

"Katherine," Marcus interrupted.

"Quiet Marcus," Katherine ordered. "Christian...seriously you have to have something stronger than Advil."

"I told you I don't," Christian said. "Ask your brother what happened to all the Oxy."

"That's bullshit!" Katherine shouted. "That's bullshit! Fucking liar!"

"Come on, we have things to do," Christian continued as he and Mr. Spahl turned and left the room.

Kerri tried several times to wake Josh from where he slept on the couch, "Josh." She said as she gently rocked his shoulder back and forth. "Josh, it's time to wake up."

"Mmm, get off me," Josh growled without opening his eyes.

"Come on Josh," Kerri urged. "You need to take your medication."

Aunt Athena slept soundly curled up on the love seat. Patrick covered her with a charcoal-colored handwoven throw blanket.

He took a seat in the recliner across the room and kept a vigilant watch over his mother. Patrick rubbed his eyes and looked down at his hands. Some part of him still wasn't convinced the last two days really happened, "Is this real? Am I here?" He whispered to himself. "Please, someone wake me up."

Ralph and Jeff crouched near the front door. Together they kept a careful watch over the front yard and street below.

"Street's filling up," Ralph said. He tapped the pump of the Mossberg 500 nervously with the index and middle fingers on his left hand. "When we went out to collect Kurt and Kim, we really stirred up the hornets' nest didn't we."

"Fuck," Jeff said as his eyes scanned back and forth from one end of the street to the other. "Getting out of here tomorrow is going to be a fucking mess."

Matt found a quiet corner of the dining room and checked his cell phone, "Still no fucking service." He said to himself. There were still so many loved ones unaccounted for, but his thoughts went first to Lauren and all the things he never got to tell her.

"Matt," Mrs. Spahl called as she appeared in the doorway.

Startled he looked up from his phone, "Wh...what?"

"Dinner in ten," Mrs. Spahl informed him. "Please let everyone know."

"I will," Matt assured her. "I just need to finish this real, quick."

"Ten minutes," Mrs. Spahl repeated as she disappeared back into the kitchen.

Matt scrolled through the phone settings until he found the automatic replies, "I can't call out." He said to himself. "But if service comes back and someone tries to call me..." His eyes narrowed as he typed feverishly on the small screen. He set automatic replies for incoming calls and text messages. He read the message back before he clicked confirm. *"Dawn, day 3, headed to the farm. Find us there. Be safe. Matt."* He nodded in approval and said quietly. "Sometimes I even amaze myself."

Everyone gathered around the dining room table. Steam rose from the Dutch oven and large bowl of egg noodles that comprised the center piece. On either side were two large plates. Each contained a dozen toasted potato rolls topped with melted butter and garlic powder.

"Alright everyone," Mrs. Spahl as cheerfully as possible. "Dig in."

The mood around the table was somber. Everyone was concerned about the prospect of leaving. Questions swirled around how to handle Anthony and whether Tyler could be moved.

Paul placed his spoon on the napkin in front of him and tore the buttered roll in half. He used it to sop up the last of the stew in his bowl, "Delicious." He declared as he reached across the table and grabbed the handle of the ladle.

"Yes, it was," Matt agreed as he took the ladle from Paul and helped himself to seconds. When his bowl was full, he looked across the table to Christian.

Christian shook his head, "No." He responded as he pushed the bowl away from him. He finished the glass of water, wiped his mouth. He rested his forearms on the edge of the table and interlocked his fingers. "We leave at dawn as planned." He said stoically.

"I think we need to reconsider that decision," Matt Chico argued.

"Chico," Christian said firmly. "It's been decided. Staying here isn't a viable option."

Matt Chico shook his head, "So that's it then? We just leave?"

"I want to leave!" Josh blurted as he slammed his fists on the table. The echo off the old wood startled everyone. "I want to go home!"

"Mom!" Matt Chico snapped as he motioned to his father. "Did he take his medication?"

"Come on Josh," Kerri urged as she hurried him out of his chair.

"I'm not done eating!" Josh insisted.

"I'm going to take your father in the other room. Yes, he took his pills, but he took them late," Kerri explained as she picked up the bowl and guided Josh into the living room. "Come on, we'll eat in here. Let them finish talking."

"Fuck them. I want to go home," Josh continued as his voice trailed off.

Things around the dining room table quickly settled down.

"What about Anthony?" Matt Chico asked. He glared as he waited for the answer he already knew.

"That's been decided also," Matt said flatly.

"That's no fucking kind of answer!" Matt Chico snarled.

"It's the only one we've got!" Matt shot back.

"You were saying," Jeff interrupted as he motioned to Christian and helped himself to another bowl of stew. "About leaving." He continued as he motioned to Ralph.

Ralph nodded, "Yeah, I'll have some more." He said as he took the ladle from Jeff.

"We'll exit through the garage. Paul and I will be the first two out. We'll provide cover for the rest of you," Christian explained. He paused as the lights throughout the house flickered.

"What is that?" Kim asked.

"With cell service out and the land line sporadic, there's a good chance we'll lose power," Matt added.

"That's not a reason to leave!" Matt Chico insisted.

"Without power, we'll be compromised more quickly than you think," Christian said unapologetically. "We're leaving and that's the end of it."

"Fucking bullshit!" Matt Chico hissed as he threw his napkin on the table and folded his arms.

"Once the garage door opens, we're going to need to move quickly," Christian explained. He knew better than to argue further with Matt Chico.

"We can't leave," Katherine blurted. "My brother can't travel with his leg and we have to bury my father."

"Tony...NO!" Aunt Athena wailed. She shrieked and covered her face.

Matt looked over at his cousin, "Pat, please take your mother to the other room."

Patrick nodded, "Come on mom, let's get away from the table for a little while."

"Your father's gone!" Aunt Athena screeched as Patrick walked her out of the dining room. "He's gone…"

"Have you looked outside recently?" Jeff asked cynically.

"No," Katherine answered coldly.

"It's crowded," Jeff informed her. "Even if we could get to your father's remains, we'd be overrun before we got him buried."

"I'm not leaving until we bury my father!" Katherine shouted defiantly.

"Enough, Katherine!" Christian ordered. "That's enough."

"Don't talk to my wife like that," Marcus demanded as he pointed an accusatory finger at Christian.

"Stay out of family business, you fucking twerp!" Matt warned.

"Don't talk to him like that!" Katherine shouted.

"I'll talk to him any Goddamn way I please!" Matt declared as he grabbed Marcus and pulled him up from his chair.

"Let him go!" Katherine ordered. Her face reddened as the volume of her voice increased. "You two think you're in charge…"

"You want to see in charge?" Matt snarled. He wrapped his hands around Marcus's throat and squeezed. "I'll show you who's fucking in charge!"

"STOP!" Katherine screamed.

Mr. Spahl got up quickly and grabbed Matt by the back of the neck, "STOP!" He ordered in an authoritative voice that no one had ever heard him use.

Matt froze and loosened his grip on Marcus's throat.

"This isn't the time to come apart," Mr. Spahl said calmly. "Let him go and sit down."

Matt paused for a moment and breathed heavily. Red faced and shaky he did as he was instructed and released Marcus, "Fine."

Mr. Spahl let go of Matt and shifted his focus to Katherine, "And you." He said as his cheeks went flush. "Calm down. Right now. We have things that need to be discussed."

"Discuss whatever you want," Katherine said angrily. She folded her arms and shook her head. "I really don't care."

"Christian," Mr. Spahl said as he sat back down.

"After we get everybody to the vehicles," Christian began. "Matt, Ralph, and Jeff are going to load the gear. I'll drive the lead car. Paul brings up the rear. Matt Chico, I want you in the second vehicle. Mr. Spahl in the third and Matt in the fourth. Stay close, watch for brake lights. We don't need an accident. Anyone gets in trouble, give one long beep. That'll be the signal for everyone to pull over."

"What about road blocks?" Ralph asked.

"We're not stopping," Christian said bluntly. He looked over the faces around the table. "Matt and I know some routes that'll keep us on back roads. I need everybody to understand something. The harsh reality is that some of us may not make it."

"That's a hell of a note to end dinner on," Jeff said as he tossed his napkin on the table.

"Better we have it said now," Christian said as he got up. "We'll stand guard in rotating shifts again tonight. The rest of you should try and get some sleep. Anyone who has fired a weapon in the last two days should come downstairs and clean your firearm. The last thing we need is to get into trouble out there and have a weapon malfunction."

After the table was cleared and tempers settled, Mr. Spahl descended the basement stairs. Sheets of newspaper covered the floor along with gun cleaning accessories and firearms in all manner of disassembly. The potent smell of powder solvent filled the air as Matt, Christian, Jeff, Ralph, and Paul all cleaned their weapons.

"Everything alright Mr. Spahl?" Matt asked as he pulled a soiled cleaning patch from the barrel of his rifle.

"Yes," Mr. Spahl said with a nod.

"How's Anthony?" Jeff asked.

"Fever's bad, but he's hanging on," Mr. Spahl answered.

"Where does that leave us?" Ralph asked as he ejected the magazine from his 1911 and cleared the chamber.

"That's one of the things I came down here to talk about," Mr. Spahl said.

"How's it looking out the front?" Ralph asked as he field stripped the 1911.

Mr. Spahl shook his head, "Fewer, but they're still out there."

"Hopefully they disperse before the garage door opens tomorrow," Paul said as he pressed 7.62X51mm rounds into a rifle magazine.

"Let's just get through the night," Mr. Spahl commented as he rubbed his head. He looked over at Matt. "You calm down?"

"Some," Matt said as he reassembled the bolt carrier group for his AR15. "Sorry about before. Temper got the better of me."

"It's a difficult situation for everybody," Mr. Spahl acknowledged. "Christian, you gave a good talk upstairs and I think it's a solid plan."

Christian nodded as he reassembled his H&K USP, "Thank you Mr. Spahl."

"All the same though," Mr. Spahl continued as he motioned towards the safe. "It's time you gave me a gun."

CHAPTER 12

exit

L AUREN STOOD WITH HER eyes closed, head tilted back and arms outstretched. The sun glistened off her long auburn hair. She wore an orange cream colored spring dress adorned with a vibrant floral pattern that wrapped around the garment. The material draped loosely around the full curves of her body. Spaghetti straps gently clung to her sunburned shoulders, while the almost transparent fabric of the dress ended just above her knees.

Disoriented and filthy, Matt stood only a few yards away. His face was speckled with gun powder residue and his sweat-soaked black t-shirt clung to his chest and shoulders. He rubbed his eyes and looked around. Confused, he tried to figure out where exactly he was. His eyes quickly found her. She stood motionless, ankle deep and bare foot among lush blades of green grass as the sun radiated warmth over her. She was a vision of poise and beauty.

"Where were you?" Matt asked. His voice carried with it a hint of despair. Despite his disorientation he couldn't help but look at her adoringly. "I was worried about you. You didn't answer the phone...I thought...I thought something might have happened to you."

Slowly, Lauren lowered her arms to her sides. Her head tipped forward as her eye lids opened. Her eyes were hypnotic; a shade of blue reserved for only the rarest of precious gem stones. Her full lips curled into a smile and her voice came sweet and softly, "I've just been here enjoying the warmth of the sun."

Matt extended his hand and took a step towards her, "You need to come with me...now." He insisted with urgency in his voice. "I can't protect you out here in the open."

"Protect me?" Lauren questioned as she pursed her lips and giggled. "I don't need you to protect me. Besides I can't go with you."

"What do you mean...why?" Matt stammered as he looked around nervously. He took another step towards her. "You must come with me. I must protect you!"

"I don't need to be protected," Lauren insisted playfully as she giggled again. She tipped her head back, closed her eyes and let out a deep sigh. "Don't be silly."

"Don't you know what's going on?" Matt asked frantically. His right hand dropped to his side and reached for his pistol. To his horror he found himself unarmed and without his gun belt. He took a step towards her as the volume of his voice intensified. "Those things are everywhere! We can't stay out in the open! Where's my pistol?"

"You don't need any of that here," Lauren assured him as her body swayed with the gentle breeze. "All you need to do is enjoy the warmth of the sun."

Matt shook his head, "What?" He questioned. Confusion clouded his thoughts as he realized after several steps, he was no closer to reaching her. His eyes scanned the field. As if a vail had been lifted he recognized where he was.

"Just enjoy the warmth of the sun," Lauren urged with a disarming smile.

"When did we get to the farm?" Matt asked bewildered as he continued to look around. Everything was as it always had been and yet he knew something was amiss. The field, tree line and rock wall were all there. The distance was wrong though. Everything was further away than it should have been; and the colors, there was a brilliance to the colors that he couldn't reconcile. "What's happening? We're supposed to leave at dawn. What time is it? When did we get to the farm?"

"We're not on the farm," Lauren said with a wink. She grinned as if she knew a secret she was yet to share with him.

"Yes, we are," Matt insisted. "I know this field. This is one of Bill's fields. I've been in this field thousands of times. The house is right back..." His voice trailed off as he motioned behind him.

"We're not on the farm," Lauren repeated as her eyes found his. "We're not anywhere."

"What? That doesn't make any sense," Matt said as he shook his head. Bewildered and frustrated he started towards her when his body jolted violently. He landed hard against the dirt road that ran along the top of the field. A cloud of dust kicked up around him. "Ah! What's happening?"

"It must be time for you to go," Lauren said as her smile turned down into a pout.

Racked with pain, Matt hurried to his feet, "What do you mean? I'm not going anywhere without you!"

"It's ok," Lauren crooned sympathetically. "You can visit me anytime."

"What?" Matt questioned. He lunged towards her but his body convulsed again. This time he stumbled backwards. He felt something in his neck pop as his body slammed against the ground. Dazed, he looked up to find her standing further across the large field.

"I told you, silly," Lauren called. She took hold of the sides of her dress and twirled playfully. "It's time for you to go."

"NO!" Matt screamed as he scrambled to get back to his feet. "Where are you going?"

"I'm not going anywhere," Lauren said as she offered a gentle wave. "You are..."

"What?" Matt called. He tried to stand but his body convulsed again. "No...NO!"

A deep voice boomed from above, "MATT!"

"What's happening?" Matt shouted. Frantic he looked to the sky. "What was that?"

"It's time for you to go," Lauren said as she blew him a kiss.

Matt forced his body up. Determination was seared across his face, "I'm not going anywhere without..."

"MATT!" The voice overhead thundered again.

"LAUREN!" Matt shouted as he struggled to remain upright. Pain shot through his neck to the base of his skull. He clamped his right hand over the back of his neck and cried. "LAUREN...WAIT!"

"I can't," Lauren said as tears filled her eyes. "It's time for you to wake up."

"What?" Matt uttered. "But I'm not..."

"MATT!" Mr. Spahl said loudly as he shook him by the shoulders. "WAKE UP!"

Matt's eyes opened wide as he gasped for air. Unsure of what was happening or where he was, he grabbed Mr. Spahl's arms and pulled him close, "Where is she?" He demanded.

"Who?" Mr. Spahl asked as he struggled to free himself from Matt's grasp.

"Lauren!" Matt insisted. "Where is she?"

"You've been asleep in the recliner for the past few hours," Mr. Spahl said sharply as he pulled free from Matt's grip. He stepped back and continued. "We were going over the details for leaving and you said you needed a minute. You came in here, sat down in the recliner and passed out...Don't you remember?"

"No...No," Matt muttered as he tried to catch his breath. He clasped his left hand over his chest and pulled at his black t-shirt. "I was on the farm. Lauren and I were standing in the field behind the house."

"It was a dream, Matt. It was a dream...or maybe a premonition," Mr. Spahl offered empathetically. "Either way, you've been asleep in this chair for the last few hours."

Matt breathed heavily as he looked around. The living room was shrouded in darkness. The last remnants of moonlight crept in through the tops of the windows. He squinted and was gradually able to make out the silhouettes of his family and friends spread out between the living and dining rooms. He turned and looked to the bright green numbers on the front of the cable box. It was just after 5 a.m., the sun would be up in less than an hour. "Why did you wake me?" He asked. His voice was uncharacteristically gravely. "It's not time to leave yet."

"Keep your voice down," Mr. Spahl urged as he got to his feet. "Most everyone's still asleep."

"Ok," Matt said with a groggy nod. Even in the darkened room, he could make out Mr. Spahl's wrinkled tan linen shirt and the brown leather holster positioned over his right hip. "You sleep in that shirt?"

"I didn't do much sleeping," Mr. Spahl answered as he rubbed his eyes.

"What'd he give you?" Matt asked as he motioned to the holster.

"1911," Mr. Spahl replied just above a whisper. "Kimber, Tactical Custom II."

"Good choice," Matt said as he tried to shake off the fog of sleep. He scratched his head and swallowed hard. His throat was painfully dry. He reached for the bottle of water on the end table next to him. "Extra mags?"

Mr. Spahl nodded, "Bianchi pouch with a pair of Wilson Combat ETM mags."

"Good," Matt responded. "Those are the best 1911 mags you can use."

"I haven't carried a side arm in a long time," Mr. Spahl continued. "It's got more heft than I remember."

"Full size .45," Matt muttered. He flinched as a sharp pain shot down his neck. He let out an uncomfortable groan and clasped his hand around the base of his skull. "Why'd you wake me?"

"There's been a development," Mr. Spahl said stoically. He knelt on the floor next to the recliner and placed his hand on Matt's shoulder. "Anthony is conscious. Christian's been with him since he came to. He's asking for you."

"He's awake?" Matt uttered as he struggled to swallow. He took a drink as he gathered his faculties. "Ok...let me go see him." He said as he pulled his stiff body out of the old recliner. The chair creaked loudly as he got to his feet.

The bedroom was still. The foul odor of rotting meat lingered in the air. Christian knelt on the floor next to Anthony. His gloved hands held tightly to Anthony's right hand.

"Just try to breath," Christian encouraged as he comforted his dying friend. "Focus on something positive."

"Please..." Anthony whimpered. "It hurts so bad..."

"Come on Ant," Christian urged. He could feel his cheeks go flush and a lump form in his throat. "Think about all the gut-wrenching workouts we survived at Powerhouse Gym. This is nothing...you got this."

"Did you get any sleep?" Matt asked from the doorway where he and Mr. Spahl stood.

"Come in and close the door," Christian instructed. He ignored his brother's inquiry and didn't turn around. "Put on a pair of gloves."

"How is he?" Matt asked as he pulled a pair of black nitrile gloves over his hands.

"He's been asking for you," Christian answered. He placed Anthony's hand in both of Matt's and got to his feet. He carefully peeled the gloves from his hands as he turned to face Mr. Spahl. "Wake everybody up. Get them downstairs and ready to go."

"Breakfast?" Mr. Spahl asked as he reached for the doorknob.

Christian shook his head, "No food prep. Only what we can eat on the drive."

"I'll get everybody up and moving," Mr. Spahl said. Even in the low light his face carried with it a fatigue that was unmistakable. "We'll be ready to go within the hour." He added as he exited the room.

Matt struggled to hold back a gasp when he saw Anthony. This was the closest he'd been to him since he'd been bit. Even bathed in moonlight the discoloration in his skin was obvious. "What can we do?" Matt asked.

"Help me," Anthony pleaded in a weak raspy voice. His body radiated heat. The high fever, blood loss and dehydration left him severely weakened and near death. Blood continued to seep from the bite on Anthony's arm. It saturated the gauze and tape that covered it. "Somethings happening to me...I can feel it."

"I'm sorry Ant," Matt said as he squeezed Anthony's hand. "There's nothing we can do."

"Christ," Christian snarled as he fought to maintain his composure. "You're the one that's supposed to be good at this."

"Good at what?" Matt retorted sharply as he fought back tears. "We've never been here before."

"The compassionate one," Christian said as he knelt next to his brother.

"Please..." Anthony begged as tears streamed down his cheeks. "Please...I don't want to hurt anymore. Please..."

Christian pressed his palms against his temples, "Fuck!"

"Stay with me...please," Anthony whimpered. "Don't let me turn into one of those things."

"It's going to be ok, Ant," Matt assured him. He looked over at Christian and quietly said. "Get me a pillow."

"Yeah," Christian said as he wiped tears from his eyes. He slowly got to his feet and made his way to the bed. "I'll get it."

"Hold on Ant," Matt said as he placed Anthony's hands across his chest. The heat from Anthony's body radiated through the nitrile gloves. He turned and took the pillow from Christian. Matt motioned towards the door with his head. "Stand back."

Christian nodded, "Yeah." He conceded quietly as he reluctantly stepped back towards the door.

Matt placed the pillow over Anthony's face, "I'm sorry." He offered as he closed his eyes and took several deep breaths.

"Can't we take him with us?" Christian asked. He knew the answer, but asked anyway out of sheer desperation.

"You know we can't," Matt reminded him. He opened his eyes and exhaled deeply.

Christian shook his head and wiped tears from his face, "Then do it quick." He said as he clamped his hands over his ears.

"Goodbye old friend," Matt said stoically as a lump formed in his throat. He slid the P220 from his holster and placed it against the pillow. "May God see you safely through the valley of the shadow of darkness."

Anthony let out a meek whimper as he struggled to take a breath. Even in his weakened state he tried to free himself.

There was a loud pop followed immediately by a bright muzzle flash that momentarily illuminated the room. Anthony's body convulsed under the impact of the .45 caliber round as it slammed into his skull and then was still.

Christian's ears rang as he retrieved the brown fleece blanket from the bedroom closet. He motioned for Matt to move back before he covered Anthony's remains. It was as much of a burial as they could give their friend and tragically more than they were able to do for their uncle.

Matt felt detached, as if watching himself move in slow motion. What little he could hear, sounded as if it were underwater. The muzzle flash left bright purple blotches at the center of his vision as he blinked, "What the fuck did I just do?" He stammered as he struggled to get to his feet. His legs felt weak as a wave of nausea hit him. "Oh, God, what did I do?"

"What you had to," Christian assured him as he grabbed his brother by the shoulders. "Fall apart later. Now we need to go."

"What did I do?" Matt repeated as he shook his head. He looked around in disbelief. "I…"

"Come on!" Christian said as he pulled Matt to his feet and hurried him to the bedroom door. "Sounds going to draw them to us. We need to leave."

Tears filled Matt's eyes as he grabbed the front of Christian's gray coveralls, "Nothing's ever going to be the same…is it?"

Christian shook his head, "No." He said bluntly as he pulled the door open. "No, it won't."

Whispered voices filled the still air of the crowded basement. Fatigue and tension covered the somber faces of their friends and family as Matt and Christian descended the stairs.

"How the fuck could you?" Matt Chico muttered. He shook his head in disgust. The look of contempt on his face left no doubt about how he felt. His parents stood huddled behind him. "He was our friend."

"Not now!" Christian said sharply as he moved across the room. He collected his AR15 from where it stood against the dresser. He checked the magazine and retracted the Raptor charging handle.

"What are they fighting about?" Josh asked confused. His hair and beard were unusually disheveled and there were deep bags under his eyes. "What was that loud sound just before?"

"I'm not sure this is a good idea," Kim confessed as she held tightly to Kurt. "What if we just tried to get to one of the FEMA camps?"

"They're not fighting. It was nothing, just a car backfiring," Kerri assured him. She rubbed her hand gently over Josh's back. "Everything's ok. We're going to leave in a few minutes. I'll help you out."

"It'll be ok," Kurt assured her. He could feel Kim tremble as he wrapped his arms around her. "We can't go to one of those camps. It won't be safe. We just need to get to the Tahoe."

Paul gave his Blackhawk Commando chest harness a final check. The eight 25-round rifle magazines added considerable weight to his large frame. He positioned the 3-point sling over his right shoulder and retracted the charging handle, "How long?"

"Almost there," Christian answered. He fastened the quick release buckles on either side of the black Spartan Armor Leonidas plate carrier and hastily shoved 6 magazines into the TACO mag pouches attached to the MOLLE webbing.

"You have plates in there?" Paul asked.

Christian shook his head, "No, just soft armor and trauma pads. Steel core plates are packed with the rest of the gear. I don't expect any incoming fire."

"Yeah," Jeff jabbed. "They're packed with the rest of the gear that we're going to carry."

"Yours are in there too," Christian reminded. "Come on. We need to get out of here before we lose anyone else."

"Please, Katherine," Aunt Athena sobbed. "I don't want to go without your father."

"We can't mom," Katherine said as she held her mother tightly. "He's gone. We must go..."

"We have to bury him at least," Aunt Athena pleaded. "We can't just leave him!"

"No mom," Katherine said firmly. "We can't. We must leave."

"NO!" Aunt Athena cried hysterically. "No...Tony...NO!"

"Do you have any more Xanex?" Matt asked impatiently as he pulled his black Sentinel plate carrier over his head and secured it around his torso.

Katherine scowled, "I'm not going to drug my mother. She's had enough Xanex." She barked. "Just because you don't care about yours..."

"Shut the fuck up and keep her quiet!" Matt ordered angrily. He was in no mood for his cousin's rebuke. He slung his AR15 over his back and tightened the Vickers tactical sling. "Maybe if you'd learn to follow fucking instructions..."

"Leave her alone!" Tyler interrupted from where he lay on the bed with his leg elevated. Beads of sweat streaked down his face as his cheeks turned a dark shade of red. He clenched his teeth and clasped his hands tightly over his chest. "Leave her the fuck alone!"

"GODDAMIT!" Christian shouted as he clipped the tactical link single point sling into the BCM Gunfighter QD mount end plate below the buffer tube on his rifle. "NOT THE FUCKING TIME FOR THIS!"

"Let's stay focused," Mr. Spahl urged from where he and Mrs. Spahl stood next to the staircase. "Lot's still to do."

"Do you want me to take his legs?" Ralph asked. He made his way over to the bed and got into position to collect Tyler.

"Yeah," Matt answered as he joined Ralph. "That'll work."

Christian unsnapped the retention band on his drop leg holster and removed his H&K USP. He hooked his left thumb in the trigger guard and wrapped his fingers over the slide. He retracted the slide just enough to confirm there was a round in the chamber, "Paul let's get set up in the garage."

"Roger," Paul responded with a nod. He opened the door and stepped into the dark room. His boots splashed across the water covered floor. "Ready!" He called.

Christian slid the pistol back into his holster and snapped the retention band into place, "Jeff, when I give the word, open the door." He instructed as he stepped into the garage.

"Got it," Jeff said as he adjusted the shoulder straps on his Ranger green Sentinel plate carrier.

"Wait!" Matt called as his eyes shifted. He hurried from the side of the bed to the laundry room. "Not yet!"

"What are you doing?" Christian barked. "We don't have time for this!"

"Matt!" Mr. Spahl called.

Matt emerged a moment later with a can of black spray paint, "Maybe it was a premonition." He said as he hurried past Mr. Spahl and up the stairs.

"This is the problem!" Tyler hissed. "My asshole cousin thinks he's in charge."

"That's not helping," Ralph said as he attempted to diffuse the situation.

"Jeff, if he's not back in 2 minutes," Christian said as he stepped back into the basement. "Go get him."

Jeff shook his head, "Your brother gets an idea in his head..."

Matt grabbed the left corner of the kitchen table with his right hand and ripped it away from the wall. It tumbled across the small room and crashed into the refrigerator. He shook the can. The paint hissed as it sprayed from the nozzle. A moment later he stepped back and looked at the large back letters against the otherwise stark white wall,

'*FARM*,' "That's what I'm talking about." He said to himself as he headed back to the basement.

"Jeff, status!" Christian called from the garage. He turned the rotary switch on his Aimpoint PRO clockwise and increased the brightness of the red dot.

"He's back!" Jeff announced as Matt rejoined the group.

"You get that out of your system?" Mr. Spahl asked.

"Not sure anybody will be around to see it," Matt said with nod. "But if anybody does make it back here, they'll know where we went."

"That actually makes sense," Mr. Spahl admitted. "Wish you thought of it earlier though."

Christian and Paul stood shoulder to shoulder in the stagnant water that covered the garage floor. Each held their rifle at the ready in anxious anticipation of what was to come.

Christan pressed the stock of the AR15 against his right shoulder and glanced over at Paul, "Ready?"

Paul clicked the button on the side of the Eotech site and the holographic reticle appeared. He adjusted his grip on the M1A Scout and answered. "Let's go."

"Jeff!" Christian called. "Open it!"

Jeff felt adrenaline surge through his body. His palms were damp and hands trembled as he reached for the gray button on the wall above the light switches. "On it." He called as he depressed the button with the heel of his left palm.

The gray hue of dawn crept into the garage as the door slowly opened. As it reached the top of the track, Christian and Paul charged outside. The brisk morning air smelled sweet. It was a welcome change from the putrid odor inside the house. Pillars of dark smoke a few streets away stood out against the light gray of the sky. In the distance the faint pop of sporadic gunfire could be heard.

Paul hurried down the steep driveway. He positioned himself in the middle of the road and surveyed the area. Almost immediately he could see movement at the far end of the street, "Let's go." He said to himself.

Christian stepped out of the garage and turned left. He positioned himself at the south east corner of the house and covered the yard and back hill. Everything appeared still but he could hear the moans and knew the quiet wouldn't last. "Move!" He called.

Jeff and Mr. Spahl hurried Mrs. Spahl, Kim, and Kurt out of the garage and down the driveway towards the Tahoe.

"Don't stop!" Jeff ordered. "Just keep moving."

Ralph and Matt followed as they carried Tyler. They were barely out of the garage when all hell broke loose.

"CONTACT REAR!" Christian shouted as a pack of grotesque figures emerged from around the corner of their aunt and uncle's house. He felt his finger take the slack out of the first stage of the trigger as he trained the red dot on the head of the closest ghoul. The rifle thundered. Skull fragments and brain tissue jettisoned into the air.

Matt's right ear absorbed the concussion of the blast. "AHHH!" He screamed and stumbled as he and Ralph fell on top of Tyler.

"FUCK!" Tyler yelped as his injured leg slammed against the concrete driveway. He squirmed in pain. "YOU MOTHER FUCKERS!"

"NO!" Ralph shouted. He tried to brace his impact but landed hard on his knees. "FUCK!"

"PICK HIM UP! PICK HIM UP AND KEEP MOVING!" Christian shouted. He placed the red dot on the head of the second ghoul and prepared to fire.

Matt Chico hurried his parents out of the garage as Matt and Ralph struggled to get to their feet.

"Grab a leg and an arm!" Matt instructed as he scrambled to his feet. Tyler had broken his fall. "Come on! We've got to move!"

"I don't know if I can walk," Ralph admitted as he struggled to get to his feet. "My knees..."

"Come on mom!" Patrick shouted as he hurried his mother out of the garage and down the driveway.

"NO!" Aunt Athena screamed. "TYLER...WE CAN'T LEAVE TYLER!"

"MOVE!" Christian ordered as he fired a second round. The contorted face disappeared behind the muzzle flash. What was left of the body jerked violently as it toppled to the ground. "NOW!"

"We're not leaving Tyler!" Patrick assured his mother as he pulled her towards the street. "Matt and Ralph have him!"

"Come on!" Matt urged. "Grab him and let's go!"

"Ok," Ralph said as he took a breath. He grabbed Tyler's left arm and leg. "Let's go!"

"GET THE FUCK OFF ME!" Tyler screamed as Matt and Ralph pulled him off the ground and hurried him towards the street.

"COME ON!" Paul shouted as he waved everyone towards the cars. "KEEP MOVING!"

"Marcus!" Katherine shouted as she followed her brother. "Marcus, hurry up!"

"I don't want to go out there," Marcus cried. He cowered terrified just inside the garage.

"We don't have a choice, Marcus!" Katherine shrieked. "Let's go!"

"MOVE!" Christian shouted. He dispatched several more ghoulish figures and turned his attention to the hill behind the house, "Oh, fuck." He muttered to himself. A horde of more than twenty undead shambled from the top of the hill towards them.

"Come on, get in!" Matt Chico said frantically as he unlocked the Roadmaster and opened the back door.

"It's my car!" Josh shouted angrily. "I'm going to drive! Now give me the keys."

"Mom!" Matt Chico called.

"Josh," Kerri pleaded as she took hold of his shoulders. "Please just get in the car."

"No!" Josh blurted defiantly. "It's..."

"CONTACT!" Paul shouted as disfigured faces came up the embankment on the opposite side of street and emerged from behind the guard rail. He raised his rifle and opened fire.

"AHHH!" Kerri screamed as she covered her ears.

"MOVE GODDAMIT!" Paul shouted as brass shell casings spit from the ejection port. Blood and skull fragments littered the street and grassy embankment as Paul continued to fire.

"GET IN THE FUCKING CAR!" Matt Chico screamed as he shoved his father forcefully into the back seat.

"LOADING!" Paul called as he snapped a loaded magazine into the magwell. He released the charging handle and continued to fire.

"My God, they're everywhere," Patrick said as he pulled his mother towards the Subaru. He watched in disbelief as a horde of figures staggered towards them from the other end of the street. "Come on mom! Get in the car!"

"NO!" Aunt Athena cried. "There's too many of them! We're all going to die!"

"LOADING!" Christian shouted. He ejected the empty magazine and shoved it in the Blue Force Gear 10-speed dump pouch attached to his Serpa belt. He pulled a loaded magazine from one of the TACO pouches and slammed it in the magwell. He released the maritime bolt catch with his left palm and continued to fire.

"Goddamn key is stuck!" Matt shouted as he struggled to open the driver's side door of the Grand Marquis.

"You mother fuckers!" Tyler hissed from where he lay on the asphalt next to the car.

"Careful!" Ralph ordered. He flinched as Paul's rifle thundered nearby. "Don't break the key!"

"GET IN AND STAY DOWN!" Mr. Spahl shouted as he hurried his wife, Kurt, and Kim into the Tahoe. He turned to his son. "JEFF, GIVE ME YOUR RIFLE!"

"WHAT?" Jeff questioned.

"NOW!" Mr. Spahl ordered. He took the Mini-14 from his son. "THE SUPPLIES JEFF! GET THE SUPPLIES!"

"LOADING!" Paul shouted as the bolt of his rifle locked open. Sweat poured from his head as he struggled to pull a loaded magazine from the chest rig.

"I'm coming mom!" Katherine shouted as she pulled Marcus towards the Subaru.

"No, Katherine!" Patrick called. "You and Marcus are in the Jeep!"

"I'm going with my mother!" Katherine insisted.

"Got it!" Matt called as the key finally turned and door unlocked.

Ralph could see his mouth moving, but the deafening sound of Paul's rifle left him unable to hear what Matt was saying, "What?" He questioned.

Matt motioned to Tyler as he pulled the back door open, "PICK HIM UP!"

"THERE'S TOO MANY OF THEM!" Christian shouted as the horde continued to grow. The undead were everywhere. The deafening crack of his AR15 echoed off the ancient aluminum siding that covered both houses. "I'M NOT GOING TO BE ABLE TO HOLD THIS POSITION!"

"HANG ON!" Jeff called as he hurried up the driveway. "WE'RE MOVING THE SUPPLIES NOW!"

Ralph and Matt hoisted Tyler up and loaded him into the back of the Grand Marquis, "I GOT THE DOOR!" Ralph shouted red faced as he swung it closed.

"FUCK!" Tyler screamed as the door slammed against his foot. His body folded in half as he grabbed for his ankle with both hands.

"OH FUCK!" Ralph gasped.

"NO TIME!" Matt called as he pulled him back towards the house. "WE HAVE TO GET THE SUPPLIES!"

"THE JEEP!" Mr. Spahl shouted as he grabbed the collar of Marcus's shirt. "PATRICK GET YOUR SISTER TO THE JEEP!"

"Come on Katherine!" Patrick urged as he pushed his sister and Marcus past Mr. Spahl to the Jeep.

"Patrick, get you fucking hands off of me!" Katherine screeched.

"They're fucking everywhere!" Mr. Spahl blurted as he hurried past the row of cars. He brought the rifle up to his shoulder. Shell casings spit from the ejection port as he engaged the horde that approached from the opposite end of the street.

Katherine screamed and covered her ears as she and Marcus stood next to Paul's Jeep, "GET IN!" Patrick shouted as he yanked the back door open. He pushed his sister in before Marcus climbed in behind her. "STAY DOWN!" He ordered. Patrick slammed the door and hurried back to the Subaru. He jumped in the back and tried to comfort his hysterical mother.

"LOADING!" Christian called as Jeff emerged from the garage with several duffle bags.

Paul glanced around and quickly reloaded. He could see Mr. Spahl positioned in the middle of the street just ahead of the Subaru. For every body that fell it was as if two took its place, "My God!" Paul said as he released the charging handle. "We're going to run out of ammo!"

Christian dropped to one knee and ejected the empty magazine. Matt took up a position next to him and unslung his rifle, "NO!" Christian ordered as he reloaded. "I'VE GOT THIS. GET THE SUPPLIES!"

"THERE'S TOO MANY OF THEM!" Matt shouted.

"I'VE GOT THIS!" Christian insisted. "GET THE SUPPLIES OR WE'RE NOT GETTING OUT OF HERE!"

"FINE!" Matt conceded. He turned and followed Ralph into the garage.

"CONTACT RIGHT!" Paul shouted wide eyed. The sound of gunfire had summoned a group of grotesque figures to his end of the street. Their contorted expressions on their faces detailed the last pain they ever felt.

"FUCK!" Mr. Spahl shouted as the bolt of the Mini-14 locked open. He slung the rifle over his back and pulled the 1911 from the holster on his hip.

"We need to leave!" Kim cried as she huddled against Kurt in the back of the Tahoe.

"Soon," Mrs. Spahl assured her as she pointed back towards the house. "They're moving the supplies now."

Jeff hurried down the driveway with his arms full. He was followed by Ralph and Matt, "Come on!" Jeff called. His face was red and sweat ran from the top of his head.

"We're right behind…" Matt shouted. His voice was drowned out as Christian fired several rounds in quick succession.

"My knees," Ralph wheezed as he carefully navigated the steep driveway.

"MOVE GODDAMMIT!" Paul yelled. "WE CAN'T STAY OUT HERE!"

"What's taking so long?" Katherine asked impatiently. She watched Jeff, Ralph, and Matt ran back and forth to the house. "How many trips are they going to have to take?"

"Come on!" Paul snarled. He zeroed the Eotech's reticle on the face of the closest creature and fired. The 7.62X51mm round ripped through most of the left side of its head. Its body spun and soaked the asphalt with blood as it fell.

"I want to leave!" Josh cried from the back seat of the Roadmaster. He clamped his hands over his ears. "I want to leave!"

"Mom!" Matt Chico shouted from the front seat. "Please keep him calm!"

"I'm trying!" Kerri blurted. "I'm trying! We need to leave!"

"TWO MORE TRIPS!" Matt shouted as he hurried past Christian.

"GOOD!" Christian called as he reloaded. "HURRY UP!"

Blood sprayed from the head of the nearby creature that lunged at Paul. Its body collapsed at his feet. Startled, Paul released the charging handle and turned quickly to his left.

"Snuck up on you," Mr. Spahl said as he motioned to the corpse. He slammed a loaded magazine into the magwell of the 1911 and released the slide. "One or two more trips, we'll be good to go."

"Hope so," Paul said with a nod. "It's getting crowded out here!" He turned his attention to the three creatures that approached and dispatched each with a double tap to the head.

Ralph limped as he carried several MTM tactical mag cans down the driveway, "I don't know if I have another trip in me." He said as Jeff hurried past him.

"Get in the Jeep," Jeff called as he headed up the driveway. "Matt and I will get the last load."

"Maybe, I should go help them," Kurt suggested.

"No!" Kim cried as she wrapped her arms around his torso.

"Don't!" Mrs. Spahl insisted as she motioned towards the house. "They're almost finished."

Ralph groaned as he pulled himself into the passenger seat of the Jeep, "You two ok back there?" He asked.

"No, we're not fucking ok!" Katherine hissed. "When are we fucking leaving?"

"FINISHED!" Matt shouted as he and Jeff carried the last of the supplies from the garage.

"Finally!" Christian said as he got to his feet. He hurried to the key pad next to the garage door and punched in the code. The door began to close as he ran down the driveway. "LET'S GO...LET'S GO!"

"LET'S GO!" Mr. Spahl shouted. He engaged the thumb safety, holstered the 1911 and got into the Tahoe. "COME ON JEFF! GET IN!"

"TIME TO GO!" Paul hollered as he pulled the driver side Jeep door open.

To the east the sun crept over the mountains. Brilliant colors filled the morning sky and illuminated the horrors. Discolored corpses and brass shell casings littered the area. Shallow pools of crimson dramatically stood out against the vibrant green of the dew-covered grass.

Only two days earlier, the radiant yellows and oranges of the sun against the cloudless baby blue of the morning sky would have been a picturesque way to start the day. If Christian was well enough, he and Matt would have spent the morning outside on the front steps.

This morning however, they stood stoically in the street and faced the house. At first neither spoke, but then they didn't have to. It went without saying that nothing would ever be the same. They each quietly said their goodbyes to the only real home they had ever known.

After a moment, Christian asked, "Did you leave it for him?"

"Yes," Matt answered.

"Where?"

"Exactly where we discussed."

"Are you sure if he makes it back here, he'll be able to find it?"

"He better," Matt answered. "He's the one who picked the spot."

"If I didn't think Giovanni could find his way back here," Christian began as he and Matt watched the yard and surrounding area swarm with the undead. "I'd burn this place to the fucking ground!"

"Everybody's waiting. We need to go," Matt urged as he glanced back at the vehicles. Exhausted faces waited eagerly to leave. "You'd really burn it down?"

"I would," Christian answered coldly. He didn't look at his brother or acknowledge that the others were waiting for them. He just clenched his teeth and shook his head. "That house is ours. It's part of our heritage, part our lineage and no one else should have it."

CHAPTER 13

a lie agreed upon

S WEATY, DIRTY, AND TIRED they clung to each other in terror as the caravan of cars moved down the road. The haunted, twisted faces kept their focus from the vibrant yellow and orange rays that glistened off the dew-covered budding green blossoms.

Christian shifted into second gear, "Hang on." He instructed as he moved his right hand from the gear shift to the grip of his USP. He slid the pistol from his holster and placed it on the seat next to him. "There's more of them up ahead."

Patrick didn't respond. He just held his mother as she cried, "It's going to be ok mom...I promise." His voice shook as he tried to comfort her.

"No," Aunt Athena whimpered as she buried her face in her son's chest. "Nothing will ever be ok again..."

The Roadmaster followed close behind the Subaru. The bumpers of the vehicles were only a few inches apart.

"What's wrong with their faces?" Josh shrieked as mangled bodies clamored down the embankment and into the street after them. "Why aren't we helping them?"

"Mom," Matt Chico called from the front seat. He stared straight ahead, afraid to look at the faces and how close they were. "A little help please."

"It's ok, Josh," Kerri urged as she pulled his gaze from the window.

Mr. Spahl could see how agitated Josh was through the back window of the Roadmaster. He pulled the Tahoe slowly into the center of the street and was careful to leave considerable distance between the two vehicles.

He slid his right hand from the steering wheel to the leather holster on his right hip, "Are you alright?" Mr. Spahl asked without looking over at his wife.

"Fine," Mrs. Spahl answered calmly. She sat quietly in the passenger seat next to her husband. Her hands were folded in her lap and she refused to acknowledge how the last 2-days affected her. "I would have liked to have showered before we left."

"That would have been nice," Mr. Spahl answered with a nod. "Jeff, how are you doing back there?"

"Fucking peachy," Jeff answered from where he sat behind his mother. His head hurt and ears rang. He rested the stock of the Mini-14 on his left thigh and tapped his index finger against the trigger guard. "Just fucking peachy..."

"There's no need for that kind of language," Mrs. Spahl scolded.

Matt pulled the gear shift into drive and pressed his foot down on the gas pedal. The large V8 engine revved and the Grand Marquis lurched forward as he hurried to keep pace with the Tahoe.

"What the fuck?" Tyler screeched. He flailed his arms to brace himself as his body slammed against the back seat.

"Sorry," Matt called. His bandaged left hand throbbed as he wrapped it tightly around the steering wheel. He paid no mind to how white his knuckles were. "I'm wearing boots...I misjudged the pedal."

"Fuck you!" Tyler hissed as he pushed his body back against the seat. "First you drop me, then you two fucking idiots fall on me and now this..."

"Shut the fuck up!" Matt ordered. He moved his right hand off the grip of his P220, reached across the passenger seat and grabbed his AR15. He pulled the rifle over to him and made sure the safety was disengaged. "I'm tired of your whining! You're nothing but a fucking liability!"

Paul pushed the shifter into first gear and traded the clutch for the gas. The Jeep with its oversized tires rumbled into motion and brought up the rear of the caravan.

"Oh, fuck," Ralph moaned from the passenger seat. He sat hunched over with his hands wrapped the front of his legs.

"What's going on?" Paul asked as he glanced over. "You, ok?"

Ralph shook his head, "Fell on my fucking knees."

"When?" Paul asked with a look of concern.

"GET US OUT OF HERE!" Katherine shrieked from the back seat as the undead filled the street around them.

"WHAT?" Paul shouted as he pressed the clutch and brake to the floor. Everyone was thrown forward as the Jeep lurched to a stop.

"AHHH!" Marcus moaned as his face slammed against the back of Paul's headrest.

"OHH!" Ralph yelped as his forehead smacked the dashboard.

"What the fuck?" Paul demanded.

"They're everywhere!" Katherine insisted. "GET US OUT OF HERE!"

"Shut the fuck up and let me drive!" Paul barked angrily. He looked over at Ralph. "You, ok?"

"Been better," Ralph answered as he cupped his hands over his face.

"How'd you fall?" Paul asked. He traded the clutch for the gas and started back after the rest of the group.

"Carrying Tyler out of the garage," Ralph answered. "I took the brunt of it on my knees."

"You dropped my brother?" Katherine continued from the back seat.

"Shut up!" Paul ordered as he shifted into second gear. "Sit back and shut the fuck up!"

One by one each vehicle cleared the stop sign at the end of the road and turned left onto Main Street. Main Street wound its way through rows of houses and shops before it finally reached the center town. Wrecked and abandoned vehicles littered the street and several yards almost immediately. Mangled human remains were scattered amongst the twisted steel and shattered glass. In the distance more pillars of black and gray smoke continued to appear.

"Pat," Christian called as he shifted into third gear and pressed down on the gas pedal. He used his right hand to wipe sweat and gun powder residue from his face. "Your mother doesn't need to see this."

Patrick gave a slight nod and used his left hand to cover his mother's face. He closed his eyes, and pressed his face against the top of his mother's head, "Please God." He whispered to himself. "Please God, keep us safe."

The Roadmaster drifted over the double yellow line as tears streamed from Matt Chico's eyes. He ran his shirt sleeve across his face and tried to focus on the road.

"You're swerving," Josh shouted from the back seat.

"Mom!" Matt Chico called as he guided the large sedan back into the proper lane. He struggled to hold his gaze on the back of Christian's car. Despite his best efforts, graphic images crept into his periphery.

"Just focus on the road honey," Kerri encouraged. Her hands trembled and heart raced as she took hold of Josh's hand. "He's ok, just let him drive."

The Tahoe slowed as Mr. Spahl took his foot off the gas.

"What are you doing?" Mrs. Spahl asked as she gently placed her left hand on her husband's right.

Mr. Spahl motioned with his head without looking over at her, "Watching them swerve. I don't want to get too close just in case."

"Josh hasn't been well," Mrs. Spahl reminded. "I'm sure that isn't helping."

"Yeah," Mr. Spahl agreed with a nod. "Kurt, how are you and Kim doing back there?"

"We're ok," Kurt answered unconvincingly. His voice trembled a little more with each blood-soaked scene they passed. "Just...ah...no...we're ok."

"It's going to be ok," Kim whispered as she moved her body away from his. She placed her hand on Kurt's cheek and looked into his eyes. "Find some solace in the fact that we're together and we're safe."

Kurt nodded. He could feel his chest tighten and a lump form in his throat as he thought about where their parents and siblings might be.

"Just breath," Jeff interjected. He could see Kurt's cheeks redden. "We're not going to let anything happen to either of you. Forget about what's going on out there and just focus on each other."

Carefully Matt guided the Grand Marquis around a wrecked vehicle and several mangled corpses.

"What's going on?" Tyler asked. His voice sounded gravely and he kept his eyes tightly closed.

"Debris in the road," Matt answered. He tried to sound as matter of fact as possible. "Nothing to worry about. How are you doing back there?"

"Shitty," Tyler answered as he clamped his hands over his face. The pain in his ankle was so severe he could feel the throb all the way to his molars. "Really fucking shitty."

Paul pushed the gear shift forward into third gear. The cold air intake gave the engine a guttural sound as he pushed the gas pedal towards the floor.

"Are you alright?" Katherine asked Marcus as she placed her hand on his back.

It was a rare moment of genuine tenderness that caught him off guard, "Wh...what?" Marcus stammered as he moved his hands away from his face.

"I asked if you were alright," Katherine repeated.

"The head rest has no give," Marcus answered sheepishly as he showed her the blood pooled in his hands from his nose and mouth.

"Oh, my God," Katherine gasped. She placed a comforting hand on the back of Marcus's neck. "Tip you head back and let me see."

"What are you looking for?" Ralph asked as Paul rummaged through the center console.

"Cigarettes and my lighter," Paul answered without taking his eyes off the road.

"Need me to look?" Ralph asked.

"No, I got it." Paul answered as he took a pack of Winston black bold 100's cigarettes and brushed copper Zippo lighter from the center console. He used his teeth to pull a cigarette from the pack and snapped the Zippo lighter open. He touched the flame to the tip of the cigarette and inhaled deeply. Paul held the smoke in his lungs for a moment and then exhaled. "I needed that."

As the procession of cars continued down Main Street the nightmare intensified. Images of carnage gave way to visceral scenes of chaos and suffering. Several houses on either side of the street were engulfed in flames. Bodies littered the yards and sidewalks.

"Hang on Pat!" Christian ordered. "We've got power lines down." He continued. He tapped the brakes several times to alert Matt Chico before he downshifted and let the Subaru drift into the oncoming lane.

"What?" Patrick asked as he opened his eyes. He watched in horror as they slowly passed a burgundy Cape Cod style home. A large portion of telephone pole protruded from what was left of the glass sun porch. Gray smoke rose from the radiator of a faded gold Chevy pick-up truck whose crumpled front end was wrapped around the base of the pole. The driver lay bloodied on the hood. His short sleeve yellow and white plaid shirt and blue jeans were soaked in deep crimson. Lacerations covered his face and head. The skin on his right arm was rolled up like a sock all the way to his shoulder. The wound exposed tendons and muscle. "My God..." Patrick blurted as began to breath heavily. "What the...Jesus, I'm going to be sick..."

Matt Chico took his foot off the gas pedal and maneuvered the large sedan into the oncoming lane behind the Subaru.

"Stop the car!" Josh demanded. He pounded his fist against the headrest. "We need to help her!"

Scraped and bruised at the bottom of a steep narrow coble stone staircase lay a young woman with fair skin and long brown hair, "Hee...hel...help me please!" She wailed. Her labored cries were mostly drowned out by the muffled crack of gunfire in the distance.

"We can't stop," Kerri pleaded as she grabbed at Josh's shoulders. "We can't!"

Jagged pieces of bone protruded through her black leggings just below her knee. Her left leg was badly contorted. "Please..." She begged as blood poured from the deep laceration that ran from her bottom lip to her chin. Tangled in an oversized black V-neck t-shirt, she struggled to reach up from the sidewalk with her badly scraped arms.

"STOP THE CAR!" Josh shouted as he repeatedly pressed his index finger against the window. "SHE'S IN DANGER!"

A black wrought iron railing accompanied the cobblestone stairs up to a white two-story colonial house whose red front door stood wide open. A disheveled figure in a blood-soaked tan bath robe lumbered from the doorway and down the stairs towards her.

"NOOOOO!" Josh cried. He slammed his palms against the window as the caravan moved on and the young woman disappeared in the distance.

"My God," Mr. Spahl said as he pointed over the steering wheel. "Josh's going to work himself in another stroke."

"Can you blame him?" Mrs. Spahl asked. "We could have stopped to help that poor girl."

"We're not stopping!" Jeff said sternly from the back seat. Despite his fatigue he remained alert.

"That's not your decision," Mrs. Spahl retorted. "I..."

"Jeff!" Mr. Spahl interrupted. "Your side."

Jeff turned his attention to the elderly white-haired man as he was besieged by the undead, "Slow down." He instructed.

"HELLLPPP!" The old man howled in agony as chunks of flesh were ripped from his back and neck. Viscera and taters of fabric from his cloths covered the lush green of the meticulously manicured front lawn.

"Dad?" Jeff questioned.

"It's mercy Jeff. End it," Mr. Spahl answered without taking his eyes off the road.

"Cover your ears," Jeff ordered as he lowered the window and leveled the barrel of the rifle.

"Jeff, wait..." Mrs. Spahl began.

"NOW!" Jeff ordered as he took aim and opened fire. The confined space of the vehicle made the thunderous crack of the rifle unbearable.

"OH, GOD!" Kim screamed as she buried her face in Kurt's chest.

"I'VE GOT YOU!" Kurt shouted as he pulled Kim against his body.

"OH MY GOD!" Mrs. Spahl cried as she clamped her hands over her ears and pressed her body against the dashboard.

"FUCK!" Mr. Spahl blurted. He winced and cupped his hand over his right ear as he struggled to keep the Tahoe on the road.

In a matter of seconds Jeff expended all 20-rounds. He dispatched two attackers, hit several others, and put the old man out of his misery. "IT'S DONE." He called as he raised the window and unsnapped the empty magazine. "Let's go."

"What's happening?" Tyler called from the back seat as the gunfire subsided.

"Jeff took care of something," Matt answered bluntly.

The caravan picked up speed as they continued towards the center of town. They passed another horrific scene in front of a red brick house, but did not slow down this time. Over the last 2-days they had seen enough suffering and carnage to last several lifetimes.

"How's your leg?" Matt asked as he glanced back at his cousin.

"Fucking hurts," Tyler answered. "I need something for the pain."

"Can't help you with that," Matt replied. "Listen, once we hit the center of town, it'll be about a mile til Main Street intersects with County Road 921, then onto the valley. That's where we're headed."

"Who fucking cares," Tyler mumbled. He covered his face with his hands and turned his head towards the back of the seat.

County Road 921 was a desolate sparsely populated fifteen-mile stretch of road which snaked through Continental Valley. As legend had it, the valley served as a camp for Washington's Continental Army during the Revolutionary War, and secured its name and place in history. It was rumored the encampment acted as a mobile hospital and was one of the final staging areas before Washington rallied his troops for their famous river crossing and push into Trenton during the terrible winter of 1776.

The valley was heavily wooded. Large pine trees covered the steep terrain on either side. It narrowed the already winding road and gave it an almost claustrophobic feel. Although not the most direct route to the farm, Matt and Christian agreed Continental Valley with its natural barriers and limited population would be the safest.

"You, ok?" Paul asked as he glanced over at Ralph.

Ralph exhaled and adjusted his grip on the shotgun, "Better when we get where we're going." He answered.

"You and me both," Paul said as he pulled another cigarette from the pack. "How are your knees?"

"Are you really going to smoke more?" Katherine chided from the back seat.

"Quiet back there," Paul ordered as he lit a second cigarette. "Your knees?" He asked again as he glanced over at Ralph.

"Not great," Ralph answered. "We'll see how bad when I have to get out of the Jeep."

They drove on. There was a straight away with a gradual decline. On either side were newly planted maple trees evenly spaced throughout the three-foot-wide stretch of grass which lined both sides of Main Street and separated the sidewalk from curb. A hundred yards beyond was a narrow turn which wound sharply to the left.

"Hold on Pat. Sharp turn coming up," Christian said as he downshifted. The driver side tires of the Subaru hugged the double yellow line as he navigated the vehicle into the turn.

"Ready," Patrick answered. He kept a tight hold of his mother with his right arm and used his left to brace himself against the back door.

Christian glanced up at the rearview mirror and watched the Roadmaster and Tahoe clear the turn before his attention was redirected to the plume of black smoke that rose from two crashed cars that partially blocked the road ahead, "We're not out of it yet Pat." He called. Christian tapped the brakes to signal Matt Chico and veered across the double yellow line into the oncoming lane.

"Ok," Patrick answered. His voice shook as he closed his eyes and waited for his cousin to tell him it was over.

"Mom, hold on to dad and brace yourselves," Matt Chico instructed. His hands shook as he jerked the steering wheel to the left. The tires of the large vehicle screeched as the front bumper narrowly missed the wreckage. Even with the windows closed Matt Chico could feel the heat as it radiated from the burning cars.

"Let me go!" Josh insisted as Kerri wrapped her arms around his shoulders and pulled him against her body.

"Get ready," Mr. Spahl instructed as he guided the Tahoe around the burning vehicles and back across the double yellow line. "You alright?" He asked as he glanced over at his wife.

"Better when we get where we're going," Mrs. Spahl answered. She adjusted the seatbelt strap and returned her folded hands to her lap. "And, I could do without any more gunfire." She added sharply.

"Next time I'll let 'em suffer," Jeff retorted as he snapped a loaded magazine into the rifle's magwell.

The battery light flickered red on the dashboard of the Grand Marquis and pulled Matt's focus from the back of the Tahoe. "What the fuck?" He muttered to himself.

"You say something?" Tyler grumbled from the back seat.

"Talking to myself," Matt answered. A surge of panic shot through him as he watched the light flash on and off several times before finally going out. "Come on baby, not today..."

"Everybody, hang on," Paul instructed as he downshifted. He took a long drag off the cigarette as he pulled the Jeep into the oncoming lane. Ash fell away towards his legs as the tobacco burned back towards the filter.

Katherine and Marcus huddled on the back seat behind Paul. Ralph turned his face away from the heat as the Jeep sped past the wreckage.

As soon as Christian saw the Jeep pass the burning vehicles, he shifted into third gear and pressed down on the accelerator. "Almost there." He called to his cousin.

"Thank God," Patrick muttered.

The caravan quickly approached the intersection that was home to the town's lone traffic light. There was a coffee shop on the corner to their left. The sand-colored stucco storefront was furnished with a bright yellow awning which started just above the windows and hung out over the sidewalk. The words "Mary's Breakfast Cafe" stood out in large red letters against the background.

On the opposite corner stood a two-story brick building which had been renovated from the town's original firehouse to a Community Theater. White paint peeled from the old wood sign which hung above the front doors of the building, faded black letters painted in Vladimir script read **"Growing Treasures Community Theater."**

Across the street stood a row of neatly kept stone cottages. Each structure was adorned with a dark gray slate roof. Though separate, the properties were surrounded by what looked like one continuous white picket fence.

"Traffic lights out," Christian called as they approached the intersection. He downshifted into second gear and tapped the brakes twice to signal Matt Chico. The community theater was much closer to the road than the coffee shop which limited his visibility. "We're going to take the right turn wide." He announced. "Hold on!"

"When will this be over?" Aunt Athena whimpered.

"Soon, mom," Patrick assured her. "We're almost there."

The tires squealed as the Subaru cleared the intersection. Just beyond the theater a geyser of water burst forth from beneath a silver four door sedan. Black tire tracks marked the asphalt where the car skidded across the double yellow line, jumped the curb, and toppled the fire hydrant.

The volume of water was more than the narrow storm drains could dispose of. With no place to go the road quickly flooded. The open hydrant sprayed across the street and soaked the four ghoulish creatures who staggered towards the disabled vehicle.

"That's not good," Christian muttered as he scanned the area. He immediately saw three more figures to his left. They turned their attention from the front door of one of the stone cottages and headed towards the silver sedan. "We need to get out of here."

Dazed from the impact a balding heavy-set man struggled to pry himself from behind the wheel of the sedan. A deep laceration above his right eye poured blood down his face and over his white t-shirt and blue jeans, "Come on you son of a bitch open!" He cried as he slammed his body repeatedly against the door. When the latch finally gave way, the man fell onto the grass.

Water logged and disoriented the man clamored to his feet and produced two revolvers from his waistband. The distinct snap and hiss of bullets erupted as the rounds missed the creatures and passed by the Subaru.

"GET US OUT OF HERE!" Patrick hollered.

As soon as he saw the other four vehicles clear the intersection, Christian shifted into third gear and gunned the engine. The windshield shattered under the impact of a stray round. The bullet lodged in the passenger side headrest next to Christian. "MOTHER FUCKER!" He snarled.

"Oh, fuck!" Matt Chico blurted as the driver side tires scraped against the curb on the opposite side of the street. He pulled the wheel hard to the right and pressed the gas pedal to the floor.

"STOP!" Josh cried. He and Kerri were thrown across the back of the car as the Roadmaster swerved into the center of the street. The car slammed into one of the ghouls and sent its broken body bouncing across the water-soaked asphalt.

"WE HAVE TO GET OUT OF HERE!" Matt Chico shouted frantically as the gunfire continued. The massive V8 engine pushed the large sedan forward. Everyone was thrown forward as the Roadmaster slammed into the back of the Subaru.

"CHRISTAIN!" Patrick shouted over his mother's terror filled screams. "GET US OUT OF HERE!"

"WORKING ON IT!" Christian called as his head bounced off the head rest. He shifted into fourth gear and slammed the gas pedal to the floor. The four-cylinder engine raced as the Subaru pulled away from the Roadmaster and the hail of gunfire.

"GET DOWN!" Mr. Spahl shouted. He grabbed the back of his wife's shirt and pulled her towards the center console.

"Hold on!" Kurt ordered. He pulled Kim to the floor and covered her with his body.

"Fuck this!" Jeff snarled. He opened the back window, leveled the barrel of the rifle, and opened fire. He hit one of the ghouls in the back. The impact spun the creature but didn't knock it down. "Slow down!"

"WE'RE NOT SLOWING DOWN!" Mr. Spahl shouted as a stray round ricocheted off the hood of the Tahoe.

The tires screeched as the back end of the Grand Marquis slid wide through the intersection, "Hang on!" Matt shouted. He spun the wheel to the left, straightened the large sedan and pressed the gas pedal to the floor.

"Ahhhh!" Tyler screamed as his injured leg crashed against the back door. "You mother fucker!"

"Oh shit!" Matt blurted as the car slammed into one of the mangled figures. There was a nauseating cracking sound as bones shattered and the body landed momentarily on the hood before it was pulled beneath the car.

Paul watched the trail of blood follow the Grand Marquis. The carcass was dragged several yards before it dislodged from the chassis, "Hang on." Paul said as he shifted into fourth gear and aimed the large tires at the remains. There was a distinct thud as the Jeep rolled over what was left of the body.

"I'M HIT!" Ralph shouted as a stray round ripped through the door and into his hip. He writhed in pain as red mist sprayed across the windshield and dashboard.

"WHAT?" Paul questioned in disbelief as he swerved sharply to the left.

"I'M HIT!" Ralph screamed. His body contorted as he clamped his hands over his right hip. "GET US OUT OF HERE!"

"HANG ON!" Paul shouted. He cut the wheel hard to the right and pressed the gas pedal to the floor. The engine roared as the Jeep lurched forward through the water-logged street and back onto dry asphalt. "JUST HANG ON!"

The caravan sped on towards the center of town. They left the heavy-set man and his pursuers in their rearview mirror.

Water logged and dizzy, the heavy-set man's body swayed back and forth as blood poured from his head. Beneath the crimson mask, the look of self-preservation gave way to the blank stare of helpless disbelief. Despite the hollow clicking sound he continued to pull the triggers of the revolvers. With all the rounds expended, the firing pins found only spent primers of empty shell casings. His panicked shots had all missed their intended targets. His efforts had only served to attract a larger hoard.

"Please God...NO!" the heavy-set man sobbed. He let his arms drop to his sides. The pistols fell away to the water-soaked ground. "I don't deserve to die...not like this." He whimpered as discolored flesh-covered hands reached for him. He looked up to the sky and continued to beg. "Please God...not like this..."

The open mouths of the undead descended on him and beckoned him to become one of them. The contorted faces and lifeless eyes would be the last thing he would ever see; the haunted image his consciousness would take to meet his maker.

CHAPTER 14

breakdown, part 1

"**I**'M FUCKING SHOT!" Ralph screamed as his body contorted. The seatbelt restricted his movement as he writhed in pain. His face turned a deep shade of red and his breathing quickened as he tried to keep from passing out. "Oh, my God...Oh, my God...I'M FUCKING SHOT!"

"What was that?" Katherine chided from the backseat. "You almost got us killed back there!"

"Hang on!" Paul ordered as he shifted into fourth gear and pressed the gas pedal to the floor. The engine roared as the Jeep raced after the rest of the caravan. He grabbed Ralph's shoulder and squeezed. "JUST HANG ON!"

"I'm trying," Ralph whimpered as his body shook. "I'm trying."

"HEY!" Katherine shouted.

"Katherine," Marcus urged as he took hold of her arm.

"No!" Katherine insisted as she pulled away from him. "What the fuck was that back there?"

"What?" Paul snarled as his eyes found her in the rearview mirror. "We were being fucking shot at; in case you missed it! Shut the fuck up!" He stammered. "Get some gauze and first aid supplies from the back and keep your fucking mouth shut!"

"Hey, don't talk to her like that!" Marcus demanded.

"I need a fucking hospital!" Ralph cried. He blinked continuously as his vision blurred. Blood poured from between his fingers and soaked the seat beneath him. "Paul, stop the Jeep...stop the Jeep...I'm bleeding...we have to stop the bleeding!"

"Hang on Ralph!" Paul ordered. "It's not safe...we can't stop here. Put some pressure on the wound!"

"I'm putting pressure on it," Ralph pleaded. "But it's still bleeding. We need to stop...I need a hospital!"

"Fuck your face pipsqueak!" Paul barked as he turned his attention to Marcus. "Another word from either of you back there and I'll leave you on the next corner. You can tell your bullshit to the undead cannibals and see how they like it. Now get the med kit from the back Goddammit!"

The battery light flickered on and off several more times as the Grand Marquis sped down the road. Matt's hands trembled and heart pounded as he watched the light finally dim and go out. He tugged at the front of his plate carrier and checked the rearview mirror to make sure the Jeep was still behind him.

"What the fuck was that?" Tyler demanded from the back seat. He grabbed for his injured leg and tried unsuccessfully to sit up. "What the fuck was that? Where'd you learn to fucking drive?"

"Didn't you see we were being shot at?" Matt retorted angrily. He used the back of his hand to wipe the sweat from his face.

"See?" Tyler questioned. "I'm laying back here! I can't see a fucking thing! You're the one fucking driving!"

"It wasn't intentional. I misjudged the turn," Matt admitted as he checked his surroundings. "And we were being fucking shot at!"

"Look at my fucking ankle!" Tyler howled as beads of sweat ran down his face. "Look at my...holy shit, it's not even facing the right direction! Oh, God what if I can never walk again?"

"Hang on...just hang on," Matt called as he glanced back at his cousin. He reached back and offered Tyler a comforting hand. "You're going to be alright. Just hang on. We'll get you patched up."

"Fuck you!" Tyler snapped as he slapped his cousin's hand away. Unable to reach his ankle he fell back against the seat and clamped his hands over his face. "You destroyed my fucking ankle! You got my father killed! This is all your fault!"

"Fuck you!" Matt snarled. He clenched his hand into a fist and swung it wildly at Tyler from over the seat. "This isn't our fault! All your parents had to do was come over and we could have protected them!"

"You, selfish prick!" Tyler accused as his face turned from red to purple. "You and your fucking brother...it's always got to be your way, doesn't it?"

"You worthless junky fuck! Leave my brother out of this!" Matt ordered. "DO YOU FUCKING HEAR ME?"

"Fuck you!" Tyler hissed. "I'm glad he's sick. I hope he fucking dies! That would serve you right, you, self-righteous piece of..."

"GODDAMN YOU!" Matt screamed. The Grand Marquis swerved across the double yellow line and into the oncoming lane as Matt grabbed a clump of Tyler's curly blond hair and pulled him off the back seat. "You fucking parasite! How dare, you! I'll kill you, you mother fucker! I'll fucking kill you!"

Mr. Spahl shifted in his seat and tugged at the seatbelt strap across his chest. He surveyed the area and glanced up at the review mirror. He shook his head and pressed the gas pedal towards the floor as he watched the Grand Marquis swerve back and forth.

"What is it?" Mrs. Spahl asked calmly.

"Not sure," Mr. Spahl answered as he motioned behind them with his hand. "Matt's all over the road."

Jeff turned and looked out the back window, "What the fuck?" He muttered to himself. "Dad, you may want to stop. It looks like there may be something wrong with Tyler."

"We're allowed to stop now?" Mrs. Spahl quipped. "I thought you said we couldn't."

"Really, mom?" Jeff answered. "I have to explain to you that we can't stop when we're being shot at?"

"Jeff!" Mr. Spahl said sternly. "That's enough."

"If it's not too much to ask," Mrs. Spahl scolded. Her head pounded and ears rang. Tired and scared she lashed out at her son. "A little more notice before you start shooting. I'm sure our guests would prefer not to be deaf at the end of our road trip."

"Are you serious right now?" Jeff asked angrily.

"I said that's enough!" Mr. Spahl shouted. He used his palm to wipe sweat from his forehead. "Christ, we don't have enough going on?"

"I'm sorry," Jeff said as he glanced over at Kim and Kurt. "About the gunfire. I know it's loud. I'll try to give you more notice next time."

"It's ok," Kim said sympathetically. "We understand."

"Yeah, Jeff. We're good," Kurt added as he wrapped his hands around Kim's waist and pulled her to him.

"When we get to where we're going can you show me how to use that?" Kim asked as she pointed to the Mini-14.

"Yeah, if you want," Jeff stammered. He couldn't remember anyone ever asking him to teach them how to shoot before and wasn't entirely sure how to respond. "Honestly though, you'd be better off having Christian teach you. He's probably the best shot out of all of us and he's proficient with the fundamentals. That's really what you need to know."

Her request caught Kurt off guard. He gave the base of her neck a light squeeze, "What's that? Suddenly you want to learn how to shoot?"

"Don't you think we should learn?" Kim asked as she turned to look at Kurt. "We don't know how long this will go on for. They've taken us in. They're protecting us..."

"Protecting us?" Kurt questioned. His eyes narrowed as his voice became more agitated. "You're mine to protect."

"Stop it!" Kim insisted. She sat up and turned to face him. "You know I don't like when you talk that way."

"What?" Kurt questioned sharply. "I don't need anybody to help me take care of you."

"The false bravado isn't helping anything," Kim said firmly. "I love you and I'm scared too. The fact is we're not prepared for anything like this and they are. If we want to be able to protect each other we need to let them teach us how."

The collision of the Roadmaster and Subaru left Matt Chico and his parents rattled. He pulled his foot back from the gas pedal and increased the distance between the two vehicles. Matt Chico rubbed his eyes as his temples throbbed. He pushed his torso away from the seat as an unfamiliar pain began in his lower back.

"I want to go home!" Josh demanded as he held his left arm immobile across his torso.

"Josh, you're bleeding," Kerri informed him as she pulled herself back onto the seat. "Your father is…"

"I don't want to fucking hear it!" Matt Chico snapped angrily. "What was Christian thinking, driving us through a hail of gunfire like that? Is he out of his fucking mind? He's going to get us all killed!"

"Excuse me?" Kerri questioned. She was unaccustomed to hearing her son speak that way. "I'm your mother…"

"I know who you are," Matt Chico retorted sharply. "Don't pull that shit with me! I'm not a fucking child!"

"Don't pull that shit with you?" Kerri repeated. "Well, your father's face slammed into the back of your seat when you ran us into Christian's car. I think he bit through his bottom lip."

"I'm bleeding," Josh blurted as blood ran from his face down the front of his shirt. "Why am I bleeding?"

"Then do something to help him Goddammit!" Matt Chico shouted. He could feel his heart race and hands shake as he tightened his grip on the steering wheel. "What do you expect me to do about it. I'm driving the fucking car!"

"That's enough!" Kerri insisted. "Stop speaking to me that way!"

"How can they expect us to just follow them to the farm," Matt Chico muttered to himself. He struggled to keep his focus on the road. "My brother…my son is out there somewhere? How can they just expect us…"

The center of town resembled documentary images of post-World War 2 Europe. Store front windows and doors were smashed and shops and businesses looted. Fire spewed from several buildings. It spread and engulfed nearby vehicles. Flames poured from second story windows and threatened power lines overhead.

The pristine white gazebo in the town square looked out of place against the twisted carnage that surrounded it. A yellow Nissan Extera was wrapped around the base of the four-sided clock. The driver hung limp over the steering wheel. Antifreeze sprayed from the punctured radiator over the engine. A foul-smelling cloud of white smoke ascended from beneath the wreck.

Bodies and broken glass littered the sidewalk on either side of the street and there interspersed throughout the carnage and chaos unrelenting in their pursuit of the living was the undead.

"Please," Aunt Athena pleaded as tears ran down her cheeks. "I just want to go home."

"That's not an option," Christian said sternly.

"We have to get off Main Street!" Patrick shouted. "We can't keep going this way, we're never going to make it!"

"We're not driving back through that!" Christian growled.

"Please," Aunt Athena whimpered. "Please just take me home...I need to bury my Tony."

"Christian!" Patrick blurted as his face turned a deep shade of red.

"We have a plan, Pat and we're sticking to it," Christian barked.

"Please," Aunt Athena cried. "Please...please."

"Keep her quiet!" Christian ordered. "I'm trying to drive."

"It's suicide to keep going this way!" Patrick said angrily. He slammed his fist into the back of Christian's head rest. "Stop the fucking car!"

"Take a look around Pat. If I stop the fucking car, how long do you think you're going to last?" Christian hissed through gritted teeth.

The anguished screams of the dying were interrupted by sporadic gunfire in the distance. The faint sound of sirens offered little in the way of hope for rescue.

"We knew shit like this was going to happen," Christian reminded his cousin. "Sit back and shut the fuck up. We're not stopping. We're not going back and that's fucking final!"

Residents who had not evacuated left their places of cover and hurried to get the caravan's attention in hopes of safe passage out of town.

"Where are they all coming from?" Patrick asked startled by the amount of people out in the open.

"The churches at either end of town, maybe," Christian answered as he watched the group increase in size. "They could have locked down and are coming out now to scavenge for food and supplies."

"What are we going to do?" Patrick asked as he frantically looked around.

"Nothing we can do," Christian said as he slid his left hand from the steering wheel and made sure that the doors of the Subaru were locked. "Hang on." He ordered as frantic hands slapped against the car and panicked faces covered the windows and screamed for help.

"Oh, my God!" Aunt Athena shrieked. "What's happening?"

"Shut her up!" Christian ordered. He checked the rearview mirror to make sure the other vehicles were still in tow and pressed the gas pedal to the floor. The engine revved as the car pulled away from the crowd. The frame of the car rocked as a desperate young man leapt from the curb. There was a loud thud as he landed and used the roof rack to pull himself onto the Subaru. "What the fuck?"

"What's happening?" Aunt Athena screamed. "Oh, Patrick!"

"I got you, mom," Patrick assured her. He pulled her against his chest. "It'll be ok."

"Mother fuckers on the roof!" Christian shouted. His gaze momentarily left the road and elevated to the ceiling of the car.

Matt Chico looked on in disbelief as people surrounded the Roadmaster.

"What's going on?" Kerri called as she tended to Josh's wounds.

"Somebody got on top of Christian's car," Matt Chico called over the cries of the crowd. "Why didn't these people evacuate when they had the chance?"

"Why didn't we?" Kerri asked.

"Take me home!" Josh hollered from the back seat as blood continued to trickle from his lacerated lip. "I've had enough! I want to go home...NOW!"

"Mom, will you shut him up!" Matt Chico demanded as he turned back and looked at his mother.

"NO!" Kerri screeched as she pointed at the windshield.

"What the fuck!" Matt Chico yelped unable to stop the large vehicle.

One of the women in the crowd jumped on the hood of the Roadmaster. She grabbed for the windshield wipers as her body bounced off the hood. She let out a high-pitched scream as she was dragged beneath the car. A considerable jolt accompanied the hollow thud as the wheels crushed the woman's torso.

"What a fucking shit show," Mr. Spahl said with disgust. "Hold on!" He ordered as desperate terrified people filled the street.

"Go around her!" Mrs. Spahl shrieked. "She's still moving!"

"No where to go!" Mr. Spahl replied. He tensed his body as the Tahoe rolled over the still breathing woman. The tires of the SUV shattered the lower half of her body.

Some of the crowd dispersed. Others shouted profanity and threw bottles and rocks.

"GODDAMMIT!" Matt shouted as a bottle shattered against the windshield. He trained the hood ornament of the Grand Marquis on the license plate of the Tahoe and followed it over the woman's broken body. Her right hand twitched and mouth moved as she struggled to take air into her punctured lungs.

Shrieks of horror replaced the cries for help as the undead descended on the living. Terror stricken residents ran in all directions and tried desperately to escape.

"Hang on!" Paul growled.

"Paul, I can't!" Ralph yelped as he started to lose consciousness. His hands and blue jeans were soaked in blood. "I can't..."

"HANG ON!" Paul ordered. He aimed the tires of the Jeep at the woman. The sound as her head was crushed was nauseating.

"You fucking monster!" Katherine cried.

"It was fucking mercy!" Paul retorted angrily. He found a measure of solace when he checked the rearview mirror and found the woman's body motionless.

Christian held the gas pedal to the floor. The four-cylinder engine raced as the car sped on.

"What are you doing?" Patrick shouted.

"Hold on!" Christian instructed. Once they were clear of the crowd, he slammed the clutch and bake pedals to the floor. The car slid to a stop and launched the young man off the roof. His body smacked against the pavement and slid to a stop in the center of the road.

Matt Chico slammed both feet on the brake pedal and cut the wheel hard to the left. The back end of the large sedan skidded across the asphalt and slammed into the rear quarter panel of the Subaru. His parents were thrown violently across the back seat.

"Ahhhh!" Kerri yelped as the back of her head smacked against the window. Her body slammed against the passenger side back door before Josh's body landed up against her.

"Mom!" Matt Chico called in a panic as he turned around. "Mom, are you ok?"

Mr. Spahl reacted quickly. He slowed the Tahoe and was able to maneuver it around the rear bumper of the Roadmaster.

"Dad!" Jeff called from the backseat.

"Everybody, hang on," Mr. Spahl instructed. He was able to bring the SUV to an abrupt stop right next to the driver's side of the Subaru.

"Excellent driving dear," Mrs. Spahl said as she placed her hand on her husband's arm. "But let's avoid any more of that if we can."

Matt gripped the steering wheel tightly as he jammed the brake pedal to the floor. The tires squealed as the vehicle slid across the asphalt.

"Fuck!" Tyler cried as his body was throw around the back of the car. "For the love of fucking Christ, why don't you just kill me!"

"Do you want to drive?" Matt snapped through clenched teeth. "Then shut the fuck up!"

Unconscious, the seat belt was the only thing that kept Ralph's body upright. Marcus held onto Katherine. He kept his legs braced against the back of the driver's seat. The engine raced and needle on the tachometer shot up as Paul downshifted. The large tires rumbled against the street as the Jeep slowed.

"Fucking great," Paul growled. He reached over and checked Ralph's pulse. "Ralph!" He called.

"What are we doing?" Katherine demanded.

"What does it look like?" Paul questioned. "We're parked in the middle of the fucking street. It must be time for a picnic."

"That's not helping," Marcus said sharply. "We can't be stopped out here. It's not safe."

"No shit genius," Paul replied. "LET'S GO!" He shouted angrily as he drove his left hand down onto the center of the steering wheel. The loud blast from the horn drew the attention of survivors and the undead.

Mr. Spahl lowered the passenger side window and motioned for Christian to do the same.

"You, ok?" Mr. Spahl called.

Christian looked up disoriented, "What?"

"Are you ok?" Mr. Spahl repeated.

Christian shook his head, "We need to keep going." He answered as he refocused himself.

"COME ON!" Paul shouted. He grabbed Ralph's shoulder and shook him. "Come on Ralph! Wake up...wake up!"

Mr. Spahl glanced at his side mirror. He could see bodies headed towards them. "We need to move. How much further until the turn off?"

"Quarter mile, maybe less," Christian answered. He shifted into first gear and released the clutch. The young man's badly scraped body convulsed in the center of the street as the Subaru pulled past him.

"Hang on. We're getting out of here." Matt Chico assured his parents. He pulled the steering wheel hard to the right and pressed the gas pedal to the floor. The V8 engine revved as the Roadmaster pulled behind the Subaru. The other three vehicles quickly followed.

The last stretch of Main Street was some of the most graphic they encountered. Buildings on both sides of the street were gutted by fire.

Downed power lines danced in between car wrecks and threw sparks like massive fourth of July fireworks. The snap and hiss of stray bullets announced their proximity. The only constant was the undead as they shambled through the mayhem in search of the living.

"Here we go," Christian said as he checked the rearview mirror and tapped the brakes twice to signal Matt Chico. The intersection was surprisingly clear compared to what they had driven through. The early morning departure from the house felt like a distant memory. Christian down shifted into second gear and turned onto County Road 921.

The other four vehicles quickly followed. No one mistook their leaving for safety. There was a long way to travel before they got to the farm. With Ralph and Tyler's injuries the group would require a hospital before long.

As the last glimpses of home disappeared, they were forced to confront the reality that their quiet little town no longer belonged to the living.

CHAPTER 15

breakdown, part 2

A S THE CARAVAN ENTERED the valley it was as if someone turned the volume down on the rest of the world. The gun shots, sirens, and pillars of smoke faded into the distance. Almost as quickly as the chaos started, it seemed to be over.

"Christian," Patrick called from the back seat as he looked desperately around. His panicked voice trembled as he continued. "We need to pull over."

"Too risky, Pat," Christian answered as he glanced up at the rearview mirror. "We need to keep going." He insisted as he pulled the gear shift back into fourth and pressed the gas pedal towards the floor.

"I can't..." Patrick stammered as the Subaru pulled ahead of the other vehicles. "I can't be in this car anymore...I need to get out."

"Just calm down, Patrick," Aunt Athena urged. She wiped tears from her cheeks as she tried to console her youngest son. "Just calm down."

"We're not stopping," Christian said firmly as the road began to twist and turn. For the first time that morning, Christian felt as though he could breathe a small sigh of relief. "Just settle back and enjoy the view."

Patrick slammed his fist against the back of Christian's headrest, "I need to get out of this fucking car! We need to stop...NOW!"

The sun was almost directly overhead. It washed the winding road in a brilliant natural spotlight. Rows of massive pine trees covered the steep valley walls and left the land on either side shrouded in dark shadows.

"MOM!" Matt Chico called as he reached over the front seat to check on his mother. "Mom, are you ok?"

"We need to pull over," Kerri wheezed. She kept her arms gently wrapped around her midsection. "Something's not right. It hurts to breathe."

"Your mother is hurt!" Josh scolded. "Something's wrong with my arm." He continued as he tried unsuccessfully to raise his left arm. "Stop the car!"

"We can't stop here, dad," Matt Chico pleaded as he tried to comfort his mother.

"Bullshit!" Josh barked as blood spewed from his mouth. "Stop the car!"

"We need to stop," Kerri pleaded as her face contorted with pain. "Please, I felt something pop when your father landed up against me. We need to pull over."

"Mom, just hang in there," Matt Chico urged. "There's a clearing a few miles ahead. We can stop there."

The caravan maintained a tight formation as they traveled along the valley floor. It was as beautiful as it was desolate. There were no other vehicles or people to speak of and no sign of the undead. Nothing in the valley moved except tree branches that swayed in the breeze and motioned the group onward.

Mr. Spahl cracked the driver's side window and wiped sweat from his forehead, "Jeff, hand me a bottle of water please."

"On your right," Jeff said as he twisted the cap loose and handed the bottle to his father.

"Thanks," Mr. Spahl said. He tipped the bottle back and took a long drink. The dryness in his mouth and throat quickly subsided. He felt some of the tension leave his shoulders. "Is everybody ok?"

"I'm ok," Mrs. Spahl said as she took the bottle from him. She casually moved several strands of hair away from her face and took a sip. She returned the cap to the top of the bottle and closed her eyes. "I'm ok." She repeated to herself.

"I think we're good," Kurt offered. He gave Kim's shoulder a squeeze. "You ok babe?"

Kim nodded, "I think so." She answered as she pressed her body against his.

"Good back here," Kurt confirmed as he pulled Kim close.

"Jeff?" Mr. Spahl asked.

"Still breathing," Jeff answered. He twisted his head from side to side until his neck released an audible crack.

"Check your ammo," Mr. Spahl instructed. "Not sure what we're going to come up against next."

"On it," Jeff said as he took the magazine from the magwell and placed it in the Ranger Green 5.11 drop pouch attached to his Mavrick battle belt. He took a loaded magazine from the mag pouch on his plate carrier and snapped it in the magwell.

"Chamber?" Mr. Spahl questioned.

Jeff retracted the charging handle enough to verify there was a round in the chamber, "Yes." He answered. "Locked and loaded."

"Good," Mr. Spahl said as he pressed the accelerator towards the floor. "Let's pray we don't need to use it."

The Tahoe pulled away from the other two vehicles and disappeared around a turn. The engine of the Grand Marquis let out a labored groan as it struggled to keep pace.

"Tyler," Matt called as he glanced back at his cousin.

"Fuck off," Tyler snarled. "Fuck all the way off."

"Keep running your mouth shit head..." Matt growled.

"Me?" Tyler questioned angrily. "You pulled me off the fucking seat."

"You said you hope my brother dies," Matt shot back. "Don't think I'm going to forget that."

"I never said that," Tyler insisted. "That's a fucking lie."

"You, junky fuck," Matt hissed through clenched teeth as he shook his head. "You're living in fucking fantasy land." He added as he glanced down at the dashboard and watched the red battery light flicker on and off several times. "You have got to be fucking kidding me! Can we not catch a fucking break?"

"What is it?" Tyler asked as he struggled to pick his head up from the seat.

Matt tightened his grip on the steering wheel, "Hopefully nothing."

The rumble of the Jeep's cold air intake echoed loudly through the cabin. The oversized tires straddled the double yellow line as the large vehicle brought up the rear of the caravan.

Ralph's arms hung limp at his sides as beads of sweat dripped from his face and beard. The shoulder strap on the seat belt was the only thing that kept his unconscious body upright. Blood continued to seep from the open wound on his right hip.

"Ralph!" Paul hollered as he shook Ralph's shoulder. "Come on buddy, wake up."

"Just pull over!" Katherine ordered from the back seat. "He's bleeding. We need to administer first aid."

"Stop?" Paul blurted. He pulled another cigarette from the crumbled pack. "Where do you want to stop? There's nothing out here but fucking trees!"

"Don't yell at her!" Marcus ordered. "Katherine's right. We need to stop!"

"Fucking child care!" Paul snarled. He threw the unlit cigarette against the windshield and gave Ralph's shoulder another shake. "Come on Ralph. I need you to open your damn eyes!"

As the road straightened a small structure partially obscured by tree branches came into view. Weathered red bricks surrounded an old white sign with black Old English lettering. Dark orange and brown rust streaks blead from ancient hinges over peeling paint which read; "Continental Valley Historic Site, picnic area and hiking trails, open to the public from dawn to dusk, four miles ahead on left."

"Did you just hit my headrest?" Christian asked angrily as his eyes found Patrick in the rearview mirror. "The fuck is the matter with you?"

"Look at the sign!" Patrick insisted as he ignored his cousin's questions. "There's a parking lot four miles ahead."

"And?" Christian questioned as he glared at his cousin.

"The trails we used to hike as kids," Patrick blurted impatiently. His cheeks reddened as he struggled to maintain his composure. "You know what I'm talking about. Just stop for a few minutes. We haven't seen any anybody or any of those things. I just need to get out..."

"Just calm down," Christian interrupted as he turned his focus back to the road. Despite the dangers, Christian knew, no good would come from his cousin's confinement. "Let's see what the parking lot looks like when we get there."

The picnic area and hiking trails were only a few minutes down the road. The historic site was surrounded by a rustic split rail fence. Square wooden posts connected by three rough cut beams provided some semblance of barrier and would buy them time if they encountered the undead.

"Hang on," Matt Chico urged as they passed the old sign. "There's an area up ahead we can stop."

"What..." Kerri asked as her voice trailed off. Her eyes fluttered and closed as her body slumped against the back door.

"MOM!" Matt Chico shouted as he shifted frantically in his seat. "Dad...DAD! Make sure she's ok!"

The tires squealed as the large sedan swerved into the oncoming lane.

"They're all over the road again," Mr. Spahl said as he took is foot off the gas pedal.

"I wonder what's..." Mrs. Spahl began before she was interrupted by the long wail of a car horn.

"What the fuck?" Jeff muttered to himself as he looked around.

It was agreed before they departed, one long beep would signal trouble and bring the caravan to a stop.

Matt could feel his stomach twist as the battery light brightened. It didn't flicker or dim this time. An uncomfortable feeling crept up the back of his neck as the light glowed red on the dashboard, "This is not happening." He said through gritted teeth.

"What'd you mess up this time?" Tyler mocked.

"Fuck off!" Matt hissed. He pushed the gas pedal to the floor. The V8 engine made a labored sound as the car lost power.

As the caravan neared the historic site, gray clouds filled the sky.

"Come on, Ralph," Paul encouraged as his focus shifted to his unconscious friend. He pressed his fingers against Ralph's neck and checked for a pulse.

"Pay attention to the road!" Katherine ordered.

"Shut the fuck up!" Paul snarled. He shot her a glance before he returned his attention to Ralph. "Come on, open your fucking eyes!"

Matt pressed the horn several more times as he guided the Grand Marquis onto the narrow shoulder, "We have to stop." He growled. Smoke rose from the grill as he pulled the hood release.

"What the fuck?" Christian questioned. He checked the rearview mirror and saw a cloud of white smoke behind them. "That can't be good." He added as he downshifted and tapped the brake pedal several times.

"WATCH OUT!" Katherine shrieked as the Grand Marquis stopped just in front of them.

"FUCK!" Paul shouted. He cut the wheel hard to the left and pressed the clutch and brake pedals to the floor.

A loud hollow bang echoed across the valley as the back end of the Jeep slid into the Grand Marquis.

"AHHH!" Matt groaned as his forehead smacked against the steering wheel.

"NOOO!" Tyler yelped as his body was thrown to the floor.

Christian grabbed his AR15 and hurried out of the Subaru as the Roadmaster and Tahoe pulled in behind him.

"OHHH!" Marcus cried as his face bounced off the back of Paul's headrest. Blood trickled from his mouth as his teeth punctured his bottom lip.

"WHAT ARE YOU DOING?" Katherine demanded as she slammed up against the back of Ralph's seat. She gasped as the wind was knocked out of her.

"SHUT UP!" Paul ordered as the Jeep came to a stop in the middle of the road. He held fast to the back of Ralph's shirt and kept him from hitting the dashboard. "SHUT THE FUCK UP!"

The sun all but disappeared as the clouds darkened and breeze picked up.

"What happened?" Christian asked as he sprinted to the Tahoe. He positioned the 2-point sling over his head and right shoulder and checked the retention band on his holster.

"Sounded like an accident," Mr. Spahl answered as he stepped into the street. He looked back at the other vehicles. "It looks like smoke's coming from Matt's car."

"I'll go check on them," Christian said. He motioned towards the Jeep and Grand Marquis that were somewhat remove from the rest of the group. "Can you hold things down here?"

"We've got this," Mr. Spahl assured him. He turned and motioned for Jeff to join him.

"Good," Christian answered. "Hopefully it's nothing too serious."

Jeff nodded and hurried out of the Tahoe, "What's the plan?" He asked as he joined his father and Christian in the road.

"We may get some rain," Mr. Spahl said. He glanced at the sky as it darkened. "Let's get everybody out of the vehicles. I think it'd be good for everyone to stretch their legs."

"I agree," Christian said as he turned back. "But we can't be out here long."

"I know," Mr. Spahl acknowledged. He slid the 1911 from the holster on his hip. "Make sure they're alright. Jeff and I will secure the perimeter."

"Got it," Christian acknowledged.

"Jeff, let's get everybody out of the vehicles," Mr. Spahl instructed as Christian took off down the road. "Then we'll establish a perimeter."

"On it, dad," Jeff answered. "I'm sure everybody could use some food and water."

"Stay here, mom," Patrick instructed as he opened the back door of the Subaru.

"Where are you going?" Aunt Athena questioned. She held tightly to her son's arms. "I don't want you to go."

"I don't know if we should get out," Kim said as she peered out the window.

"It'll be good to get out and stretch our legs," Kurt assured her.

Kim looked skeptical, "I...I'm just not sure."

"It'll be ok honey," Mrs. Spahl added as she unfastened her seatbelt and opened the door. "We could all use a break."

"I'll be right back," Patrick assured his mother. "I just have to check on Tyler and Katherine."

"Come right back," Aunt Athena insisted.

"I will," Patrick said as he placed a comforting hand on his mother's back before he hurried off. "I'll be right back."

White smoke continued to drift up from under the hood. Dazed, Matt pushed the driver side door open with his left leg and staggered into the road, "What just happened?" He mumbled to himself as his head pounded.

"Hey," Paul called as he climbed out of the Jeep. "You, ok?"

"Been better," Matt answered with a slight wave. He blinked several times and tried to get his eyes to focus.

The pine trees appeared a deeper shade of green as dark gray clouds rolled across the sky.

"Mom!" Matt Chico called. He shouted to Jeff as he ran around the front of the Roadmaster. "Jeff, give me a hand with my mom. She's hurt."

"Right there," Jeff said as he ran over to help his friend.

"Ralph's been shot," Paul called as he hurried over to Matt.

"Shot?" Matt questioned as he struggled to regain his balance. "What do you mean? When?"

"You mother fuckers!" Tyler screamed from the floor. "Get me out of this fucking car!"

"He's unconscious," Paul added. He motioned to the back of the Grand Marquis. "Is your cousin alright?"

"My fucking cousin," Matt said as he shook his head. He made his way to the back of the car and pulled the door open. "He's been running his mouth since we got on the road."

"Must run in the family," Paul added. "His sister's been up my ass the whole trip."

"Get me out of this fucking car!" Tyler demanded as he struggled to pull himself back on to the seat.

"You want out of this car?" Matt asked.

"Get me out this fucking car!" Tyler repeated.

"My cousin said something very unkind about my brother," Matt said. He grabbed Tyler's left pant leg and belt.

"What are you doing?" Tyler whimpered. "Get off me!"

"Matt!" Christian called as he quickly approached. His light assault boots made a distinct sound as they pounded against the road. "MATT!"

"Right behind you," Patrick called as he ran after Christian.

"Did he now?" Paul said sharply. He joined Matt at the back of the Grand Marquis. "And what exactly did he say?"

"He said, he hoped my brother would die," Matt announced. In a single violent motion Matt yanked Tyler from the back seat. His narrow body landed with a painfully loud slap against the asphalt several yards from the car. His head bounced twice against the road. "Can you believe that?"

"Fucking scumbag," Paul said as he shook his head.

"NO!" Patrick shouted. His heart pounded and arms pumped up and down as he pulled ahead of Christian. "Tyler...NO!"

"What are you doing?" Katherine screamed. She pulled Marcus out of the Jeep behind her as she hurried to her brother. "Tyler...Tyler, are you ok?"

"Dad!" Jeff called as he and Matt Chico tried to move Kerri from the back of the Roadmaster. "Dad, she's hurt bad. We need your help."

"Keep her head and neck immobilized," Mr. Spahl called as he hurried over to them.

The first drops of rain fell from the sky as thunder rumbled in the distance.

"Matty!" Patrick blurted as he reached his cousin. He grabbed Matt by the plate carrier and slammed him up against the car. "Why'd you throw him?"

"Get off me!" Matt shouted as he tried to push his cousin away. "Get the fuck off me!"

"Tyler!" Katherine called as she placed her hands on either side of her brother's face. "Tyler, can you hear me?"

"HEY!" Paul shouted. He wrapped his thick arms around Patrick's chest and pulled him off Matt. "That's enough!"

"What happened?" Tyler muttered as he tried to open his eyes. "Where am I?"

"Hang in there Tyler," Marcus urged from where he knelt next to Katherine. "You're going to be ok."

Patrick stumbled, "FUCK!" He blurted as he landed on his hands and knees in the middle of the road.

"CUT THE SHIT!" Christian hollered. His chest heaved as he reached the Grand Marquis and Jeep. "What the fuck? We don't have enough going on?"

Rain drops morphed into a constant mist as the breeze picked up significantly.

"Just lay her on the road," Mr. Spahl instructed as they carefully moved Kerri out of the back of the car.

"Not on the road," Matt Chico pleaded.

"It's ok," Mr. Spahl assured him. He could see the worry on Matt Chico's face. "It's just so we can assess her wounds."

"It's ok, Chico," Jeff offered. "My dad knows what he's doing."

"We've got this, Jeff," Mr. Spahl said as he placed his hand on his son's shoulder. "We need to secure the perimeter. Position yourself about fifty yards ahead of Christian's car."

"I can do that," Jeff said with a nod as he got to his feet.

"Be careful," Mr. Spahl instructed. "It looks like we're alone out here, but there's a lot of ground to watch over especially with so much tree cover. You see anyone or anything call it out."

"I will," Jeff said as the light rain saturated his head and neck.

"We need to cover my mother," Matt Chico insisted. "She's getting wet."

"We will," Mr. Spahl assured him. He turned back to his son. "Go, Jeff...get out there."

Jeff hurried back to the Tahoe. He grabbed his raider desert camouflage hat with the BCM logo embroidered in black across the front and hurried with his rifle down the quiet stretch of road.

"You alright?" Christian asked red faced as he tried to catch his breath. He motioned to Matt's forehead. "You've got a lump forming."

"Yeah," Matt said as he staggered towards his brother. He touched his fingers against his forehead. "That's nothing compared to how bad my neck hurts."

"You see this?" Christian asked as he motioned to the cloud of white smoke that rose from the hood of the Grand Marquis. "What happened?"

"Battery light came on, car lost power," Matt answered as he moved slowly around the front of the car. He reached under the hood and released the latch. A foul-smelling cloud of white smoke rose from the center of the engine as he lifted the hood. "That's not good."

"How is he?" Patrick asked as joined his sister and Marcus. "Is he conscious?"

"Look at his ankle," Katherine blurted angrily. "It's not facing the right way...look at it!"

"It's going to be alright, Katherine," Marcus assured her as he took hold of her arm. "We're going to..."

"Get off me!" Katherine shrieked as she pulled her arm away. "Don't touch me! I'm going to check on my mother and I'm not riding with this asshole!" She shouted red faced as she stormed off.

"Don't," Patrick insisted as Marcus tried to follow. "Just let her go and cool down."

Some of the smoke dissipated and engine sizzled as droplets of water landed on it.

"Doesn't look like the radiator's overheating," Matt mumbled to himself.

"Any ideas?" Christian asked as he joined his brother in front of the car. "I don't want to be out here any longer than we have to."

"Not sure," Matt answered. The lump on his head began to throb. "I can't tell exactly where the smoke is coming from."

A large cloud of dark smoke wafted up from the engine. It was followed by audible pops and hisses and the yellow glow of flames.

"That's not good," Christian said as he pointed to the small fire which erupted from the center of the engine.

"Fuck!" Matt blurted. "The alternator's on fire."

"Fire extinguisher?" Christian questioned.

"No," Matt answered.

"How do you don't have a fire extinguisher?" Christian asked.

"Give me a fucking break," Matt snapped. He hurried to the back of the car, opened the trunk, and retrieved a thick dark colored wool blanket. "The only preparedness item I don't have..."

"What are you going to do with that?" Christian asked as Matt returned with the blanket.

"Smother the flames," Matt answered.

A flash of lightening overhead momentarily pulled everyone's focus to the sky.

"Storm's getting close," Kurt said. "You can feel the temperature's dropped."

"I don't think we should be out here," Kim said with a shiver. She held fast to Kurt as the two of them stood next to the Tahoe.

Kurt looked around, "It'll be ok." He assured her. He wrapped his arms around her shoulders and held her close. "Jeff's keeping watch."

"What about his mom and dad?" Kim asked.

"I think they're taking care of Kerri and Josh," Kurt answered as he looked back towards the Roadmaster.

Thunder rumbled in the distance as the mist became a steady rain.

"Here we go," Matt said as he pressed the thick wool blanket against the flames that jumped from the alternator.

"Careful," Christian urged as he stepped out from behind the open hood.

The passenger side door of the Jeep was open. The contents of the first aid kit were laid out on the hood. Ralph was still unconscious as Paul tended to his wounds.

"I think we're good," Matt said as he lifted the blanket off the engine. There was a hiss and pop followed by dark gray smoke and flames. "FUCK!" He shouted as he covered the flames with the blanket. "It's not working!"

"PAUL!" Christian called. "Do you have a fire extinguisher in the Jeep?"

"What's going on over there?" Patrick shouted from where he knelt next to Tyler. What's on fire?"

"Yeah," Paul answered as he retrieved some gauze and bandages from the first aid kit. "In the back of the Jeep."

"What's on fire?" Patrick asked again as Christian retrieved the fire extinguisher.

"Come on!" Matt snarled. Flames jumped from the engine as he pulled the blanket away.

"Move!" Christian ordered as he appeared at the front of the car with the fire extinguisher. The flames danced tauntingly under the open hood. Christian pulled the pin, aimed the nozzle, and squeezed. The carbon dioxide extinguisher coated the engine in a cloud of white.

"Is it out?" Matt asked as he balled up the singed blanket.

Christian nodded, "Yeah, it's out." He let the empty extinguisher fall to the ground in front of him. "That's enough for one day."

"I've got Ralph patched up as good as I can," Paul said as he joined Matt and Christian.

"What happened?" Matt asked. "You said he got shot."

"The guy we passed. The open fire hydrant before we got to the center of town," Paul explained. "Stray round, right through the door. Hit him in the hip."

"How is he?" Christian asked.

"Still unconscious," Paul answered. "I packed it with gauze to stop the bleeding, but he needs a hospital."

"So does my brother," Patrick announced as he joined the three of them. "What was that? Why'd you throw my brother out of the car?"

"We don't need to get into that right now," Matt said as he glanced over at his cousin.

"We are going to get into it," Patrick said firmly as he took a step forward.

"How is Tyler?" Christian interrupted.

"He needs a hospital," Patrick answered. His face turned a deep shade of red and his breathing quickened. "His foot is facing the wrong direction and I'm sure he's got a concussion from his head smacking against the road."

"Easy, Pat," Christian urged. He put his hand on his cousin's shoulder to calm him. "Let's get Tyler in the Jeep with Ralph, so they're not in the open."

"And then what?" Patrick asked angrily. "We need a hospital."

"I second that," Paul agreed. "We're not equipped to handle injuries this serious."

"Agreed," Christian said. "First thing, we need to check on the rest of the group. We'll unload the supplies from the Grand Marquis and divvy them between the other vehicles."

"I don't know about you guys," Matt interjected. "But I need something to eat and drink."

"Yeah, fucking food," Paul added. "I'm not going to get much further without something to eat."

"None of us are," Christian said. He motioned to Matt. "Your forehead is swelling. We need to get you a Dynarex cold pack for that."

"That'd be good," Matt said as he ran his fingers over the lump on his forehead. "My head is fucking throbbing."

"Come on," Christian said as he motioned to where his cousin lay. "Let's load Tyler in the Jeep and eat. I want to get back on the road as quickly as possible."

"And the hospital?" Patrick questioned.

"Yeah, Pat," Christian answered. "A detour to the hospital is looking more and more inevitable."

CHAPTER 16

apart

J EFF STOOD STATUESQUE IN the middle of the road. His boots straddled the double yellow line. He held his rifle at the low ready position. His left hand was wrapped around the rifle's forend and his right index finger tapped against the trigger guard as his eyes scanned the terrain from beneath the brim of his hat, "Let's go." He muttered to himself. "We can't be out here."

"It's ok, mom," Matt Chico offered. He did his best to make his mother comfortable as lightening flashed overhead and rain soaked the back of his shirt.

"It hurts to breathe," Kerri whispered as she kept her eyes closed tightly. She was slumped against the back seat and the color all but drained from her face.

"Christian, help me sit her up please," Matt Chico asked as he climbed in the back of the car.

"Chico, I'm not sure if that's a good idea," Christian said. "We don't know how severe her injuries are. It may be better if we give her something for the pain and lay her across the back seat."

"I want to go home!" Josh demanded from where he sat in the passenger side of the front seat. He pressed a Dynarex cold pack against his swollen face.

"Yes, dad. I know you want to go home," Matt Chico acknowledged. "Try not to talk. We just got your lip to stop bleeding."

"Chico, your mother's pulse is shallow but steady," Christian informed him. "All we've got for pain is ibuprofen. See if you can convince her to take some. I need to check on Tyler and Ralph. Mr. Spahl and I will come back after."

"Yes, please bring him back with you," Matt Chico said with a nod. "Mom...mom, come on open your eyes. I need you to take some ibuprofen. It'll help with the pain."

The rain slowed to a drizzle and after a few minutes stopped completely. The sky was an intense shade of white as thick clouds kept the sun hidden. The breeze settled and the musky scent of pine returned to the valley. In the distance the low rumble of thunder continued as most of the group gathered next to the Subaru and Tahoe.

"Come on, you need to eat," Mrs. Spahl insisted. She stood at the back of the large SUV and handed out sandwiches and bottles of water from a red igloo cooler. "You need to keep up your strength. We're not out of the woods yet."

"I don't know Matty, that just doesn't sound like something Tyler would say," Patrick insisted. His hands trembled as he twisted the plastic cap off the bottle of water and took a long drink. "It just doesn't."

"Thanks, Mrs. Spahl," Matt said as he pulled the Ziplock bag open and took a bite of the peanut butter and jelly sandwich. He closed his eyes and savored his first taste of food for the day. When he opened his eyes, he locked eyes with his cousin. "Tyler said it Pat. I don't know what else to tell you. He said it."

"Well, Matty," Patrick continued as his face reddened. "He's in a lot of pain. Maybe he didn't know what he was saying."

"That's possible, Pat," Matt said before he took another bite of the sandwich. "But he said it and he paid the price."

"Thank you," Kurt said with a nod. He took a bottle of water and sandwich from Mrs. Spahl and turned back towards Kim. "Here, take this."

"I'm not sure I can eat," Kim said as she shook her head. She placed her hands over her stomach. "I just...I don't..."

"Nonsense dear," Mrs. Spahl said as she carried a sandwich and bottle of water over to Kim. "You need to eat something."

"I know," Kim insisted. Her gaze shifted uncomfortably to Kurt and back.

"I'll eat it if you can't," Kurt offered.

"You will not," Mrs. Spahl said sternly. "Kim, sweetie. Look at me." She insisted. "You need to eat something."

"I'm not sure what you're looking for Pat," Matt said sharply as he finished the last of the sandwich. "If it's an apology, don't hold your breath."

"Matty," Patrick growled. "I'm not looking for an apology."

"I can't get those images out of my mind," Kim pleaded through tear filled eyes.

"I know," Mrs. Spahl said empathetically. "I can't either, but you need to get some fuel in your system."

Kim winced as she wiped a tear from her cheek, "How could this be happening?" She whispered.

"That's not for us to figure out right now honey," Mrs. Spahl said quietly as she took another step towards Kim. "You need to eat and drink something. If your blood sugar drops off, it'll start with a pounding headache followed by nausea."

"Nausea?" Kim questioned.

"If you let yourself get dehydrated," Mrs. Spahl continued. "That'll be much more serious."

"I understand," Kim said sheepishly as she took the items from Mrs. Spahl.

"There will be time to deal with what's happened," Mrs. Spahl assured her as she rubbed Kim's arms. "Right now, our safety is in each other's hands. That begins with getting yourself fed and hydrated."

"What then?" Matt demanded. "Hmmm, what do you want?" He tipped his head back and took a long drink from the bottle. The cold water felt good against the back of his dry throat. He ran his bandaged left hand across his mouth and continued. "Nobody, family or not wishes my brother ill and gets away with it."

"Don't hurt him again!" Patrick blurted. "You want to know what I want...that's it! Don't hurt my brother again!"

"Fine, Pat. So long as he watches his mouth," Matt agreed with a shrug.

"How are Josh and Kerri?" Mrs. Spahl asked as Mr. Spahl returned to the group.

"Not great," Mr. Spahl answered as he peeled the black Nitrile gloves off his hands. He motioned to the cooler. "May I get a bottle of water please?"

"Of course," Mrs. Spahl answered as she reached in the cooler. "Were you able to help them?"

"We got Josh's lip to stop bleeding and gave him a cold pack for the swelling," Mr. Spahl explained. He took a long drink from the bottle. A look of deep concern covered his face. "There's nothing I can do for Kerri. Her injuries are internal. She needs a hospital."

"What about Ralph?" Matt asked as he turned his attention away from his cousin. "How is he?"

"Ralph?" Mr. Spahl asked before he took another long drink from the bottle. "Still unconscious, but we stopped the bleeding."

"QuikClot comes in handy," Christian added as he joined the group.

"Yes, it does," Mr. Spahl agreed. He finished drinking and turned back to his wife. "Another bottle please."

"Where are we with cell service?"

"It was out last I checked," Kurt answered. He took his phone out of his pocket and looked at the screen. "No, still nothing."

"No bars?" Christian asked.

"Not evening roaming," Kurt answered.

"It's only day three," Christian muttered as he turned his attention back to Mr. Spahl. "Did you use packing gauze?"

Mr. Spahl nodded, "Yes, and the emergency trauma dressing."

"North American Rescue," Christian said. "That company makes exceptional products."

"Yes, they do," Mr. Spahl agreed as he twisted the cap off the second bottle.

"How is my brother?" Patrick asked.

"He's concussed," Mr. Spahl answered.

"How bad?"

"I'm sorry, Patrick," Mr. Spahl said before he took another sip of water. "I don't feel qualified to answer that."

"What about his ankle?" Patrick asked as his cheeks turned a deep shade of red.

"Not great," Mr. Spahl answered bluntly. He motioned towards Christian. "We splinted it as best we could but he needs X-rays and possibly an MRI."

"Bottom line?" Patrick asked as he became visibly agitated.

"Your brother needs a hospital," Mr. Spahl answered. "The injury to his ankle is substantial. It could result in a blood clot and be fatal if left untreated."

"Christ," Patrick uttered as he looked up towards the sky. He exhaled deeply and clasped his hands behind his head. "Can I see him?"

"Of course," Mr. Spahl answered. He motioned towards the Jeep. "You mother and sister are with him and Marcus is over there too."

"Thanks," Patrick said as he cleared his throat. "Let me go check on him." He added before he hurried off.

"Where's Paul?" Matt asked.

"With Ralph," Mr. Spahl replied. "He'll be over in a few to eat." He continued. "Let me see your hand."

"It's fine," Matt said as he looked at the soiled bandages that covered his left hand. "It just throbs a little."

"Stop being stubborn and let me see your hand," Mr. Spahl ordered. "We need to change the bandages."

As the cloud cover broke, golden rays of sunshine illuminated the valley. Droplets of water glistened as they fell from the pine branches. The joyful chirp of birds returned and filled the air as it warmed.

Jeff adjusted his stance. He could feel his lower back tighten. His stomach growled as a headache started behind his eyes. He glanced around, "We need to leave." He said to himself. "We shouldn't be out here in the open like this."

"We can't go to the farm," Kerri whispered from where she lay. The ibuprofen did little to temper the pain. "We can't..."

"I know, mom," Matt Chico said. He gently slid a rolled-up sweatshirt under her head as a makeshift pillow. "Here this should make you a little more comfortable."

"Your mother and I need medical care," Josh grumbled from the front seat.

"I know dad," Matt Chico acknowledged. Exhausted his legs weakened and his body slowly dropped to the ground. He pressed himself against the back tire and covered his face with his hands. "I just need a minute..."

"Your brother should be to the house soon," Josh continued. "I doubt the rain slowed them down. We need to hurry or they'll get home before us."

"Please dad," Matt Chico pleaded as tears poured from his eyes. "Just...just stop."

Jeff exhaled and felt his shoulders relax and drop slightly. He closed his eyes, tipped his head back and let the sun warm his face. The valley had a peaceful quality he wasn't sure if he appreciated until now. He let the sling take the weight of the rifle as his arms dropped to his sides. "I need to eat something." He said to himself.

"I've been meaning to ask you two," Mr. Spahl began. He soaked several pieces of gauze with peroxide and used them to clean the lacerations on Matt's left hand. "How did you guys accumulate all this stuff?"

"All what stuff?" Christian asked as he took a sandwich and bottle of water from Mrs. Spahl. "Thank you." He said with a nod. "The medical supplies?"

"That and...well all of it," Mr. Spahl said as he used his forearm to wipe sweat from his forehead. Fatigue consumed his body as the adrenaline high subsided. "The medical supplies, firearms, ammunition, gear. All of it."

"If I said it was about being prepared, I don't think that would surprise anyone," Matt offered as he glanced over at Christian. "Beyond that though there's a historical precedent. You want to explain?"

"Historical precedent?" Mr. Spahl questioned curiously. "That's interesting. Let's hear it."

"The American Revolution," Christian began. He motioned back towards the sign for Continental Valley. "The war effort was funded by the Continental Congress, and also by a number of private citizens."

"It's been a long time since I took a history class," Mr. Spahl admitted as he placed several pieces of gauze over Matt's palm. "But that sounds vaguely familiar."

"The one I'm speaking of," Christian continued. "Has to do specifically with Ethan Allen."

"He was instrumental in founding the Republic of Vermont, if I'm not mistaken," Mr. Spahl offered as he rebandaged Matt's hand.

"That's correct," Christian said with a nod. "He also founded and led the Green Mountain Boys and is probably best known for capturing Fort Ticonderoga from the British in 1775."

"That sounds familiar also," Mr. Spahl replied. "What's the connection?"

"Ethan Allen, outfitted the Green Mountain Boys himself," Christian explained. "Out of his own pocket. He made sure they had food, clothes, weapons, whatever they needed. He made sure they were trained and together they did the impossible."

"I don't think I knew that part of the story," Mr. Spahl acknowledged. He wrapped three long strands of white medical tape around Matt's hand. "There!" He spoke. "Try not to do anything to strenuous. Those cuts are starting to heal."

"Thanks," Matt said as he looked at his palm. "Do we have any more food?"

"I'm sure we can find you something," Mrs. Spahl said as she opened the cooler.

"So, if I understand," Mr. Spahl began. "Those who have the ability, have the responsibility?"

"Something like that," Christian answered. "We set out to equip ourselves. After we did, the next logical step was to outfit and equip the people we trust."

"Building a community?" Mr. Spahl clarified.

"Exactly," Matt said as he opened another sandwich and took a bite.

"There's also a biblical precedent," Paul announced as he joined the group.

"And what's that?" Mrs. Spahl asked as her ears perked up.

"Abraham and the battle of Siddim," Paul answered.

"If I remember correctly, Siddim was also known as the valley of the salt sea or dead sea," Mrs. Spahl added.

"The very same," Paul said with a nod. "Somebody knows their good book."

Mrs. Spahl grinned and nodded, "I've felt the need."

"Outstanding," Paul bellowed. "Abraham armed and trained 318 of his own men. He led those men at the battle of Siddim. There he defeated the four kings and rescued his nephew Lot."

"I'm embarrassed to say I'm less familiar with Abraham's exploits," Mr. Spahl said. "Please explain the connection. What does it all mean."

"To me?" Paul asked. "It means we take care of our own. These two maniacs." He continued as he motioned to Matt and Christian. "These two have given us gun belts, holsters, magazines, IFAKs. They didn't wait until something happened. They've been slowly equipping us for years, and now here we are..."

"And where's that?" Kurt interrupted. "It looks to me like we're broken down on the side of the road and some of us are badly injured."

"No plan or preparation is flawless," Paul answered as he shot Kurt a stern look. "The fact of the matter is, there are more of us standing than aren't."

Mrs. Spahl tapped her husband on the shoulder, "Call him back please. He needs to eat."

Mr. Spahl nodded, "Jeff!" He called as he stepped into the middle of the street and motioned with his arm. "Come on back!"

Jeff turned, looked back towards the group, and gave a wave of acknowledgement.

"Maybe so," Kurt admitted. "But from where I'm standing broken down on the side of the road is a long way from being safe."

"Stop it," Kim insisted as she jabbed Kurt in the ribs with her elbow. "Just stop it."

"No, that's alright. Let him talk," Paul said as he took a step towards Kurt. He continued as he pointed a knife hand at Kurt's chest. "We may not be safe…yet. But we're alive and there are enough of us proficient with firearms to keep the rest of YOU safe."

Mr. Spahl motioned again for Jeff to return, "Come back and get something to eat."

Jeff hurried back to the group, "Everything alright?" He asked as he reached the Tahoe and saw the look on Paul's face.

"Everything's ok," Mrs. Spahl answered. "Just a heated discussion. We're all a bit on edge. Here, you need to eat something." She said as she handed her son a sandwich and bottle of water.

"Thanks," Jeff said as he sunk his teeth into the sandwich. "Food always tastes better when you're starving." He added as he took another bite. He motioned to lump on Matt's forehead. "You alright? You look like you lost a fight."

"Thanks Jeff," Matt said as he shook his head. "I assure you I feel worse."

"Paul, would you like something to eat?" Mrs. Spahl asked.

"Please," Paul answered as he lowered his hand and took a step back. "I almost forgot how hungry I was."

"What would you like?" Mrs. Spahl asked. "We've got turkey and cheese or salami and cheese."

"One of each please," Paul answered. "Do we have coffee by any chance?"

"No, I'm sorry," Mrs. Spahl said as she handed him the sandwiches. "Only water."

"Try this," Matt offered. He took a plastic bag from the cargo pocket on his tactical pants.

"What are those?" Jeff asked. "They look like hand rolled cigarettes."

"They're not," Christian said. "It's something far worse."

"It's not worse," Matt said as he opened the bag. "It's just coffee grounds wrapped in a small coffee filter." He explained as he removed one from the bag and shoved it in the left side of his mouth between his cheek and gum.

"Definitely worse," Paul said with a smirk. "Let me eat these and then I'll try one."

"How's your car?" Jeff asked. "It looked serious."

"The car's done," Matt answered as he moved the coffee filter around in his mouth. "We'll need to unload everything and figure out where we have room in the other vehicles."

"So, what's the plan?" Jeff asked as he finished the sandwich.

"Unload the Grand Marquis and get back on the road," Matt answered.

"We need to get to a hospital," Mr. Spahl said. He cupped his hands around the red Bic lighter as he held the flame to the tip of the cigarette clenched between his teeth. "There's no way around it." He continued as he handed the crumpled pack and lighter to Paul.

"Thanks," Paul said as he removed a cigarette and lit it. "Agreed, we need a hospital."

"The way I see it," Christian began. "We have three options. The only problem is all three have received wounded personnel from the arsenal."

"Given what we know now, that definitely increases the risk," Jeff added.

"Which one's the closest and won't put us too far off our route?" Matt asked.

"Saint Peters, is the furthest I think," Mr. Spahl said. "Not to mention it's back the way we came and well out of our way."

"Two towns over," Christian added. "That's not going to work."

"Let me have the lighter please," Jeff said as he bit down on the end of the cigarette between his teeth.

"Sure thing," Paul said as he handed Jeff the lighter. "There's the Good Shepard."

"That's back the way we came also," Christian explained. "That would take us right back through the center of town."

"We can't do that again," Mr. Spahl said.

"Please," Kim pleaded. "We can't go through that again."

"Don't worry, honey," Mrs. Spahl assured her. "We're not going back through that."

"Neither of those sound feasible," Jeff said. He took a long drag off the cigarette and handed the lighter back to his father.

"There's Saint Mary's in Stone Land Park," Christian explained. "I think that's going to be our best bet."

Matt nodded, "Yeah, probably. When we come to the end of the valley, we'll have to go a few miles in the opposite direction but it'll put us closer to the farm than either of the other two."

"They're supposed to have the best trauma center in the area," Christian added.

"Let's just hope it's still intact," Mr. Spahl said. He used his thumb to flick ash from the end of his cigarette. "Tyler's ankle, Ralph's gunshot wound and Kerri's internal injuries…"

"We're not going with you," Matt Chico interrupted as he joined the group. No one heard him approach. It startled everyone momentarily when he spoke. His voice was raspy and his eyes had a fatigue about them a good night's sleep would not correct. "I'm sorry, but we can't go with you."

"Chico, what are you talking about?" Christian asked as he turned to face his friend. "Of course, you're coming with us."

"I can't," Matt Chico said bluntly. His voice was shaky and his mind was made up. "I'm taking my parents to Good Shepard hospital, then I'm taking them home."

"Chico, are you sure?" Matt asked.

"I am," Matt Chico answered with a nod. "I can't take the chance my brother will get home and we won't be there. I can't put my son through that."

Everyone was quiet for a moment. The only sound as they stood on the desolate stretch of road was the chirp of birds and rustle of wind through the trees.

"Sounds like you've made up your mind," Christian said as placed his hand on Matt Chico's shoulder.

Matt Chico nodded, "I have." He said as he rubbed his eyes.

"Do what you need to do," Christian said empathetically.

"I'm sorry," Matt Chico began. "I didn't want to let you guys down..."

"You didn't let anybody down and no apologies," Christian insisted as he hugged his friend. "Take care of your parents and stay safe. You know where we'll be."

"Yeah," Matt Chico said as he nodded and wiped tears from his eyes. "I know."

"Get your parents to the hospital and fixed up," Christian encouraged. "Once you've got your brother and son squared away, if this isn't resolved, get to us. No matter what it takes, get to us."

"I will," Matt Chico assured him as a lump formed in his throat. His cheeks reddened and the tears at the corners of his eyes streamed down his cheeks. "Come hell or high water, I will see you both on the farm."

"I know you will Chico," Matt said as he put his hand on his friend's shoulder. "I just wish we could send someone with you."

"I appreciate that Matt," Matt Chico said as he brushed tears from his face. "This is something I've got to do myself. Just keep everybody else safe and look after each other."

"We will," Christian assured him.

"Tell Bill I'll be over in a bit and to please save me a seat at the table," Matt Chico uttered before he covered his face with his hands and began to sob.

"We'll let him know," Matt assured him. He wrapped his arms around Matt Chico and hugged him. "We'll have a seat at the table saved for you. Just make sure you get there."

"You guys are more than my friends. You're my brothers," Matt Chico said as he cleared his throat and composed himself. "Thank you."

"Give me a squeeze Chico," Christian said as he embraced his friend. "Don't make us come looking for you."

"I won't," Matt Chico assured him. "I won't."

Jeff waited with open arms to say goodbye to his friend, "You better come back, cause somebody's got to help me keep an eye on these two maniacs." He joked as he motioned towards Matt and Christian.

Matt Chico scoffed and nodded, "You got it, Jeff."

"Alright, that's enough of all this emotional stuff," Christian insisted as put his hand on Matt Chico's shoulder. "I'm going to take Chico and get him outfitted with some gear."

The mood was somber as the cloud cover dissipated and midday sun radiated warmth over the valley. Christian guided Matt Chico to the back of the Subaru and began to organize supplies.

"HEY!" Patrick shouted from the middle of the road. He waved his arms frantically. "HEY, RALPH IS AWAKE!"

"Come on!" Paul shouted as he slapped Mr. Spahl on the back. "Ralph's awake. We've got to check on him."

"Let's go," Mr. Spahl said as the two of them hurried down the road towards the Jeep.

"Kim," Matt said as he motioned to Kurt. "May I borrow him for a minute?"

"Sure," Kim answered skeptically. "Is everything ok?"

"Of course," Matt said with a nod. "I just need to talk to Kurt for a minute."

"Matty?" Kurt stammered.

"Come on, let's walk out a ways," Matt encouraged. He positioned his rifle sling over his right shoulder and motioned for Kurt to follow him. "We can keep watch while they're getting squared away."

"Matty," Kurt inquired as they walked out well beyond the rest of the group. "Where are we going?"

"What are you doing?" Matt asked as he finally stopped and turned to face Kurt. The expression on his face was stern.

"What do you mean?" Kurt stammered.

"What do I mean?" Matt questioned. "Getting mouthy with Paul. That's what I mean." He said as he pointed an accusatory finger at Kurt. "So let me ask you again. What are you doing?"

"Matty..." Kurt began.

"You realize none of us can physically stop him?" Matt stated bluntly. "So, if you go picking a fight with him..."

"Matty," Kurt pleaded as he held up his hands. "That's not what I was doing."

"Are you sure?" Matt chided. "Because from where I was standing it looked like you were."

"What do you want me to say?" Kurt asked with a deep look of concern on his face.

"I'm just trying to figure out where your head's at," Matt explained.

Kurt stood for a moment as his face reddened. He shook his head and looked away, "Matty, I'm scared."

"We'll all scared," Matt said bluntly. "All of us."

"Not like this!" Kurt blurted as he rubbed his eyes. "I'm fucking terrified."

"Terrified?" Matt repeated.

"Yes, goddammit. I'm terrified of what's happening," Kurt admitted. His body trembled as his breathing quickened. "I'm terrified of not knowing if we're going to see our parents or siblings again. I'm terrified that I'm not going to be able to protect her." He blurted as his face contorted and tears ran from his eyes.

"Ok, ok. It's alright," Matt offered. He cupped his right hand around the back of Kurt's neck and pulled him close. "It's going to be alright." He assured Kurt. "You know that you and Kim are my favorite young couple. We're not going to let anything happen to either of you. Everything's going to be alright."

"Promise Matty?" Kurt asked desperately.

"I promise," Matt said as he locked eyes with Kurt. "But listen to me, you need to blow off steam you tell me. No more poking the bear."

Kurt cleared his throat and tried to regain his composure, "Alright, Matty."

"Good," Matt said. "We've got you. Christian and I have got you both. We're not going to let anything happen to you." He added as they started to walk back towards the rest of the group. "Come on, I've got to say good bye to Chico."

"How much did you say was in here?" Matt Chico asked as he placed the large duffle bag in the trunk of the Roadmaster.

"You've got enough food and water for three days," Christian explained. "Take these." He continued as he handed Matt Chico a Mossberg 500 shotgun and OD green ammo can. "Here, there's fifty 2 ¾ inch 00 buck shells."

"Are you sure you can spare them?" Matt Chico asked.

Christian nodded, "Yes. Here take this." He added and handed Matt Chico a Ruger P89DC pistol, three fifteen round magazines and a box of ammunition.

"Thank you," Matt Chico said with a grateful nod.

"You've trained with both of these," Christian reminded him. "Do you remember how to use them?"

"I do," Matt Chico assured him. He checked the magwell and retraced the slide to ensure the chamber was empty. "How many 9mm rounds?"

"That's a Federal, hundred round range pack," Christian answered. "Plus, each of the three magazines holds fifteen rounds. Go ahead and load it."

Matt Chico slammed one of the magazines in the magwell and racked the slide. He used his right thumb to depress the decocking lever, "Heavier than I remember." He said as he slid the pistol in his waistband.

"Stress and adrenaline," Christian said as he slammed the trunk closed. "Keep the extra mags close by. Hopefully you won't need them...but just in case."

Matt Chico nodded, "Will do." He said and checked on his mother one more time. "You alright mom?"

Kerri gave a slight nod but didn't open her eyes.

Matt Chico gave Christian one last hug before he got in the car, "We'll see you soon." He said as he started the engine.

"Looking forward to it," Christian said. "Be careful!"

"We will," Matt Chico assured him without looking up. He pulled the gear shift down into drive. Too upset to watch his friends vanish from the rearview mirror, Matt Chico kept his eyes on the road and his thoughts focused on the journey ahead.

Matt and Christian stood stoically in the middle of the road and waved as the Roadmaster pulled slowly away. They watched as the large sedan maneuvered around the first bend and disappeared. Neither of them was sure if they would ever see Matt Chico or his parents again.

"Do you think we made the right decision bringing everyone out here?" Matt asked.

"We didn't force anyone to come with us," Christian answered. "You drove through the same town I did. Do you think we could have stayed?"

"No, I don't think we could have stayed," Matt answered as they turned back to the rest of the group. "What now?"

"We made a plan," Christian said. "Keep our people safe and get to the farm."

"We didn't plan for a detour to the hospital," Matt reminded.

"Some things are out of our control," Christian said as they walked. Their boots made a distinct sound against the asphalt. "Sometimes even the best plans need to be altered."

"Then let's finish the journey," Matt said with a nod.

"Agreed," Christian said as they reached the rest of the group. "Let's finish the journey."

CHAPTER 17

welcome to wherever you are

S HADOWS RETURNED AS THE sun again slipped behind dark gray clouds. The breeze slowed and an oppressive veil of humidity descended on the valley.

"You see the irony in it?" Matt asked as he gave the charred engine a final look.

"In what?" Christian responded impatiently as he scanned the area. "Come on we need to get back on the road."

"We couldn't take Anthony to the hospital," Matt said as he pressed his hands against the open hood and shook his head. "And now we're headed there anyway."

"Anthony wouldn't have made it," Christian insisted as he squeeze the Hogue grip on his AR15. "You saw what kind of shape he was in at the end. I mean you..."

"I know!" Matt interrupted sternly as he held his hands up. "You don't have to remind me. Believe me, that's something I'll never forget."

"We need to leave," Christian said as he quickly changed the subject. "Is the gear loaded?"

"Yeah, it's all loaded," Matt answered as he slammed the hood closed. He shook his head and rubbed his eyes. "I loved this car."

"It's just a car," Christian reminded him. "Let's go. We've got more important things to take care of."

"Yes, we do," Matt agreed. He adjusted the rifle sling over his right shoulder before he picked up the large black duffle bag and Pelican V700 rifle case from where they lay on the road. "How long have we been stopped?"

"Less than twenty minutes," Christian answered as he glanced down at the Garmin Instinct Crossover Tactical watch fastened around his left wrist.

"Christ, it feels like we've been out here for hours," Matt commented as he shook his head. His gaze moved skyward as he continued. "We might get some more rain."

"Come on," Christian urged as he continued to scan the area. "We've been out in the open long enough."

All around droplets of water fell from dark green needles at the end of pine branches. They glistened against sparse golden rays that escaped through breaks in the cloud cover as they dropped towards the ground. Hungry and exhausted, Matt and Christian moved slowly back towards the group. As they neared there was an unmistakable fatigue on the faces and in the posture of their friends and family.

"We can't stay with them," Katherine said quietly. She huddled next to her mother, Patrick, and Marcus away from the rest of the group. "We'll end up like Tyler or worse."

"Oh, Katherine," Aunt Athena whimpered. "Don't say that."

"It's true mom," Katherine hissed through clenched teeth. Her cheeks reddened as she continued. "You know I'm right!"

"Katherine," Patrick growled. "How can you say that?"

"They're not taking us to the farm to keep us safe," Katherine said bluntly.

"Katherine, please," Aunt Athena pleaded. "I need to get home. I need to bury your father..."

"Katherine!" Patrick interrupted. "What are you saying? Of course they're trying to keep us safe!"

"You know Matt's mind," Katherine insisted. "He doesn't want to live on the farm...that's where he wants to die."

"Katherine...NO!" Patrick blurted as his eyes widened. "No...that's not..."

"Where would we go?" Marcus interrupted. He was visibly flustered and his hands trembled. "How would we get there? We don't have a car?"

"Later," Katherine said as she looked around. "They might hear us. We'll discuss it later."

"Come on, everybody," Mrs. Spahl insisted as she continued to hand out bottles of water. "You need to stay hydrated."

"Are there any more sandwiches left?" Kurt asked as he guided Kim towards the Subaru.

"No, I'm sorry. Just a few granola bars," Mrs. Spahl answered. "We should have made more. I didn't know we were going to skip breakfast."

Jeff took a seat on the ground. He let out a sigh of exhaustion as he rested his body against the back tire of the Tahoe, "Thanks, mom." He said as he gladly accepted the bottle of water from his mother. He unscrewed the cap and took a long drink.

"I could have really used another sandwich," Kurt mumbled as he opened the back hatch of the Subaru. He motioned to Kim. "Come and sit down."

"I'm not sure I'll want to get back up," Kim said as she took a seat on the back bumper next to Kurt. Her cheeks were flushed and her blonde hair was soaked with sweat. "I feel like I could fall asleep right here."

"Come on," Kurt encouraged as he wrapped his arm around her. "Close your eyes for a minute and rest you head on my shoulder."

Paul pulled the back door of the Jeep open, "Ralph." He growled. "You ok back here?"

"He's out again," Tyler muttered just above a whisper. His face contorted with pain. "When are we leaving?"

"Soon," Paul assured him as he pressed his fingers against Ralph's neck. He was somewhat relieved to find Ralph's pulse steady. "We're leaving soon. Just hang in there."

Mr. Spahl looked down at the Expedition North Ridge watch on his left wrist, "Come on." He whispered to himself as he shook his head. Beads of sweat ran down his face. His right hand rested on the grip of the 1911 as he kept watch. "It's time to go."

"What do you think we'll find once we leave the valley?" Matt asked. Their boots echoed against the wet asphalt as they walked.

"Can't imagine it's going to be better than what we've seen," Christian answered. He used his left hand to retrieve his inhaler from the pocket of his coveralls.

"What about the hospital?" Matt asked as he adjusted his grip on the rifle case and duffle bag.

"I think it'll be a mess," Christian replied. He shook his inhaler and took two quick puffs. "But we have to try."

"Yeah," Matt agreed. "I guess we do."

"We couldn't have saved them," Christian said bluntly.

"Uncle Tony and Anthony?" Matt asked. He twisted his head from side to side and attempted to keep the fatigue that clamored up the back of his neck at bay.

"Yes," Christian answered. "We did everything possible."

"I know," Matt acknowledged. "But we're here now and I'm not ready to lose anybody else."

"Neither am I," Christian said quietly.

Matt glanced over at his brother as they neared the group. He noticed Christian's right hand moved from the grip of his rifle to his abdomen, "You alright?"

"Fine," Christian answered. His tone indicated he didn't want to be asked again. "I just hope Chico makes it to the farm."

"Me too," Matt replied. "I understand why he left though."

"Doesn't make it any easier," Christian said as they joined the rest of the group near the vehicles.

"No, it does not," Matt acknowledged. "You alright Jeff?"

"I'm good," Jeff answered from where he sat. "Just thinking."

"What about?" Matt asked.

"Alaska," Jeff said as he rubbed his temples. "Our trip up north to visit Aaron."

"That was a good time," Matt said as he placed the rifle case and duffle bag on the ground. "The look on his face when I showed up at the baggage carousel."

"He didn't you know were coming," Jeff said as he managed a slight grin.

"That was a hell of a trip," Matt said stoically.

"Yes, it was," Jeff agreed. "One hell of a trip."

"What's got you thinking about that?" Matt asked as he knelt next to the duffle bag and rifle case.

"Just the trees," Jeff answered. "The quiet."

"Yeah, the quiet," Matt said as he looked around cautiously.

"Rember Crow's Pass?" Jeff asked as he closed his eyes and tipped his head back. "The only sound was the wind through the trees and the river..."

"We need to get back on the road," Mr. Spahl interrupted. "Are all the supplies loaded?"

"They are," Matt answered as he opened the rifle case. "Most everything is in the Subaru and Tahoe."

"What about the Jeep?" Mr. Spahl asked.

"Had to make room so we could put the seats down," Paul answered as he joined the group. The M1A hung on the 3-point sling in front of him.

"How's Ralph?" Matt asked as he unzipped the duffle bag.

"Unconscious again," Paul answered. He lit another cigarette and took a long drag. Gray smoke snaked from his nostrils as he spoke. "His pulse is steady. What's the plan?"

"I was wondering when you were going break those out," Jeff said as he pulled himself off the ground and walked over to Matt.

"It's time," Matt replied with a nod. "Alright, Christian and I will be in the lead vehicle with Aunt Athena, Katherine and Marcus."

"What about Patrick?" Aunt Athena cried.

"He's in the Jeep with Paul, Ralph and Tyler," Matt answered.

"I want Patrick with me," Aunt Athena protested.

"Paul since you've got the wounded, we're going to put you in the middle," Matt continued as he ignored his aunt.

"Copy that," Paul said as he flicked ash from the end of his cigarette.

"No!" Aunt Athena shrieked. "Patrick needs to be with me."

"Christ," Matt muttered dismissively as he shook his head. "Mr. Spahl can you pull up the rear?"

"So long as we hurry up and get back on the road," Mr. Spahl answered.

"Two minutes," Christian interjected. "We don't know what we're going to find when we get to the hospital so we need to get this straight now."

"Jeff, give your father the Mini-14," Matt instructed. "Get your AR15 and make sure you swap the mags in your plate carrier."

"On it," Jeff said as he handed his father the rifle. He hurried to the back of the Tahoe and retrieved his AR15 from the black polymer Bushmaster case. He filled the magazine pouches on his plate carrier with PMAGs and hurried back to the group. "Mags!" Jeff called as he handed his father three aluminum rifle magazines.

"Front seat," Mr. Spahl instructed as he motioned to the SUV. He retracted the charging handle enough to verify there was a round in the chamber, engaged the safety and slung the Mini-14 over his left shoulder. "Alright, what's next?"

"Let's hurry before the rain starts again," Paul said as the low rumble of thunder echoed in the distance. He took a final drag from the cigarette and flicked the smoldering butt towards a shallow puddle on the side of the road.

"Did you check your gear?" Matt asked. He took two Omega Elite drop leg magazine pouches from the duffle bag and handed them to Christian and Jeff. "Loop these through your battle belts."

"I did," Paul answered as he motioned to his chest rig and drop leg holster. "Loaded and ready."

"Pat, it's time," Christian said as Matt handed him an Omega Elite tactical vest and shell pouch from the duffle bag.

"For what?" Patrick asked timidly.

"You're proficient with a firearm," Matt said.

"I...I," Patrick stammered as he took a step forward. "I mean, I've shot with you guys and hunted with my dad."

"I don't want him carrying a gun," Aunt Athena insisted. She grabbed Patrick's arm and tried to pull him back towards her.

"STOP!" Christian ordered. "We don't have time for this!"

"We don't know what we're going to find when we get to the hospital," Matt began. He pointed at his cousin from where he knelt and spoke sternly. "Unless the building is on fire or the parking lot is the wild west, we're going in."

"NO!" Aunt Athena shrieked.

"We need every able-bodied man," Christian said firmly as he handed his cousin the tactical vest. "Put it on."

"Katherine, take her please," Patrick said as he struggled to break free from his mother's grasp. He took the vest from Christian, pulled it on over his t-shirt and zipped it up. "Ok, now what?"

"Come on mom. It's ok," Katherine said. She took her mother by the shoulders as she glared at her brother. "He's made up his mind."

"You've got a Glock 19, compact 9mm in the cross-draw holster," Christian explained. "The magazine is loaded but the chamber is empty. Remember that."

"Got it," Patrick said as he tapped the holster cautiously with his left hand. "Mag loaded, chamber empty."

"Yes," Christian acknowledged as he continued. "The mag pouches over your left chest have three additional 15-round pistol magazines. The larger mag pouches on your right side have three 30-round PMAGs. Those are back up in case we run out."

"Come on Marcus," Katherine instructed as she pulled her mother away from the group. "Help me get my mother to the car."

"Should we wait?" Marcus asked cautiously.

"No," Katherine chided. "Let them play their macho bullshit."

"Ok," Patrick said with a nod. "I remember you taught me how to shoot the Glock."

"Good," Christian said. "You're also going to need a long gun."

"We're giving you Christian's Mossberg 590 shotgun," Matt said as he handed the shotgun to Patrick. "The safety's engaged. You've got seven shots in the magazine and another six on the side saddle and four in the speed feed stock."

Patrick took the shotgun cautiously and kept the barrel pointed towards the ground, "Seven in the magazine." He repeated with a nod. "Ok."

"There's a shell in the chamber," Christian informed his cousin. "To disengage the safety, you need to push the button on top of the receiver forward. When you see the red dot, you're ready to fire. Any questions?"

"No," Patrick answered. He looked at the shotgun and shook his head. "I shot this before. I remember the stock and the ghost ring sights."

"Fasten this around your waist," Matt instructed as he handed Patrick the brown leather shell pouch. "You've got thirty extra shells in there."

"If something happens, Pat," Christian began as he locked eyes with his cousin. "If you run out of shells, the gun jams, anything and you need to transition to your pistol put the empty magazines down the front of your shirt. Without the magazines the pistol is useless."

"I understand," Patrick acknowledged confidently. "I can do that."

Matt unclipped the Kydex holster from the tactical mount on his Scorpion belt. He placed it and the P220 in the duffle bag along with the magazines and retrieved another holster and pistol.

"What about us?" Kurt asked from where he and Kim sat.

Christian glanced over at Kurt and shook his head, "Not until we've trained you."

Matt released the retention canopy and slid the Sig 1911 Emperor Scorpion from the holster. He disengaged the thumb safety and checked the chamber. Satisfied, he returned the pistol to the holster and fastened it to the mount.

"Just passengers again," Kurt muttered with a yawn. "Oh, well."

"Stop," Kim insisted. She gave Kurt a stiff jab in the ribs with her elbow. "Just stop."

Matt took a Sig 1911 Emperor Scorpion Fastback from the duffle bag and secured it in the Condor HT holster on the front of his plate carrier. Then he filled the mag pouches on his belt and plate carrier with Wilson Combat ETM mags, "Last thing." He called. "From here on out we stay in constant contact. Each vehicle gets a Midland GXT720 walkie talkie. Keep them set to channel 10 subchannel 10. If the channel gets compromised, call Delta Hotel. That'll be the signal to switch to channel 2 subchannel 1."

"When we get to the hospital, Jeff and I will take point," Christian explained. "Matt, you and Paul will need to carry Tyler and Ralph."

"We can do that," Matt said as he got to his feet.

"Mr. Spahl, we'll need you and Pat in the parking lot to secure the perimeter," Christian continued. "Everybody else stay in the vehicles until we've got things secured."

Mr. Spahl nodded and looked over at Patrick, "You up for this?"

Patrick gave an unconvincing nod and stammered, "Ye...yeah. I'm good."

"What if the hospital's compromised?" Jeff asked as he positioned the AR15's two-point sling over his right shoulder.

"We're taking the detour," Christian answered. "We're going to find a doctor, even if we have to fight our way through."

"Once we're inside, we need to move fast," Matt added. "The longer we take the more exposed we are. If we have to engage, do it quick. Put the threat down and keep moving forward. Don't get distracted. Don't get separated and..."

"Hey!" Paul interrupted as he held his left hand up. There was an urgency in his voice. "Do you hear that?"

"Hear what?" Jeff asked as he looked around.

"The birds stopped chirping," Paul explained as he stepped into the middle of the road and looked back the way they came. An eerie silence fell over the valley. "We're leaving. Everybody in the vehicles now!" He ordered. "Move!"

Raindrops splashed against the windshields as the caravan departed from the side of the road. The stop provided a much-needed break and opportunity to take a breath, but the group found a level of safety in not remaining static.

The vehicles were cramped with bodies and supplies. A few minutes down the road, they passed the entrance to the historic site, with its picnic tables, hiking trails and memories. It marked the half way point through the valley and an innocence this life no longer afforded them.

Christian glanced into the rearview mirror to ensure the other two vehicles were still behind him, "Places to be." He said as he shifted into fourth gear and pressed the gas pedal to the floor.

Pine trees moved quickly past the windows as the caravan sped through the winding road. The trees became sparser as they neared the end of the valley.

Matt brought the walkie talkie up to his mouth and pressed the PTT button, "County Road 118 turn off, two hundred yards." He called as the Subaru passed the blue and gold metal sign. "Repeat, County Road 118 turn off two hundred yards on the right."

The speaker crackled, "Copy that." Paul's voice boomed.

"Roger," Mr. Spahl called. "We are clear back. How's the front?"

"Front is clear," Matt answered. "Pine trees and storm clouds."

The vehicles quickly arrived at the turn off. It was not a heavily traveled stretch of road. Despite its beauty, there was something unsettling about the area. An urban legend dated back to the turn of the century and claimed the area to be haunted.

Christian took his foot off the gas and let the Subaru slow down. The area looked clear as he scanned the terrain, "Here we go." He said as he tapped the breaks twice as a signal to Paul and downshifted into third gear.

"Keep it tight," Matt called into the walkie talkie.

One after the other the vehicles navigated through the turn.

"Good," Paul called.

The speaker crackled again, "Tahoe is clear." Mr. Spahl called.

"Everybody's through," Matt announced.

"Great," Christian said as he pulled the gear shifter back into fourth gear. "Let them know what's coming."

Matt pressed the PTT button, "County Road 118 for a few miles, then the four-way intersection." He explained. "Right turn puts us in New Haven town and three blocks from Saint Mary's hospital."

"Roger that," Paul's voice boomed. He glanced over at Patrick. "How you doing?"

"Nervous," Patrick admitted as he wiped sweat from his forehead.

"Yeah," Paul answered. "Me too."

"Good copy," Mr. Spahl responded. He glanced over at his son who occupied the front passenger seat. "You ready?"

Jeff nodded as he squeezed the AR15's black Hogue grip, "I'm ready."

The rain tapered off and in the distance the sky cleared. As they approached the intersection, a pillar of white smoke became visible as it rose from between the trees.

"An accident?" Matt suggested. He brought the AR15 up to his eye line and used the G33 magnifier behind the Eotech holographic sight to try and get a better look.

"Probably," Christian answered. "Based on the color of the smoke."

"Punctured radiator," Matt offered. "Antifreeze pouring over a hot engine."

"That'd be my guess," Christian said. "Better let everybody know."

"Can't make it out from here," Matt said as he lowered the rifle. He pressed the PTT button. "Smoke up ahead. It may be an accident. Keep the formation tight, watch for brake lights. Over."

"Copy that," Paul called.

"Copy," Mr. Spahl answered.

Christian took his foot off the gas and let the Subaru drift into the middle of the road. He glanced up at the rearview mirror and watched as the other two vehicles followed suit.

As they neared, a black Cadillac Escalade came into view. The front tires were flat and the vehicle was disabled diagonally in the center of the intersection. Shattered glass littered the area. A portion of the front end lay in the street several yards away. The hood was crumpled and white smoke poured from the exposed radiator.

Thick black skid marks covered the asphalt. They followed the path of a red Ford Transit van through the intersection, off the road and into the tall green grass where it overturned just before the tree line.

"What a mess," Christian said. He tapped the brakes twice and downshifted into second gear. The Subaru rolled slowly towards the stop sign. "I don't see anybody." He said as he surveyed the area. "We need to keep going."

"Movement!" Paul's voice boomed over the walkie talkie. The passenger side door of the Escalade creaked open. A bloody man with short sandy blond hair struggled to climb out. He pulled a short redhaired woman behind him.

"We don't have time for this!" Christian growled.

"Stop the car," Matt insisted as he checked the side mirror.

"What?" Christian questioned. "We can't stop!"

"Mr. Spahl already pulled over," Matt said as he opened the door. "Stop the car and let me out. I'll get everyone moving."

"This is a bad idea," Christian said as he stopped the Subaru. He moved the gear shifter back and forth and pulled the emergency brake up. "Nobody gets out of the car." He instructed. "Matt and I will check things out."

"I don't want to stop!" Katherine shouted from the back seat.

"Sit tight!" Christian ordered. "We'll be right back."

Matt scanned the road and tree line. He kept the AR15 at the low ready position as he made his way around the front of the car to his brother, "Clear." He called.

Christian was visibly agitated as he pulled the single point sling over his head and right shoulder, "How are we going to help these people? We don't have room for any more wounded."

"I know," Matt said as he pressed the PTT button on the walkie talkie. "Jeff, rear guard. Patrick, get up here and cover the front."

"On it," Jeff called. He positioned himself twenty yards behind the Tahoe. Jeff held the AR15 at the low ready position as he scanned the area for movement.

Patrick hurried to where Matt and Christian stood, "Where do you want me?"

"Twenty yards out," Christian said as he motioned to the intersection. "On the outside of the two disabled vehicles. Keep visual contact."

"Ok," Patrick answered. "Do you want to check the red van for survivors."

"NO!" Christian snapped. "I want you where I can see you. Safety off, eyes open. No cowboy shit."

"Got it," Patrick replied as he hurried to get into position. He held the shotgun at the high ready position as he looked nervously around.

"Help us," the man called. He steadied himself against the side of the Escalade. Blood ran from his nose down the front of his face. It saturated his goatee, white polo shirt and aqua colored cargo shorts in bright crimson.

The woman tried to walk but her legs gave out and she landed in a heap on the asphalt, "Ahhhh!" She moaned. Her upper body slumped against the running board. Dark red poured from an open wound on her left shoulder. Blood ran down her arm and soaked her white and blue floral pattered spring dress.

"Please help us," the man begged as he struggled to remain conscious. He used his left hand to check the front of his face. "Please, we need to get to a hospital."

"Hang on! We're coming to help," Mr. Spahl shouted. He pulled a pair of black nitrile gloves over his hands and collected gauze and bandages from the first aid kit.

"Right behind you," Paul called as he pulled a pair of gloves on and followed Mr. Spahl towards the Escalade.

"My wife has a fever and she's having trouble breathing," the man called as they approached. "Please hurry. She needs a hospital."

"Alright," Mr. Spahl answered. "Just hang on. We're going to get you checked out."

"I don't like this," Christian said as he scanned the area.

"You're bleeding badly from your nose and mouth. Try not to move," Mr. Spahl said as he put his hand on the man's left shoulder.

"My wife," the man pleaded as his eyes began to roll back in his head.

"Stay with me!" Mr. Spahl ordered. "Come on, stay with me."

"My wife," the man repeated. "She needs a hospital."

"We're going to help her next," Mr. Spahl assured him. "I want you to tip your head forward and hold this gauze against your nose. Do you understand."

"Please help her," the man insisted. His hand swayed as he tried to take the gauze.

"Your depth perception is off," Paul observed. "I think you've got a concussion."

The man blinked several times but didn't answer. He finally took the gauze and held it against his nose, "Please my wife." He pleaded as he motioned towards the woman. Blood and broken glass surrounded her motionless body.

"Fuck!" Christian snarled as he motioned to Matt. "Come on. We need to get over there."

"Paul, see if you can find him a place to sit down off the street," Mr. Spahl began. "I'm going to examine her and it would probably be better if he wasn't here."

"Hey!" Christian called as he and Matt hurried over. "We don't have time for this. We need to go!"

"We can't just leave them out here," Paul shouted. He turned his back to Christian as he helped the man to his feet. "Can you walk?"

"The fuck we can't!" Christian barked. "They're not our problem, and don't turn your back on me. I'm talking to you!"

"ENOUGH!" Mr. Spahl shouted. He knelt next to the woman as he continued. "They're injured and we need to..." He stopped abruptly, got to his feet, and backed up. He pointed to the wound on the woman's shoulder. "Is that a bite?"

Paul stepped back from the man, "Are you fucking bit?" He questioned as his right hand moved quickly to the grip of his 1911.

"Please my wife," the man sobbed. "I was trying to get her to the hospital..."

Matt brought the AR15 up to his shoulder and placed the Eotech's reticle on the back of the woman's head, "She's bit!"

"On your six," Christian said as he put his left hand on Matt's shoulder. He pulled the USP from his drop leg holster and moved behind his brother. He brought the pistol up as he checked the Escalade. "Is there anyone else in the vehicle?"

"Please the hospital is just down the road," the man pleaded as he held the gauze against his face. "My wife needs a doctor."

"Are you fucking bit?" Paul demanded.

"Please we need to get my wife to the hospital," the man continued as he ignored Paul's inquiry.

"Is there anyone else in the Escalade?" Christian demanded.

"No," the man whimpered. "It's just us. Please I was just trying to get her to the hospital. She's hurt."

"Is that a fucking bite?" Paul barked.

"Please help my wife…" the man groaned.

"Fuck your wife!" Paul snarled. "Answer my fucking question!"

Without warning the woman's body jerked. She lunged forward, grabbed her husband's left leg and sunk her teeth into his calf.

"NO, SUZANNE!" He screamed as his back arched and body convulsed with pain.

"Get behind me!" Matt ordered. He stepped forward and squeezed the trigger. The rifle thundered as the 5.56mm round ripped through the top of the woman's head. Blood and brain tissue rained down over her corpse.

"No!" the man cried as he dropped to his knees. Blood poured from the bite on his calf. He sobbed as he turned to his right and reached for the woman's body. "Suzanne, no…NO!"

Matt stepped back, trained the reticle on the man's head, and fired. The shot ripped through the man's temple. His head gave an audible smack as it bounced once off the asphalt as his body fell atop hers.

"What happened?" Jeff called as he and Patrick hurried to the Escalade.

"Is everyone alright?" Patrick asked.

"Safety!" Matt called as he pointed to the shotgun. His ears rang as he stepped away from the blood that pooled around the bodies.

"Got it," Patrick said as he engaged the safety on the shotgun. "Should we check the other vehicle?"

"Fuck no," Matt answered as he turned back towards his brother. "Leave it alone."

"This is why we don't stop to play red cross," Christian snarled angrily as he pointed at the bodies.

"We can't just leave people in need," Mr. Spahl argued as he peeled the gloves off his hands and threw them towards the road. "We can't!"

"We're not equipped to help," Christian said. He holstered the USP and fastened the retention band. "We don't have room. Two of our own need medical attention as it is. We can't afford to lose any more man power or resources."

"Easy," Matt said as he tried to defuse the situation. "We've still got a ways to go. Let's just get out of here."

"We're not stopping again until we get to the hospital. Is that clear?" Christian barked as he pointed an accusatory finger. "I don't care if we pass twin girls with pig tails and overalls, on the side of the road selling lemonade and giving puppies away. We're not fucking stopping!"

CHAPTER 18

and they are us

S TORM CLOUDS CLOSED IN. They held the sun hostage and shrouded the sky in dark gray. Bolts of purple and white lightening flashed over the tree tops, followed by the deep rumble of thunder. A substantial breeze picked up and ushered the caravan along.

"Storm's moving in," Matt said as he watched the sky ahead of them darken.

"That's alright," Christian answered. "We should be at the hospital in a couple minutes."

"The storm should cover any noise we make when we get there," Matt continued as he scanned the area.

"If it's anything like it's been, we'll need all the cover we can get," Christian said. There was a hint of disgust in his voice as he downshifted into third gear. "Better let them know."

"We're all struggling," Matt offered. He brought the walkie talkie up to his mouth and pressed the PTT button. "Vehicles up ahead. Looks tight, be careful. Over."

Abandoned and disabled vehicles littered both sides of the street. Blood pooled on the sidewalks and lawn around the remains of the unfortunate. The viscus substance appeared a deeper shade of red under the dark clouds that rippled across the sky.

"Why are you slowing down?" Katherine questioned from the back seat. She held tight to her mother, who was seated in between she and Marcus. "What are you waiting for? We need to get out of here!"

"What a fucking mess," Christian said. He held fast to the gear shift as he guided the Subaru around a white 4-door Tesla whose front end was crumbled under a silver Ford F250 Super Duty XLT truck. The interior of the truck's shattered windshield was covered in deep red. The driver of the Tesla was visibly impaled against the steering wheel. Blood ran from the motionless body of the passenger sprawled across the hood. "I can't imagine what we're going to find at the hospital."

"Christian!" Katherine hollered. Her shrill voice made her mother flinch. "CHRISTIAN..."

"Katherine," Marcus interrupted timidly.

"Quiet Marcus!" Katherine hissed. "Christian, did you hear me?"

"Katherine," Aunt Athena pleaded. "Please stop."

"Shut up mom!" Katherine barked. "CHRISTIAN!"

"Knock it off Katherine!" Christian ordered. "I fucking heard you! I'm working on it. Just keep quiet!"

"Don't tell me to be quiet!" Katherine shouted as she slammed her hand against the back of Matt's headrest.

"What the fuck Katherine?" Matt blurted as he sat forward in his seat. He looked back and glared at his cousin. "Are you out of your fucking mind? We don't have enough going on?"

A blinding flash of lightening lit up the sky overhead as the caravan drove on. In between thunder claps the low ominous moans of the undead could be heard somewhere in the distance.

"You with me?" Paul asked as he glanced over at Patrick. His 1911 rested cocked and locked on his right leg.

"Something...the seat's wet...I don't know," Patrick stammered as he squirmed.

"It's Ralph's blood," Paul said bluntly. "I tried to clean it all before we left the valley. There wasn't time."

"Ralph's blood?" Patrick questioned with a grimace. He glanced back at his brother and Ralph. "Do you think..."

"Stay alert," Paul interrupted. "We'll be there soon."

Patrick breathed heavily as he kept a tight hold on the shotgun positioned in between his legs, "I'm watching." He assured Paul with a nod. "I'm watching."

"What is it?" Paul asked as Patrick rocked back and forth in his seat.

"This is too tight," Patrick said as he tugged at the front of the vest. "It's making it difficult for me to breath."

"It's not the vest," Paul said empathetically. "Adrenaline and cortisol are pumping through your body."

"I..." Patrick began as his face reddened.

"It's not," Paul insisted. "Unzip it if you have too, but you need to focus on your breathing."

"My breathing," Patrick repeated as his chest heaved.

Paul nodded, "Steady cadence. Five count. In through your nose, out through your mouth."

"Just shut up," Tyler whispered to himself. He kept his eyes closed tight and hands clenched in fists over his chest. The pain from his lower leg was so severe it pulsed up into his temples. "Please God, just get us there soon."

"Paul," Ralph uttered. His voice was weak and gravely. "Paul, where are we?"

"Ralph!" Paul blurted as he glanced back at his friend. "Just hold on. We're almost there."

"Where are we?" Ralph repeated. He struggled to pick his head up so he could look out the window. "My body hurts Paul. Why does my body hurt so bad?"

"Hang in there Ralph!" Paul ordered. "We're almost there. We're going to get you fixed up."

"What's going on?" Ralph asked. An intense flash of lightening momentarily blinded him. "My eyes!" He groaned as he struggled to cover his face.

"Hang on!" Paul instructed as he guided the Jeep around more debris in the road.

"What's going on?" Ralph stammered. "I can't move. Why does my body hurt so bad?"

"You were shot," Paul explained. "We're on the way to the hospital. We're going to get you fixed up. Just hang on!"

"Shot?" Ralph questioned. "Who shot me?"

Another blinding flash was immediately followed by the deafening crack of thunder. The sky opened and rain poured down in sheets. It soaked the windshield and echoed off the hood of the Tahoe.

"I think you did the right thing," Jeff said. His tone was intentionally matter of fact and he didn't look over at his father. "Back there I mean."

"Back where?" Mr. Spahl asked as rain continued to coat the windshield.

"The accident," Jeff answered. "I think you did the right thing, trying to help those people."

"Thanks," Mr. Spahl muttered uncomfortably. He had no interest in reliving what had happened.

"There's no way we could have known the woman was bit," Jeff continued. "I just think you did the right thing trying to help them."

"Wipers, dear" Mrs. Spahl interrupted calmly from the back seat. She was well versed in her husband's body language and knew despite her son's good intentions it was a topic better left alone.

"What?" Mr. Spahl questioned as he looked around.

"It's raining hard. You need to turn the wipers on," Mrs. Spahl repeated. "No headlights. We don't want to draw attention."

"Oh, you're right," Mr. Spahl replied as he turned the windshield wipers on. He shook his head as if to clear his mind. "I've been up too long."

"Brake lights, dad," Jeff said as he pointed to the back of the Jeep. "Looks like there's more debris in the road."

"I see it," Mr. Spahl acknowledged. He carefully maneuvered the large SUV into the oncoming lane. "How's everybody in the back?"

"Fine," Mrs. Spahl replied. She sat with her hands folded in her lap. "Just fine."

"Are you ok?" Kurt asked quietly as he pulled Kim close.

Kim nodded, "Yes, I think so."

"We're good back here," Kurt announced.

"Alright, everybody, hang tight. We should be through this soon," Mr. Spahl explained. "Jeff, what do you see out your side?"

"Nothing good," Jeff answered. "Looks like a slaughter from here."

"They definitely got hit hard here," Mr. Spahl said. He drew the 1911 from his holster and placed the pistol on the center console next to him. "You ready?"

Jeff nodded. He switched his grip on the AR15 and brought the rifle up to his left shoulder, "I'm ready."

"Off hand?" Mr. Spahl questioned. "Since when can you shoot left-handed?"

"I've been practicing," Jeff said as he glanced back at his father.

"That's good," Mr. Spahl said. "That's really, good. Matt and Christian?"

"Of course," Jeff answered. "The three of us have been working drills since the start of the year."

"Where?" Mr. Spahl asked.

"The farm," Jeff answered. "Bill constructed a backstop at the far edge of one of the hayfields."

"That's excellent," Mr. Spahl added with a deep sense of pride.

"More sporadic lately, since Christian's been out of remission," Jeff added.

"All the same," Mr. Spahl said as he increased the speed of the wipers. "It's a good skill to have."

Sheets of rain continued to strafe the area and limit visibility. The caravan slowed so as not to collide with any vehicles and human remains that cluttered the roadway. The sounds of the undead intensified as they carefully navigated the roadway.

"Movement!" Matt called. His head whipped to the right as something caught his eye. "I've got movement to my right!"

"GET US OUT OF HERE!" Katherine demanded.

"Alive?" Christian asked. He cut the wheel and pulled the Subaru into the oncoming lane and around several more wrecked vehicles.

"Not by the looks of it," Matt answered as he brought the AR15 up to his eye line.

"CHRISTIAN!" Katherine shouted. "GET US OUT OF HERE!"

"Shut the fuck up Katherine!" Christian ordered. He glanced over at Matt. "Better let them know."

"Christian," Marcus said sheepishly.

"Shut up Marcus!" Matt instructed as he brought the walkie talkie up to his mouth. "We don't have time for your cuckhold bullshit." He continued as he pressed the PTT button. "Movement right side. Repeat, movement on our right side. Over."

The walkie talkie crackled before Paul's voice came over the speaker, "Left side. We've got movement on our left side too. Over."

"Both sides and behind us," Mr. Spahl added. There was considerable concern in his voice. "They're getting close to our vehicle. We need to get off this street. Over."

"Fuck! They're everywhere," Matt snarled as he looked around. He pressed the AR15's stock against his left shoulder. He could feel the laceration on his left-palm reopen as he twisted his hand around the BCM pistol grip. He glanced over at Christian. "We need to move."

"CHRISTIAN!" Katherine screamed.

"Katherine, shut the fuck up!" Matt ordered.

"Hang on!" Christian said. The wipers moved the excess water from the windshield as he looked around hurriedly. "Fuck, it's tight."

"There's no place to turn around," Matt said. His voice was agitated as he swept the barrel from the windshield to the passenger side window and back.

"We're not going back," Christian hissed through clenched teeth. "We've come too far not to make it to the hospital."

"What's the plan?" Matt asked as he brought the walkie talkie up to his mouth.

"Straight through," Christian said. He tried to shift into third gear but another multi-car wreck prevented it. "FUCK!" He snapped. He slid the gear shift back into second gear and traded the clutch for the gas. "Tell them."

"Straight through," Matt called into the walkie talkie. "Keep the formation tight. Keep moving. Watch for brake lights. Do not engage unless you absolutely must. Gunfire is only going to draw more of them to us. Over."

Despite their awkward movements, the undead shambled purposefully. The rain soaked their tattered cloths and bloodied carcasses. Water ran from their discolored outstretched limbs as they moved amongst the wreckage towards the caravan. As they neared their haunted moans intensified.

"FUCK!" Paul snarled. "We cannot be out here. Get me the map!" He ordered as he pointed to the glove compartment.

"What?" Patrick questioned as he looked back terrified from the window. "They're getting closer."

"THE MAP!" Paul growled as he pointed again to the glove compartment. "Get me the fucking map!"

"The map?" Patrick repeated. "What about the GPS?"

"Fuck the GPS!" Paul snarled. "Paper maps dammit!"

"Got it," Patrick said as he tugged at the latch. He pulled several folded maps from the compartment. "Which one?"

"They're closing in!" Paul said. He took the maps from Patrick as he maneuvered the Jeep around more bodies and debris in the road.

"They're everywhere!" Patrick blurted. "We can't outrun them, not at this speed."

"This one!" Paul said as he rifled through the maps. "Help me unfold it."

"Paul..." Ralph wheezed from the back of the Jeep. His breathing was labored and voice weak. "What's happening?"

"Hold on Ralph!" Paul ordered. He glanced over at Patrick. "Got it? Here let me have it."

"What do you want me to do?" Patrick asked as he handed Paul the open map.

"Get your pistol ready," Paul instructed as he folded the map in half. "If you need to fire, make sure you get the window down. You don't want glass blowing back in your eyes."

"Ok," Patrick said nervously. He pulled the pistol from the cross-draw holster on the vest and looked down at the door.

"Not there," Paul growled. He pointed to the four switches under the climate control dials. "Here! If you need to put the window down, that's the button."

The walkie talkie crackled and Mr. Spahl's voice echoed over the speaker, "We've attracted a crowd. We need a detour so we can lose them. We don't want to bring them to the hospital with us. Over."

"Roger that," Paul called into the walkie talkie. He folded the paper in half again and peered down at it. "Working on it! Over."

"Getting closer!" Patrick shouted.

Paul quickly traced a route with his index finger and pressed the PTT button, "New plan. Take the next right onto Elm, the second left onto Racine. Over."

"Right on Elm, second left onto Racine," Matt repeated. "Good copy, over."

"Racine to 7th Avenue," Paul continued. "7th Avenue to Hospital Drive. That'll get us there and should give us some room to maneuver. Over."

"Roger," Matt said as he released the PTT button. "You good with the route?"

"Got it," Christian answered without taking his eyes off the road.

"NOOOO!" Aunt Athena screamed.

Several figures lurched from either side of the street towards the Subaru. Their discolored flesh clamored against the back windows as they tried to get at the living.

"GET US OUT OF HERE!" Matt shouted.

"CHRISTIAN!" Katherine screeched as the passenger side back window cracked under the weight of undead hands.

"MOTHER FUCKERS!" Christian blurted. He pushed the gas pedal towards the floor. The engine raced as he spun the steering wheel to the left and back hard to the right. There was a distinct thud as the tires pulled one of the creatures under the car.

"WHAT ARE YOU DOING?" Katherine shrieked. Her body was thrown against the back door as the Subaru swerved to the left.

"KATHERINE!" Aunt Athena cried as she slammed up against her daughter.

"HOLD ON!" Christian ordered. He shifted into third gear and spun the steering wheel back to the left. The front quarter panel of the Subaru pushed one of the ghouls against a light blue minivan on the side of the road. There was a nauseating crunch as the lower half of the creature's body was crushed.

"CAREFUL!" Matt shouted. "IF WE PUNCTURE THE RADIATOR OR BLOW A TIRE WE'RE FUCKED!"

"CLEARING A PATH!" Christian snapped as he straightened the wheel and sped down the road. He glanced up at the rearview mirror to make sure the other two vehicles were still behind them.

"THE TURN!" Matt called. He pointed to the faded green sign obscured by low hanging tree branches. "THAT'S THE TURN!"

"GOT IT!" Christian said. He tapped the brakes twice, downshifted into second gear and spun the wheel hard to the right.

The engine whined and tires squealed as the Subaru skidded over the wet asphalt.

"What the fuck is your cousin doing?" Paul asked as the back end of the Subaru slid across the intersection.

"I have no idea," Patrick said as he shook his head. "I just hope my mother's alright."

"We can't afford to lose another vehicle!" Paul said as he pushed the clutch and brake pedals towards the floor and prepared to downshift.

"CHRISTIAN!" Katherine yelled as she was thrown across her mother.

"UHHHH!" Marcus groaned from the back seat as he was sandwiched against the door.

"HANG ON!" Christian ordered. He shifted into third gear and straightened the wheel. He watched as the Jeep and Tahoe cautiously followed them onto Elm Street. "What do you see?"

"They're more spread out," Matt answered as he lowered the AR15. "Not as many vehicles either."

The rain continued to pour down and soak the area. Thunder and lightning dissipated some as the caravan drove in the opposite direction of the storm. As they moved further from the center of town, the carnage lessened.

Collective relief was shared as the vehicles turned onto Racine Avenue without incident. Things quieted further as the caravan reached 7th Avenue. Less than twenty minutes later they turned onto Hospital Drive. A much-needed glimmer of hope arrived in the form of the large medical facility as it came into view at the end of the road.

"Finally," Matt said as he engaged the safety on his AR15. He tucked the stock under his left arm and pressed the PTT button on the walkie talkie. "Parking lot, 300-yards. I repeat, hospital parking lot 300-yards. Stay alert. Over."

"Thank God," Aunt Athena whimpered. She dropped her head into her hands and wept. "Thank God..."

"It's alright mom," Katherine urged. She put her arm around her mother's shoulders and tried to comfort her. "It's alright, we're almost there."

"What do you think?" Matt asked as he glanced over at Christian.

"Too quiet," Christian answered as he shook his head. He took his foot off the accelerator and looked around. "Too, fucking quiet."

"It all looks untouched," Matt observed with noticeable surprise in his voice. He scanned the area. "Are they still with us?"

Christian glanced up at the rearview mirror as he tightened his grip on the steering wheel, "Yeah." He muttered with a nod. "Still with us."

The rain slowed to a light drizzle as the storm passed. There was no movement on either side of the street as the caravan approached. There were no disabled vehicles or human remains in sight.

"Alright," Paul said as he wiped the sweat from his forehead. He glanced back at Ralph. "Hang on brother, we're almost there."

Ralph managed a meek nod of acknowledgement, "That's good." He said as he blinked several times. "My vision's blurry. I can't..." He said as his voice trailed off.

"Check on him!" Paul ordered.

"What?" Patrick stammered.

"NOW!" Paul growled.

"Hang on Ralph!" Patrick called. He reached back and grabbed Ralph's shoulder. "Ralph, can you hear me? Ralph!"

The hospital campus looked pristine. The lush green of the perfectly manicured lawn appeared intact. There were several cars parked throughout the lot but no movement to speak of.

"Look sharp Jeff," Mr. Spahl instructed.

"I'm on it, dad," Jeff said as he sat straight up and shifted his position on the seat.

"If something's going to happen," Mr. Spahl said as he moved the 1911 from the center console and placed it on his right leg. "It's going to happen now."

Erected at the far end of the parking lot were 3-FEMA emergency relief shelters. The large white structures faced the emergency room entrance and were outfitted with blue doors and awning ways. Nothing appeared out of place except the large tan and gray Winnebago with out-of-state plates parked at the rear of the lot.

"What about that?" Matt asked. He motioned towards the Winnebago. "Looks out of place. Doesn't it?"

Chrisitan shrugged, "Patient maybe. Family member." He offered as he guided the Subaru off the street and into the parking lot.

"From Virginia?" Matt said curiously as he caught a glimpse of the license plate. "Doesn't track."

"Didn't you take a rental car from Jersey and visit Chico at the hospital in North Carolina after his accident?" Christian asked.

"Yes, but..." Matt began.

"Let's just focus on finding a doctor," Christian interrupted. Brilliant rays of golden yellow escaped through breaks in the cloud cover as the caravan circled the lot. "We've got enough to worry about without trying to solve the mystery of who the Winnebago belongs to."

"Can't we go any faster?" Katherine snapped from the backseat. "Tyler needs a doctor!"

"Katherine!" Matt said sternly.

"Fuck off!" Katherine barked. "Why are you taking the long way around? Just pull under the archway and take them to the emergency room entrance."

"We will, Katherine," Christian assured her. "After what we've been through, we're not taking any chances."

"What chances?" Katherine insisted. "There's nobody around!"

"We need to be sure," Christian said as he gritted his teeth. His patience was exhausted as it concerned his cousin. "We can't take the chance there's any more of those things nearby or another group waiting to ambush people in need of medical attention."

"Now you're worried about another group?" Katherine chided loudly. "That's ridiculous! There's no one here. Just pull up to the ER entrance!"

Matt glanced over at his brother, "Do you want me to?"

"No," Christian said quietly as he shook his head. "Katherine." He said sternly. "Just be quiet. I've got this."

"Yeah, right," Katherine muttered to herself. Red faced she waved at him dismissively. "You've got this, what a fucking joke."

"What was that?" Matt blurted as he whipped around in his seat.

"Leave it alone!" Christian ordered. "We've got more pressing matters."

"Fine," Matt agreed as he repositioned himself. "This conversation isn't finished."

"I'm going to pull through the portico and park along the sidewalk," Christian explained as he completed the loop around the perimeter. "It'll be easier to unload Ralph and Tyler."

"We'll be facing the right direction if we have to get out in a hurry," Matt said with a nod. He pressed the PTT button on the walkie talkie. "Parking just beyond the portico. Repeat, we will park just beyond the portico. Over."

"About damn time," Paul said. "Take this." He continued as he handed Patrick the walkie talkie. "Hang on Ralph! We're almost there."

"Get ready," Mr. Spahl instructed. "This is it, Jeff."

"I got it dad," Jeff assured his father with a nod.

The emergency room entrance appeared dark as they drove past. The portico was a large structure covered in red brick. It extended well past the face of the building. Eight large pillars, four on either side of a cobble stone causeway supported the structure. The area beneath the portico was large enough to accommodate multiple ambulances in the event of a mass causality incident.

Most of the cloud cover dissipated and revealed a pale blue sky. A layer of humidity blanketed the area as the sun shone down like a spot light over the hospital campus.

Matt and Christian hurried from the Subaru as the other two vehicles came to a stop under the portico. Mr. Spahl and Jeff hurried from the Tahoe and met the brothers in front of the Jeep.

"What the fuck are we waiting for?" Paul questioned as he pushed the driver's side door open. "We've got to get these two inside!"

"Is everyone good with what needs to happen here?" Matt asked hurriedly. He held his left hand up to block the sun from his eyes. "Through those doors and into the ER."

"We've got it," Mr. Spahl said as he checked the Mini-14. He gave Patrick a nod. "You good?"

"Come on!" Paul barked. He opened the back of the Jeep and prepared to move Ralph's body. "Let's go!"

"Yes," Patrick answered. "I'm good. You guys go ahead. We've got this."

"See if you can find a place with cover and a good vantage," Christian instructed. "Alright, Jeff you..." He began before he stopped abruptly.

"What is it?" Matt asked as he raised the AR15 to the low ready position.

"Movement," Christian answered cautiously.

"Movement?" Matt repeated. "Where?"

"Winnebago," Christian said firmly. He brought the AR15 up to his shoulder.

"Fuck!" Paul snarled as he carefully repositioned Ralph in the back of the Jeep.

"Ahhh!" Ralph groaned.

"Stay down Ralph," Paul ordered. He hurried to retrieve his M1A Scout. "Just hang on. We'll have you inside soon!"

"Spread out!" Matt ordered. "Find cover!"

Mr. Spahl hurried back to the Tahoe, "Everybody down!" He shouted as he positioned himself behind the passenger side rear quarter panel.

"Come on!" Mrs. Spahl called as she pulled Kim and Kurt off the back seat and onto the floor with her.

"What's going on?" Kim shrieked. "I thought we were going inside?"

"Just stay down!" Mrs. Spahl ordered.

"Paul!" Christian shouted. "We need a base of fire!"

"On it!" Paul called back. He moved past where the Tahoe was parked, to the furthest of the large red brick covered pillars. He raised the rifle, pressed the stock against his shoulder and trained the Eotech's reticle on the driver's side compartment of the Winnebago. "Move!"

Matt sprinted to the pillar immediately to the right of Paul, "MOVE!" He shouted as he raised his rifle and scanned the area.

"Patrick!" Mr. Spahl shouted.

"Yeah?" Patrick answered as he looked around hurriedly. His expression was a mixture of confusion and fear. "What?"

"Get over here and cover the ER entrance!" Mr. Spahl insisted.

Patrick hurried behind the Tahoe, "Where do you want me?"

"Behind the passenger side front tire," Mr. Spahl answered. "Cover the doors behind us. Make sure we don't get ambushed."

"Jeff, with me!" Christian shouted.

"GO!" Jeff shouted. The two of them moved quickly to the furthest pillar at the end of the portico.

"Paul?" Matt called as his eyes found the nearest car in the parking lot. "I'm going for the white Audi."

"I got you brother," Paul answered. He glanced over at the white Audi S5 convertible parked less than 30-yards from their position. "GO!"

Matt's boots pounded against the asphalt as he bolted across the lot. In a matter of seconds, he reached the back of the car. Adrenaline pumped through him as his chest heaved. He flipped the G33 magnifier in front of the Eotech site and used the body of the car as cover as he peered around the passenger side. "MOVE!" He called.

"Cover me, Jeff," Christian instructed.

"I got you," Jeff assured him. "GO!"

Christian hurried from the pillar as Jeff took up the position to cover Christian as he ran, "On your six!" He called as he came up behind his brother.

"I don't see any movement!" Matt answered as he kept his eyes locked on the Winnebago.

"We need to get them over here and check it out," Christian said. He pressed his back against the rear bumper as he squatted behind the car. "I'm bringing Jeff over." He said as he motioned with his left hand and pointed past the Audi to a black Suburban with heavily tinted windows a few spaces over.

"Ready," Matt answered.

Jeff sprinted passed the Audi to the large SUV. He used the passenger side rear of the vehicle to cover their flank. "MOVE!" He shouted when he found the area clear.

Christian motioned to Paul.

Paul nodded and glanced back at Mr. Spahl, "You got me?"

"I've got you," Mr. Spahl answered with a nod. "GO!"

Paul's large frame hurried across the open lot. He could feel his lower back strain under the weight of the chest rig loaded with the eight 25-round magazines. His face was red and chest heaved as he reached the back of the Audi, "Fuck this running shit!" He muttered as he wiped sweat from his face and tried to catch his breath. "Anything?"

"Not that I can see," Matt answered.

"Take a second and catch your breath," Christian urged.

Paul nodded, "I'm ok." He assured them. "This chest rig is fine to wear, but I didn't expect to have to run in it."

"7.62 ammunition is no joke," Matt offered from where he knelt.

"Yeah, you're telling me," Paul said with a smirk. "Alright, what's the plan?"

"You two cover me," Christian instructed. "I'm moving up to Jeff's position."

"GO!" Paul ordered as he brought the rifle up to his shoulder.

Christian hurried past Matt, "Jeff!" He called as he reached the Suburban. "You see anything?"

Jeff glanced back, "Nothing." He answered. "Everything's a little too still."

"Tell me about it," Christian said as he looked back and motioned to Matt and Paul. "Move!"

Paul nodded, "Go." He called to Matt. "I'll cover you."

"Moving!" Matt announced. He hurried from the back of the Audi to a silver 4-door BMW parked several spaces away. He posted up behind the car and scanned the area. "GO!" He called.

Paul moved cautiously through the lot and stopped at the blue Nissan Rogue ahead of Matt's position, "Move!"

Matt ran past the Rogue to a thunder gray Volvo S60 sedan parked less than 50-yards from the Winnebago. He was about to call for Paul when a glimmer of light reflected off something and caught his eye, "Contact 11 o'clock! Contact 11 o'clock!" He shouted as he placed his index finger on the trigger and prepared to fire.

"Wait! Don't shoot!" A man's voice called from behind a hunter green Jeep Cherokee parked 2-spaces to the left of the Winnebago. "We're alive! Don't shoot!"

"MOVING!" Paul shouted, startled by the man's voice. He took off running towards a vanilla white Chrysler 300 parked two spaces from Matt's right flank. "SHOW YOURSELF!" He ordered as he reached the sedan.

"We're alive!" The man's voice called again. "Don't shoot!"

"We fucking heard you the first time!" Paul shouted. "Show yourself!"

"Alright," The man agreed with a shaky voice. "We're coming out just don't shoot!"

"Hands and weapons in the air!" Christian shouted as he joined Matt at the back of the Volvo. "In the air...or we will open fire on you!"

"Ok, ok," the man insisted. The shakiness in his voice now sounded panicked. "We can do that. Please just don't shoot...don't shoot!"

Slowly the high-power scope and bolt action rifle it was attached to emerged from behind the green Jeep Cherokee followed by the man who held it. As he stood up, he was careful to keep his left hand on the stock and away from the trigger. His right hand was gripped tightly around the barrel to demonstrate he was not a threat, "My name's Shaw. We don't want any trouble. One of our group is injured and she needs medical attention."

Shaw appeared to be in his early-50's. He was stocky with broad shoulders. His hazel eyes were surrounded by deep lines. A faded blue baseball cap with a minor league team logo covered his bushy salt and pepper hair. His face was covered with a scruffy 3-day beard of the same color. He wore a light blue denim shirt with dried sweat stains in the under arms. The sleeves were rolled up to his elbows and exposed tattoos on both forearms.

"Keep those arms raised!" Christian ordered. "How many more with you?"

"Six," Shaw answered. "Two out here with me and three more in the Winnebago. We don't want any trouble. We've got an injured person who needs medical attention. Please don't shoot."

Paul kept the reticle of his Eotech trained on the windshield of the Winnebago, while Jeff continued to scan their right flank.

"Matt!" Christian said.

"I've got him," Matt answered as he kept the Eotech's reticle on the center of Shaw's chest.

"Jeff, you got our right flank?" Christian called.

"Right flank secure!" Jeff called back.

"Mr. Spahl?" Christian shouted.

"Roger!" Mr. Spahl shouted back. "Left flank secure!"

"What do you want to do?" Matt asked.

"Get this sorted so we can get inside," Christian answered. He turned his attention back to Shaw who was still standing with the rifle over his head. "Shaw, we've got our own people who need medical attention so let's cut the bullshit. Tell the rest of your group to come out slow!" He ordered. "I want to see their hands. If we see a weapon we will fire!"

"If I bring my people out, do I have your word you won't shoot?" Shaw asked nervously.

"We won't shoot unless you give us reason to," Christian assured him.

"Alright!" Shaw said with a nod. "You heard the man. Weapons on the deck! Everybody, step out slowly with your hands up."

The first to emerge was a man who looked to be about the same age as Shaw. He was tall and lean with the same deep lines seared into his face. His dark hair was parted to one side and there was a thin mustache above his upper lip. A black leather vest partially covered a white linen button down shirt. He placed a Beretta A300 Ultima Patrol 12-gauge shotgun on the roof of the Cherokee and stepped out from behind the vehicle.

"You got him?" Matt asked.

Christian placed the Aimpoint's red dot on the center of the man's chest, "Yeah, I got him."

A younger man with short brown hair appeared next. He was stocky and muscular. His white t-shirt was tucked into the waist of well-worn blue jeans. He placed an SKS rifle with folding stock on the roof of the Cherokee next to the shotgun, raised his hands and stepped out next to Shaw and the other man.

"Paul!" Christian called.

"I got him!" Paul answered. He moved the reticle from the windshield of the Winnebago to the base of the third man's throat.

"All right," Christian shouted. "Now everybody in the Winnebago!"

"Easy," Shaw said with a nod. "Dominick, Barbara, you need to come out."

"You said there were three!" Christian shouted.

"There are," Shaw explained. "But my sister is injured. We're trying to move her as little as possible until we can get her inside and find a doctor."

"Jeff, move up!" Christian ordered.

"Moving!" Jeff called. He hurried from the Suburban across the parking lot to a granite-colored Jeep Wrangler Unlimited parked just opposite of the Winnebago. "In position!" He called.

"Cover the side door of the Winnebago," Christian instructed.

"Got it!" Jeff answered as he trained the Aimpoint's red dot on the door.

"You better not be fucking with us!" Christian snarled.

"We're not," Shaw reassured him. "We just need a doctor, same as you."

"Get the other two members of your group out here," Christian ordered. "Do it now!"

"Go easy fellas," Shaw encouraged as he placed the rifle on the ground in front of him. "Dominick, Barbara, you need to come out here now!"

The side door of the Winnebago opened slowly, "Don't shoot!" Dominic called. His voice trembled as he continued. "We're coming out!"

"SLOWLY!" Christian shouted.

"I heard you!" Dominic called again as his arms emerged from the doorway.

Dominic stepped from behind the door and into the parking lot. He was an older gentleman and appeared to be in his early-70's. His head was covered with silver-gray hair. He was husky with a powder blue button-down shirt tucked into a pair of gray flannel pants.

"I got him!" Jeff said as he placed the red dot on the center of Dominic's chest.

"Step off to your right!" Christian ordered. He didn't want the next person out of the Winnebago to use Dominic as cover and get the drop on them.

Dominic kept his hands raised and did as he was instructed. Once he was next to the other 3-men, he turned his head and looked back to the individual still inside the vehicle. He gave a nod before he turned his attention back to Christian, "She's coming." He offered with a nod.

A few moments later Barbra appeared from the vehicle. She was petite with short auburn hair and freckles. She was visibly nervous as she held her hands in the air. She wore a white blouse tucked into a black skirt, with black stockings and no shoes.

"Any other firearms?" Christian called.

"I have a revolver in a holster on my waist," Shaw answered. He motioned to the man next to him with the mustache. "Holden has a 1911 in a shoulder holster under his vest."

"Slowly!" Christian instructed. "Thumb and index finger only. Both of you!"

Shaw nodded and looked over at Holden, "Nice and easy." He said as he lowered his hand to his right hip and retrieved the revolver.

"Yep," Holden agreed in a raspy voice. He shook his head and pulled his vest open with his left hand. With his right, he slowly reached for the 1911. "Tell me again why we came through New Jersey."

"Don't start that shit," Shaw insisted. He drew the revolver from the holster and threw it out in front of him. "Just be cool and don't get us killed."

"This is the last time I surrender my firearms," Holden said with obvious disdain in his voice. He threw the pistol on the hood of the Jeep Cherokee and held his hands up to show they were empty. "The last fucking time!"

"Jeff, Paul, base of fire," Christian ordered. "Matt and I are going to clear the Winnebago."

"Roger!" Paul called. "MOVE!"

"I'm scared," Barbra said as her hands trembled. "What if they..."

"It'll be ok," Shaw assured her. "Just stay calm. It's almost over."

"Are we really going to stand here and let this happen?" Holden asked as Christian and Matt approached.

"If they wanted to kill us, they could have," Shaw answered. "Just be cool and don't provoke them."

Christian lowered his rifle as he reached the five of them, "This is nothing personal, but we don't know you." He said as he came face to face with Shaw.

"The country being what it is now, I understand," Shaw said with a nod. "But it sounds like we've both got wounded who would be better served inside. How do we convince you we're not a threat and after the same thing?"

"My brother's going to check you for weapons. Then we're going to check your vehicle," Christian explained. "If everything is as you say we'll dispense with the formalities."

"And if not?" Holden snarled.

"That's enough!" Shaw insisted.

Matt circled behind the group, "Nice and easy fellas." He said as he frisked Shaw first.

"No need to search the young lady," Christian said as he motioned towards Barbra. "You can put your hands down miss."

Barbra nodded and lowered her arms, "I'm Barbra. These are my older brothers Shaw and Holden." She explained.

"What about him?" Christian asked as he motioned to the younger man in the white t-shirt.

"Our nephew, Roderick," Barbra answered.

"And the older gentleman?" Christian inquired.

"Dominick," Barbra answered. "He's a family friend, well more like an adopted uncle I guess."

"Nice to meet you Barbra," Christian said. "I'm sorry it has to be under these circumstances."

No one noticed how beautiful the day was or how brightly the sun shown overhead.

"What's going on?" Patrick called.

"Not sure," Mr. Spahl answered. "Just keep watch over the entrance. We don't want anyone coming up behind us."

"I am," Patrick assured him as beads of sweat ran down his face.

"Can you see anything?" Mr. Spahl asked.

"No," Patrick answered. "The corridor is dark. I can't see anything except the exit sign at the far end of the hall."

Mr. Spahl shook his head, "We need to get inside." He muttered to himself. "We can't have made this trip for nothing."

Despite the sparse cloud cover, the air was humid and thick. Beads of sweat ran down Matt's back as he frisked Holden and moved on to Roderick.

"Matt?" Christian called.

"All clear!" Matt answered as he turned his attention to the Winnebago.

"My sister needs a doctor," Barbra insisted as she glanced over her shoulder towards Matt.

"That's your sister in the Winnebago?" Matt asked. "What's her name?"

"Yes, our sister, Katlyn," Barbra answered with a look of deep concern on her face. "She's not armed. She fell running from those things. I think she broke her collar bone. She's in a lot of pain and we only have Aspirin."

"We'll be as gentle as we're able," Matt assured her as he moved to the open door of the Winnebago, "Katlyn, we're coming in. Put any weapons down. Place your hands in the air. I do not want to hurt you but if you're armed, I will fire!"

"I'm not armed," Katlyn's weak voice called from inside the Winnebago.

Christian slapped Matt on the back, "Go!" He said as the two of them disappeared into the large vehicle.

Jeff and Paul cautiously approached the group while Matt and Christian checked on Katlyn and cleared the Winnebago.

"Put your hands down," Paul insisted as he lowered his rifle. "Don't worry, we're the good guys."

"Funny way of showing it," Roderick scoffed as he wiped sweat from his forehead.

"Don't question it kid," Paul growled. "We're looking after our own same as you."

"Easy," Shaw said. He extended his right hand to Paul. "I'm Shaw."

"Paul," Paul said as he shook Shaw's hand. "What brings you to the Garden State Shaw?"

"My brother wants to know the same thing," Shaw said as he motioned to Holden. "We're from Virginia. A little town near Ft. Lee. Things got bad there a couple days ago. Looked like it spread across the country before the news broadcasts stopped, so we decided to head north. Dominick's got family in Alaska."

"Alaska?" Jeff questioned. "I've been there. My brother used to be stationed there."

"Ft. Richarson?" Dominick asked.

"Yes," Jeff answered with a nod. "That's an ambitious journey, Alaska."

"We thought the isolation would provide a measure of safety," Shaw explained.

"That and maybe the cold weather would have some kind of effect on the undead," Holden added.

"Things fell apart quick by us. We weren't sure what to do," Shaw explained. "When Dominick showed up with his Winnebago, we collected everything we could and headed out."

"What happened to your sister?" Paul asked.

"Katlyn and I worked for the same law firm. I passed the bar exam last month and she was working as a paralegal and getting ready to take the exam too." Barbra explained as she wiped a tear from her cheek. "The streets were a mess. People were in a panic and then those things showed up. We were headed out of the building when someone pushed Katlyn out of the way. She fell down the concrete steps outside the building. We lost two of Rodrick's friends saving her."

"I served with those guys," Rodrick said as he buried his head in his hands. "They were like my brothers."

Shaw put a reassuring hand on Rodrick's shoulder, "It's going to be alright."

"There was nothing you could have done," Holden added. "They got bit. It was a mercy killing."

"Doesn't make it any easier," Roderick said as he wiped his eyes.

"No, it doesn't," Matt said as he and Christian emerged from the Winnebago. "We've lost loved ones too. There's a young lady in here in need of medical attention. What do you say we continue this conversation inside and see if we can keep from losing anybody else?"

"Let's do that," Dominic agreed. He managed a slight smile and patted Shaw on the back. "Come on, let's go." "Yeah, let's get everybody inside," Roderick added as he ran his hands over his face. "There is one thing I'm curious about though."

"What's that?" Paul asked.

"Do you always treat out of towners this way?" Roderick inquired as he regained his composure.

"Don't take it personal kid," Paul encouraged with a slight chuckle. "That's just hospitality, Jersey style."

CHAPTER 19

emergency

"T HEY'RE STUCK!" MATT SHOUTED. The sling held the rifle across his back as he tried to pry the doors open that led to the emergency room. "I can't..."

"Get out of the way!" Paul ordered as he pushed his friend aside.

"Patrick!" Mr. Spahl called. There was noticeable fatigue in his voice. "Position yourself at the rear of the Subaru. I want you to watch everything to the right." He instructed. Mr. Spahl held the forend of the Mini-14 in his left hand as he motioned with his right. "Everything from the corner of the building to the FEMA shelters. Got it?"

"I got it," Patrick answered. He gave a quick nod and hurried across the portico to the Subaru.

The grating sound of metal on metal echoed across the parking lot as Paul forced the doors off their track. "MOTHER FUCKER!" He snarled. He dug the tips of his fingers in between the cold steal as he pried them apart. Paul wedged his large arms in between the doors and forced them open.

"Christ," Holden mutter. His mouth hung open in disbelief. "Where'd you find this fucking guy?"

"Never hurts to have a Paulerbear on your side," Matt said as he pulled himself up from the sidewalk. "We were in Arizona a few years back and he almost impaled me on a wrought iron fence."

"Really?" Holden questioned with a grimace. "Why'd he do that?"

"Somebody insulted a friend of ours," Matt explained. "I just happened to be in the way."

"Enough small talk!" Paul growled as his chest heaved. "I'm going to get Ralph!"

"Listen up!" Matt called. "Christian and Jeff are on point. I'll carry Tyler. Paul's got Ralph." He continued before he glanced back at Shaw. "Who's taking your sister?"

"Roderick and I will carry Katlyn," Shaw answered.

"What about us?" Kurt asked as he and Kim stood near the passenger side of the Tahoe.

"Out here with us," Mr. Spahl answered. He glanced back at Matt. "Get going. I don't want to be out here any longer than we need to be. We need to get everyone inside or get out of here."

Matt nodded, "We'll hurry." He assured Mr. Spahl. "Let's move!"

"I want to go too," Barbra pleaded as she pushed her way to the front of the group. "She's, my sister. I need to be with her."

"I don't think that's a good idea," Matt said as he shook his head. "We don't know what we're going to find in there. We may need to exit in a hurry."

"But..." Barbra began before Christian cut her off.

"It's her sister," Christian said bluntly. "She's coming."

"You sure?" Matt questioned.

"If it was you or I would anyone be able to stop us?" Christian asked.

"No, they would not," Matt answered stoically. He glanced back at Barbra. "Alright young lady let's go. Stay behind your brother and nephew. Keep your eyes open, be ready to move."

Barbra nodded and managed a meek smile, "I can do that."

"Holden, you and Dominick stay out here with us for the time being," Mr. Spahl instructed. "There's a lot of open ground and I need all the eyes I can get keeping watch."

"Yeah, we can do that," Holden said. He rubbed his blood shot eyes. They underscored the look of exhaustion seared across his face. He ran his hands through his hair and tried to shake off the feeling of dread that crept up the back of his neck. "I'll cover the far side."

"Keep your walkie talkie close," Matt urged. Tyler groaned as Matt hoisted him up across his shoulders. "We'll keep you updated."

Mr. Spahl nodded without looking back, "Yeah, get going!"

"Jeff, rifle up, safety off," Christian instructed.

"Got it," Jeff answered as he followed Christian through the open doorway.

The light from the entranceway was minimal and all but dissipated after a few feet. It left the long narrow corridor darkened and visibility limited. A few faint beams of light streamed through a small set of windows at the top of another set of sliding doors at end of the corridor. The sparse light washed the far end of the hallway in a haunting hue of pale blue. The air in the corridor was stale. The enclosed space was filled with an unsettling smell, heavy with the scent of chemical disinfectant and iodine. It was the kind of odor that made you wish you were someplace else.

"Lights!" Christian ordered. He pulled the Surefire E2D Defender flashlight from the MOLLE webbing on his plate carrier with his left hand and clicked it on.

"On it," Jeff replied as he did the same with his Surefire Aviator flashlight.

The beams of light illuminated the narrow space. They danced over the sterile stark white walls and mosaic slate pattern vinyl floor as they moved cautiously forward. The hallway was empty except for several burgundy polyester fabric couches evenly spaced along both walls. Opposite the emergency room doors at the far end was a large silver and tan semi-circular receptionist desk.

"God, I hope someone's in there," Christian said. Beads of sweat ran from his hairline down his forehead. The soles of his boots squeaked against the vinyl floor as his pace quickened.

"You think we'll get to see Paul rip another set of doors open?" Jeff asked with a nervous chuckle. He breathed heavily as he hurried to keep pace with Christian.

"Always possible," Christian answered without looking back. He used the back of his left hand to wipe the sweat from his forehead. "Stay focused, keep moving!"

"What are you doing?" Matt questioned angrily as Tyler squirmed on his back.

"Your shoulder is crushing my fucking balls," Tyler hissed as he continued to writhe in pain.

"Shut him up!" Paul ordered as he followed behind Matt.

Matt wrapped his left arm around the back of his cousin's neck and pulled down forcefully, "Shut up!" He ordered.

"Uhhhh!" Tyler let out a meek whimper and complied.

The 3-point sling kept the M1A in front of Paul as he carried Ralph unconscious through the darkened hallway. He could feel something warm and sticky against the back of his neck and realized the quick clot had given way and Ralph's wound had reopened. "Come on!" He hissed. "Can't we catch a fucking break!"

"Be careful in there," Holden offered.

Shaw gave his brother a nod as he and Roderick made a seat with their arms. They passed through the doorway and carried Katlyn in between the two of them.

"We will," Barbra assured Holden as the four of them passed through the open doors and quickly disappeared into the darkened hallway.

The lean features of Katlyn's face were contorted in pain. Her cheeks were flushed which gave her naturally fair skin a sickly pale coloration. Her shoulder length dirty blonde hair was sweat soaked and matted to her head. Her torso was covered in what was left of a cream-colored blouse. The white straps of her bra were visible through the tattered garment. Her left arm was folded across her body and an ice pack rested atop her broken collar bone. A pair of skinned knees peaked out from the torn fabric of her dark slacks.

"Easy," Katlyn whimpered as her body stiffened. "Please, just go easy. I don't know how much more I can take.""It'll be ok," Barbra assured her. She placed her hands gently against her sister's back to keep her body immobile.

"I don't know," Katlyn moaned. "I feel nauseous. I'm afraid I might vomit."

"Just breathe sis," Barbra urged. She was terrified and desperate for what her sister was going through. She did her best to sound brave and hoped that would be enough to provide Katlyn some measure of comfort. "We've come this far. We're going to get you fixed up. Just hang on."

Everything under the portico remained quiet. The tree branches danced in the distance as the breeze picked up again.

"Ok fellas," Dominick asked as he squatted down between Mr. Spahl and Holden. He used a white handkerchief to dab beads of sweat from his forehead. "What do you need me to do?"

"At the moment, nothing," Mr. Spahl said calmly. He glanced over at Dominick. "You look like you could use some water."

Dominick nodded, "Now that you mention it young man. I am thirsty."

"Young man," Mr. Spahl scoffed from where he knelt. "Another few minutes in this position and I'll be lucky if I can stand up straight."

"Just wait til you get to be my age," Dominick jabbed. "They only keep me around because I can drive the Winnebago."

"Don't say shit like that," Holden scolded. "You're family and you know it."

"I appreciate that," Dominick said as he ran the handkerchief over the top of his head. "You were saying about getting some water?"

"Go see my wife," Mr. Spahl urged. He motioned to where Mrs. Spahl stood with Kim and Kurt. "She's in charge of the cooler. She'll get you squared away."

"Thank you, young man," Dominick offered as he struggled to get to his feet. "Oh, this getting old stuff. You two want some water?"

"Yes, please," Holden answered. "And something to eat if there's any food."

"Ok," Dominic said as he returned the handkerchief to his pants pocket. "What about you, young man?"

"Water please," Mr. Spahl answered. "Hey while you're up..."

"What's that?" Dominic asked as he turned back.

"Check on Patrick," Mr. Spahl said as he motioned to the far end of the portico. "He's got the reddish blond hair, over by the Subaru."

"Will do," Dominic said with a nod.

"Let him know you're coming," Mr. Spahl instructed. "He can be jumpy especially under the circumstances."

"Good to know," Dominic said as his eyes widened. He pressed his hands against his lower back and let out a groan as he made his way over to Mrs. Spahl. "Oh, my back is tight."

"Hold them up," Christian instructed as he and Jeff reached the emergency room doors.

Jeff turned and raised his left arm. The beam from the flashlight illuminated the area around him. He let the sling take the weight of the rifle as he brought his right arm up and made a fist.

"Stop," Matt said quietly as he turned back towards Paul.

Paul turned back to Shaw and Roderick, "Hold up." He said as he shifted Ralph's body across his shoulders.

"What's happening?" Barbra asked.

"Not sure," Shaw answered. "They want us to stop."

Jeff turned back to Christian, "We're good."

"It fucking stinks in here!" Christian said as he clipped his flashlight to his plate carrier. He took his inhaler from his pocket and shook it before he pulled two quick puffs into his lungs. "Come on, help me get these doors open."

The foul medicinal odor mixed with the smell of sweat permeated the narrow space. It was almost unbearable as Christian and Jeff struggled unsuccessfully to pry the doors apart.

"FUCK!" Christian snarled after several minutes. He held his hands out in front of him. The tips of his fingers were raw. They looked pink against the LED light from his flashlight as it shown towards the floor. "It's not going to open."

"I've got no leverage on this side," Jeff said through gritted teeth. He wiped the sweat from his forehead. "I'm too close to the fucking wall!"

"What are we doing?" Paul demanded as he shifted Ralph's body again.

"Working on it!" Jeff called. "Just…"

"Hold up!" Christian interrupted as he held up his hand. He looked back towards the long corridor. Even in the darkness he could see the desperation etched into the faces.

"What is it?" Jeff asked.

Christian shook his head, "Fuck it!" He said as he pounded his fist against the door.

"What are you doing?" Jeff questioned.

"Somebody's got to be in there!" Christian shouted as he continued to slam his fist against the door.

"Alright then, fuck it!" Jeff added as he began to pound his fist against the other door.

"Something moved in there! There's somebody in there!" Christian shouted as he peered through the small window at the top of the door. "HEY! We need a doctor! We've got injured people out here! We need a doctor!"

"OPEN UP!" Jeff shouted as he continued to bang his fist against the door. "WE NEED A DOCTOR!"

"Movement!" Christian hollered as he pointed at something on the other side of the window. He continued to slam his fist against the door. "Somebody's in there! We've got injured! We need a doctor!"

Christian and Jeff stopped to catch their breath. There was a long pause before a man's voice called out cautiously from the other side of the door.

"Has anyone in your group been bitten, scratched or had any contact with the infected?" The man called.

"NO!" Christian called back. "Gun shot and broken bones. No bites, scratches, or contact."

"How many in your party are injured?" The man questioned.

"Three injured," Christian answered. "We need a doctor!"

"Are you armed?" The man asked.

Christian glanced at Jeff and then back at Matt, "We are, but we're not looking for a fight. We just need a doctor!"

There was an uncomfortable moment of silence before the florescent lights overhead hummed and flickered on. In the few seconds it took for everyone's eyes to adjust, the light on the sensor above the automatic doors illuminated a bright red and then green.

Christian held his rifle at the low ready position as the doors slowly parted, "Here we go!"

"Ready!" Jeff replied as beads of sweat ran down his temples. His index finger tapped anxiously against the lower receiver.

As the doors opened a cold gust of air offered a momentary distraction. Christian felt his shoulders slump and eyes grow heavy as cool air filled his lungs. Jeff gave a slight shiver as the air washed over his sweat covered head.

An older man stepped cautiously from behind the wall. He was tall with broad shoulders and looked to have been an athlete in his youth. Dark eyebrows protruded over the top of his wire rimmed glasses. His cheeks were flush and a bushy gray beard covered his round face. Thinning silver-gray hair covered his head. He wore a white lab coat over a pastel yellow button-down shirt, black slacks, and black orthopedic shoes.

The man stood motionless for a moment. He glanced back and forth at Christian and Jeff, before he finally removed his hands from the pockets of his lab coat. They were startled back to reality as light reflected off something metallic.

"HANDS!" Christian shouted. His eyes opened wide as he brought his rifle up to the firing position. "SHOW ME YOUR HANDS!"

"WAIT!" The man cried as he threw his hands up. "It's just my watch! I'm not armed! Please don't shoot!"

"DON'T YOU FUCKING MOVE!" Christian ordered as his finger moved from the lower receiver to the trigger. "Is anyone else here with you?"

"WAIT!" The man cried again. "I'm a doctor...I'm a doctor."

"Easy!" Jeff encouraged as he lowered his rifle. "He said it was his watch. He doesn't look to be armed and I don't see anyone else."

Christian's hands trembled as he lowered the rifle, "What's your name?"

"Dr. Edwards...I'm Dr. Edwards," he answered. "May I put my hands down?"

"Yes," Christian responded with a nod. "It's been a difficult couple of days."

"I can imagine," Dr. Edwards offered empathically as he slowly lowered his hands. He pulled the sleeve of his lab coat to the middle of his forearm. Fastened around his left wrist was a stainless-steel Timex easy reader watch. "See, it was just the light reflecting off my watch."

"Thanks Doc," Jeff said as he placed his left hand on Christian's shoulder. "Glad we got that sorted out."

Dr. Edwards motioned towards Christian and Jeff. "You weren't kidding about being armed."

"No, we were not," Christian said flatly.

"That's good," Dr. Edwards said as he took a cautious step towards them. "Because we need your help."

"We've got wounded Doc," Christian said as he engaged the safety on his rifle.

"What do you need our help with?" Jeff asked.

"Well, we've got..." Dr. Edwards began.

"We've got wounded!" Christian interrupted in a more forceful tone.

"Yes, of course. We can table that discussion for now," Dr. Edwards said uncomfortably as he motioned for them to enter. "Please bring your people in. Let's have a look."

"Move!" Christian ordered as he took a step back. He raised the rifle to the low ready position and ushered everyone quickly through the open doors. "Let's go!"

Light cascaded down from the few perimeter lights that were on. They flicked, hummed, and cast long shadows over the large room. The dim setting and white noise in the background gave the emergency room an unsettling feel.

Barbra let out a deep sigh of relief as the cool air filled her lungs. She kept her hands pressed firmly against her sisters back as she momentarily closed her eyes. Her tranquil moment was cut short. "Ahhh!" Barbra yelped. She flinched as the automatic doors closed behind her.

"What happened?" Christian demanded as he and Jeff turned quickly.

"Nothing," Barbra insisted. "I'm sorry. I'm sorry. The doors closed. I didn't expect it. I just got spooked."

Christian shook his head and reengaged the safety on his rifle, "Pay more attention please. We don't need to have a mishap now."

"She just got spooked," Roderick reiterated as he and Shaw carefully carried Katlyn into the emergency room. "Just cut her some slack. She's scared."

"Come on," Jeff encouraged. He placed his hand on Christian's shoulder and put himself between Christian and Roderick. "Let's find a place to sit down."

"We're all scared kid," Paul growled as he glanced back at Roderick. "Now, drop it."

"Samantha, they're in," Dr. Edwards called to someone out of sight. "Please shut down the power."

Shaw looked around nervously as he watched the corridor go dark behind them, "I don't like this." He muttered to himself.

"Come in, come in please," Dr. Edwards said. He motioned towards several open beds against the far wall. "Put your folks over there and we'll have a look at them."

"Wait!" Christian said as he looked around. "Who else is here with you?"

"We'll get to the introductions," Dr. Edwards assured him. "First, get your folks situated and we'll have a look at them."

"Who else is here with you?" Christian asked again. "How many?"

"There are six staff members," Dr. Edwards answered. He held his hands up and attempted to put everyone at ease. "Actually; there are five of us now. We will explain everything later. For now, let's..."

"Tell them to come out!" Christian interrupted.

"Young man," Dr. Edwards began as his cheeks reddened. "You knocked on our door remember?"

"Ahhh," Tyler whimpered timidly as Matt repositioned him across his shoulders.

"We've had a couple really trying days, Doc," Matt said through clenched teeth. "What my brother's getting at is it would put us all at ease to meet your staff right now."

"What is this?" Doctor Edwards asked with a look of confusion. "I thought you weren't looking for a fight?"

"We're not," Christian answered stone faced. "We're also not looking to get ambushed. Now tell your people to come out here."

"I guess this is what the world is now," Doctor Edwards said with disappointment in his voice. He placed his hands in the pockets of his lab coat and shook his head. "The staff are taking care of other patients. This is still a hospital after all. Please use the beds against the far wall for anyone in need of medical attention and I will collect my team."

The beds were simply adjustable gurneys that could be wheeled in and out of the ER as needed. A 4-inch-thick piece of foam covered with a fitted white sheet served as a makeshift mattress.

"Easy," Barbra instructed. She grimaced as Shaw and Roderick lowered Katlyn onto the bed closest to the doors they entered through. "Go easy."

"Wait, wait, wait," Katlyn whimpered as her body tensed. Waves of pain seared through her with every movement.

"Watch my ankle," Tyler hissed. "Watch my fucking ankle!"

"Stop fucking squirming!" Matt ordered. He all but dropped Tyler on the bed against the opposite wall.

Tyler's face tightened and he let out high pitched yelp as his ankle smacked against the metal bed frame, "Ahhh! You fucker!"

"I don't like this," Christian said quietly. The florescent lights continued to emit an eerie hum. He motioned to Jeff as he looked around the ER. "Make sure nobody else is in here with us."

"On it," Jeff said with a nod. He made his way methodically around the perimeter of the room. He paused at each ER bay and pulled the curtain back to ensure they were empty.

"You're alright sis," Shaw insisted as he and Roderick carefully placed Katlyn on the bed. He held his sister's hand and looked up at Roderick. "See if you can find a pillow or something she can rest her head on."

"I'm on in it," Roderick said with a nod. He was better with a task to focus on. That's what his time in the military taught him. Too much downtime made a man soft. He lost too many brothers in arms to ever let his guard down again. "I'll find you something." He assured his aunt.

"Where are we?" Ralph whispered. His voice was gravely and breathing labored as Paul lowered him on to the bed in the middle of the row.

"Easy, brother," Paul encouraged. He was relieved to see Ralph regain consciousness. "We're in the hospital. We're going to get you fixed up."

"Sounds great," Ralph muttered as his eye lids fluttered. "Are there pretty nurses?"

"Clear!" Jeff called out as he rejoined Christian. "It's just us in here."

"We'll use the nurse's station as a base of fire," Christian said as he pointed to the large square structure in the center of the room. The top of the station stood almost 4-feet high. Computer terminals, chairs and cabinets with patient file folders occupied the work space. "It's central and there's cover."

"Wait," Shaw insisted as he joined Christian and Jeff. "What are we doing? They took us in. We need their help. My sister…"

"We're not taking any chances!" Matt barked as he joined the three of them. He adjusted the rifle sling and checked his magazine. "Find an empty bay you can move your sister into. We need to keep the injured out of the line of fire."

"Fucking hospitality, Jersey style," Roderick scoffed as he returned with an arm full of white cotton towels. "No pillows, but I found these."

Shaw nodded, "They'll work. Come on help me wheel Katlyn's bed into one of the bays."

"We don't have to listen to them," Roderick insisted. He could feel the hair on the back of his neck stand up.

"No?" Shaw questioned. "They're armed and we're not. So how about you don't provoke them and help me get your aunt into one of the bays and out of sight."

"This is fucking bullshit!" Roderick snapped. "This is why they wouldn't let us bring our weapons in?"

"Help your uncle kid," Paul said calmly as he wheeled Ralph's bed into one of the empty bays. "With any luck this will be resolved soon and we can have everyone seen to."

"Christ," Roderick blurted as he shook his head in disgust. His face reddened as he made his way over to his aunt. "I can't wait to get out of this fucking state."

"Jeff, right side," Christian ordered. He motioned towards cabinets across the room that protruded several feet from the wall. "Use those as cover."

"On, it," Jeff answered as he moved quickly into position. He kept his rifle trained on the double doors Dr. Edwards exited through.

"Paul, we need you on the left flank," Christian said as he and Matt moved to the corners of the nurse's station.

"In position," Paul announced as he stepped into the first ER bay and checked his rifle.

"How are you fixed for getting through those doors if things go south?" Christian asked as he looked over at Paul.

Paul glanced around the corner at the door they entered through. Unimpressed he brought his rifle up to the firing position and simply said, "Fuck those doors."

"Please reconsider this," Barbra pleaded as she approached the nurse's station. "My sister needs medical attention."

"And we aim to see that she gets it," Paul replied without looking back. "Stay with your sister."

"But..." Barbra began.

"No," Paul interrupted. "This is happening. Take your brother and your nephew and look after your sister. Stay out of sight until this is resolved."

Thirst and hunger contributed to the fatigue and agitation. The stress of the last 3-days only served to compound the exhaustion everyone felt.

The time it took for Dr. Edwards to return felt like an eternity. Finally, there was an audible click as someone on the other side of the doors pressed the button on the wall which activated the electric motor.

Dr. Edwards was the first to emerge as the large doors slowly parted. He was followed by two women and a man who all wore light blue hospital scrubs. A third woman also in a white lab coat was the last to enter the room.

The first woman through the doors was the shortest of the group. She had a round freckled face and long blonde hair pulled back into a pony tail. Her scrubs appeared to be at least a size too large. It looked as if she could disappear inside them if she wanted to. Her pant legs were rolled several times so as not to get caught on her white and pink sneakers. White long sleeves protruded from her scrub top and almost covered her hands. She shrieked in terror and threw her arms up when she saw the rifles, "AHHHH! Please don't shoot!" She cried. "We surrender!"

"It's alright Lexi. Get behind me," Dr. Edwards instructed as his face went flush. He could feel his heart pound in his chest. He slowly removed his hands from the pockets of his lab coat as his eyes found Christian's. "What is this?"

"Be calm!" Christian instructed. He kept the Aimpoint's red dot trained on Dr. Edwards chest. "Just be calm."

"What's happening?" Lexi cried as she darted behind Dr. Edwards.

"We welcomed you in," Dr. Edwards said sternly as he shook his head in disgust. "And this is how you treat us? I told you we would look after your injured. I told you we meant you no harm."

"All we want to do is make sure of that," Christian said as he glanced over at Matt. "My brother is going to check all of you for weapons."

"Is this really necessary?" Barbra pleaded from the back of the room. She swatted Shaw's hand away as he tried to pull her back into the ER bay and out of sight.

"Barbra, get back in here," Shaw ordered from where he stood just behind the wall.

"Stop it!" Barbra demanded. "Somebody must put a stop to this before it escalates." She continued before she turned her attention to the rest of the group. "Please, my sister needs medical attention."

Paul glanced back at her, "Get back in there." He growled. "We'll let you know when it's safe."

"Civilities can commence once we're satisfied, you're well intentioned," Christian said.

"We're well intentioned?" Dr. Edwards questioned angrily. "You're the ones pointing guns at us!"

"Have your people spread out," Christian ordered as he lowered his rifle and glanced over at Matt. "Ready?"

"Doc..." Lexi questioned nervously as she folded her arms. Her hands closed tightly around the sleeves of her scrub top as her cheeks reddened. "Doc, what's happening?"

"It's ok Lexi," Dr. Edwards assured her. He put a comforting hand on her shoulder. "Come on everyone. Do as they say. Spread out."

"Nice and easy," Matt said almost to himself. He lowered his rifle and moved around the nurse's station. "Jeff."

"I got you," Jeff answered. He lowered the barrel of his rifle as Matt passed in front of him. "You're clear."

The thin man next to Dr. Edwards breathed heavily. His eyes darted nervously from side to side as he took a step forward. Wirey sand color hair covered his head. His face was lean and cheeks a deep shade of red. The scrub top he wore appeared too wide for his narrow shoulders. Thick blond hair covered his forearms and his hands trembled visibly, "NO, FUCK THAT!" He blurted as he raised his left hand to reveal a scalpel and lunged forward.

"NO TOBIAS!" Lexi shrieked.

"WEAPON!" Christian shouted as he swung the barrel of his AR15 to the right.

"DON'T SHOOT!" Dr. Edwards cried. He threw his hands up and stepped in front of Tobias. "DON'T SHOOT!"

"PUT IT DOWN!" Matt ordered as he quickly brought his rifle up to the firing position and trained the Eotech's reticle on the Tobias's face.

"TOBIAS, STOP!" The woman in the white lab coat cried as she grabbed hold of his left arm. "THEY'LL KILL YOU!"

"NO!" Tobias hollered as he struggled to pull free of the woman's grasp. "LET ME GO!"

"PUT IT DOWN!" Matt repeated as his index finger moved to the trigger. "NOW!"

"DON'T SHOOT! DON'T SHOOT!" Dr. Edwards cried. He grabbed Tobias from behind and pinned his right arm against his body. "DR. SINGER, THE SCALPEL! GET THE SCALPEL!"

"Come on Samantha!" Lexi blurted. She took hold of the woman's scrub top and pulled her backwards as Dr. Edwards and Dr. Singer struggled to subdue Tobias.

"DO NOT FIRE!" Paul ordered.

"I don't have a shot!" Matt called from the other side of the room. White lab coats obstructed his view as the doctors struggled to disarm Tobias.

"THE SCALPEL, DR. SINGER!" Dr. Edwards cried as he struggled to turn Tobias's body away from the rifle barrels. "GET THE SCALPEL!"

"TOBIAS!" Dr. Singer screamed as she fought to keep hold of his left arm. "DROP IT TOBIAS! DROP IT!"

Christian's heart pounded as his index finger pulled through the first stage of his rifle's Geissele SSA trigger, "ENOUGH!" He bellowed in a voice that sounded as if it thundered down from the heavens.

The smack of metal against the vinyl floor quickly followed. It echoed across the room as Matt charged forward, "STEP AWAY FROM HIM!" He ordered.

"PLEASE!" Dr. Singer cried as she let go of Tobias's arm. She threw her hands in the air and kicked the scalpel away. "DON'T SHOOT!"

"STEP AWAY FROM HIM!" Matt repeated more forcefully.

"It's done!" Dr. Edwards called as he struggled to catch his breath. He pushed Tobias towards the double doors they entered through before he turned and pulled Dr. Singer behind him. "It's done!"

"The hell it is!" Tobias blurted. His eyes narrowed as he turned and charged back towards the nurse's station.

Matt lunged forward and shoved the 4-prong muzzle break on the end of his rifle in Tobias's face, "ON THE FUCKING GROUND!" Matt demanded as adrenaline pumped through his body. "ON THE FUCKING GROUND NOW!"

"Please!" Dr. Singer pleaded as she pushed her way around Dr. Edwards. "Please, just stop!"

Dr. Singer was tall and lean with an athletic figure. Dark rimmed glasses did little to hide her seductive green eyes. Full lips complemented her olive complexion. A head of long silken dark brown hair was pulled back in a tight bun. Beneath her white lab coat, she wore a satin white blouse tucked into black slacks and a pair of black non-slip shoes.

"On your stomach, arms out in front of you!" Matt ordered as he pressed the barrel of the rifle against the base of Tobias's neck. "Do not fucking move!"

"Please," Dr. Singer repeated. "Please, just stop."

Paul could see the desperation in her eyes and hear it in her voice. He lowered his rifle and tried to slow his breathing, "Stop." He managed as his chest heaved.

"As soon as I've checked him," Matt answered as he knelt next to Tobias. He used his left hand to quickly check Tobias for weapons.

"Stop!" Paul repeated. His throat was dry and voice gruff. The straps on his chest rig dug into his shoulders as a headache began behind his eyes. He didn't want to take any unnecessary chances, but the look of anguish on Dr. Singer's face was more than he could bear. This isn't who they were and not why they fought their way there. "That's enough!"

"Matt?" Christian called as he lowered his rifle.

"Clear," Matt answered as he finished with Tobias and stood up. He kept the rifle against the back of Tobias's neck as he turned and looked at Dr. Singer.

"You don't need to check us," Dr. Singer pleaded. "Please, we're not armed."

"THAT'S ENOUGH!" Paul barked. "You neutralized the threat. We've got bigger problems to deal with."

"Four more people to check," Matt said. He wiped sweat from his face as he motioned to the rest of the hospital staff.

"No!" Paul said sternly. "This ends now!"

"How's that?" Christian asked as he glanced over at Paul. "He had a weapon. What's to say the rest of them don't?"

"You heard me," Paul answered. "We've scared these people half to death and we need their help."

"We need to be safe," Christian snarled. "Are you forgetting that?"

"I'm not forgetting anything," Paul retorted as his eyes narrowed. He motioned towards Tobias. "He's face down with a rifle against his head. You think he's still a threat?"

Christian's eyes closed momentarily as pain ripped through his abdomen. He felt dizzy and nauseous. His eyes opened slowly and he glared at Paul. "If anything happens to our people because we didn't check them, that bloods on you." He snarled through clenched teeth as he reached for the corner of the nurse's station to balance himself.

"I'll take that chance," Paul said as he wiped the sweat from his forehead. He could see Christian was hurting and tried to diffuse the situation. "For now, we've got people who need medical attention."

"When I get off this floor," Tobias hissed. "I'm going to fuck you up."

"What was that?" Matt asked as if he hadn't heard the threat.

Tobias turned his head, "I said…"

"Threaten me again motherfucker!" Matt shouted as he drove the barrel of the rifle down at Tobias.

"AHHH!" Tobias yelped as the muzzle break caught him just above the left eye. His face smacked against the floor. He covered his face with his hands and curled up in the fetal position.

"STOP!" Paul demanded. He motioned for Matt to move away from Tobias. "ENOUGH! LEAVE HIM ALONE!"

"Fuck you!" Matt snarled. The sling held the rifle in front of him as he stood over Tobias with his fists clenched.

"GET AWAY FROM HIM!" Paul ordered as he took an imposing step forward. "NOW!"

Dr. Singer hurried to where Tobias lay. She knelt next to him, glanced up at Paul and mothed the words, "Thank you."

Paul answered with a slight nod of acknowledgement.

Matt picked up the scalpel, walked around the nurse's station and took a seat in one of the rolling chairs. His hands trembled as he tugged at the front of his plate carrier. "Fucking scalpel. Who pulls a fucking scalpel?"

"Lexi, Samantha, help me please," Dr. Singer called as she checked Tobias. She placed her hands over his. "Here let me take a look."

"Coming Doc," Samantha answered as she and Lexi hurried over.

Samantha was average height and petite. Her light brown hair was pulled tightly into a bun on the top of her head. A ball point pen protruded from her hair just above her hair tie. Rectangular framed clear rimmed glasses rested on the bridge of her freckled nose. Her scrubs appeared to be freshly pressed and she had a clear plastic clipboard tucked under her right arm.

Christian's body swayed slightly as he pushed himself away from the nurse's station, "He threatened my brother. Did you hear that?" He said with a scowl.

"And he paid for it," Paul said calmly. He could see the pain in Christian's eyes. "It's done now."

"If this goes south..." Christian began.

"I heard you the first time," Paul interrupted as he turned and walked away to check on Ralph.

Christian engaged the safety on his rifle, turned and locked eyes with Dr. Edwards. "Our wounded are over here."

Dr. Edwards hands trembled as he scowled, "You hold us at gun point and just like that you want to care for your people?"

Christian's eyes felt heavy and his breathing slowed. He could feel his legs weaken as the pain in his abdomen intensified, "I guess this is what the world is now." He said coldly.

"Let go of me! It's over!" Barbra said as she pulled free from Shaw's grasp. She stepped out of the ER bay and waved her arms. "We need help over here. Please my sister is hurt!"

"Lexi, please check on the woman in bay one," Dr. Singer instructed as calmly as she could, while she and Samantha helped Tobias to his feet.

"Yes, Doc," Lexi answered. Her cheeks were a deep shade of red and she looked at the floor as she shuffled past Christian. "Excuse me." She said in a timid voice as she hurried across the room.

"How's your balance?" Dr. Singer asked. "Do you need a wheelchair?"

"I don't need a chair," Tobias mumbled. He kept his hands over his left eye as he staggered towards the double doors. "My vision is blurry."

"Samantha, get a cold pack please," Dr. Singer said as she glanced over at the young nurse.

"Are you sure you have him?" Samantha asked. She was hesitant to let go of Tobias's arm.

"I've got him," Dr. Singer assured her. "Meet us in room three." She instructed as Samantha disappeared through the double doors. "You may have a mild concussion and we need to address the swelling above your eye."

"Miss," Paul called in a gruff tone as Lexi stepped into the first bay. He motioned to the next bay over where Ralph lay barely conscious. "When you're done there, my friend's been shot."

"Yes of course," Lexi said as she disappeared around the corner. "I'll be right there."

Matt bit down on his knuckle as his hands trembled, "The fuck did I almost do?" He whispered to himself.

Jeff stepped into the nurse's station and took a seat across from Matt, "You alright?" Jeff asked as he placed his hand on Matt's shoulder.

Matt shook his head and pushed Jeff's hand away, "I almost fucking killed him." He managed before he took several deep breaths. "What the fuck is happening?"

"Let's hope this gets sorted out soon," Jeff offered with all the empathy he could muster. "Just sit for a few minutes. I'll find you something to drink."

Matt glanced up to say something when the walkie talkie crackled.

"Burning day light out here," Mr. Spahl called. "What's the status? Over."

Matt unclipped the walkie talkie from his plate carrier and looked at it for a moment before he pressed the PTT button, "We're in. Found a doctor. Stand by for update. Over."

"Tobias is our orderly," Dr. Edwards explained as the doors closed behind Dr. Singer. He returned his hands to the pockets of his white lab coat and took a cautious step towards Christian. "We've had our issues with him, but he didn't deserve that."

"He had a weapon and he threatened my brother. If all he's got is a concussion, he got off easy," Christian said sharply through clenched teeth. "Our people need help. Are they going to get it or not?"

Dr. Edwards nodded as his gaze lowered to the floor, "Yes, we will help your people."

"Thank you," Christian said. His voice was raspy as the pain in his abdomen intensified. "This isn't who we are."

Dr. Edwards brought his gaze up, "Am I correct that nothing like this will happen again?"

"No, it will not," Christian answered as he locked eyes with Dr. Edwards.

Dr. Edwards could see the pain seared into Christian's face, "Are you alright?" He asked as he cleared his throat.

"Fine, Doc," Christian answered as he motioned towards the other side of the room. "We have wounded in the first three bays."

"Of course," Dr. Edwards said. "Nurse Lexi is attending to your people now. I'll send nurse Samantha over as soon as she's finished with Dr. Singer."

"Doc," Jeff said as he joined Christian. "I'm sorry we came upon you this way."

"Yes," Dr. Edwards said with an exhausted nod. "So am I."

"Doctor," Lexi called as she pushed Ralph's gurney towards the double doors. "The young woman in bay one will need x-rays, but I'm almost certain she has a broken collar bone."

"What about this gentleman?" Dr. Edwards asked as he motioned towards Ralph.

"Gunshot wound," Paul answered as he followed close behind. "He caught a stray round as we were making our way out of town. What are you still doing here?"

"Only staff beyond those doors please, until we determine a course of treatment," Dr. Edwards said. He held up his hand as Lexi continued with the gurney. "How much do you know?"

"Aside from being in the thick of it," Christian answered as he rubbed his temples. "Just what we've seen on TV and the internet."

"Then you know what happened at the arsenal, correct?" Dr. Edwards asked.

"We saw the reports," Matt called from where he sat.

"Well," Dr. Edwards began. "We received a number of their wounded."

"What happened Doc?" Paul asked.

"I promise you the broadcasts did not do the situation on the ground justice," Dr. Edwards answered. He glanced back to ensure his staff was out of the room before he continued. "I've been practicing medicine for the better part of four decades and I've never seen the kind of carnage that was air lifted here. Not even as an Army medic in Vietnam."

The room went quiet. An uncomfortable stillness covered the room like a heavy blanket as everyone tried to process what they just heard.

Samantha's voice startled everyone as she and Lexi returned, "Dr. Edwards." Samantha began as she and Lexi headed to the bays at the far end of the room. "We're going to bring the other two back now. Dr. Singer would like you to prep for surgery for the gunshot wound."

"Of course," Dr. Edwards replied. "Please let Dr. Singer know I'll be along momentarily."

"Thank you, Doctor," Samantha said as she and Lexi pushed the gurneys through the double doors.

"What are we dealing with?" Christian asked as the doors closed behind the nurses.

"It appears to be viral," Dr. Edwards answered. "But it's unlike any virus we've ever seen. As far as we can tell it's spread through bites, scratches, most skin-to-skin contact."

"Any kind?" Matt asked. His mind flashed back to Anthony and how many people carried him into the house after he was bit.

"Let me clarify," Dr. Edwards said as he held up his hand. He cleared his throat and twisted the band of his watch around his wrist. "There seems to need to be transmission of blood or saliva. I hypothesize other bodily fluids would be infectious also. Although, I have no data to back that up."

"Do you know where it started?" Christian asked. "Or how?"

"We do not," Dr. Edwards answered bluntly. "Early reports indicated outbreaks originated on military installations, first in the Continental United States. I can't confirm the accuracy of those reports. Some of the final broadcasts reported outbreaks of infected on every continent."

"Christ," Matt said as he let out a deep exhale. He dropped his head into his hands and rubbed his eyes. "That doesn't sound promising."

"No young man it does not," Dr. Edwards said. He adjusted his glasses and ran his hands through his silver and gray hair. "Keep in mind, I can't confirm all of this. I can only tell you the reports we saw and what happened here."

"So, what did happen here?" Paul asked.

Dr. Edwards looked down at his watch and then back at the group, "Gentlemen, I need to prepare for surgery."

"Humor us Doc. Just for a minute," Christian insisted. "Our people are with your staff. They're in good hands."

"Helicopters brought the wounded in faster than we could care for them," Dr. Edwards began as a haunted look overtook his eyes. "The ER became a triage center. We did our best to stabilize patients, but..." He paused, took his right hand from his coat pocket, and ran it uncomfortably over his chin. "The consensus between the doctors was that we were dealing with a fast-acting virus that was transmitted through the saliva in the bites."

"Accompanied by a high fever?" Christian asked.

"Yes," Dr. Edwards answered. "We saw temperatures as high as 106-degrees. We packed patients in ice to try and break the fever, but..." His voice trailed off for a moment as he paused to compose himself. He cleared his throat and continued. "After the fever came the change in flesh color. It began with a yellowish gray discoloration around the wound. Then spread throughout the body."

"Any viable treatment options?" Paul asked as he tugged at his beard.

"No," Dr. Edwards answered bluntly. He shook his head and looked around the room uncomfortably. "No, we did not. Their screams as the virus progressed and the lifeless hollow look that came over their eyes. Just terrible, unforgettably terrible. When you see it up close..."

It was quiet for a moment as Dr. Edwards voice trailed off again. He fidgeted with the watch band around his left wrist. The sound of the double doors as they opened redirected everyone's attention.

"Dr. Edwards," Dr. Singer called from the doorway.

"Yes," Dr. Edwards answered. He was visibly startled as he turned around. "Yes, Dr. Singer."

"We're prepping the patient with the gunshot wound for surgery," Dr. Singer explained. "We'll need you in OR-4 in ten minutes."

Dr. Edwards nodded, "I'll be along in a moment."

"Thank you, Doctor," Dr. Singer said as she nodded and turned to leave. "I'll let the team know."

"Dr. Singer!" Paul called as he walked over to where she stood.

"Yes," Dr. Singer replied. She stopped abruptly and turned back. "And, it's Tamara please."

"Tamara," Paul repeated as he managed a slight grin. "How's Ralph? My friend with the gunshot wound. How is he?"

"He's in good hands," Tamara assured him. She felt herself blush slightly as Paul approached. "He's going to be fine. I...I must prep for surgery." She added as she turned and passed between the doors as they closed behind her.

"What about the wounded Doc?" Christian asked.

"They died," Dr. Edwards answered. "We did everything we could but…"

"They didn't stay dead, did they?" Christian pressed.

"No. No, they did not," Dr. Edwards answered uncomfortably. "The reanimation times were unpredictable, minutes, hours. There was no way to determine when the infected would return. When they did, we weren't ready for it. They attacked patients and the hospital staff. It didn't take long for the top three floors of the hospital to be overrun."

"What about FEMA and the National Guard?" Paul asked as he returned to the group.

"Left almost as quickly as they arrived," Dr. Edwards answered. "The National Guard was here less than eight hours before they were redeployed to Trenton."

"And FEMA?" Christian asked as he adjusted his rifle sling. "The shelters in the parking lot were impossible to miss."

"They departed not long after the National Guard," Dr. Edwards explained. "FEMA personnel were redeployed to region 3."

"Region 3?" Matt questioned as he paced.

"FEMA has the country broken out by zones or regions," Dr. Edwards explained. "New Jersey and New York are part of region 2."

"Do you know where they were redeployed to?" Jeff asked.

"Region 3," Dr. Edwards answered. "Washinton D.C."

"Figures," Matt snarled. He twisted his head from side to side and tried to crack his neck. "Fucking figures…"

Christian glanced at Matt and then back at Dr. Edwards, "Anybody give you an explanation or a timeframe for return?"

"They're not coming back," Matt said angrily. "We're on our own."

"I was in the operating room for most of it," Dr. Edwards answered. "But no, the staff here never received any information. By the time I finished in the OR, the upper floors were chaos and we had to deal with that."

Paul rubbed his temples, "Why'd you stay?"

"I took an oath," Dr. Edwards answered. He took a white handkerchief from his pocket and dabbed at the tears that formed at the corners of his eyes.

"An oath?" Paul repeated.

"I'm a widower," Dr. Edwards admitted as his cheeks reddened. "Our son in the Navy. He's on a ship deployed to the South China Sea. There's no one to go home to. Circumstances being what they are, I thought I'd honor my oath and care for our remaining patients."

"Honorable," Paul said as he motioned towards the double doors. "Why'd the others stay? What about the rest of the staff?"

"Questions you'll have to ask them," Dr. Edwards answered as he wiped his nose. "They each have their reasons. I thank God, we're all here together. Most of the staff left after the National Guard pulled out. Unfortunately, everyone that stayed except for those you met, fell victim to the infected as the virus spread throughout the hospital."

"How many patients are left?" Matt asked.

"Seven, not including your people," Dr. Edwards answered. "One is touch and go, an older gentleman with a heart condition. I see no reason why the others won't make a full recovery. That is as long as you're willing to help us."

"Help you how?" Christian asked.

"The original hospital was constructed as the cold war was beginning. It consisted of the first floor, where we are now. Along with multiple OR rooms, patient rooms, offices, and a massive sub-basement that doubled as a fallout shelter," Dr. Edwards began. "Construction of the upper floors began in the late 70's. The elder care and physical therapy wings were added in the mid-90's."

"Do you have something more than a bathroom down here?" Jeff asked. "I've been in the same cloths for a couple days and I could use a shower."

"Yes," Dr. Edwards answered. "A portion of the sub-basement was renovated into locker rooms for the staff. They have sinks, showers, toiletries. Everything you may need. You and your people are welcome to use them."

"We've got anxious people out here!" Mr. Spahl called as his voice crackled over the walkie talkie. "What's the status? Over."

Matt clicked the PTT button, "Ralph is going in for surgery. Details to follow. Over."

"Let's get to it Doc," Paul said. "We've got people hanging fire outside. What do you need from us?"

"We have access to everything on the first floor and sub-basement," Dr. Edwards explained. "That includes the generator, backup power controls, and incinerator. The emergency controls are set up so that in the event of a disaster, man-made or otherwise, power can be diverted to whatever sections of the hospital require it. That's how we were able to power up the foyer and electric doors to allow you access. Power can be routed from floor to floor or more narrowly to refrigeration units to keep food and medicine viable."

"Get to the Goddamn point!" Christian growled. The mask of pain was etched across his face as his body contorted.

"The rest of the hospital," Matt interrupted. "What about it?"

"We're running out of food and medicine is the short of it," Dr. Edwards finally admitted. "There are refrigeration units on the 2nd and 3rd floor that we are continuing to run, but we have no way of getting to them."

"How's that?" Jeff asked.

"Yesterday against my direction, Nurse Reed left the 1st floor, for what she described as a supply run," Dr. Edwards said. "She was going to retrieve some of what we needed, but hasn't returned. I don't know if she's alive or dead. We have no way to get to her. We don't have weapons. We're not equipped to deal with the infected and we're running out of what we need to keep our patients alive."

"Do you have floor plans?" Matt asked. "It's a big hospital. We can't just venture off and look for your nurse."

"We have the floor plans," Dr. Edwards answered. "They're in my office just down the hall."

"We need the lights on both floors on," Matt said. "I don't want to be up there stumbling around in the dark."

"We should be able do that," Dr. Edwards assured him.

"Do you have a list of exactly what we need?" Christian asked.

"Need?" Dr. Edwards questioned. "We need everything. There's a cafeteria on the 2nd floor with a large walk-in freezer and a secure medication room with two refrigeration units on the third floor. We need it all."

"Empty a walk-in freezer?" Christian questioned. "That's not practical. Besides you have a day maybe two before whatever you don't consume spoils."

"Do you have a better plan?" Dr. Edwards asked.

"Doc," Matt said as he forced a grin. "We always have a plan."

"Get our people fixed up so we can get back on the road," Christian began. "In return we'll collect the medication from the third floor and clear out enough of the second floor so you and your staff can get back and forth to the cafeteria safely."

"Do you think you can do that?" Dr. Edwards asked. "The rest of the hospital was..."

"Take care of our people," Christian interrupted as he extended his hand for Dr. Edwards to shake. "Do that for us and we'll find your nurse and get you what you need."

CHAPTER 20

danger close

AN UNNERVING HOLLOW ECHO accompanied each step as Matt and Christian ascended the metal stairs. The stairwell was dark except for the emergency lights mounted at the top of each landing. The small, poorly angled lights did little to illuminate the area. Even in the dim light, moisture was visible on the concrete block walls and a musty odor filled the confined space.

"One more flight," Matt said quietly as he reached the top of the landing. He depressed the pressure pad with his left thumb and activated the Surefire Scout M600V weapon light mounted just behind the barrel of his rifle. The 350-lumen LED light cut through the darkness. "Stairs are clear. Let's go."

"In a second," Christian mumbled from where he stood on the lower landing. His right hand was wrapped tightly around the railing while he pressed his left against his abdomen.

"What?" Matt questioned as he looked back at his brother.

"I said in a second," Christian repeated without looking up.

"You alright?" Matt asked as he hurried back down the stairs. Even in the low light he could see Christian's face was more pale than usual. "Here let me help you."

"I'm fine," Christian insisted as he waved his brother off. "I just need a second."

"Sit this one out," Matt suggested. "We'll go back downstairs and I'll get Jeff and Paul."

"No!" Christian hissed as he looked up at his brother. The low light cast a dark shadow across most of his face. "I told Dr. Edwards we'd get this done."

"I don't think it matters which of us..." Matt began.

"We started this," Christian interrupted. "We're going to finish it."

"Jeff..." Matt offered.

"Jeff and Paul are busy bringing our people and our gear in," Christian interrupted again, this time through clenched teeth. "We don't need to ask any more of them. We can do this ourselves."

"Fine," Matt said as he turned back. "Then let's go. The 3rd floor entrance is at the top of the next flight of stairs."

"What about the 4th floor?" Christian asked. He knew the answer, but his body wasn't ready to move.

"Administrative offices mostly," Matt replied as he glanced back. He knew by Christian's voice he needed another minute and decided it best not to push him to continue. "Everything the staff needs is on the 2nd and 3rd floors. We start on three and work our way back to the emergency room."

"Hopefully we find their missing nurse," Christian added as he stood up straight. He could feel his body relax as the pain subsided.

"Yeah, hopefully," Matt said with a nod. "You ready?"

"Yes," Christian answered. He adjusted his rifle sling, made sure his safety was off and started up the stairs. "Let's get this done."

The steel diamond floor plating that covered the landing was noticeably slick. The emergency lights flickered and hummed over the flat cream color paint that covered the metal door. There was a large number '3' stenciled in black on the wall next to the door.

Christian breathed heavily as he pulled himself up the last few stairs, "Ready?" He asked as he positioned himself next to the entrance to the 3rd floor.

Matt nodded, "I'm good." He answered as he brought his rifle to the low ready position.

"The lights should be on," Christian explained. "When I open the door, you push in. I'll be right behind you."

"I know," Matt said. He let out a deep exhale, steadied himself and motioned towards the hinges. "The door opens towards the wall. We go on three."

"On three," Christian said as he took hold of the door handle. "One...two...three!"

"CONTACT!" Matt immediately shouted as the stairwell door swung open. The air on the 3rd floor was putrid and rife with the odor of decay. To their horror the hallway was filled with undead whose attention was immediately drawn to the arrival of the living.

"LEFT SIDE!" Christian ordered. He placed his left hand on Matt's right shoulder and pushed his brother into the corridor.

"THEY'RE EVERYWHERE!" Matt called as he opened fire. Shell casings spit from the ejection port of his AR15 as he eradicated the infected.

"PICK YOUR TARGETS!" Christian instructed. He stepped into the hallway behind his brother, turned and pulled the door closed behind them. "WE NEED TO CONSERVE OUR AMMO!"

Drawn by the thunder of gunfire, infected flooded the corridor. Blood-stained hospital gowns did little to cover what was left of their mangled bodies.

"THERE'S MORE COMING!" Matt shouted. He momentarily let go of the MLOK rail and pointed to the end of the corridor. "COME ON!"

"FOUR O'CLOCK!" Christian called as he took up a position diagonally behind his brother. He raised his AR15 and systematically dispatched infected as they approached.

The hallway was long with patient rooms evenly spaced on either wall like tracks of a zipper. Dr. Edwards delivered on his promise to turn the lights on. Unfortunately, this did not include the HVAC system. The buildup of moisture left the space sultry and floors unusually slippery.

"MOVE!" Matt ordered. He motioned for Christian to move past him as he continued to fire. "WATCH THE FLOOR, IT'S SLICK."

"MOVING!" Christian called as he hurried past Matt and stopped at the first doorway. He checked the door and found it locked. The stench made him gag. It was everything he could do not to vomit. His eyes watered as he raised his rifle, trained the red dot on the head of the nearest ghoul, and squeezed the trigger. "I DIDN'T EXPECT THIS MANY!"

Viscus dark red blood painted the walls and brass shell casings littered the floor as the brother's laid waste to the undead. The foam ear plugs did little to deaden the sound as the rifle blasts reverberated through the confined space.

Matt was startled when the bolt of his AR15 locked open, "LOADING!" He shouted as he ejected the magazine into his left hand and shoved it quickly into the Blue Force Gear 10-speed dump pouch attached to his Scorpion belt.

"HURRY!" Christian called without looking back. He could feel his chest tighten as he struggled to draw air into his lungs. Gun powder residue speckled his face as 79-grain hollow point rounds shattered skulls and decimated undead flesh.

"MOVING!" Matt yelled. He slammed a loaded magazine into the magwell and slapped the maritime bolt catch with his left palm. He grabbed the thick wooden rail attached to the wall with his left hand as he made his way past his brother. His eyes watered as he neared the corpses that cluttered the floor in front of them. "My God." He muttered to himself as he looked over the contorted faces and discolored remains.

"AHHH!" Christian hollered as a hot brass shell casing jettisoned from the ejection port of his rifle, bounced off the wall and caught him just above the right eye. "FUCK!"

"CHRISTIAN!" Matt called as he hurried to his brother. He lowered his rifle and tried to pull Christian's hands away from his face. "WHAT HAPPENED!"

"GET OFF!" Christian demanded as he pushed his brother away. "It was just a shell casing." He said as he motioned to the burn mark above his right eyebrow. "I'm fine."

"You sure?" Matt asked as haunted moans intensified from the opposite end of the hall.

"YES!" Christian snarled. He glanced at his brother as he struggled to catch his breath. "Come on, rifle up!" We need to push them back so we can get out of this hallway."

"You need your inhaler?" Matt asked.

"We need to get out of this hallway!" Christian repeated. "Let's go!"

Matt nodded and moved to engage the horde, "Ahhh!" He shouted as his boot slid across a puddle of blood that collected around the floor in front of them.

"MATT!" Christian called as he watched his brother stumble.

"FUCK!" Matt yelled as he felt his lower back twinge. He pushed the rifle away from his body as he landed hard on his left side.

"GET UP!" Christian shouted.

"Oh, that's not good," Matt moaned. Pain seared through his lower back as he tried to sit up.

"GET UP!" Christian ordered. He redirected his focus to the infected who staggered towards them, raised his rifle, and opened fire. "COME ON! GET UP!"

"My fucking back," Matt muttered to himself as he struggled to get to his feet. He grabbed for the railing with his left hand and used it to pull himself up. He winced as the laceration on his palm reopened.

With the last of the thirty rounds expended, Christian felt the bolt of his AR15 lock open, "LOADING!" He called as he dropped to one knee.

Pain shot down Matt's left leg, "Come on!" He grumbled as he struggled to stand up straight. He steadied himself, placed the Eotech's reticle between the closest set of lifeless eyes and pulled the trigger. Clumps of brain matter and skull fragments jettisoned across the corridor.

Christian shoved the empty magazine in the dump pouch on his web belt. He pulled a loaded magazine from a TACO pouch on his plate carrier as he got to his feet, "Fucking infected." He hissed to himself as he slapped the maritime bolt catch with his left hand and reengaged the mob.

They expended more ammunition during the initial contact than anticipated. The brothers were careful to keep at least 10-feet of open ground between themselves and the undead. Matt and Christian checked each door as they moved carefully along the corridor. They waded through pools of infected blood and mounds of decayed flesh as they pushed forward.

"Hold the line!" Christian shouted as he advanced. He squared his stance, placed the red dot on the haunted expression of the closest face, exhaled and squeezed the trigger.

"Loading!" Matt shouted as he tried to pull a loaded magazine from the pouch on his plate carrier. He watched in horror as it slipped from the saturated medical tape around his palm and tumbled to the floor. "FUCK!"

"PICK IT UP!" Christian shouted as he glanced over at his brother. "HURRY!"

"ON IT!" Matt called. A surge of adrenaline raced through him as he scrambled to retrieve the magazine.

"We're almost there!" Christian hollered as the bolt locked open again. His eyes widened with surprise. "LOADING!"

"What?" Matt questioned as his hand found the loaded PMAG. He slammed it in the magwell, released the bolt catch and opened fire from where he knelt.

"ON IT!" Christian answered. He let the single-point sling hold the rifle in front of his body as he quickly drew the H&K USP from his drop leg holster and opened fire. When the slide locked open, he returned the pistol to his holster, reloaded his rifle, and continued to fire.

Viscera and decayed flesh erupted across the corridor as rifle rounds pulverized the skulls of the infected. Mangled remains crumpled to the floor as the brothers pushed forward.

"Fuck," Matt muttered to himself. His body trembled as he took his finger off the trigger and steadied himself. "They just keep coming."

"COME ON!" Christian shouted as he glanced over at his brother. "We're almost there."

Matt shook off the fatigue and raised his rifle, "We're almost there." He repeated to himself as he took several deep breaths. A little longer and they'd be safely back downstairs he thought to himself as he placed the bright red reticle on the head of the nearest ghoul and squeezed the trigger. The contorted body collapsed in a heap without most of its face. Skull fragments and brain matter dripped down the wall where it stood.

"MOVE!" Christian shouted.

"MOVING!" Matt called back as he hurried through the pile of remains to the next doorway. "MOVE!" He called as he opened fire.

"MOVING!" Christian answered as he followed suit. He dispatched the last group of infected in the hallway before the bolt locked open. "LOADING!" He called as he quickly switched out magazines.

"CLEAR!" Matt called as the last body fell. His ears rang as he wiped gun powder residue from his face. He looked back and forth several times and cautiously surveyed the area. "We're all clear!"

The smell of sweat and gun powder hung in the stagnant air. It did little to mask the oppressive odor of decay.

Matt looked over at Christian, "You good?" He asked as he gave the hallway another look.

Christian retrieved his inhaler, shook it, and pulled two puffs into his lungs, "Better now." He answered.

Matt ejected the magazine from his rifle and replaced it with a fully loaded one from his plate carrier, "We need to move."

Christian pulled the USP from his holster. He ejected the empty magazine, replaced it with one from the mag pouch on the front of his plate carrier and racked the slide, "We expended too much ammunition." He said as he returned the pistol to his holster and fastened the retention band.

"Yes, we did," Matt responded as he peered cautiously down the hallway.

"You have extra magazines on the back of your plate carrier?" Christian asked.

"Two," Matt answered as he held up 2-fingers and glanced over at Christian. "In the pouch next to my med kit."

"Same," Christian answered as he motioned behind him. "Give me a hand." He said as he pulled two empty magazines from his dump pouch.

Matt hurried through the heap of bodies that filled the middle of the hallway. He pulled the Velcro cover open and collected the magazines, "Here." He said as he handed them to his brother.

"Thanks," Christian said. He placed the magazines in the TACO pouches on the front of his plate carrier and handed his brother the two empty ones. "Here, put these in the pouch."

"My turn," Matt said as he fastened the cover and secured the pouch on his brother's carrier. He turned so Christian could retrieve his magazines.

"You're good," Christian said as he secured the empty magazines in the pouch.

"You ready?" Matt asked as he placed the loaded magazines in the pouches on the front of his plate carrier.

Christian nodded. "I'll take point." He said as he smacked the maritime bolt catch with his left hand. "Watch the doors. There may be more infected in these rooms. We don't need any surprises."

The brothers knew the harsh odor and twisted faces would haunt them for the rest of their days. They watched for movement as they carefully maneuvered through the blood-soaked pile of carcasses.

They almost reached the end of the hallway when an open door caught Christian's eye, "Open door right side." He called. Christian barely got the words out when a pair of discolored hands lunged at them from the darkened room.

"CONTACT!" Matt shouted.

Christian quickly stepped back, raised his rifle, and fired. There was a thud as the body smacked against the floor, "Tango down." He paused to make certain there was no other movement. Satisfied, he pulled the door closed as they continued.

"Watch the corner!" Matt instructed as they neared the end of the corridor.

"What's down the next hallway?" Christian asked. The MLOK rail felt warm against his left palm as he adjusted his grip.

"More patient rooms," Matt answered as he pressed his body against the wall for balance. The pain down his left side intensified with each step.

"That means more infected," Christian said quietly. He stopped just before the end of the wall and looked back at Matt. "I've got the right side."

"I'll clear the left," Matt responded. "We don't need those things coming up behind us."

"Ready?" Christian asked as he took a cautious step forward.

"Ready," Matt answered as he mirrored his brother's movement.

"Go!" Christian called. He pivoted to his right and stepped around the corner into the next hallway.

"CONTACT LEFT!" Matt shouted as he came face to face with two infected who lumbered towards them.

"CONTACT RIG..." Christian hollered. His voice was quickly drowned out by the thunderous crack of Matt's rifle.

Matt's first shot tore through the throat of the infected. His second shattered the creature's forehead. Its body stumbled backwards and smacked against the floor, "Tango down!" He called as he turned his focus to the second ghoul.

Christian's first shot found its mark. A thick mist of blood rained across the floor as the mangled body spun and bounced off the wall before it slammed face first into the floor, "Clear right!" He called.

Matt trained the reticle on the face of the second infected and squeezed the trigger. The round struck the chin and pulverized its jaw. The impact snapped its head back and knocked it backwards, "Tango down!" Matt called as he stepped forward. He fired another round into the contorted face. Dark red blood spilled from the exit wounds and coated the floor around what was left of its head. "Clear left!"

"Let's go!" Christian ordered.

The gentle hum of the florescent lights and squeak of their boots were the only sounds in the hallway as they hurried on. As they neared the end of the next corridor Christian noticed another open door and stopped abruptly.

"What is it?" Matt asked.

"Open door," Christian answered as he motioned with his left hand. "Right side."

"Cover me," Matt instructed as he moved to the doorway.

"I've got you," Christian said. He moved to the opposite wall and scanned both sides of the hallway.

Matt cautiously entered the room and swept the barrel of his rifle from left to right, "Clear!" He called. He pulled the door closed behind him. "Let's go."

Christian wiped sweat and gun powder residue from his face, "Hang on." He said as he retrieved his inhaler. He gave it a quick shake and took two more puffs. He inhaled as deeply as he could and pulled the medication into his lungs. He held his breath for a few seconds before he slowly exhaled through his nose.

"You alright?" Matt asked as he joined his brother.

"Fine. I just need a second," Christian answered. "How's your hand?" He asked as he changed the subject.

"Fucked," Matt said as he looked down at the gauze and medical tape that covered his left hand. "The laceration keeps pulling open."

"Crazy glue," Christian said as he tipped his head back and took several deep breaths. "When we get back downstairs clean it out and try some crazy glue."

"That might work," Matt agreed. "I've got a couple tubes in my go bag."

"That should hold," Christian said as he pushed his body away from the wall. "Alright, what's next?"

"End of this hallway, we turn left," Matt explained. "There should be a bank of elevators and pair of bathrooms in the next hallway."

"After that?" Christian inquired as he adjusted his rifle sling.

"After that," Matt began. "We find ourselves at the center of the 3rd floor."

"Almost there," Christian mumbled. He forced a slight smile as he struggled to conceal the obvious pain, he was in.

"It's a large open atrium," Matt explained as they readied to move. "Kind of an all roads lead here central hub for the 3rd floor."

"Sounds like the place we need to be," Christian said as he gave the hallway behind them another glance.

"Dr. Edwards said the administrative offices on the 4th floor were constructed around a massive sky light that overlooks the atrium," Matt continued. "There are decorative fountains on the north and south walls. A secure records room on the west and secure medication room on the east."

"Let's get to it then," Christian said as he moved his rifle to the low ready position.

"There's going to be a lot of open ground to and from the medication room," Matt said as he adjusted his rifle sling. "Depending on the level of infestation we could have our hands full."

"Hit and run," Christian said bluntly. "Shoot ourselves an opening big enough to get into the room. Collect what we need and Wild Bunch it out of there."

"I appreciate the reference," Matt said with a grin. "But you remember how that movie ended?"

"I do," Christian answered. "But the infected won't be shooting back. Once we've got what we came for it won't matter if the infected are trapped up here."

"Let's get this done," Matt said as he put his hand on his brother's shoulder. "Come on."

The heat became oppressive as the brothers hurried down the hall. Without the sound of gunfire to drown out, the foam ear plugs felt more awkward than helpful. Their pace slowed and they moved cautiously as they neared the end of the corridor.

Matt twisted his right hand around the BCM grip as he readied himself to clear the hallway to the right, "Ready?" He asked as he glanced over at his brother.

Christian nodded as he prepared to clear the left side, "Go." He said as he raised his rifle. They moved in unison around the corner.

"CONTACT RIGHT!" Matt shouted as he discovered a ghoulish figure in a blood-stained lab coat who reached for him from the floor. The infected tried to clamber to its feet with what was left of its legs.

"CONTACT LEFT!" Christian shouted as he came face to face with three infected who lumbered purposely towards him. Their discolored mouths hung awkwardly open and emitted an unsettling moan. Shredded hospital gowns clung to dried blood on the disfigured bodies. Christian raised the rifle and quickly dispatched the first ghoul. "Tango down!" He called as he prepared to dispatch the other two.

Matt zeroed the reticle on top of the creature's head and pulled the trigger, "Tango down!" He called as the body convulsed under the impact of the 62-grain green tip round.

"Two more!" Christian called as he swung the rifle barrel. His second shot tore through the creature's throat. The body tumbled backwards to the floor. Its head snapped violently back as the round exited just above the left temple.

"Clear right!" Matt called as he turned to join his brother.

Christian didn't look up. He kept the rifle stock under his cheek bone. The Aimpoint site allowed him to operate the rifle with both eyes open. In one fluid motion he maneuvered the rifle right and squeezed the trigger. The shell casing spit from the ejection port as the 77-grain OTM round ripped through the discolored flesh of the creature's skull. The blood-stained hospital gown followed the contorted body as it slammed against the wall and left a smear of blood as it toppled towards the floor, "Tango down!"

"Where's that coming from?" Matt shouted as the haunted moans of the undead began to fill the hall.

"Behind us," Christian answered. He could feel the hair on his neck stand up. "They're behind us. Come on we've got to move."

The moans faded into the background as the brothers hurried towards the atrium. As they approached the end of the long corridor, they could see the colossal fountain chiseled out of deep blue clouded marble on the south wall.

"That's huge," Matt observed they neared the center of the 3rd floor. "I bet it was as expensive as it is beautiful."

"When we get to the end of the hall, I want you to cover me," Christian instructed. "I'll move to the fountain and set up a base of fire."

"Got it," Matt answered. "When you're in position call it out. I'll cover you from the end of the nurse's station so you can get to the medication room."

"Once we punch the code into the cypher lock," Christian said as they continued. "We're in."

"Collect the meds, clear a path to the cafeteria and back to the ER," Matt added.

"Sounds like a plan," Christian said as he gave his brother a nod.

A grin stretched across Matt's face, "I love it when a plan comes together."

They stopped when they reached the corner of the wall. The atrium was much larger than they anticipated. From where they stood the area appeared clear, but there was a significant portion of the floor that was not visible to them.

"Fuck," Matt snarled. "Visibility is shit from here."

"Nothing we can do about that," Christian said as he surveyed the area.

Matt pressed his left shoulder against the wall and looked back towards his brother, "Ready?"

"Ready," Christian answered. "Let's go."

Matt stepped out from behind the corner and pivoted to his left, "Move!"

Christian took off in a sprint. His boots pounded against the floor and his chest heaved as he ran. He stopped just as he reached the marble fountain. He swept the atrium from his position and to his relief found it empty, "Clear!" He called.

"Clear!" Matt echoed as he lowered his rifle. He hurried to join his brother. "I've had enough trigger time for one day. The recoil is starting to make me shaky."

"Your blood sugar is dropping off," Christian said as he continued to look around. "Come on let's get the med room open."

The otherwise pristine white of the atrium was repeatedly interrupted with the unmistakable crimson red of blood. What concerned them more though was the trail of blood that led directly to the door of the secure medication room.

"Oh, what the fuck?" Matt questioned as he pointed to the trail of red that ran from the nurse's station to the heavy metal door with the cypher lock below the knob. "That's not good."

"Whatever it is we'll deal with it," Christian assured him. He let the single point sling take the weight of the rifle as he drew the USP from his holster and checked the chamber. "What's the code?"

Matt tightened the quick adjust tab on his Vickers tactical sling and maneuvered the AR15 behind him, "The code is 0-5-0-8-1-2." He said as he drew his 1911 and checked the chamber.

Christian repeated the numbers as he typed them into the cypher lock, "0-5-0-8-1-2." There was a brief pause before the lock buzzed. "We're in. Let's go!" He said as he turned the knob and pushed the door open.

Cool air washed over them as the heavy metal door swung open. To their surprise, at the other end of the room with her back to them stood a woman. She wore a white wool sweater over blue scrubs.

"Hey!" Matt called as he hurried into the room. "Are you alright? Do you need help?" He was in mid step when Christian grabbed the drag handle on the back of his plate carrier and pulled him back. "What the fuck?" Matt called as his body jerked backwards.

"I don't think she's alright," Christian said as he let go of his brother and pulled the door closed behind them. He pointed to the smear of blood that covered the linoleum and ran the length of the room. The woman's sneakers and most of the left leg of her scrub pants were covered in dark red.

They stood shoulder to shoulder for a moment in the small room. Their hearts pounded and they felt a slight chill as the cool air dried their sweat. Neither spoke, they just stared at the woman as her body teetered unnaturally from side to side.

Quietly at first the low ominous moan began. It got louder as the woman slowly turned to face the brothers. The front of her sweater was saturated with blood from the gaping wound on the left side of her neck. Pinned to her sweater partially obscured by red was a white plastic nurses' badge. There was an uncomfortable moment as the brothers realized the name on the badge was 'REED.'

Nurse Reed's head cocked to the side as her mouth hung open. The final measure of excruciating pain she experienced in life was imprinted across her contorted face. Her hollow eyes offered no remnants of humanity. Her arms slowly raised as she reached for them.

"Fuck this!" Christian growled as he raised the USP and stepped forward. There was a deafening crack and blinding muzzle flash. The .45 caliber slug struck Nurse Reed between the eyes. Her body was thrown backwards against the wall. It came to rest in a heap on the floor.

They stood for a moment in silence and tried to collect their thoughts. Neither knew what to say.

"I was hoping that would have gone differently," Matt finally said as he looked at nurse Reed's remains. There was a slight tremble in his hands as he engaged the thumb safety and returned the 1911 to his holster.

"Yeah, me too," Christian said as he depressed the decocker with his thumb.

"What now?" Matt asked as he ran his hands over his face.

Christian returned the pistol to his holster and retrieved his inhaler, "We finish what we started."

CHAPTER 21

my brother's keeper

"**S**ECURE THE STRAP AROUND the door handles!" Matt shouted as he threw his body against the large pair of fire doors. He struggled to hold them closed as the infected pushed from the other side. "HURRY!"

"HOLD THEM CLOSED!" Christian ordered. Discolored flesh squeezed between the doors as infected piled against the other side.

"I'M TRYING GODDAMMIT!" Matt blurted as his face reddened. "THESE THINGS ARE FUCKING STRONG!"

"They're hungry!" Christian retorted. He wrapped the thick cloth straps used to restrain hostile psych ward patients around the metal door handles several times. The heavy doors moved back and forth as the bodies pressed against them. "You want to be lunch? Put your fucking legs into it!"

"FUCK!" Matt snarled as he put his back against the doors and squatted down low. A guttural scream worthy of a medieval battle field emanated from deep in his gut as he pushed. "AHHHHH!"

There was a loud bang as the doors slammed closed against the metal brackets attached to the top of the frame. Matt held the doors in place as Christian tightened the straps around the door handles and finally secured them.

"We had access to the Winnebago, so it only made sense to use it," Dominick explained to Mrs. Spahl before he finished the last swallows of water from the plastic bottle. "The thing you have to remember about large recreational vehicle like that..."

"DAD!" Jeff called as he hurried from the darkened corridor.

"What happened?" Mr. Spahl demanded as he clambered to his feet. "Where is everyone? Is that gunfire we keep hearing?"

"How's my sister?" Holden called as he hurried over from where he stood at the far end of the portico.

"We found the medical staff!" Jeff blurted as he stopped and caught his breath.

"Oh, thank God," Mrs. Spahl said. She placed her hand on her chest, closed her eyes and tipped her head back. "Thank God."

"How is my sister?" Holden repeated. "Has she been seen to?"

"I think we're going to be here awhile," Jeff informed the rest of the group. "We need to start bringing everything inside."

The straps pulled tight around the door handles as the infected trapped on the other side tried desperately to get through.

"Are we good?" Matt asked as the collective moan of the undead intensified. His quadriceps burned as lactic acid built up in his legs.

"We're good," Christian answered as he gave the straps a final check.

Matt let out a deep exhale and slumped down against the door, "Fucking hell." He mumbled as the infected scratched and clawed from the other side. "How long do you think the straps will hold?"

"Don't know," Christian answered. He took a few steps back and placed his left hand over his abdomen. "Long enough for the Doc and his staff to reinforce them with something else, I'm sure. Where to next?"

"Let's take a look," Matt said. He pulled a paper copy of the floor plans from the cargo pocket on his left pant leg and unfolded it.

Christian slowly sat himself next to his brother. He used the sleeve of his shirt to wipe his forehead. The sweat left a visible streak against the already moist fabric, "What's the verdict?" He asked as he pressed his fingers against his temples.

"Whoever designed this place was a maniac," Matt declared as he held the plans out in front of him.

Christian rubbed his eyes, "That's what happens when you put multiple additions on an existing structure."

"Didn't the Doc say they had different contractors for the early additions to the building?" Matt asked as the noise on the opposite side of the door began to subside.

"Something like that," Christian answered without opening his eyes. "Problems with the budget or architect or zoning or some bullshit."

"Mystery solved," Matt said as he stared at the floor plans.

"Ok," Christian said with a deep exhale. He opened his eyes and refocused his attention. "Where are we?"

"Here," Matt answered as he placed his finger against the paper. He used his index and middle fingers to trace the route as he spoke. "We came down the south stairwell here. This is where we need to be and this is the path, we need to take to get there."

"Ok...ok," Christian uttered as his jaw tightened.

Matt could see his brother was in a significant amount of pain, "How bad?" He asked.

"I can keep going," Christian answered. He closed his eyes and tipped his head back against the cold metal door. "I just need a minute."

There was a noticeable pause in the muffled pop of gunfire from the floors above. The lull left the gentle hum of equipment as the only sound. Tensions in the emergency room began to subside, aided in no small way by the cool dry atmosphere.

"Where do you want me to put these?" Kurt asked as he entered the emergency room with a large duffle bag slung over each shoulder.

"What?" Paul questioned almost startled as he turned from where he stood at the nurse's station.

"Oh, it's nice in here," Kurt observed as cool air washed over his face and head. He stood for a moment as his shoulders relaxed. "Where'd you say to put them?" He asked again from an almost trance like state.

"Where's Jeff?" Paul asked as he collected his rifle from where it stood next to him.

"How's behind the nurse's station?" Kurt asked as he made his way slowly over to where Paul stood. "Where's Jeff?" Paul asked again as he positioned the rifle sling over his shoulder.

"Outside," Kurt answered. He placed the duffle bags behind the nurse's station and sat down in one of the rolling chairs. "That's nice." He continued as he exhaled. His body slumped forward until his elbows rested on his legs just above his knees.

"JEFF!" Paul repeated more sternly.

"Yeah," Kurt said with an exhausted nod. "Jeff's getting the gear together and he's bringing everybody in."

"Does he need help?" Shaw called from where he and Roderick stood at the back of the room.

"Probably," Kurt answered as he glanced back. "I'm going head back out. I just need to sit for a minute."

"You relax kid," Shaw offered. He motioned to his nephew. "Roderick and I will head out and see if we can help."

"Where's your other half?" Paul asked as Shaw and Roderick passed through the automatic doors on their way out.

"Kim's coming in I think," Kurt assured him. There was a noticeable tremble in his hands. "She's helping Katherine with her mother."

"Is everything alright out there?" Paul inquired.

"Quiet," Kurt answered with a nod. "It's almost too quiet out there." His voice shook as he continued. "Feels like you're holding your breath waiting for something to happen."

"I know that feeling all too well," Paul said in a gruff voice. He unslung the rifle and leaned it against the counter next to him. "Why don't you sit for a minute."

"Yeah," Kurt said as he slowly cracked his knuckles. The uncomfortable sound echoed across the open space. "Cloud cover's back. Looks like it may storm again."

The moans of the infected trapped on the other side of the large doors gradually subsided. It left the hallway with only the eerie buzz of the florescent lights overhead. The air was stale and rife with the odor of decay.

"You ready?" Matt asked as he got to his feet.

Christian nodded but didn't open his eyes, "Yeah." He muttered quietly.

"Come on," Matt encouraged. "We need to move."

"Just give me a minute," Christian said as he tried to gather his strength.

Matt could see his brother was in pain, but knew not to insist they go back or Christian remain behind. Christian repudiated pity of any kind. Matt rested his hands on his gun belt and waited until his brother was ready to push on and finish what they started.

"Why are you staring at me?" Christian asked as he opened his eyes and looked up at his brother.

Matt shook his head unable to formulate a witty answer, "Just keeping an eye on you."

"Well knock it off," Christian instructed with a grimace. He began to pull himself up from the floor. "I'm fine."

"I know," Matt agreed as he extended his hand. "Here, let me help you."

"I said I'm fine," Christian insisted as he waved his brother's hand away. He grabbed hold of the cloth strap wrapped around the door handle and slowly pulled himself to his feet. He stood statuesque as the pain eventually subsided. "You don't need to keep an eye on me."

"No, I don't," Matt said as he brought his hand back to his gun belt. "But if I didn't, I'd be somebody else. So, you're just going to have to live with it."

"Hmm," Christian scoffed with a slight grin as he rubbed his temples. "Fine. I'll live with it." He conceded. He adjusted the rifle sling and retracted the charging handle enough to make sure there was a round in the breach. "Let's go."

There were no fewer infected on the 2nd floor. They wandered and staggered seemingly oblivious until the sound of gunfire drew their attention. Matt and Christian found the undead more spread out than on the floor above. It allowed the brothers to barricade several pairs of large fire doors as they secured a route to and from the cafeteria.

"Any word from the doctor?" Jeff asked as he entered the emergency room. He placed two large ammo cans down next to the nurse's station and used a small towel to wipe the sweat from his face.

"No," Paul answered impatiently. He motioned to the set of doors that led to the operating and recovery rooms. "One of the nurses was by a few minutes ago but all she could tell me was that we'd have to wait for the doctor."

"Maintain protocol while the rest of the world collapses," Jeff said before he finished the half full bottle of water on the counter. Muffled pops pulled his attention to the ceiling. "Sounds like they're back at it."

Paul shook his head and pulled on his beard before he slammed his fists down on top of the nurse's station, "Mother fucker!" He blurted.

Jeff flinched at the unexpected outburst, "What the fuck's gotten into you?"

"Jesus Christ!" Paul snarled. "We should be up there with them!"

"They're fine," Jeff insisted. "Besides, they were clear about needing us down here to watch over everything."

"Fucking watch over everything," Paul hissed. "There's been a lot of shooting. They didn't take that much ammunition. They might need our help. What if they're in trouble?"

"As long as they're still shooting," Jeff offered. "They're fine."

"Bullshit!" Paul scoffed. "A hundred things could have gone wrong up there."

"They've got a walkie talkie in case they get into trouble," Jeff reminded him.

"They took a walkie talkie," Paul corrected. "We don't know that they still have it or that it's working."

"They're fine," Jeff repeated. "Come on. I'm getting hungry and we've got more stuff to bring in."

Outside, the humidity returned. The green of the trees appeared darker as the sun was eclipsed by thick smoke-colored clouds. There was a substantial breeze and it appeared as though a thunder storm was on the horizon.

Mr. Spahl and Patrick pulled their perimeter back. They gathered everyone under the portico as they continued to keep watch. The last of the weapons, ammunition cans and supplies sat piled on the sidewalk next to the darkened corridor.

"Those are gun shots," Mr. Spahl said as the muffled pops continued.

Patrick nodded as he scanned the parking lot and hospital grounds, "Yeah, that's what they sound like to me too."

"Where's Jeff?" Mr. Spahl asked with considerable agitation in his voice. He looked around hurriedly. "We've been out here long enough."

"He was bringing gear in last I saw him," Patrick offered. "I'm sure he'll be back after."

"The sooner we're all inside the better," Mr. Spahl muttered.

"Here he comes," Patrick announced as Jeff and Paul emerged from the building.

"Dad!" Jeff called as he hurried to where his father stood. "Let's get the rest of the gear and bring everybody in."

"How is everyone?" Mrs. Spahl called to her son. She stood with her arm around Aunt Athena's shoulders.

"Waiting on the doctor," Jeff answered as he glanced back.

"Everybody's in good hands," Paul assured them.

"Are you sure?" Aunt Athena asked as she struggled to hold her composure.

"I'm sure," Paul answered. "Tyler will be fine. Just keep praying for him."

"I will," Aunt Athena said as she managed a meek smile.

Mrs. Spahl mouthed the words, "Thank you."

"Sure," Paul replied with a nod. He quickly turned his attention to Mr. Spahl and the rest of the group. "Come on." He bellowed. "Let's collect the rest of the gear and get inside."

"Was Kurt with you?" Kim asked. The concern was visible on her face as she picked up a rifle case and backpack. "He carried some bags in and I haven't seen him."

"He's inside," Paul informed her in a softer tone. "He looked exhausted so I made him sit down. He's in at the nurse's station."

"Thank you," Kim said as a look of relief washed over her face. "The nurse's station you said? I'll find him."

"Yes," Paul answered as she disappeared into the corridor. "Just beyond the automatic doors to your right."

"Where are they?" Mr. Spahl asked as he motioned behind him to the building. He slung the rifle over his left shoulder.

"Sounds like the second floor," Jeff answered.

"Sounds like a lot of shooting," Mr. Spahl commented before he finished the last swallows of water in his bottle. "Do we know if they help?"

"My question exactly," Paul interjected. "We could have cleared the second floor while they cleared the third and we'd be done by now."

"We don't know that," Jeff argued. "Besides, the fewer rounds being fired the safer we all are. Anyway, like I keep saying, they've got a walkie talkie and if they needed us, they'll call."

"Fine," Paul growled. He grabbed a rifle case and ammo can and walked back towards the building.

"You coming back?" Jeff asked.

"No," Paul answered. "You don't need me. There's enough man power out here to bring the rest of this stuff in."

"Where are you going?" Jeff called after him.

"To find the Doc," Paul growled without turning back.

"He said he'd be out to talk to us later..." Jeff began.

"Not him," Paul interrupted as he disappeared into the darkened corridor. "The attractive one!"

The velocity of the 5.56mm round shattered the skull. Blood and brain tissue stained the ceiling tiles. The rest of the limp body followed what was left of the head as it collided with the floor.

"Tango down!" Matt shouted. "Two more!" He called as he swung the barrel of his AR15. He placed the reticle on the closest face and fired. A small cloud of red mist hung briefly in the air where the creature's head had been.

Matt advanced and zeroed the reticle on the face of the last infected. In his haste to clear the hallway, he failed to notice his brother hadn't kept pace with him. Christian stopped about 30-feet back. He hung onto the thick railing that the lined the wall and struggled to stay on his feet.

The last of the infected shambled awkwardly. A narrow plastic tube dangled from the I.V. needle which protruded from the discolored flesh on its arm.

"Take your time," Matt muttered to himself as a surge of adrenaline hit him. He exhaled and tried to steady his breathing. The recoil and sound of gunfire left him fatigued and shaky. "Take your time and make the shot count."

A few more twists and turns and they'd arrive at the cafeteria. They managed to secure almost all the necessary corridors and trap most of the infected behind the substantial metal fire doors. Another few minutes and Matt and Christian would be on their way back to the emergency room to deliver the backpack full of medication. They would be able to eat, drink and if they were lucky sit for a few quiet minutes. Hopefully there would be good news about Tyler and Ralph. With any luck they'd be back on the road and on their way to the farm within the hour.

The outstretched arms of the ghoulish figure closed in. Matt exhaled and slowly squeezed the trigger. There was a hollow ping as the firing pin hit the primer and the round failed to discharge, "MISFIRE!" He shouted. Certain Christian would make short work of the infected, he didn't move. When his brother's rifle failed to sound a surge of panic raced up the back of Matt's sweat-soaked neck. Frantically he turned in search of his brother.

Christian's eyes rolled back as his eyelids fluttered. His face was paler than before and his lips had all but turned blue. He gasped and tried desperately to catch his breath as he used his left arm to support the entirety of his weight on railing.

"CHRISTIAN!" Matt screamed as his eyes found his brother. "CHRISTIAN!"

Christian's mouth moved as if he were trying to speak but no words were audible. He let go of the AR15's pistol grip and tried to find the railing with his right hand.

"NO!" Matt shouted as undead hands descended on him. He felt a tug as the discolored fingers grabbed hold of the drag handle on the back of his plate carrier. "GET OFF ME, GODDAMMIT!" He shouted as he forced his body forward and let go of his AR15. The sling held the rifle at his side as he pulled the 1911 from his drop leg holster and twisted his body forcefully to the left. He brought his left arm up to cover his nose and mouth and fired 4-shots. The infected figure staggered back as the 230-grain bullets slammed into its chest.

Exhausted and dehydrated, Christian finally lost his grip on the railing. He stumbled and landed hard on his knees as he dropped to the floor.

Free from his pursuers grasp, Matt spun and brought the pistol up to his eye line. He clasped his left hand over his right and fired twice. Both rounds struck the creature in the forehead. Matt didn't wait for the decrepit body to hit the floor, "CHRISTIAN!" He called as he hurried to help his brother.

"I'm ok," Christian mumbled as he struggled to pull himself up.

"I've got you!" Matt blurted. He grabbed Christian under the arms from behind and locked his hands around his brother's chest. "Just hang on!"

"Let go of me," Christian managed to utter. "I'm fine."

"Just hang on!" Matt ordered. He ignored Christian's protest as he squatted down and pulled his brother up from the floor. "Can you stand?"

"I'm fine," Christian repeated unconvincingly. His legs buckled as he grabbed for the railing. "I..."

"Can you stand?" Matt demanded.

Christian shook his head as his eye lids fluttered, "I don't think so..."

"I've got you," Matt assured him. "Just hang on. We're getting out of here."

Dr. Singer's office was sparsely decorated. A calendar of National Park landscapes hung on the wall behind a plain metal desk. A framed picture of a young girl in white shorts and bright orange life vest on a sail boat hung next to the calendar. The lights in the office were off except for a lone desk lamp with a bronze-colored pull chain. An LED bulb shown from beneath an emerald-colored glass cover and illuminated the patient charts as Dr. Singer reviewed them.

"Doc?" Paul said softly as he presented himself in the doorway.

Dr. Singer gasped and sat straight up in her chair, "You startled me." She said as her cheeks reddened.

"Sorry about that, Doc," Paul said with a grin. "Got a minute?"

Matt no sooner pulled Christian from the floor, than the moans began to echo from down the hall. There were several hallways which connected the second floor like a labyrinth they had yet to secure. Much as it had done on the 3rd floor, the gunfire attracted the infected in droves.

"Hang onto the railing!" Matt instructed as he pressed his shoulder against Christian's chest to keep him upright.

"I don't know if I..." Christian's voice trailed off as his head swayed.

"I need you to hold on," Matt insisted as he placed each of Christian's hands on the railing. "Just hold on!"

Dr. Singer closed the file and placed her glasses on the desk next to her. She smiled and motioned for Paul to enter.

"Thank you," Paul said as he unslung his rifle. He leaned it against the door frame as he stepped into her office. "May I?" He asked as he motioned to the dark gray metal chair with faded green vinyl covered cushion in front of the desk.

"Please," Dr. Singer answered as she motioned with her left hand. "I don't know how comfortable it'll be. I think that chair has seen better days."

"So have I," Paul said lightheartedly as he took a seat. "Who did your decorating?"

Dr. Singer grinned as she glanced around the room, "It's pretty awful, isn't it?"

"Just a little sterile," Paul answered. He pointed to the photo on the wall behind her and changed the subject. "Is that you?"

Dr. Singer nodded as the redness left her cheeks. She glanced at the picture and then back at Paul, "Yes, it is."

"I like your life vest," Paul said playfully. "Very fashionable."

"Oh, really?" Dr. Singer questioned. "That vest was so constrictive it was difficult to smile for that photo."

"Well, safety first I guess," Paul offered as he tugged at his beard. "Do you sail?"

"No, not me," Dr. Singer answered with a slight shake of her head. "My parents were the sailors. That was their boat. They had a shore house in Ocean Grove. That's where we would spend our summers. What about you?"

"Sail?" Paul questioned. "Not since the Navy."

"Oh my," Dr Singer teased. "A man in uniform."

"Yes, ma'am," Paul said with a nod. "At your service."

"No wonder you're concerned with my décor," Dr. Singer chided playfully. "Did they have you mop the deck and make sure the ship was bright and shiny?"

"Nothing like that," Paul answered. "I was in the Honor Guard."

Dr. Singer sat back in her chair and folded her hands. Her smile faded into a somber expression, "You carried the caskets."

"I did," Paul answered as his smile faded. "More than I'd like to remember."

"I'm sorry," Dr. Singer offered.

Matt retracted the Raptor charging handled and cleared the misfired round from the breach as the moans grew louder. He swapped the rifle magazine with a fully loaded one from a pouch on his belt.

"They're coming," Christian mumbled as he struggled to open his eyes.

"That's alright," Matt snarled as the infected approached. Their awkward gate and twisted faces sent a surge of fear through him. He removed the retention band that secured the 1911 Fastback in the horizontal holster at the top of his plate carrier. "I've got something for them."

The office was uncomfortably silent. Dr. Singer and Paul sat across the desk from each other but neither knew what to say.

"You know about the Honor Guard?" Paul finally asked.

"Some," Dr. Singer answered with a nod. She glanced down at her desk and then back at Paul as she searched for the words. It was an uncomfortable feeling to be speechless. She couldn't remember the last time it had happened to her.

"What about the local police?" Paul asked as he leaned forward and rested his thick forearms on the edge of the desk.

"What?" Dr. Singer asked as if unprepared for the question.

"The local police," Paul repeated. "Did they offer any assistance?"

"No," Dr. Singer answered bluntly. "The Chief was here with two officers to meet the National Guard Commander. That was the last we saw of local law enforcement."

The old chair creaked as Paul sat back against it, "They really left you on your own here, didn't they?"

"Not sure they had a choice," Dr. Singer answered nervously. She hurriedly organized the files in front of her as her cheeks again reddened. "I can't imagine what's happening out there. How bad it's gotten."

Paul could see the fear and concern on her face, "I didn't mean to upset you." He offered. "I just wanted to ask after our people."

Dr. Singer nodded and brushed a tear from the corner of her eye, "I'm optimistic." She said as she forced a slight smile. "We should know something more definitive shortly."

"Thank you," Paul said as he started to stand up.

"You seem close," Dr. Singer blurted as if to preempt his departure. "Your group I mean."

"We are," Paul said as he turned and sat back down. "We've had our struggles the last few days, but we're intact."

"These are unprecedented times," Dr. Singer offered. "Still though, you need to protect the people you love."

"Agreed, Doc," Paul said with a grin.

"Tamara, please," Dr. Singer said. She fidgeted with her glasses for a moment before she finally put them on. "I need to do my rounds. Was there something else?"

"I was just wondering what you were doing after this?" Paul asked. His eyes narrowed as he leaned forward in the chair again. "Tamara."

"After what?" Dr. Singer asked with a look of innocent bewilderment.

"The apocalypse," Paul answered with a smile. "I was just wondering what you had planned for the rest of your life?"

Dr. Singer chuckled slightly unsure if Paul was joking or not, "Alright sailor." She said as she stood up. "Let's table the heavy discussion until I've completed my rounds."

The oppressive stench of rotting flesh filled the long corridor as the infected neared.

"I've got you," Matt said as he struggled to keep Christian on his feet.

"I can't..." Christian mumbled. His voice trailed off as his head slumped forward.

"I've got you!" Matt repeated more forcefully. He shifted his focus to approaching horde. He knew he couldn't clear the hallway by himself. "Fuck! Hang on, I'm going to pick you up."

"Don't..." Christian managed. He struggled to remain conscious as he felt his legs weaken.

"Hang on!" Matt ordered. He held Christian against the wall with his left arm and used his right to pull the AR15 tight against his shoulder. He released a volley of rounds that dispatched the nearest infected. He let go of the rifle and grabbed the walkie talkie. "JEFF!" Matt shouted. "JEFF!"

"Is everything alright?" Dr. Singer asked as her expression turned to one of deep concern. She pointed to the walkie talkie. "He doesn't sound alright."

"No, he doesn't," Paul said. He shook his head and pressed the PTT button. "Matt, it's Paul. What's going on up there?"

"I need you up here!" Matt shouted. "We're about to be overrun. South staircase...Use the South staircase."

"I gotta go!" Paul blurted. He grabbed his rifle and took off down the hall. "HANG ON! WE'LL BE RIGHT THERE!" He shouted into the walkie talkie. "JEFF! JEFF, GET YOUR RIFLE! THEY NEED US!"

"What happened?" Jeff called as Paul hurried past him.

"South staircase! South staircase!" Paul shouted. "They need us!"

Jeff unslung his rifle and took off after Paul. He was renowned for his speed and agility, "COME ON!" He shouted as he bolted past Paul, through the south stairwell door and up the stairs.

Matt sent another volley of rounds into the horde before he grabbed Christian above the left wrist. He bent down hooked his right arm around Christian's left leg. In one motion he pulled Christian's body across his shoulders and stood up, "Hang on!" He ordered.

Jeff's chest heaved as he took the stairs two at a time, "I'm coming." He muttered to himself as he clicked the safety off.

"Fuck!" Matt groaned. He winced under the weight of Christian's body and tactical gear and immediately felt pressure in his lower back. "Hang on brother, I've got you."

Christian didn't respond. His body hung limp over Matt's shoulders.

Matt pulled the 1911 Fastback from the holster on his plate carrier and depressed the thumb safety. He turned to engage the horde when the stairwell door burst open.

"BEHIND YOU!" Jeff shouted. He charged into the hall, moved past Matt and Christian and opened fire.

"MOVING!" Matt called over the thunder of rifle fire. He pushed off hard with his right leg and moved as quickly as he could towards the stairs.

"MOVE!" Jeff shouted. Bodies fell and blood erupted across the corridor as Jeff used his AR15 with surgical precision.

Paul emerged from the stairwell just as Matt reached the door, "IS HE ALRIGHT?"

"I DON'T KNOW," Matt answered hurriedly.

"GO!" Paul ordered. He raised his rifle and moved into the hallway. "GET DOWNSTAIRS. WE'VE GOT THIS!"

Gun shots echoed in the stairwell like firecrackers exploding in a metal garbage can.

Matt scrambled down the stairs, "Are you ok?" He called as he struggled to catch his breath.

Christian didn't respond.

"CHRISTIAN!" Matt shouted as he hurried down the stairs. He misjudged the step and caught the heel of his boot on the landing. He tried unsuccessfully to grab the railing. His foot landed awkwardly and he felt something in his right hip pop as pain shot from his lower back down his right leg. "Mother fucker!" Matt shouted as he stumbled down the next few stairs. Finally, he was able to steady himself as he reached the bottom of the staircase. He pushed the stairwell door open and limped into the emergency room. "I NEED A DOCTOR!"

Dr. Singer hurried to help, "What happened?" She called.

"HELP ME!" Matt shouted.

"Get a gurney!" Dr. Singer ordered as she motioned to Mr. Spahl and Patrick.

"Here," Mr. Spahl offered as he and Patrick gabbed a gurney from the far wall and quickly wheeled it over.

"What happened?" Dr. Singer asked again. She helped Matt lower Christian off his shoulders.

"I don't know," Matt answered frantically. Tears streamed down his cheeks as they placed Christian on the gurney. "He was fine and then he couldn't stand. I was talking to him and then he couldn't answer me."

"Ok," Dr. Singer said as calmly as she could. "Did you see him take anything?"

"Help him," Matt pleaded desperately. "Please just help him."

"We're going to do our best to take care of him," Dr. Singer assured him. She turned back towards the doors that led from the emergency room. "Lexi, Sam, I need the two of you out here now!"

"We're coming," Samantha called as she and Lexi hurried to help Dr. Singer.

"Get him into exam room 1 and get him started on a saline drip. Draw blood for a panel and alert Dr. Edwards. I'll be down in a moment," Dr. Singer instructed. She turned back to Matt. "Is your brother allergic to anything?"

"Not that I know of," Matt answered as he shook his head. He wiped tears from his cheeks as emotion overtook him. Exhausted, Matt's legs felt like rubber beneath him. "Doc, is he going to be..."

"Come with me," Dr. Singer ordered. "I need a complete health history."

The large doors began to close as the gurney disappeared around the corner, flanked by the nurses, Dr. Singer, and Matt.

"Let me have the walkie talkie," Mr. Spahl ordered as he tapped Patrick on the shoulder.

"What?" Patrick questioned as he stared at the large doors. He could feel his stomach churn as his thoughts spiraled.

"The walkie talkie," Mr. Spahl repeated. "Let me have it!"

"Oh, right," Patrick answered as he fumbled to unclip the walkie talkie from his belt. "Here."

"Status!" Mr. Spahl shouted into the microphone. He waited a moment and depressed the PTT button again. "STATUS!"

"BUSY!" Paul called as gun shots thundered in the background.

"What's going on up there?" Kurt asked as he and Kim joined them at the nurse's station.

Mr. Spahl shook his head, "Not sure."

It took Jeff and Paul almost 30-minutes to clear out the infected and secure a route to the cafeteria. They found a linen closet after they secured the last set of fire doors. With a pair of clean sheets, they gathered all the food and water they could carry and headed back to the emergency room.

"You're back!" Mr. Spahl blurted. He was relieved to see them return. "How was it up there?"

"Shit show," Jeff answered. His ears rang as he placed the make shift sack on the nurse's station. "Food and water!" He announced. "How's Christian?"

"Still waiting on the doctor," Mr. Spahl answered.

"Thank you," Shaw said. He, Holden, Roderick, and Dominick collected food and water and resigned themselves to the back of the room where they discussed the quickest route out of the Garden State.

Paul wiped sweat from his face and opened a bottle of water as the double doors parted and Dr. Singer returned. She wore a set of blue scrubs and carried several patient charts, "Hopefully she's got some good news for us." He said before he took a long drink.

"Thank you for your patience," Dr. Singer said. She placed the patient charts on top of the nurse's station. "And thank you for everything you were able to collect. You've saved lives."

"We told you we'd take care of it, Doc," Jeff said as he reloaded his rifle. "How are our people?"

"Katlyn is doing well," Dr. Singer began as she shuffled the charts on the counter. "Her sister is with her. She has a fractured clavicle and her shoulder was dislocated. We were able to get her shoulder back in place without any trouble. She won't need surgery but she will need to be in a sling for at least six weeks. She had some other scrapes and bruises which we cleaned and bandaged as needed. We've given her something for the pain but she is awake and you can go and see her if you'd like."

"Where is she Doc?" Shaw asked as the four of them approached the nurse's station.

"Recovery room 3," Dr. Singer answered. "Through the doors and straight down the hall. Nurse Lexi is with her."

"Thank you, Doc," Shaw said with a sigh of relief. He shook Dr. Singer's hand before the four of them hurried through the double doors.

"What about my brother?" Patrick asked. "Tyler. He had the injured ankle."

"Tyler cracked a bone in his lower leg and dislocated his ankle," Dr. Singer explained. "We've got the ankle back in place. Based on the X-ray and MRI we're not recommending surgery. He does need to rest and keep the leg elevated for at least two weeks. After that he'll need to be on crutches for another four and a walking boot for two weeks after that. If he follows the protocol, he should be fully healed in about eight weeks."

"Ralph?" Paul questioned. "How's he doing?"

"His injuries were more serious," Dr. Singer said bluntly. "The good news is we've got him stabilized."

"Thank God," Paul said as he let out a deep sigh of relief.

"We removed the bullet and stopped the bleeding," Dr. Singer began. "It was a lead tip which helped. If it had been a full metal jacket round it would have been more serious. There would have been considerably more damage. Thankfully the door and his hip slowed the bullet significantly."

"I'm impressed," Paul admitted. "You're the first doctor I've ever met who knew about ammunition."

"Sadly Paul, your friend isn't the first gunshot victim we've treated," Dr. Singer said stoically. "Thankfully the bullet didn't shatter the bone. At the very least though we need to keep him overnight for observation. After that he'll need to keep the leg elevated for a few weeks and slowly transition to crutches before he's able to start walking again."

"When can we see him?" Paul asked.

"He's still heavily sedated," Dr. Singer answered. "Give him another hour or so before you go to see him."

"What about Christian?" Jeff asked. "How is he? Is Matt still with him?"

"Yes, Matt is still with him," Dr. Singer replied as she glanced down at the charts. "Christian's going to be ok. We're primarily giving him fluids and some other medications to help with his condition. My recommendation would be to let him rest at least overnight."

"Thank you, Doc," Jeff said as he tipped his head back. "Thank you."

"Everybody, get comfortable!" Mr. Spahl called. "We're staying the night."

"We're grateful to you," Paul said as he took Dr. Singer's hand in both of his. He paused awkwardly as he gazed into her eyes.

"Tamara," Dr. Singer said with a grin. "It's ok to use my first name."

"Of course," Paul said as his cheeks reddened slightly. "Thank you, Tamara."

"You're welcome, Paul," Tamara answered.

"Tamara," Paul crooned. "That is a beautiful name."

Tamara blushed, "Now that we know everyone is on the mend, maybe we could finish our conversation."

Paul's eyes narrowed as his lips curled into a playful grin, "I think we should."

"If you're free," Tamara began. "Would you care to accompany me to my office?"

"I am, and I would…Tamara," Paul said in a much more relaxed tone.

Jeff and Kurt watched as Dr. Singer wrapped her arm around Paul's and the two walked through the double doors towards her office.

"Just like that?" Kurt asked. "How does he do it?"

"Stressful situations affect people differently," Kim said as she took Kurt's hand in both of hers.

"He's the Paulerbear," Jeff said with a shrug. "Women love the Paulerbear."

"I guess so," Kurt said as he put his arm around Kim.

"Speaking of stressful situations," Kim began as she looked up at Kurt. She pressed her thumb into his ribs just above his waist. "Don't ever disappear and leave me to wonder where you are again."

"About that," Kurt offered with an uncomfortable grimace. "I'm sorry."

"We've got undead cannibals running around and I don't want to worry about where you are," Kim insisted. She removed her thumb from Kurt's ribs and opened a bottle of water. "We don't know what the world is coming to?"

"The rest of the world can wait until tomorrow," Jeff muttered. He stood for a moment, listened to the quiet of the emergency room and tried to make sense of the last few days. He wondered if he'd be able to go back to his old life or if he'd even want to. His thoughts drifted to his brothers and sister, all of whom were still unaccounted for. He wiped sweat and gun powder residue from his face and cleared his throat. "Right now, we've earned ourselves some downtime."

CHAPTER 22

a perfect world

MORNING CREPT THROUGH THE large office windows on the 4th floor. Tamara stood statuesque; a vision of poise and beauty as she looked out over the rose garden behind the hospital. A thin layer of fog covered the bottoms of the bushes. It looked as if the red and white roses had grown out of a whitish gray cloud.

Tamara held a linen sheet from the pull-out couch where she and Paul spent the night over her breasts. The sheet hugged the curves of her naked body as it wrapped around her and completely covered her from the waist down. The fabric was cool against her skin. Her long brown hair hung almost to the center of her bare back.

There in the quiet of the morning, her thoughts drifted back a few days before the outbreak began. A single tear ran down her left cheek as she remembered the garden filled with staff and patients. She brushed a second tear from her right cheek and thought about how the patients benefited from their visits to the garden.

The secluded area with all its beauty had been a sanctuary for patients who faced a long and difficult recovery and even more so for those who knew their condition was terminal. It was an escape that made hope an option again, even if only briefly.

Paul lay asleep only a few feet from where Tamara stood. His large frame spread across most of the mattress. Tattoos were scattered across his torso and arms. His chest moved up and down with the steady rhythm of his breathing. A cream-colored bed sheet barely covered his lower half.

Tamara glanced back at him and wiped another tear away. Paul appeared so peaceful she was hesitant to rejoin him for fear of waking him, "Rest now, my sweet." Tamara whispered.

She turned and watched the rose garden for a few more quiet minutes until she heard Paul stir behind her. As much as she wanted to share the morning with him, Tamara hoped for a little more time to capture every detail of the garden in her mind's eye. The image would serve as a refuge. A place she could return to find strength and solace against the uncertain days ahead.

The ceiling was blurry as Paul tried to blink the sleep from his eyes. He didn't immediately remember where he was, but he was comfortable and felt no urgency to move. He glanced to his right and saw his 1911 on the end table and rifle leaned against the door frame. He rubbed his eyes as his head left the pillow. A smile crept across his face as his eyes found Tamara. The early morning light cascaded in and gave her skin the look of porcelain, "Good morning," Paul uttered in a gravelly voice.

"Good morning," Tamara said quietly without turning around.

"What are you looking at?" Paul asked as he propped himself up on his left arm.

"Something beautiful," Tamara answered.

"Hmmm," Paul began. "So am I."

She blushed as she turned to face him, "You're sweet." Tamara said as the ends of her mouth curled into a smile. "How did you sleep?"

"Good, I think," Paul answered. "The last few days really took it out of me."

"You seemed to have a lot of energy last night," Tamara teased as she adjusted the sheet around her body.

"Well," Paul began. "I do aim to please."

"You did indeed," Tamara said with a giggle.

Paul rubbed his eyes and yawned deeply as he sat up. The rest had done him good, but he wasn't ready to concede his time with her, "How'd you know this office had a pull-out couch?" Paul asked curiously.

"It was part of the sales pitch," Tamara explained. "It was supposed to sweeten the deal when the head of the cardiology department propositioned me."

Paul's face dropped, "I'm sorry." He offered. "Men can be pigs."

"Hmmm," Tamara began. Her left eyebrow crept up as her head lowered. "The head of cardiology wasn't a man."

Paul's eyes opened wide, "Oh, really?" He questioned curiously.

"Yes," Tamara said with a smirk. "Really."

"And?" Paul teased.

"And, nothing," Tamara quipped. "I told her I was very flattered but women were not my preference."

"Lucky me," Paul crooned.

"I would say so," Tamara replied as she matched Paul's cadence. "Are you hungry? Should we get breakfast?"

"Not yet," Paul said with a wink. He pulled the sheet off himself and let it fall to the floor. "Your turn."

Tamara's cheeks reddened again. "My turn?" She questioned full of giddy excitement. She stood for a moment before she let the sheet drop from her body.

"We'll get breakfast in a little bit," Paul said as he admired her. The natural light surrounded her in a radiant angelic glow. "For now, come back to bed."

The emergency room was dark except for the red glow of exit signs. The central air system offered the low hum of ambient noise as it kept the room at a cool 67-degrees. The beds were filled with the sleeping. Exhausted and scared they welcomed a few restful hours safely behind the metal doors that separated the emergency room from the long corridor which led to the chaos of the outside world.

Patrick tossed and turned. His haunted mind raced and replayed the sight of his father with the rifle under his chin. Unable to sleep he rolled onto his back and stared at the ceiling, "Come on." He grumbled and clamped his hands over his face. "Stop!" He demanded as he sat up, and tried to shake the image from his mind. Patrick's eyes adjusted to the dark room and he realized he was the only one awake. Slowly he got to his feet. His muscles tightened and he knew he needed water. Quietly he made his way down the hallway towards the recovery rooms.

Tamara lay with her head on Paul's arm, her back against his chest and felt safe. She closed her eyes and quietly reveled in how good the warmth of his body felt against hers. Goose bumps formed under Paul's finger tips as he gently caressed her soft skin, "That tickles a little." Tamara said as she pulled her arms into her chest.

"Want me to stop?" Paul whispered.

"No," Tamara said as she rubbed her cheek against his bicep. "It feels good."

"Good," Paul replied softly. He leaned over and kissed her neck.

Patrick was surprised to find Matt stretched out between two chairs in the hallway just outside Christian's room. Matt's head was cocked uncomfortably to the side as he snored.

"Matty," Patrick whispered as he gently shook Matt's arm. "Matty."

Startled Matt sat up quickly and grabbed for his pistol. He was momentarily panicked when his hand couldn't locate the holster on his right hip, "What?" Matt sputtered. "Where's my pistol?" He blurted and almost fell off the chair.

"Matty, it's just me," Patrick said as he grabbed his cousin's shoulder. "It's just me."

"What's going on?" Matt questioned as he struggled to get to his feet. He blinked, shook his head, and tried to escape the fog of sleep. "Pat, what's going on?"

"Everything's ok," Patrick assured him. "You looked uncomfortable so I thought I'd wake you up."

"What's going on?" Matt asked again. He held onto his cousin's arms as his legs wobbled underneath him.

"Nothing. Nothing's going on," Patrick insisted as he eased Matt back onto the chair. "Everything's ok. Here just sit down."

"Where's my gun belt?" Matt asked frantically.

"On the back the chair," Patrick answered as he motioned behind him.

"Thank God," Matt said relieved. He sat up, rested his elbows on his legs and let his head drop into his hands. "My fucking body hurts."

The chair creaked as Patrick sat down across from his cousin, "What are you doing out here?"

Matt twisted his head from side to side and tried to get his neck to crack, "Christian kicked me out. He told me he didn't want me to watch him sleep."

Patrick chuckled uncomfortably, "Were you watching him?"

"I was worried about him," Matt answered as he glanced up at his cousin. "If you saw how he was up there, you'd be worried too."

"I was worried about him," Patrick insisted and quickly changed the subject. "You came out here to sleep?"

"This was as far away as I was going, without a small army to drag me away," Matt explained as his neck finally released an audible crack.

Tamara slid her body across the bed away from Paul. She rolled onto her left side and faced him. She ran her fingers tenderly through his hair as she brought her eyes up to meet his.

"What is it?" Paul asked as the expression on her face intensified.

"I need you to know something," Tamara began. "I don't jump into bed with every stranger I cross paths with."

"I never thought you did," Paul said with a smile.

"It's just," Tamara continued as her eyes dropped. "There was someone I used to be involved with."

"We've each got a past," Paul said quietly as he moved several strands of hair away from her face. "It's nothing we need to discuss if you don't want to. It doesn't matter."

"It does matter," Tamara insisted. Her bottom lip quivered as she continued. "The past always matters."

"If you need to talk about it," Paul offered. "I'll listen."

"Thank you," Tamara said quietly as her face tightened. "They were dangerous men, involved with organized crime. They followed a code, but I know they hurt and killed people."

"You were with one of them?" Paul inquired. He hoped his expression wouldn't show the judgement he felt.

"Yes," Tamara answered with a slight nod. "His name was Jack Tallon. He was in charge."

"Where is he now?" Paul asked.

"I don't know," Tamara admitted as she shook her head. There was a blankness about her expression as she continued. "We were supposed to meet a few days ago and he never showed. He could be dead for all I know."

"Did you love him?" Paul questioned. No sooner had he uttered the words than he wished he hadn't.

"No," Tamara answered without hesitation. "I was drawn to the element of danger. I loved the idea of risk."

"I'm sure it was exhilarating," Paul offered sympathetically.

"That's not why I needed to tell you," Tamara explained as her eyes dropped. A mixture of sorrow and regret covered her face.

"Why then?" Paul questioned.

"I won't..." Tamara began as a tear escaped down her left cheek. She brushed it away, took a deep breath and continued. "I won't have that kind of violence in my life again. I don't know what I was thinking. Being here with you now, has made me remember how healthy is supposed to feel."

"When the world feels upside down and nothing makes sense, it's normal to want to feel safe in someone's arms," Paul offered tenderly. He gently brushed another tear from her cheek. "Everybody needs that. It becomes precious to them."

"Thank you for understanding," Tamara whispered as she wrapped her arms tightly around Paul's neck. Tears filled her eyes as she pressed her lips against his. He kissed her back before he gently used his thumb to wipe the tears from her cheeks.

"What came before doesn't mean as much as this moment in time," Paul said quietly. "We belong to each other. For us, right now the rest of the world doesn't exist."

Patrick helped his cousin to his feet. Matt felt unsteady as he reached for his gun belt. The prior day's exhaustion and stress gave way to pangs of hunger.

"You alright Matty?" Patrick asked.

"Feel like I got hit by a truck," Matt said. He clipped the Cobra buckle around his waist and fastened the retention strap around his right leg. He depressed the thumb break, drew the 1911 and checked the chamber. He rubbed his temples and tried to straighten his body. "Other than that, I feel fucking great."

"You sure Matty?" Patrick pressed. "You seem off balance."

"I need to move around some and loosen up," Matt said. He rubbed his stomach. "I need to eat and I need a shower."

"Me too," Patrick agreed. "The doctor said there were locker rooms down the..."

"Is anybody else awake?" Matt interrupted as he looked up and down the hallway.

Patrick shook his head, "Not that I saw."

Matt collected the AR15 from where it rested against the door frame. He retracted the Raptor charging handle and checked the breach before he positioned the sling over his right shoulder, "You missing something?"

"My guns?" Patrick questioned. "I left them in the ER." No sooner had the words left his mouth than he watched his cousin's expression drop. He quickly changed the subject. "What's the plan?"

The dark clouds that threatened rain the day before retreated from sight. A brilliant morning sun hung in a cloudless sky. The layer of fog that surrounded the rose bushes all but dissipated.

"Are you related to any of your group?" Tamara asked as she ran her fingers through the hair on Paul's chest.

"Not by blood," Paul answered. "But Matt, Ralph and I refer to each other as brothers."

"Which one is Matt?" Tamara asked curiously.

"Matt and Christian retrieved the medicine," Paul answered. "They found your missing nurse."

"Ok," Tamara replied as she thought. "Christian is the brother who collapsed?"

"Yes," Paul said with a nod. "Christian collapsed."

"How do you and Matt know each other?" Tamara inquired.

"You ask a lot of questions," Paul playfully observed. He lifted the sheet and looked over her naked body. "You wearing a wire?"

"Stop," Tamara chided. "I just want to know you."

Paul smiled and gently pulled the sheet back over her, "Matt and I worked together years ago. Turns out we had a mutual love of John Wayne, red meat, and firearms. We've been friends ever since."

"The Duke," Tamara said as she tugged gently on Paul's beard, "What about the others?"

"We're all friends or family of Matt and Christian," Paul revealed. "I've met them all before, but it wasn't until this started that I spent any real time with most of them."

Tamara tenderly placed her hand on Paul's cheek, "How did you all end up in the same place?"

"They called everybody," Paul explained. "Matt and Christian called everybody when this started and tried to bring everyone together. They knew from the first news broadcasts this was something serious."

"They seem close," Tamara said as she kissed Paul's chin ever so gently.

"Close is an understatement," Paul said with a chuckle. "It's more like two halves of the same coin. Yin and yang."

"How so?" Tamara asked curiously.

"They're each other's, other half," Paul said as caressed the back of Tamara's head. "That's the way Matt's described it over the years. Their individual strengths complement each other and make up for any weaknesses the other has."

"Impressive," Tamara commented with a smile. "Who's older?"

"Matt by a couple years," Paul answered. "He's the planner. Everything's got to have a plan and two to back it up in case things go wrong."

"Sounds very serious," Tamara observed as she furrowed her brow. "Did he plan for this?"

"Not specifically this," Paul offered with a slight shake of his head. "But they've been preparing for years."

"If not for this," Tamara began. "Then for what?"

"Something, anything," Paul said with a wink. "Civil unrest, cyber-attack, global pandemic, food shortage, train derailment of toxic chemicals, act of God." He added as his eyes opened wide. "Take your pick."

"Does he have a sixth sense?" Tamara asked as she rested her chin on Paul's chest.

"Not that I'm aware of," Paul said with a chuckle. "Matt's a paranoid student of history who's been saying ever since I've known him that something big would happen in our lifetime and we needed to be ready."

"Are you still paranoid if you turn out to be correct?" Tamara questioned.

"Good point," Paul answered. "In his case though, he's still paranoid."

"What about Christian?" Tamara asked.

"I don't know him as well," Paul replied. "He keeps to himself more, but he's very smart and extremely mechanically inclined."

"Is he as paranoid as his older brother?" Tamara inquired.

"Not sure," Paul said as he ran his fingers through her long hair. "Either way, they're usually on the same page. They watch out for each other. Matt's overprotective, which I never understood because Christian looks like he could handle himself."

"What about the others?" Tamara asked.

"The other group?" Paul clarified.

"Yes," Tamara answered as she gently pressed her lips against Paul's.

"Met 'em at gun point in the parking lot," Paul said bluntly. "Pleasantries commenced once we determined they weren't a threat."

Matt slowly pushed the door to Christian's room open and stepped inside. Patrick followed close behind his cousin. Despite the dimly lit room, they could see most of the color had returned to Christian's face.

"Why are you two sneaking into my room?" Christian demanded as he opened his eyes.

"We're checking on you," Matt said as he moved to the side of the bed. "I wasn't sure if you were still sleeping."

"Sleeping?" Christian questioned. He pressed the button on the side rail. The motor whined as the back half of the bed moved forward and brought him up to the seated position, "I was until you two started having a conversation outside my door."

"Sorry Christian," Patrick offered. "I was trying to be quiet."

"You can't be quiet Pat," Christian teased. "You're too passionate."

Patrick's face reddened as he chuckled, "Never gonna live that down."

"Doubt it," Christian said as he managed a slight smile. "What was that, Easter dinner, forever ago?"

"Yeah, Easter," Patrick answered.

"You show up wearing red shorts, red t-shirt and a red hat," Christian began. "Your face is bright red because you've been on the phone arguing with your girlfriend. What did you think Tyler was going to say?"

"Tyler!" Patrick shouted in a playful falsetto as he shook his fist at the ceiling. "Tyler kept saying that red was the color of passion and he kept calling me passionate Pat. I was so mad at him."

They laughed raucously as the three of them enjoyed a much-needed moment of levity and relived the absurd adolescent memory.

"Passionate Pat and I wanted to see if you were ready for breakfast," Matt finally blurted after he unsuccessfully tried to hold his composure. "Goddamn, it feels good to laugh!"

"Matty!" Patrick shouted. He feigned outrage at his cousins' comment as his chest heaved. "It really does. If only to take the edge off."

"Yes, it does," Christian agreed. "Things got too dark for a bit." He added as he pushed his head back against the thin hospital pillow. "Alright, breakfast? I think I could eat. Can we get to the cafeteria?"

"Yes, we can," Matt answered. "Jeff and Paul picked up where we left off and finished securing the route."

"That must've been something to see," Christian said proudly. "I'd like to hear all about it. Maybe it's time to wake everybody up and discuss it over breakfast."

Several quiet taps on the door startled them. Matt's thumb depressed the canopy release and he pulled the 1911 from his holster as the door opened.

"Am I interrupting?" A woman's voice asked softly.

"Put it away," Christian ordered as he motion towards Matt. "Pat, see who that is."

Nurse Samantha stood sheepishly in the doorway. Her light brown hair was pulled into a tight bun at the back of head. She smiled and adjusted her glasses as she stepped into the room, "Oh, I'm sorry," She blurted when she saw the pistol in Matt's hand. Samantha cringed and turned to leave. "I didn't mean to..."

"It's alright," Matt said apologetically. "Please don't go. I was startled, that's all. I'm still jumpy from yesterday. Please come back in."

"I didn't mean to interrupt," Samantha said as she returned. "I need to check on our patient."

"Of course," Matt said as he motioned towards Christian. "Please, come in."

"Christian, how are you feeling this morning?" Samantha asked. She placed the clipboard on the foot of the bed next to his feet and readied her pen.

"Still a little sleepy," Christian confessed. "All things being equal though, Nurse Samantha I'm much improved from yesterday."

"That's good," Samantha said as she captured his response. "Please just call me Sam. Everybody here does."

"Does that go for us too?" Patrick joked.

"Of course, it does," Samantha said with a smile. She made her way around Christian's bed and replaced the saline bag on his I.V. pole. She glanced back at Patrick as she wrapped the blood pressure cuff around Christian's arm. "As long as I get to call you passionate Pat."

"What?" Patrick blurted as his face turned bright red. "Ah...no!"

"She's got your number Pat," Matt teased. "Looks like someone was listening at the door."

"Be quiet Matty!" Patrick shouted playfully. He laughed so hard it sounded like he was going to hyperventilate.

"Admit it Pat," Chrisitan encouraged. "That was a good one?"

"Yeah, it was," Patrick acknowledged as he tried to catch his breath. "Sam, have you met my cousins?"

"Only at gun point," Samantha chided as she annotated Christian's blood pressure. "Not formally though."

"Shit," Matt scoffed. He shook his head and holstered his pistol. "I think she's got all our numbers."

"This is my older cousin, Christian," Patrick said as he motioned to Christian.

"Very nice to officially meet you," Samantha said with a nod. "Your blood pressure is much improved by the way."

"Good," Christian acknowledged as he rubbed his eyes. "That's good."

"This is my even older cousin Matty," Patrick sputtered as he laughed through the introduction.

"Even older?" Matt questioned as he shook his head. "In that case, I hope there's Ensure in the cafeteria for breakfast."

"If you want, I'm sure I could find you some stool softener to keep your old bowels regular," Samantha offered.

"Oh, boy," Matt scoffed. "I guess we know who the resident ball buster is."

Samantha checked Christian's temperature, "At your service." She said as she pretended to curtsy. "I'll be here all week."

"How's he looking?" Matt asked as he refocused the conversation.

"Much improved from yesterday," Samantha said confidently. "I'm going to draw some blood. How's your pain level this morning?"

"Less," Christian answered.

"Give me a number," Samantha insisted.

"Two," Christian said and held up the requisite number of fingers.

"Much improved," Samantha said as she jotted his answer on his chart. "Dr. Edwards will be in a little bit to check on you. Is there anything any of you need in the meantime?"

"Advil," Matt replied. "A lot of it, please."

"Something stronger?" Samantha offered.

Matt shook his head, "No, just Advil."

"Not a problem," Samantha said with a smile. "We can get that for you. Anyone else?"

"I'm good for now thanks," Christian said. He dropped his head back against the pillow. "We're going for breakfast in a bit. Will you join us?"

"Sure, I'd love too. I've been in the ER too long and I'm starting to get stir crazy," Samantha said before she turned her attention to Patrick. "How about you? Is there anything I can get for you?"

"My muscles are starting to spasm," Patrick explained. "Do you have anything for dehydration?"

"Wait here," Samantha said as a devilish grin crept across her face. "I have just the thing."

Paul and Tamara lay quietly wrapped in each other's arms. Sunlight filled the office, but neither were ready to leave their warm sanctuary.

"Do you have any loved ones you haven't been able to reach?" Tamara asked just above a whisper.

"Yes," Paul answered as a lump formed in his throat. "Several. You?"

Tamara nodded, "My younger sister Hayley is at TCU. I haven't been able to reach her since this all started."

"TCU?" Paul questioned.

"Texas Christian University," Tamara explained. "She's a Bio-Chem major."

"Very impressive," Paul said.

"My sister's ambitious," Tamara continued. "It's a seven-year PhD program."

"That can't be cheap," Paul began. "Are your parents helping with tuition?"

"My parents?" Tamara said as tears filled the corners of her eyes. "My parents are gone."

"I'm sorry," Paul offered empathetically.

"Car accident, not long after I graduated medical school," Tamara explained. "They were on their way home from dinner one Saturday night and a drunk driver ran a stop light."

"I'm so sorry," Paul offered.

"Thank you," Tamara said quietly. "After they were killed, I threw myself into my work. My sister felt like she needed to get as far away as she could. She said it was too painful to come home every day to that empty house."

"Do you have any other family here?" Paul asked.

"Our grandmother on my mother's side," Tamara answered. "She's the only one left of my immediate family and she's the only one still in New Jersey. My grandfather was a successful investment banker with a sizable life insurance policy. He always told her she'd be well taken care of."

"Did he expect to pass first?" Paul asked curiously.

"He was ten years her senior," Tamara explained. "He always figured she'd outlive him. She became a multi-millionaire when he passed."

"Money certainly helps," Paul began. "But it doesn't take the sting out of losing someone you love."

"...And it didn't," Tamara agreed. "They were as close as I've ever seen two people. She was devastated when he passed. She helped me pay off my loans and now she's helping my sister through TCU. It was everything I could do just to get her to spend some of that money on herself."

"Where is she now?" Paul asked. "Why aren't you with her?"

"I talked her into one of those senior citizen cruises," Tamara admitted as a gush of tears followed. "It's a ten-day trip. She left two days before all this started. I have no way to reach her."

"Don't give up on her," Paul encouraged. "On either of them."

"I'm not giving up," Tamara assured him. "It's just so difficult...the not knowing..."

"I understand," Paul said as he closed his eyes. "All too well."

"I don't know where they are, if they're alright, or if I'm ever going to see them again," Tamara sobbed before she buried her face in Paul's chest.

"There was some discussion before we got on the road yesterday," Paul whispered as he held her tightly and gently caressed her skin.

"Once we get to where we're going and get situated, the plan is to form a search and rescue team and find our loved ones."

Tamara looked up at him red faced, "Really?" She asked as she wiped away tears.

"Yes," Paul answered firmly. "I think you should come with us."

"Leave the hospital?" Tamara questioned. "You would help me find my sister? Why?"

"Because," Paul said as he leaned forward and kissed her forehead. "I'm a sucker for a fairytale ending."

CHAPTER 23

the toll, part 1

THE LARGE HINGES RELEASED an audible squeak as Dominick pushed the heavy metal door open. Cautiously he entered the cafeteria's kitchen. The dark space smelled of cleaning products as his hand searched the wall for the light switch.

"Where are you?" Dominick muttered to himself as he ran his hand up and down the cold tile that covered most of the interior wall. Finally, his husky fingers found the plastic switch cover. "There you are." He said to himself with a sigh of relief.

The florescent lights hummed overhead as Dominick acclimated himself to the large room. He found a white apron on a hook next to the large stainless-steel door that provided access to the walk-in freezer. He chuckled to himself as he crossed the apron strings behind his back, pulled them tight around his waist and tied them in a bow just above his belt buckle.

"I might have to think about skipping a meal," Dominick said playfully to himself as he gave his protruding midsection a smack. "First things first though, I need to find my glasses then I'm going to cook these folks up something delicious for breakfast."

Dominick looked confused as he grabbed at his pants pockets and tried to remember where he put his glasses case. He was relieved, though not entirely surprised to find them in the breast pocket of his shirt.

"There you are," Dominick said with a bewildered smirk. "How the heck did you end up in that pocket?" His thick liver spotted hands trembled slightly as he struggled to pry the case open. The hinge was stiff but finally opened and surrendered a pair of narrow framed dark rimmed reading glasses affixed to a long-beaded chain with a small crucifix attached to the end. "Now we're in business." He said with a smile as he placed the beaded chain around his neck. "Ok, now we're in business."

The aroma of fresh food wafted from the kitchen. It aided the jovial atmosphere in the cafeteria. The hospital staff was elated to finally be out of the emergency room. They reveled in the warmth of the sunlight as it poured in through the windows.

"I almost forgot what the sun felt like on my skin," Lexi confessed as she tied her long curly blonde hair into a pony tail at the back of her head. "I was terrified we may never get out of the emergency room."

Dr. Edwards stood next to her in stoic wonderment as he watched the outside world through the large windows. His hands were tucked away inside the large pockets of his white lab coat. He quietly fought to hold his composure as he spoke, "I'm embarrassed to admit, I was worried about that also."

Barbra had remained at her sister's side since being allowed to see her. She was relieved to see the color return to Katlyn's face. Even as they neared the cafeteria, Barbra held Katlyn's left hand in both of hers.

"We're almost there," Katlyn commented as they walked slowly.

"I don't know about you sis," Barbra began. "But I'm starved."

Katlyn managed a slight nod, "Yeah, me too."

"Are you alright?" Barbra asked as they continued down the hallway.

"No," Katlyn answered as she shook her head, "The strap is rubbing against the side of my neck."

"Wait a second," Barbra instructed as the two of them stopped just ahead of the cafeteria doors. She carefully lifted the white strap attached to the blue sling that held Katlyn's right arm immobile. She pulled the collar of the oversized white t-shirt Shaw donated between the sling strap and her sister's neck. "Here, this should help."

"Thank you," Katlyn said quietly. She still felt drowsy from the pain medication, but managed to give her sister a smile.

"How are you feeling?" Barbra asked as she fussed with a few rogue strands of Katlyn's hair.

"Still pretty numb," Katlyn answered. She didn't mind that her sister fixed her hair. Over the years she became accustomed to way Barbra doted on her. From as far back as she could remember Barbra looked out for her and treated her more like a daughter than a younger sister. "I'm fine Bar. It's almost time to take another pain pill and I can't do it on an empty stomach."

"It's a little early for more pain medication," Barbra said empathetically.

"Bar," Katlyn began sheepishly. "The pain was terrible. All those hours laying the back of the Winnebago. I can't hurt like that again."

"Don't worry honey," Barbra offered as she took her sisters hand. "I'll talk to the nurse and we'll get your next dose ready."

"Thanks Bar," Katlyn said with a sleepy smile. "You always take such good care of me."

"That's what big sisters are for," Barbra said as she pushed a few more strands of hair behind Katlyn's left ear. "Uncle Dom's in the kitchen. I'm sure he's creating a small feast."

"Is he?" Katlyn asked excitedly. "These folks have no idea what kind of treat their in for."

"Are you ok to keep going?" Barbra asked.

Katlyn nodded, "Yes. Let's just go slow."

Aunt Athena gathered her two oldest children and son-in-law around the table closest to the window. They joined hands and prayed quietly as the warmth of the sun radiated over them.

"Amen," Aunt Athena said quietly as she ended the prayer. "Tyler, how are you feeling?"

"Come on mom," Tyler snapped. "Stop asking me that!"

"Tyler," Aunt Athena pressed as she ran her hands through his wavy blond hair. "Do I need to get the doctor?"

"No," Tyler insisted as he brushed her hand away. "I'm fine. I just need to keep my leg elevated is all."

"Don't get snippy Tyler," Aunt Athena demanded. She continued to run her fingers through his hair. "I was worried sick about you. I'm just glad the doctors were able to take care of you so quickly."

"I know mom," Tyler offered as he softened his tone. "I was worried too. I was worried that someone else might close a car door on my foot or someone might throw me over their shoulder and carry me around..."

"I don't appreciate your sarcasm," Aunt Athena scolded. "Matthew and Christian were only trying to help you. It would be nice if you showed some gratitude."

Tyler shook his head and looked away, "It's been a rough couple of days." He mumbled.

"I know," Aunt Athena said. She wrapped her arms around her son's head.

"What are you doing?" Tyler asked as he tried to squirm away.

"I don't care how old you are," Aunt Athena said as she pulled Tyler's head towards her cheek. "You'll always be my little boy and you'll never be too big to hug."

Mrs. Spahl wrangled some of the man power and had several of the rectangular tables reconfigured into a large "U" shape in front of the east facing windows. The newly formed banquet area offered a tranquil view of the rose garden and was large enough for everyone to congregate around.

No one seemed to notice Tobias as he somberly shuffled into the cafeteria. The swollen egg-shaped lump over his left eye was a deep shade of purple. His wrinkled scrubs looked as if they'd been slept in and his unkept hair added to his overall disheveled appearance.

"Dr. Edwards," Tobais uttered in a gravelly voice as he approached. "I'd like a word."

"Tobias?" Lexi questioned as she turned away from the window. "Oh, my God your eye!" She blurted. "What are you doing up?"

"You really should be laying down," Dr. Edwards added. "You have a significant concussion."

"I'd like a word," Tobias repeated. His right eye lid twitched as he glared at the two of them. "Now."

"Tobias..." Lexi began.

"It's alright," Dr. Edwards interrupted as he held up his hand. "I think I know what this is about. Let's talk away from the others."

"I don't care who hears," Tobias hissed through clenched teeth.

"Well, I do," Dr. Edwards responded sternly. He motioned towards the entrance. "We can talk over there, then I expect you back down stairs. You need to lay down and I recommend you put more ice on that eye."

Mrs. Spahl stepped back to admire her creation when she heard Dominick's voice behind her.

"Excuse me young lady," Dominick politely interrupted.

"Young lady?" Mrs. Spahl questioned as she turned around.

"Would you care to help me?" Dominick asked as he gazed at her from over the narrow frame of his reading glasses.

"I don't go by young lady," Mrs. Spahl said curtly. "My parents were kind enough to give me a proper name thank you."

"Oh, I'm sorry, ma'am," Dominick stammered. "I didn't mean anything by it. It was just a term of endearment."

"Please endear yourself to an unmarried woman," Mrs. Spahl said as she folded her arms.

"Nothing like that," Dominick chuckled uncomfortably. "Oh, my nothing like that. I was just wondering if you'd like to help me prepare breakfast?"

Tobias walked slowly towards the cafeteria entrance. It was apparent by the way he moved that his balance was compromised by his injuries.

"Tobias," Dr. Edwards said insistently. "Let's just speak here."

"I'm fine," Tobias growled without turning around.

"No, you are not," Dr. Edwards said empathically. "Say your peace and then I want you back downstairs."

"I don't want them here," Tobias said coldly as he moved to the wall. He pressed his back against it to steady himself. "They shouldn't be here."

"Tobias," Dr. Edwards began frustratedly. "We've been over this. This is a hospital and our entire purpose is to help those in need."

"They're parasites," Tobias insisted as his eyes narrowed. "They forced their way in at gun point and they're taking what's ours."

"I allowed them in," Dr. Edwards reminded him. "And those parasites as you called them secured the food and medication necessary to keep ourselves and our other patients alive."

Undeterred, Tobias tugged at his sparse blond beard and scowled, "She spent the night with one of them!"

"She?" Dr. Edwards questioned as he rubbed his forehead. "I assume you're speaking of Dr. Singer?"

"Yes!" Tobias hissed as droplets of spit spewed from his mouth. "She spent the night with one of them!"

"Alright, stop!" Dr. Edwards ordered. He held his index finger up to underscore the seriousness of his words. "We have been over this. Dr. Singer made it very clear several times that she had no interest in being romantically involved with you."

Tobias looked away angrily and muttered something inaudible under his breath.

"You don't have to like what I just said," Dr. Edwards offered. He preferred to avoid conflict whenever possible but this was not the first time, he and Tobias had had this conversation. "How Dr. Singer spends her time or who Dr. Singer spends her time with is none of your business."

"But..." Tobias stammered.

"Do you remember how uncomfortable you made Dr. Singer feel?" Dr. Edwards demanded. "How many times you showed up with gifts? How many times you followed her to her car?"

"I was escorting her to her car!" Tobias insisted. "That, Jack whatever his name was a dangerous man. I was trying to protect her!"

"Do you recall Dr. Singer pleading with you to stop?" Dr. Edwards asked as he ignored Tobias's claims of chivalry.

"I was just trying to protect her," Tobias contended. "If you had just explained it to her, she would have listened."

"Stop it, Tobias!" Dr. Edwards ordered. "You made Dr. Singer so uncomfortable; she felt she had no other choice than to file a complaint against you with the human resource office."

"You could have talked her out of it," Tobias asserted as his face reddened. He squirmed uncomfortably as Dr. Edwards continued.

"Your behavior towards Dr. Singer was unprofessional and bordered on stalking," Dr. Edwards said sternly. "The board of directors was prepared to have you removed, but Dr. Singer felt sorry for you and withdrew the complaint, against my insistence I might add."

"Fuck this," Tobias growled. His eyes avoided Dr. Edwards. "You never fucking liked me."

"Do not use that kind of language towards me!" Dr. Edwards demanded. "Dr. Singer is an adult. She can make her own decisions. She does not require your approval or protection. Is that clear?"

Tobias shook his head, "Fuck you!" He muttered.

"Excuse me?" Dr. Edwards asked as his large frame moved towards Tobias. "What did you just say to me?"

"Fuck this place!" Tobias snarled. "Fuck you and fuck that ungrateful whore!"

"Back to the emergency room!" Dr. Edwards ordered. His face reddened as he pointed to the door. "NOW!"

"I'm not going anywhere!" Tobias vowed.

"You do not belong here right now," Dr. Edwards said as he took a step back. "I would like you to leave."

"I have as much right to be here and eat as any of those fucking parasites!" Tobias growled as he stormed off. He all but fell into a chair at the far end of the cafeteria away from everyone else.

Olive oil warmed in two sizable skillet pans on the stove. It filled the kitchen with a savory aroma.

"Is that a southern accent I detect?" Dominck asked as he showed Mrs. Spahl how he staged everything.

"A bit, yes," Mrs. Spahl answered with a nod.

"Where from?" Dominick asked. "Originally I mean?"

"South Carolina," Mrs. Spahl answered. "But we moved around a lot."

"Was your father in sales?" Dominick asked as he tugged at the strings that held the apron in place.

Mrs. Spahl exhaled impatiently, "My siblings and I were Army brats. My father was a full Colonel when he retired. We moved a lot as you can imagine, but we spent a great number of years between Fort Benning and Fort Bragg."

Dominick stood for a moment and listened intently, "Wonderful, that's just wonderful."

"Dominick," Mrs. Spahl said firmly to recapture his attention. "What did you need my help with?"

"Breakfast," Dominick blurted excitedly. "I was hoping you'd help me make breakfast for everyone."

"Breakfast," Mrs. Spahl repeated.

"Yes," Dominick replied. "You see I have this recipe; I call harvest breakfast. It'll feed everybody, but it's always easier if you have two people working on it."

"Harvest breakfast?" Mrs. Spahl questioned as she moved curiously towards the stove. "What's in this masterpiece of yours?"

"I've got everything staged here on the counter," Dominick explained. He motioned to the eight onions, eight green peppers, twenty potatoes, forty eggs and four pounds of bacon strategically placed on the butcher block counter top. "I'm warming the olive oil in these two large skillets."

"That's quite the spread," Mrs. Spahl commented. "Very impressive."

"This is something I perfected when I was in the Navy," Dominick explained. He turned the knobs clockwise and increased the flame under each pan. "You've got to get creative when you're on a ship with limited resources and you're cooking for the whole crew."

"Navy," Mrs. Spahl commented with a smile. "Well, thank you for your service. My husband's an Army vet."

"Vietnam?" Dominck asked as he took his glasses from the end of his nose. The chain held them just above the top of his apron.

"Yes," Mrs. Spahl answered with a nod.

"Combat NCO?" Dominick inquired. He made a circular motion with each skillet and moved the olive oil around the bottom of each pan.

"Yes," Mrs. Spahl answered more stoically.

"I could tell," Dominick said as he glanced back at her. "By the way he handled himself outside yesterday. I could tell he knew what he was doing."

The conversation around the newly organized banquet area picked up as more people entered the cafeteria. What began as somber and reflective essentially evolved into something more lighthearted.

No one was phased when Matt and Samantha propped the entranceway doors open so Christian and Patrick could wheel their I.V.

poles in from the hallway. The plastic wheels made a distinct sound as they rolled onto the linoleum floor of the cafeteria.

Aunt Athena shrieked when she saw the I.V. pole attached to her youngest son, "Oh my God! My baby, what happened to my baby?"

"Calm down mom!" Patrick insisted as his face turned bright red. "Sam, will you tell my mother please, will you tell her I'm, ok?"

"Your son's fine. I'm sorry I don't know your name," Samantha stammered as she hurried to comfort Aunt Athena. "Patrick's mom. Your son is fine. He was just dehydrated. I set him up with a saline drip and in an hour or so he'll be as good as new."

"MY BABY!" Aunt Athena wailed.

"Christ, mom the nurse said he's fine!" Tyler shouted over his mother's anguished cries. "Jesus, Patrick gets a hang nail and suddenly the world's coming to an end. You treat me like garbage. Being the oldest sucks!"

Patrick rolled the I.V. pole to the table and sat down next to his mother, "Don't worry little mommy." He joked. "I was dehydrated and Sam's getting me fixed up so we can get back on the road. There's nothing to worry about."

"The dead are returning to life to eat the living," Katherine reminded everyone. "Don't tell me there's nothing to worry about."

"Thanks Katherine," Tyler chided. "Glad we can always count on you for something positive."

"Well..." Patrick stammered as he looked at his sister. "Besides that, there's nothing to worry about."

"I was so worried when I saw you," Aunt Athena said as she squeezed Patrick's face between her hands.

"Come on Tyler," Christian offered as he took a seat next to his cousin. "You had to know that reaction was coming."

Tyler waved his hand dismissively towards his mother, "I'm already yesterday's news. I'll have to lose a limb before anybody gives a shit about me."

Dominick took two chef's knives from the magnetic strip on the wall behind the counter. He wiped them off on a dish towel he had tucked into the front pocket of his apron.

"Alright, what's first?" Mrs. Spahl asked.

"Well," Dominick began. "If it's ok with you, I'd like you to peel and dice the potatoes, while I dice the onions, peppers and cut up the bacon."

"I think I can handle that," Mrs. Spahl said as she took the smaller of the two knives from him.

"We'll let the olive oil get a little warmer than we'll add the diced onions," Dominick explained. "After the onions soften, we'll add the green peppers."

"Sounds good," Mrs. Spahl replied with a nod. She traded the knife for the potato peeler. "Let me get started on these."

"Once the potatoes are diced, we'll season them with salt and pepper. We'll add them once the green peppers soften," Dominick continued. "When the potatoes begin to crisp, we'll add the bacon. Then we can add some half and half and whip the eggs."

"Sounds like you've done this a few times," Mrs. Spahl teased.

"Oh, much more than a few," Dominick said with a smile. "Once the bacon is cooked, we'll add the eggs. Then we cook everything until the eggs are no longer moist, add a little salt and ketchup and we've got our masterpiece."

"...And that's the harvest breakfast?" Mrs. Spahl asked.

"That's it," Dominick said as he sliced through the first onion. "Then we feast."

Matt slung his plate carrier over the chair back next to where Christian sat. He could feel the Advil start to kick in, that coupled with moving around helped loosen up his stiff muscles. He engaged the safety on his AR15 and leaned it against the table, "I'm going to check on everybody," Matt said as he gave Christian's shoulder a squeeze.

Christian nodded, "Sure."

"You need anything?" Matt asked as he turned back.

"I'm ok," Christian assured his brother. "Go ahead and make sure everybody else is alright."

"How are you two holding up?" Matt asked as he approached Kurt and Kim.

"Ok, I think," Kurt said with a nod. "Still in a bit of shock, but overall ok."

"How about you Kim?" Matt inquired.

"I'm ok, I think," Kim answered. "My ears are still ringing a little bit."

"Mine too," Matt said as he managed a smile. "It might take some time but that should go away."

"Do we have a plan?" Kurt asked.

"Breakfast!" Matt answered energetically. "Then we'll check with the Doc. If everybody is road ready, we'll head out."

"Are you sure everybody's alright to travel?" Kim asked with considerable concern in her voice.

"We'll find out," Matt offered. "Tyler's over there cursing up a storm so he should be good to go. Ralph's the one I'm worried about, but we'll see what the Doc has to say. Let me go talk to Jeff. Hang tight I think they'll have breakfast ready shortly."

Dr. Edwards motioned to Tobias to join the rest of the group around the table, "Since you insist on staying, you could at least join everyone."

At first Tobias ignored the request and pretended not to have heard it.

"Tobias," Dr. Edwards repeated as he motioned again.

"I'm fine," Tobias growled as he defiantly looked away.

"Hang on Doc. Let me," Lexi insisted. "TOBIAS!" She shouted. "Come over and join the rest of us!"

"Fine," Tobias snarled unable to ignore the volume of Lexi's voice. He got to his feet and slowly walked over.

"How you doing, Jeff?" Matt asked as he made his way over to his friend.

"I'm good," Jeff answered. "Got some sleep, got some coffee and it smells like we're going to eat soon."

"How'd you sleep?" Matt asked.

"Better than I had any right to," Jeff joked as he sipped hot coffee from the cream color mug. "I never would have guessed a gurney could be that comfortable."

"Funny how that happens when you're exhausted," Matt commented.

Tobia's shoulders were slumped forward and his hands were shoved in the pockets of his scrub pants as he made his way across the cafeteria.

"Did you really need to shout?" Tobias asked as he reached the table.

"No, not really," Lexi jabbed. "I just figured you couldn't ignore my voice the way you ignored the Doc."

"Maybe I ignored him because I don't care for the company," Tobias said loudly.

"TOBIAS!" Dr. Edwards said sternly. "We don't need that kind of talk!"

"I don't much care what you need Doc," Tobias taunted. "That conversation isn't finished as far as I'm concerned."

"What are you talking about?" Lexi asked.

"Nothing, forget it," Tobias said harshly. "Alright, I'm here. What?"

"Tobias, I do not like your tone or overall attitude," Dr. Edwards stated firmly. "I understand that you do not like that these people are here, but they helped us and every patient in that emergency room. So, if you are going to stay here, please act civil."

Matt and Jeff were too far away to hear the particulars of what was being discussed by Dr. Edwards, Lexi, and Tobias. The facial expressions and hand gestures indicated to them the conversation was tense.

"You think their discussing Ralph's condition?" Matt asked.

"I don't think so," Jeff said as he shook his head. "I think they're arguing. Especially, what's his name there." He continued as he pointed to Tobias. "That guy seems pissed."

"Maybe we should make sure they're ok," Matt suggested.

"You looking to throw down?" Jeff asked.

"Not at all," Matt assured him as he got to his feet. "Just want to make sure everyone is ok. You coming with?"

"Sure, why not," Jeff said as he got to his feet. "Maybe breakfast will be ready by the time they tell us their conversation is none of our business."

"Always possible," Matt agreed as he and Jeff started over.

As Matt and Jeff neared, they could see Tobias was increasingly more agitated. His hand gestures were animated and the pitch of his voice was much higher.

"I don't want to have anything to do with them!" Tobias seethed. "They're trash, all of them."

"How dare you say something like that," Dr. Edwards scolded. "If you don't want to socialize that's fine, but you could at least contribute. They're making breakfast for us."

"Contribute? How do you want me to contribute?" Tobias asked rhetorically. "Should I show them to the exit?"

"How about making some more coffee?" Dr. Edwards suggested. "This way you don't have to interact with anyone."

"Coffee?" Tobias scoffed. "You've got to be fucking kidding me. Let the parasites make their own coffee."

"I already told you about that language..." Dr. Edwards began.

"Who's a parasite?" Jeff interrupted.

Startled, Dr. Edwards face turned bright red, "This is a staff discussion. Please excuse us."

"We didn't mean to interrupt," Matt said as he glared at Tobias. "But we heard there might be coffee. How's your eye?"

"Fuck this!" Tobias shouted as he got up and turned to storm off.

"Does this mean you're not making coffee?" Matt taunted.

The conversations around the table stopped abruptly as Tobias's voice echoed across the cafeteria. Everyone took notice of the situation as it escalated. Shaw and Holden moved closer to Barbra and Katlyn who were still seated at the center of the far row of tables.

"Why don't you go fuck yourself!" Tobias barked as he tried to push past Matt.

"Don't put your fucking hands on me!" Matt ordered. He grabbed the lump above Tobia's eye and squeezed.

"AHHH!" Tobias screamed as he stumbled backwards. "You fucker!"

Christian grabbed Matt's AR15 from where it leaned. He checked the magazine to make sure it was seated properly, clicked the safety off and made sure there was a round in the chamber.

"Come on," Kurt said as he hurried Kim to her feet.

"What's going on?" Kim asked.

"Just come on," Kurt insisted as they moved quickly behind where Christian was seated.

Roderick scanned the room as he moved away from the rest of the group and closer to the entranceway.

"Get the fuck out of my way asshole!" Tobias ordered as he tried to push past Matt a second time.

"The fuck is your problem?" Matt questioned as he pressed his right forearm against Tobias's throat and shoved him backwards.

"Make them stop!" Lexi begged as she grabbed Dr. Edwards arm. "Please!"

"My problem?" Tobias hissed as he pressed his finger into Matt's chest. "You're my fucking problem! You and your entire fucking group are my fucking problem!"

"Tobias, stop!" Lexi shouted.

"This isn't a fight you want to start," Matt insisted with a deadpan expression.

"Tough guy with a gun," Tobias mocked as he motioned to the lump above his eye. "I bet without that gun you're a pussy just like the rest of you friends."

"Tobias!" Dr. Edwards demanded. "STOP!"

Adrenaline pumped through Matt's body as his fists clenched, "Keep running your mouth cock sucker."

"Matthew!" Aunt Athena called. "Just walk away."

"You're a bunch of fucking parasites," Tobias continued. "You come in here take our medicine, eat our food..."

Jeff grabbed Matt's right arm and pressed his right palm against Matt's chest, "Come on, let's not do this."

"Let him go Jeff!" Christian ordered from where he sat.

"What are you going to take next, one of our ambulances?" Tobias chided. "Huh? You took everything else!"

"JEFF!" Christian called again. "Let him go!"

"Oh, look at this pussy," Tobias taunted as he pointed at Jeff. "Taking orders from an invalid hooked up to an I.V. pole."

"Jeff!" Mr. Spahl said as he got to his feet.

Jeff let go of Matt's arm and turned to face Tobias, "Hey pal, where are you from?"

"Where am I from?" Tobias asked with a confused expression on his face.

"Yeah, where are you from?" Jeff asked again.

"Ohio," Tobias answered. "Why?"

"Ohio?" Jeff repeated.

"Yeah," Tobias said with a confused look on his face. "Ohio. Why?"

"Are they all assholes in Ohio?" Jeff asked with a smirk. "Or just you?"

"Oh, funny," Tobias scoffed. "You can go fuck yourself too."

"Tobias, that's enough!" Dr. Edwards shouted.

"Tyler, do something," Aunt Athena insisted.

"What do you expect me to do?" Tyler asked frustratedly. "I'm on fucking crutches."

Matt took a step towards Tobias, "Did you just tell my friend to fuck himself?"

"Fuck you! If it wasn't for us, your brother would be dead!" Tobias shouted as he pointed at Christian.

Mr. Spahl felt a wave of exhaustion hit him, "Oh fuck, why did he have to say that?" He muttered to himself.

"What'd you say tough guy?" Matt snarled.

"I said, your brother would be fucking dead..." Tobias blurted.

Matt charged him before the words had fully left Tobias's mouth, "Mother fucker!" Matt screamed. His face was a deep shade of red and the guttural scream which emanated from him sent a chill through the room. "AHHHH!"

"No!" Tobias managed. He tried to move back but Matt was on top of him immediately. His hands wrapped tightly around Tobias's throat. His knees buckled under Matt's weight and the two of them crashed to the floor.

"Oh my God!" Lexi shrieked as she jumped to her feet. "Somebody, make them stop!"

"Matthew!" Aunt Athena screamed as she got up hurriedly. "Stop it!"

"Talk shit now mother fucker!" Matt taunted as his hands tightened around Tobias's throat. "Come on, talk shit now!"

"Oh my God!" Katlyn shrieked as she looked away.

"Don't look!" Barbra insisted. She grabbed Katlyn, pulled her sister close to her chest and used her left hand to cover her sister's eyes.

Tobias gasped for air. His face turned a deep shade of red as Matt squeezed. Tobias pulled at Matt's arms but couldn't free himself.

"Talk shit now motherfucker!" Matt continued to taunt.

"Please, somebody do something!" Aunt Athena begged.

"Nobody interferes!" Mr. Spahl announced as he stood up and drew the 1911 from the holster on his hip.

"WHAT?" Dr. Edwards questioned. "This has to stop!"

"Your man started it," Mr. Spahl said bluntly. "This situation demands resolution."

"What's going on?" Mrs. Spahl shouted as she and Dominick hurried from the kitchen.

"He picked a fight with Matt, now he's got to deal with the consequences," Mr. Spahl said without turning around.

"What happened?" Dominick called. "Shaw what's going on?"

"I'll kill you motherfucker," Matt screamed as Tobias's face turned purple. "Nobody hurts my brother! I'll fucking kill you!"

"He said what?" Mrs. Spahl inquired.

"Not now!" Mr. Spahl ordered as he cut her off.

"This isn't our fight Dom. Don't get involved," Shaw instructed. "The little guy started it. It's on them to figure it out."

"But he can't breathe," Dominick argued.

"Fuck you!" Matt snarled as he pressed his weight onto Tobias's wind pipe. "Fuck you!"

"Somebody, help!" Lexi cried. "He's going to kill him!"

"ENOUGH!" Dr. Edwards yelled as he threw up his hand and moved towards Matt. "THAT'S ENOUGH!"

"JEFF!" Mr. Spahl shouted.

That was all Jeff needed to hear. His father's tone said more than a sentence of words ever could. He pulled the P90 from his holster and stepped in front of Dr. Edwards. He brought the pistol up and placed the front sight post between Dr. Edwards eyes, "Don't!" Jeff said as he shook his head. "Just don't!"

"Please no!" Lexi screamed at the sight of Jeff as he pointed the pistol at Dr. Edwards. She clamped her hands over her mouth to muffle her reaction as tears ran down her cheeks.

"It'll be good to get some coffee," Tamara said. She gave Paul's offer to leave with them serious consideration as they walked arm in arm down the hallway.

"I need some chow," Paul said with a grin. "I'm famished. You wore me out."

"That was all you marathon man," Tamara teased as they neared the cafeteria. "I don't know what they're preparing but it smells good.

"Yes, it does," Paul agreed as he inhaled deeply. He kissed the top of her head ever so tenderly. She glanced up at him. They stared into each other's eyes and shared a loving moment of contentedness and peace.

"Talk shit now motherfucker!" Matt shouted as he bounced Tobias's head repeatedly off the floor. Tobias's head sounded like a ripe melon as it smacked again and again against the linoleum. "You don't talk about my brother," He screamed red faced as Tobias's eyes started to roll back in his head. "You don't talk shit about my brother!"

The doors parted. Tamara's head rested on Paul's shoulder as they entered the cafeteria.

"What's going on?" Tamara shrieked as she saw the chaos they walked into.

"I'LL KILL YOU, MOTHERFUCKER!" Matt screamed. His knuckles whitened as his hands constricted around Tobias's throat.

"OH MY GOD, WHAT ARE YOU DOING?" Tamara screamed when she realized what was going on.

"MATT!" Paul called. He unwrapped himself from Tamara and lunged forward. The surge of adrenaline that shot through his body made everything appear as if it were happening in slow motion.

Tobias's airway was so compressed no sound emanated from him. His vision blurred and his extremities had the feel of pins and needles.

With no strength left, his hands smacked against the floor as the last moments of his life slipped away.

"NO!" Lexi shrieked.

"HE'S GOING TO DIE!" Samantha shouted.

Paul grabbed Matt around the torso. He locked his hands around Matt's chest and pulled up with a measure of force that surprised even him. "STOP!"

"GET THE FUCK OFF ME!" Matt ordered as he released his hold on Tobias's throat.

Tamara hurried past Paul, "TOBIAS!" She cried as she knelt next to his motionless body. "Can you hear me? Lexi, Samantha we need a crash cart. We're going to need to open his airway. HURRY!" She called as the two nurses ran from the cafeteria. "Tobias! Tobias, can you hear me?"

CHAPTER 24

the toll, part 2

"GET OFF ME!" MATT shouted as he struggled to free himself from Paul's grasp. "GET THE FUCK OFF ME!"

"CALM DOWN!" Paul barked as he fought to maintain his grip. "CALM THE FUCK DOWN! WHAT HAPPENED!"

"LET ME GO!" Matt demanded. "I'M GOING TO KILL THAT MOTHER FUCKER!"

"Is he breathing?" Dr. Edwards called as he hurried to help Tobias. "Tamara, is he breathing?"

"He's turning blue!" Tamara cried as she worked feverishly to revive Tobias. "Where's Lexi and Samantha with the cart?"

"They'll be back," Dr. Edwards assured her as he knelt next to Tobias. "Here let me help. Tip his head back. We need to start mouth to mouth."

"PAUL!" Christian shouted as he slowly got to his feet. He brought the AR15 to the low ready position as Paul dragged Matt towards the kitchen, "LET HIM GO!"

"What happened?" Paul questioned as he and Matt stumbled backwards. "Calm down and tell me what happened!"

"Put it away Jeff," Mr. Spahl instructed as he holstered his pistol.

Jeff looked around the room, glanced back at his father and nodded, "Yeah." He said as he followed suit and returned the pistol to his holster.

"I SAID, LET HIM GO!" Christian repeated as he raised the rifle.

"We've got the cart!" Samantha announced as she and Lexi burst through the cafeteria doors. The plastic wheels rattled as Samantha and Lexi hurried the large white metal cart full of equipment to where Tobias lay. "Is he breathing?"

"What?" Paul asked startled. He looked towards Christian. "Easy."

"Not going to say it again!" Christian growled as he took a step forward.

"You want to know what happened?" Mr. Spahl interjected as he came around the table. "The pile of shit on the floor decided to tell Matt that Christian would be dead if it wasn't for these fucking snowflakes."

"He did what?" Paul questioned in disbelief. "What did he say?"

"You heard my father," Jeff said. The tone of his voice was a mixture of sarcasm and hostility. "What the fuck do you think about that?"

"That piece of shit," Paul blurted as he released Matt. "That, mother fucker!"

"Fuck him," Matt hissed. His legs felt like rubber beneath him. It was everything he could do not to drop to the floor as the adrenaline began to subside. "I hope he fucking dies."

"I'm sorry brother," Paul said bewildered as he breathed heavily. He bent over and placed his hands on his legs as he tried to catch his breath. "I didn't know."

"I'm going to finish what I started," Matt mumbled as he drew the 1911 from his holster. He started towards where the hospital staff worked to revive Tobias.

"DON'T!" Mr. Spahl directed loudly. He held his hands up. "You made your point. Don't do something that's going to put you in the wrong."

"My father's right," Jeff insisted as he stepped in front of Matt. He put his hand on Matt's shoulder. "You won. He's down. No need to destroy him."

Matt stood for a moment and glared at Tobias. He reluctantly returned the pistol to his holster and shook his head, "Fine. Fuck him." He snarled before he turned to face Paul.

"Go easy brother," Paul said as he straightened his body and wiped sweat from his face.

"You want to know what happened while you were off playing house?" Matt asked angrily as his chest heaved. "Motherfucker got what he deserved. That's what the fuck happened."

"I didn't know," Paul said as he shook his head. "I thought you were gonna kill him."

"That's what I was aiming to do," Matt explained unapologetically. "You should have backed my play."

"Backed your play?" Paul questioned. "That's not the kind of guilt you want to be carrying around."

"That's for me to worry about!" Matt snapped as he pointed his index finger menacingly at Paul. "From here on out, you just back my play and trust my judgement until I can fill you in on the full fucking particulars."

"Table it," Paul calmly insisted. "Until you've calmed down."

Tamara counted as she pushed on Tobias's chest. After every thirty compressions, Samantha used the valve mask CPR resuscitator to force oxygen into Tobias's lungs.

"Is it working?" Lexi asked desperately.

"I've got a pulse!" Dr. Edwards announced.

"Oh, thank God!" Lexi cried.

Gradually Tobias's eye lids began to flutter and the color returned to his cheeks and lips.

"He's breathing!" Samantha shouted excitedly.

"Ahhhh," Tobias groaned as he began to regain consciousness.

"Stabilize his head and roll him towards me," Dr. Edwards instructed as he motioned with his hands. "Carefully now."

"What…" Tobias gasped and coughed as he struggled to take a deep breath. "Ahhh."

"Easy son, just try and breathe," Dr. Edwards encouraged as he placed his hand on Tobias's shoulder. "Nice and easy."

"Where…" Tobias wheezed.

"Tobias?" Tamara called. "Tobias, can you hear me?"

"Well, what do you know," Matt sneered as a look of contempt covered his face. "I guess I didn't kill the motherfucker after all."

"Matthew," Aunt Athena said sternly. "Is that really necessary?"

"Not at all," Matt answered curtly. He grabbed the back of the chair next to Christian to steady himself. He tried not to let on how lightheaded he was or how weakened the incident with Tobias left him. The feet made a shrill screech as Matt forcefully yanked the chair from beneath the table. He smirked as he dropped his body down on the seat. Spots danced before his eyes and he thought he may vomit. "But fuck him anyway for starting it!"

"Matthew!" Aunt Athena scolded. "That kind of talk isn't helping."

"Oh, fucking well," Matt responded with a shrug. His deception required a certain amount brazen bravado. He didn't care if anyone liked him, only that for the near term no one challenged him.

"My throat…" Tobias muttered. He continued to cough and sputter as he rubbed the front of this throat.

"Can you hear me?" Tamara asked again. "Tobias, can you hear me?"

"We should take him downstairs to the ER," Samantha suggested. "We need to check his wind pipe and determine the level of damage."

"Absolutely, Samantha," Dr. Edwards agreed. "That's a good idea."

"I'm fine," Tobias wheezed as he struggled to lift his head.

"Tobias, don't worry. You're going to be ok," Tamara assured him as a look of relief overtook her face. "We're going to take you downstairs and check you out. Can you…"

"Get your hands off me you fucking cunt!" Tobias growled.

"Tobias!" Dr. Edwards blurted forcefully. "Stop that!"

"What?" Tamara stammered. "Tobias…"

"This is all your fault, you fucking cunt!" Tobias continued as he rolled onto his stomach and pulled himself up to his knees.

Tamara was horrified by what she heard, "Tobias, no…"

"I loved you, you fucking cunt! That wasn't good enough for you. You had to go and fuck that piece of shit!" Tobias wheezed as he motioned towards Paul.

"How can you speak to me like that?" Tamara questioned.

"Tobias, that's enough!" Dr. Edwards ordered.

"You disgust me!" Tobias hissed. He swung his left arm around and struck the left side of Tamara's face.

"Ahhh!" Tamara yelped as she was knocked her from where she knelt to the floor.

"NO!" Paul shouted as he charged forward.

"Dr. Singer!" Dr. Edwards called as he reached for her.

Tobias's outburst brought all the men to their feet. Before anyone could react, Paul yanked Tobias up by the back of his scrub top and spun him around, "That's enough cock sucker!" He growled.

"Fuck you!" Tobias hissed as he tried to squirm out of Paul's clutches.

"Fuck me?" Paul questioned. Tobias's cheek bone gave an audible crack under the force of Paul's right hand as he drove it down into Tobias's face. "NO! FUCK YOU!"

"AHHH!" Tobias cried as blood squirted from his mouth. He grabbed Paul's left hand in a feeble attempt to free himself.

Paul twisted the fabric in his fist and tightened the scrub top around Tobias's neck. Tobias gasped as he reached for Paul's face. Paul swatted Tobias's hand away before he drove his fist into Tobais's face a second time, "I'm going to teach you some fucking manners." Paul growled.

"Fuck you!" Tobias muttered defiantly as blood ran from his nose and mouth.

"You should know better than to hit a woman," Paul barked before he hit Tobias again. He glanced over at Tamara, who was still laying in the fetal position on the floor. She had her hands cupped around the left side of her face as she wept.

"Fuck that bitch!" Tobias managed in a raspy whine as droplets of blood spewed from his mouth.

"Keep talking scumbag," Paul hissed as his eyes narrowed. Tobias's eyes bulged as Paul twisted the scrub top tighter. He reared his right arm back again. There was an audible crack as Tobias's jaw shattered under the force of the blow.

"Ahhh!" Tobias cried. His head snapped back as blood and several teeth jettisoned from his mouth.

"FUCK YOU!" Paul yelled through clenched teeth before he threw Tobias's limp body to the floor.

There was a collective gasp as Tobias's body smacked awkwardly against the cafeteria floor. He came to rest in a bloody heap in front of Dr. Edwards.

"STOP!" Dr. Edwards pleaded. "FOR THE LOVE OF GOD, STOP!"

"What the fuck is wrong with the people in this state?" Roderick muttered as he hurried to rejoin the rest of his group.

"Get that mother fucker out of my sight!" Paul ordered as he pointed to Dr. Edwards. He turned his attention to Roderick. "Any more about this state or the people in it and you'll be riding the Goddamn gurney with him. Understand?"

Roderick held his hands up and backed away slowly, "Yeah, I understand."

"That's enough," Dr. Edwards insisted. He turned to Shaw, Holden, and Roderick. "Please help me get him to the emergency room."

"Sure Doc," Holden said as he cautiously got to his feet. "Maybe a little space would do everybody good."

The atmosphere remained tense, even after they transported Tobias out of the cafeteria.

"Where are we with breakfast?" Mr. Spahl asked. He was hungry and thought it best to change everyone's focus.

"What?" Dominick stammered.

"Breakfast," Mr. Spahl repeated. "Is it ready?"

"I...I don't know," Dominick answered. "I have to check."

"If you'd be so kind," Mr. Spahl said as he motioned to kitchen. "There's a room full of hungry people who would very much like to eat."

"Of course," Dominick said with a nod. He looked around almost confused and mumbled. "Breakfast, really?"

"Come on," Mrs. Spahl encouraged. She took Dominick by the arm and guided him back to the kitchen. "Let's finish up and get everybody fed."

Patrick wheeled his I.V. pole across the cafeteria and proceeded to make two pots of fresh coffee, "This morning is off to a great start." He muttered quietly to himself.

Everyone sat in an uncomfortable silence. No one was quite sure what to say about what had happened. There was collective relief when Dominick and Mrs. Spahl returned from the kitchen and served breakfast.

Matt stayed close to Christian. Neither said much. They were content to have a few quiet minutes while they devoured their meal.

"Coffee's good," Kurt said as he took a sip from the cream-colored mug.

"Thanks," Patrick said with a nod. "It's not too bad."

"It's actually really good," Kim added. "How'd you make it?"

Patrick shook his head, "Family secret." He said with a grin. "I can't say."

"Well however you did it," Kim said. "It's delicious."

"Thank you," Patrick said with a nod. He picked up his fork and dug in. "Talk about delicious." He continued with a mouth full of food.

Paul took his plate and found a table away from everyone else. Steam rose from the Styrofoam cup as he moved it between his hands, "What a fucking mess." He said to himself. Paul looked out over the rose garden, thought about what he'd just done and wished he and Tamara were still upstairs wrapped in each other's arms.

"That fucking cock sucker," Matt mumbled. He held the white mug with the hospital logo printed in black on either side tightly to keep his hands from trembling. "I should have stomped on his throat."

"Eat something," Christian directed. "We're going to have to get back on the road. I think we've worn out our welcome here."

"Yeah," Matt agreed as he shoved a fork full of food in his mouth. "Fuck them too."

"Barb, Katlyn" Shaw asked as he returned to the cafeteria and checked on his sisters. "How are you two doing?"

"I've never seen anyone get angry like that," Katlyn said quietly. "I'm scared. I want to leave."

"It's going to be alright Katlyn" Shaw assured her. "Barb, what do you think?"

"I would like to have stayed one more night," Barbra offered. She rubbed her eyes and used her fork to move food around her plate. "But after what happened. Maybe it would be better to leave."

"We shouldn't stay here," Katlyn continued. Her eyes darted nervously around the room. "As long as they give me something for the pain, I think I can travel."

The emergency room felt chaotic as the staff worked to stabilize Tobias.

"They really did a number on him," Samantha observed as she hung a bag of saline from the I.V. pole next to where Tobias lay.

"Samantha, when you're done there check his pressure," Tamara instructed.

"Yes, Dr. Singer," Samantha answered.

"Lexi," Tamara called.

"On my way," Lexi answered as she hurried back to the room. "I'm here."

"Can you clean him up a little please?" Tamara asked as she motioned to the blood on Tobias's face and neck. "We've got to get him in for x-rays."

"Right away Doc," Lexi said with a nod.

"Dr. Singer," Dr. Edwards said as he pulled a pair of gloves over his hands.

"Yes, Dr. Edwards," Tamara answered.

"When we've finished here," Dr. Edwards began. "I'm going to tell them they have to leave."

"I understand doctor," Tamara acknowledged with a nod.

"What happened up there," Dr. Edwards said as he shook his head. "Was completely unacceptable."

The cafeteria was uncomfortably quiet. It seemed that even the sunlight that streamed through the windows had lessened.

Paul deposited his plate and silverware in the large stainless-steel sink in the kitchen and headed towards the exit.

"Where you going?" Matt called loudly as if daring someone to challenge him. "Something wrong with the company?"

Paul stopped abruptly but didn't look over, "Going downstairs." He answered. "You can find me there if you need me."

"Don't be a stranger," Matt continued before he turned back and finished what was left on his plate. "I think I'll have a second cup of coffee." He announced as he stood up and slid his chair across the floor.

"What the fuck has happened to us?" Paul muttered as he left the room. The metal stairs echoed under his feet as he made his way to the first floor. He needed to make sure Tamara was alright. There was a sense of loss he couldn't reconcile when he watched her leave the cafeteria. All he knew was the sooner they were in each other's arms, the sooner the world around them would feel less crazy.

Holden was startled when he pulled the stairwell door open only to find Paul's large frame headed towards him, "Whoa!" He blurted as he moved aside.

"Where is she?" Paul demanded as he stepped out of the stairwell.

"Who?" Roderick asked defiantly.

"No," Holden said as he shook his head. He grabbed his nephew and pushed him into the stairwell. "Get going." He instructed before he turned back to answer Paul. "Everyone's beyond the double doors tending to the little guy."

"Roger," Paul replied without looking back. He stormed past the nurse's station and headed through the double doors.

"Ahhhh!" Lexi yelped in a high-pitched voice as she rounded the corner and unexpectedly came face to face with Paul.

"Really kid?" Paul grumbled as he shook his head. "I had a feeling you were the jumpy one. Where's Tamara?"

"You startled me," Lexi said. She pressed her hand against her chest as she cautiously looked Paul up and down. "I didn't think anyone else was down here."

"I'm looking for Tamara," Paul repeated. "Have you seen her?"

"Dr. Singer?" Lexi questioned. "Yes. She's with Dr. Edwards. They're taking care of Tobias. She'll be a bit. I can let her know you're waiting."

"Let her know, I'll be in her office," Paul instructed.

"I will," Lexi assured him as she nervously hurried off.

It took more than 30-minutes before Tamara appeared in the doorway of her office. She peeled the latex gloves from her hands and removed the face mask as Paul approached her. It wasn't lost on him that despite his best efforts to be gentle, Tamara flinched when he gently caressed her face. He guided her head to the right to get a better look at the bruise on her left cheekbone.

"Are you alright?" Paul asked. It was difficult for him to mask how upset he was that she had been hurt. "Is there anything…"

"You two almost killed him," Tamara said coldly.

"What?" Paul questioned. "But…"

"His wind pipe and larynx are bruised," Tamara interrupted. "He was already concussed from yesterday and now he's had his head bounced off the floor, I don't know how many times."

"He hit you," Paul reminded her as he stood perplexed for a moment.

"Thanks to you," Tamara continued. "His cheek bone is fractured. His jaw is broken in two places and was dislocated. Not to mention you knocked out four of his teeth and broke two more at the gum line."

"He hit you!" Paul repeated. "What did you expect me…"

"You overreacted!" Tamara accused as she pointed a finger sternly at Paul. "We expended a lot of resources to address something that shouldn't have happened."

Paul shook his head in disagreement, "He hit you and he threatened Christian."

"First of all, we helped your people," Tamara said tersely. "We were never not going to help your people despite what Tobias said because he was upset. We are medical professionals, that's what we do."

"Yeah," Paul responded. He could feel his blood pressure rise as Tamara lectured him.

"Second of all," Tamara continued. "I've been hit harder by worse guys than Tobias. He's a cupcake. I was in no real danger."

"Right," Paul said coldly. "That's not how it looked when you were curled up in the fetal position crying on the floor."

"You two overreacted," Tamara repeated as she ignored Paul's comment. "I told you; I couldn't have that kind of violence in my life."

"You've been hit harder by worse guys?" Paul questioned. There was disgust in his voice as he continued. "And somehow me standing up for you is the kind of violence that's intolerable?"

"You were out of line," Tamara insisted. There was a coldness about her eyes as she continued. "What happens to me is none of your business."

"None of my business?" Paul questioned angrily. "You would have let me go searching for your grandmother and your sister; and what happens to you is none of my business? Am I hearing this right?"

"You offered," Tamara snapped harshly. She pushed past Paul and took a seat behind her desk. "I never asked you to do that."

"You never asked?" Paul repeated. He could feel his heart pound in his chest. "Wow...ok then."

"I don't need to be saved," Tamara declared as she slammed her hand down on the top of her desk. "By you or anyone else."

"Saved?" Paul questioned as he leaned against the door frame. He couldn't reconcile the space between them. Paul was tired and there was disappointment in his voice as he continued. "That's great. I get it now."

"You get it now," Tamara repeated angrily. "You get what now?"

"You're one of them," Paul said plainly and turned to leave.

"What do you mean one of them?" Tamara demanded as she stood up. "Where do you think you're going?"

"You know what," Paul said calmly as he turned back to face her. There was sadness in his eyes as they found hers. "I was hoping for a fairy tale, not the twilight zone. Good luck with the rest of your life."

Christian finished the last fork full of breakfast and pushed his plate towards the center of the table. He sat back, scanned the room, and tried to gauge the mood by the facial expressions. He noticed Shaw glance up several times as if he couldn't decide whether to approach. When Shaw finally stood up, Christian gave Matt's arm a nudge to alert him.

"Mind if I sit down?" Shaw asked nervously. He used his left hand to stir a thin red plastic straw around the rim of the ceramic mug he held.

Matt motioned to the chair to his right, "Please."

"I thought we could speak briefly," Shaw said as he slid the chair from beneath the table and sat down.

"What about?" Matt asked disarmingly. "The amount of sugar you use?"

"Good catch," Shaw said as he chuckled uncomfortably. He hadn't expected anyone to notice how much sugar he poured into his coffee cup.

"I'm surprised the straw doesn't stand straight up like a flag pole with all that sugar," Matt observed.

"My wife would agree," Shaw said with a smirk. He looked down at the table and cleared his throat. "Would have agreed with you."

It wasn't lost on him, that Shaw amended his comment to reflect the mention of his wife in the past tense. "I'm sorry." Matt offered as genuinely as he was able.

"Thank you," Shaw said before he took a sip from the mug. "She used to tease me. She'd ask me if life was too easy and I was trying to make it more difficult by adding diabetes to the mix."

Matt nodded unsure of how to respond, "What'd you want to talk about?"

"I'm not saying you were wrong..." Shaw began.

"Good, because I wasn't," Matt snapped.

Shaw let go of the straw and held his hand up, "If it was my brother, I probably would've done the same."

"Then it's settled," Matt responded unimpressed with Shaw's approach. "So, what's the public service announcement?"

"The what?" Shaw asked unsure of what the reference meant.

"The public service announcement," Matt repeated. "The lesson. The moral of the story. The thing you needed to say that brought you over here." He continued as his posture straightened, voice intensified and heart pounded. He wasn't about to be lectured. "What in the fuck exactly do you want?"

"I'm not trying to upset you," Shaw assured him. He glanced at Christian in the hope of eliciting some measure of support. "I just wanted to say that what's happening out there, whatever it is, may not be over quickly."

"What a revelation," Matt chided. He turned to his brother. "Are you getting all this?"

Christian leaned forward, turned, and glared at Shaw, "It's time to come to the point."

"Fine," Shaw began. He was disappointed they weren't more receptive to his attempt at civility. "We'll be parting ways soon enough." He began. "I'm grateful to you both for the help you gave my family. I just hope you'll keep something in mind as you get to where you're going…"

Matt leaned in curious as to the words of wisdom Shaw was about to leave them with. His eyes narrowed as he rested his chin on his fist. A sinister grin spread across his face and he let his right hand drop from the table to his holster, "My brother asked you to come to the point."

"I'm not armed," Shaw explained as he glanced at Matt's hand on his holster.

"I know," Matt said calmly. "We weren't about to trust strangers with firearms. So how about the punchline?"

"I didn't come over here to challenge you," Shaw explained. He struggled not to show how uncomfortable he was. "I'm not looking to start a fight."

"What then?" Matt asked antagonistically.

Katherine could hear the way Matt taunted Shaw. It was not a tone she was accustomed to and certainly not one that instilled confidence. She shot Christian a look from across the table and hoped he would not allow things to escalate, "Do something." She mouthed.

Christian returned the look with a stern glare and defiant head shake. He would afford Shaw no easy way out of the conversation he started, "No." He said coldly.

"I don't want any trouble," Shaw assured them both. "I just want to say something I hope you both will consider."

"Please then," Matt offered sarcastically. "Illuminate us."

"I understand if you need to puff your chest up and make sure everybody knows you're the craziest guy in the room. I get that," Shaw began as his voice trembled. He slowly pushed the chair away from the table and stood up. He could see Katlyn and Barbra were concerned about where the conversation was headed. He gave them a nod before he returned his attention to Matt and Christian. "I hope you remember who the real threat is. The fight isn't in here with the living. It's out there with the dead."

"The fight?" Matt growled through gritted teeth. He forced his body up from the chair as he glared at Shaw. "The fight is with whoever gets in my fucking way!"

CHAPTER 25

epilogue

AN AWKWARD SILENCE DESCENDED upon the cafeteria after Tobias's semi-conscious body was removed. Without the HVAC system, the brilliant mid-day sun kept the room uncomfortably warm. The stagnant air blanketed the space with an oppressive aura which contributed to the collective discontent.

Kim glanced anxiously around the cafeteria, "We can't just sit here." She said to herself as she nervously rubbed the fingernail on her right index finger against her thumb.

"You alright?" Kurt asked as he glanced up from his plate. "Eat a little more if you can. This is really good."

"We can't just sit here," Kim repeated. The metal feet of the chair scraped against the floor as she slid it away from the table. Kim blushed slightly as she stood up and all eyes turned towards her.

"What's going on?" Kurt asked as he reached up for her.

Kim shook her head, "We've been here long enough." She said as she collected her plate, silverware, and mug.

"What?" Kurt questioned as he loaded up his fork. "Here, sit back down."

"No," Kim said as she took a step back from the table. "It's time we collected our things and got on our way."

"Hang on," Kurt insisted. "Just let me finish eating and I'll..."

"Eat," Kim instructed. She made her way around the perimeter of the banquet table and collected empty dishes and mugs. "You finish. I'll clean things up. I want to go downstairs, take a shower and then we'll find Matt and Christian and tell them it's time to leave."

Kurt nodded before he glanced down at the mound of food on his plate, "Ok." He agreed, unsure of how exactly to respond.

As Kim exited the kitchen, she was surprised to see Katherine approach with an arm full of plates and bowls.

"I'm sorry," Kim said. She didn't know Katherine well and wasn't sure what else to say.

"For what?" Katherine questioned. "It's not right that you do all the cleanup."

"I can take those," Kim offered as she reached to take the stack of dirty dishes from Katherine.

"I can manage," Katherine assured her. "Where do you want them?"

"Here," Kim answered as she turned and held the kitchen door open. She motioned to the counter top just beyond the stove. "I put everything over by the sink."

"Good," Katherine said. She stacked the plates and bowls next to the pile Kim created and turned back. "Ok, what's next?"

"I don't know," Kim admitted. She shook her head as the two headed back to the table. "I was getting anxious just sitting around so I thought I'd clean up. I'm sorry. I didn't want you to think you had to help me."

"Don't apologize," Katherine insisted. "These guys should be apologizing for not clearing the table for us."

"Did you hear that, Kurt?" Kim asked with a smirk.

"I didn't hear anything," Kurt pretended. He grinned and didn't look up from his coffee cup. "I'm finishing my meal like you told me to."

"Sounds suspect," Katherine groaned. "Well, I know Marcus heard me."

Marcus looked up bewildered, "What?"

"Don't *what* me Marcus," Katherine scolded. "Get up and help us finish clearing the table."

Dominick returned to the kitchen, where he scooped the last of his breakfast creation into two large bowls, "I didn't think we'd have left overs." He said to himself as he covered the bowls with sheets of tin foil.

"It wasn't for a lack of quality," Mrs. Spahl assured him as she entered the kitchen.

"Oh," Dominick yelped as his posture straightened. He glanced back at Mrs. Spahl. "I didn't realize you were here."

"The meal was exceptional," Mrs. Spahl said. She placed a comforting hand on his shoulder. "Thank you for sharing your special recipe with us."

"It was my pleasure," Dominick said with a smile as his cheeks reddened slightly. "It was a shame, things happened out the way they did. I guess that's just the world now."

"I've known those young men since they were children," Mrs. Spahl explained. "Matthew and my Aaron went to first grade together."

"Oh, you've known them a long time," Dominick observed. He moved the pans off the stove and placed them in the large basin sink on the opposite wall. "A long time."

"Yes," Mrs. Spahl responded. "A long time and when we get to where we're going, I'm going to have a long talk with both of them about what happened here."

"I hope you do," Dominick said. He used the dish towel to wipe his hands. "It can't be healthy to go through life with that kind of rage."

"No, it certainly cannot," Mrs. Spahl agreed. As she turned, the small crucifix at the center of the chain attached to Dominick's glasses caught her eye. "May I ask what that is?"

"What's that?" Dominick replied.

"The chain attached to your glasses," Mrs. Spahl answered. "Is that a crucifix hanging from the back of it?"

Dominick nodded as he turned, "Yes, it is." He answered as he leaned against the sink and took the glasses from around his neck. "It is a crucifix."

"This is so unique," Mrs. Spahl commented as she took the glasses from Dominick. "I've never seen a chain like this on a pair of glasses before. It almost looks like Rosary beads."

Dominick smiled and folded his arms in front of him, "Those are Rosary beads."

"They are?" Mrs. Spahl questioned unable to hide her surprise.

"Yes, they are," Dominick answered as his eyes lit up. "They were my grandmothers Rosary beads. She used to tell me that she'd pray extra hard with them every day that I was in the Navy."

"That's very sweet," Mrs. Spahl commented with a smile.

"She was a saint, my grandmother," Dominick said wistfully.

"I think that's wonderful," Mrs. Spahl said. She could see the corners of Dominick's eyes get moist as he looked away.

"As she was getting up there in years, she told me she wanted me to have her Rosary beads," Dominick explained. "It really meant a lot to me. I never wanted to lose them, but I wasn't sure how I could keep them with me all the time. I came up with this idea, but wasn't sure what the rules were."

"What the rules were for what?" Mrs. Spahl questioned curiously.

"As far as making modifications to the Rosary," Dominick explained.

"How'd you figure it out?" Mrs. Spahl asked.

"I told my grandmother my idea and asked for her permission," Dominick explained with a shrug. "She loved the idea. She used to say, even if I wasn't praying the Rosary, Jesus still had my back."

Christian and Patrick each held onto one of the metal railings that lined either side of the stairwell. Matt carried the I.V. poles just ahead of them and was careful not to put any tension on the plastic tubing as they descended the stairs. To their surprise the door opened just as they reached the bottom of the staircase.

Samantha hurried into the stairwell. She carried a plastic bin filled with gauze, white medical tape, and latex gloves, "I thought you three would still be in the cafeteria." She said startled as she stopped abruptly. I was coming back to remove your I.V.s."

"Thought I'd save you the trip," Matt said. He lowered the wheels on the bottoms of the poles on the floor and glanced back at his brother and cousin. "So, I brought the patients down to you."

"That works," Samantha said with a nod. "Let's go to the nurse's station and we'll unhook you both."

The air in the emergency room was cool and dry. It was a dramatic change from the cafeteria. The gentle hum of the equipment was the only constant sound.

"Matt, would you bring one of the gurneys over here please?" Samantha asked as she placed the plastic bin on the nurse's station.

"Got it," Matt answered as he wheeled one of the gurneys over to where the three of them stood.

"Thank you," Samantha said. She lowered the gurney to chair height and motioned to Christian and Patrick. "Sit down please."

"I'm going to skip this part," Matt said as he looked away.

"Yeah, no one likes needles," Samantha said as she put on a pair of latex gloves. "How are you feeling?" She asked as she slid the needle from Christian's arm.

"Better now," Christian answered as he watched the thin piece of metal leave his vein.

"Good," Samantha said with a grin. She held a folded piece of gauze against his arm. "Hold that right there please."

"I've got it," Christian said as he pressed his index finger against the gauze.

"You're doing great," Samantha encouraged as she placed a strip of white medical tape over the gauze. "There you go. All done."

"Thanks Sam," Christian offered with a nod.

"Sure," Samantha replied. "Big brother, how are you doing over there?"

"Just fine," Matt scoffed without looking back. "Thanks for asking."

"Your turn," Samantha announced as she redirected her focus to Patrick, "Are you ready?"

"Do I have a choice?" Patrick asked uncomfortably.

"Not if you want to leave," Samantha said as she readied the gauze and white medical tape.

The sound of the double doors as they opened drew Matt's attention. Paul arrived in the emergency room with a seldom seen scowl on his face. Not far behind, Dr. Edwards emerged about twenty paces removed.

"Everything alright?" Matt asked as Paul approached.

Paul shook his head, "I've had enough of this place. It's time to leave."

"What happened?" Matt asked. He could hear the agitation in his friend's voice. "I thought you and Dr. Singer hit it off."

"Until I broke what's his names face," Paul grumbled.

"What's that?" Matt questioned.

"Nothing!" Paul said angrily. "She's a fucking headcase. It's time to go. We can take our chances on the road."

"Doc's coming up behind you," Matt called as he motioned with his hand. "As soon as he clears everybody we'll get going."

"How are you two doing?" Paul asked as he motioned towards Christian and Patrick.

"Samantha's getting them squared away," Matt answered. "They're both ready to travel."

"I wouldn't mind staying one more night," Patrick admitted as he slowly got to his feet.

"We're not staying," Paul said coldly as he passed the nurse's station on his way to collect his gear.

"Let's see what the Doc has to say about Ralph," Matt suggested.

"My only concern there," Paul continued without turning back. "Is how we're going to transport him without reinjuring him."

"I've been working on that," Matt said as Dr. Edwards approached. "I think I've got it figured out."

Eventually everyone returned from the cafeteria. They huddled around the nurse's station as Dr. Edwards shuffled through his stack of charts. He provided an update on Ralph, Tyler, and Katlyn. He also detailed how best to care for each of them in the days and weeks ahead. With the diagnosis positive most everyone dispersed.

"That's all well and good Doc," Matt began as he and Christian remained. "Sounds like everyone's on the road to recovery, but what about my brother?"

"More difficult to predict," Dr. Edwards answered as he placed Christian's chart on top of the pile. "I'm going to prescribe several medications along with dosage and consumption instructions for you."

"You have those here?" Matt asked.

"Yes," Dr. Edwards answered. "We'll have everything ready for you to take with you."

"What else Doc?" Christian asked.

"Well," Dr. Edwards began. "I recommend an easy to moderate activity level for the next few weeks and a significantly restricted diet. I understand that under the circumstances this may be more difficult."

"Alright," Christian agreed as he reviewed the instructions and list of medications. "I'll do what I can."

"One more thing Doc," Matt interrupted.

"What is it?" Dr. Edwards asked as he nervously shuffled the files across the top of the desk. "I've got patients I need to see."

"I wanted to thank you for taking care of my brother and the rest of our group," Matt said earnestly.

"It's our job," Dr. Edward replied somewhat standoffish. "And you're welcome."

"We appreciate it all the same," Matt assured him. "I also wanted to say I'm sorry again about your nurse."

"Judy Reed was a good nurse and a sweetheart of a person," Dr. Edwards said as he shook his head. "She didn't deserve that, to end up that way."

"None of us do, Doc," Matt added.

"I suppose you're right about that," Dr. Edwards agreed. "I guess there is some measure of solace in knowing what happened to her."

"Agreed," Matt said plainly. "At least you know she's not suffering."

"It's a small consolation, but a consolation all the same," Dr. Edwards acknowledged as he adjusted his glasses. "Was there anything else that you wanted to discuss?"

"As a matter of fact, there is," Matt said. "We're going to need to take one of your ambulances."

"One of our ambulances?" Dr. Edwards questioned.

"I noticed yesterday while my brother and I were clearing out the 3rd floor," Matt started. "You've got a fleet of ambulances parked in a designated lot off the north-east corner of the building."

"We do," Dr. Edwards admitted begrudgingly. "Yes, five or six I think."

"Seven actually," Matt informed him. "But we only need one."

"May I ask why?" Dr. Edwards questioned impatiently.

"Sure, you can ask," Matt quipped.

"We don't have a vehicle that can transport Ralph safely," Christian interjected. "So, we're going to need an ambulance."

"Fine," Dr. Edwards conceded. "I suppose we can spare one."

"That's mighty generous of you Doc," Matt said sarcastically. "If we hadn't shown up, you and your staff probably would have never seen those ambulances again. In fact, you probably would have ended up like the Donner party after the food ran out."

"That's a disgusting reference," Dr. Edwards scolded. "I agreed to let you take an ambulance. Can we just leave it at that."

"Yes," Christian answered firmly. "We'll leave it at that."

"Yeah, we'll leave it at that," Matt repeated as he turned to leave. "Much appreciated Doc. We have gear to pack."

"When you said there was one more thing," Dr. Edwards blurted before Matt stepped away. "I thought you wanted to apologize for what you and Paul did to Tobias."

"No," Matt said coldly as he turned to face Dr. Edwards. "I'll never apologize for that."

"This..." Dr. Edwards began. He was visibly flustered as he crossed his arms and shook his head.

"If I had my druthers," Matt said angrily as he stepped towards Dr. Edwards. "That motherfucker would be a blood stain on the floor upstairs. I..."

"That's enough!" Christian ordered as he stepped in front of his brother. "Doc, don't you have patients to see?"

"Yes. Yes, I do," Dr. Edwards answered. The color drained from his face as he fidgeted with the files. "I hope you get to where you're going without any more violence." He added before he turned and left.

Christian turned to face Matt, "No more." He said sternly.

"No more what?" Matt asked as his chest heaved. "We helped them. Without us..."

"They helped us," Christian reminded. "We still need their help, so drop the attitude."

"Why is it always on me to play nice?" Matt questioned angrily. "What, that cock sucker Tobias..."

"Tobias isn't a factor in this equation!" Christian growled as he pointed a knife hand at his brother. "Every time you're antagonistic, you put this group at risk. Stop, before something escalates to the point where one of us is forced to take a life!"

Outside, the sun hung directly overhead and bathed the surrounding area in warmth. The air was still and humidity low. There was no trace of the rain from the day prior.

Despite the earlier events, morale was high largely due to a good night's sleep and hardy breakfast. Matt and Jeff secured an ambulance and parked it under the portico.

"Nice and easy," Mr. Spahl instructed. He had the Mini-14 slung over his left shoulder as Paul, Kurt, Jeff and Matt guided Ralph and Tyler into the back of the ambulance. "Good job!" He offered as they secured the doors. "Alright, what's the plan?"

"I'll drive the ambulance," Matt said as he collected his rifle. "I want Christian to ride shotgun with me."

"Who's driving the Subaru?" Mr. Spahl asked.

"I want Patrick to drive the Subaru," Christian answered. He zipped his coveralls and fastened his plate carrier over his chest. "You good with that Pat?"

"Yeah," Patrick said with a nod. His strawberry blond hair was still damp from the shower. He tugged at the tan t-shirt that clung to the moisture on his back and shoulders.   "I can drive the Subaru."

"Good," Christian replied as he fastened his Serpa belt around his waist. "You've got your mom, Katherine and Marcus."

"I've got room in the Jeep," Paul announced as he made his way over. He took the pack of cigarettes from his pocket. "Kurt and Kim, do you want to come with me?"

"As long as you don't smoke," Kim said as she pulled her long blonde hair into a ponytail. She adjusted the black t-shirt that was a size too large for her and pointed to the pack of cigarettes. "We'll ride with you as long as we don't have to breathe that."

Shaw, Holden, and Dominick joined Dr. Edwards, Tamara, and Samantha under the portico to see everyone off. Roderick hurried across the parking lot to collect their firearms from the Winnebago. Lexi remained inside to monitor Tobias and the other patients. Barbra and Katlyn found an empty conference room on the first floor. They laid out the map and double checked their planned route north.

"Thank you, Doc," Mr. Spahl said as he extended his hand. "For taking care of our people and for use of your shower."

"Of course," Dr. Edwards replied. He took Mr. Spahl's hand in both of his and shook it firmly. "Do you have everything you need?"

"I think we do," Mr. Spahl said as he glanced over at the ambulance. "Thank you for this also."

"Safe travels to you and yours," Dr. Edwards offered. "Our very best wishes for your continued wellbeing."

Dominick made a point to walk Mrs. Spahl to the Tahoe, "Let me get that." He insisted as he opened the door for her.

"Thank you, Dominick," Mrs. Spahl said as she stepped up on the running board and pulled herself into the passenger seat. "Take care of yourself."

"I will," Dominick assured her. He forced a smile over the look of concern he was unable to hide. "You keep these young fellas fed and keep yourself safe."

"I will," Mrs. Spahl said confidently. She gave a final smile and nod before she pulled the door closed.

Matt stepped back from the Jeep where he loaded gear and supplies only to find himself face to face with Shaw.

"Thank you for not turning us away," Shaw said appreciatively as he extended his hand.

Matt gave Shaw a firm handshake, "Sorry for the way I acted." He said with genuine embarrassment.

"I don't know how I would have acted if it was my brother and I was in your position," Shaw offered. "Anyway, it's over. I hope you get to where you're going."

"Thank you," Matt said. "I hope you do too and I hope your sister's alright."

"She's on the mend," Shaw answered. "Thank you."

"What's your plan?" Matt asked before he threw the last duffle bag in the back of the Jeep.

"Stay here another day or two, until my sister's ready to travel," Shaw answered. "Then we're off."

"Canada, was it?" Matt inquired.

"Alaska," Shaw corrected. "Dominick's got people there from his Navy days. The thought is between the terrain, weather, and lack of population it may be the perfect place to be."

"Yeah, I can see that," Matt said with a nod. "Good luck and be careful."

"You too," Shaw said as he turned to leave.

"Um, hey," Matt called as Shaw turned back. "You made a good point about who the fight's really with. I won't be quick to forget it."

"Glad to hear it," Shaw replied. He paused for a moment and asked. "What's the end goal, for you I mean?"

Matt stood for a moment as he contemplated Shaw's question, "What's the end goal? You mean beyond the obvious survival?"

"Yes," Shaw answered. "Beyond that. What do you need to get out of this?"

"I need to maintain normalcy for the people I love," Matt answered as his eyes narrowed. "That's my end goal."

Tamara stood towards the back of the group. Her arms were crossed and she was visibly upset. She had a difficult time as she tried to maintain her composure, "Paul." She began in a shaky voice as she nervously stepped forward.

"Hey," Paul said gently as he looked up at her.

No sooner had their gaze met than tears burst from her eyes, "Paul, I'm..." Tamara sputtered.

"I know," Paul said tenderly. He could feel a lump form in his throat. The argument didn't seem to be theirs anymore. It felt more like a conversation between two strangers. "I'm just so sorry."

"It's just..." Tamara began as tears ran down her cheeks.

"A lot all at once," Paul offered as he put his arms around her. "I know. For me too."

"I wish we could..." Tamara started as she sobbed into his chest.

"I do too," Paul whispered. "The world's a more dangerous place now. Violence is bound to be part of it and I don't want you subjected to that side of me."

Samantha took Tamara by the shoulders and guided her away from Paul. She handed Tamara a tissue and put a comforting arm around her, "It'll be ok." Samantha offered as she tried to reassure her.

Paul and Tamara stood for a moment on the sidewalk and stared at each other. They were only feet apart but the space between them felt infinite. Silently they longed for their perfect world where they could be together.

"Keep yourself safe," Paul said as he searched for the right words. "With any luck this'll all get sorted out quick and we can see about picking up where we left off."

Tamara nodded and wiped her eyes, "I'd like that."

They stood for another quiet moment before Paul turned to walk away. His exit was interrupted by Samantha.

"Not even a kiss goodbye?" Samantha inquired with a puzzled look on her face.

"No," Paul answered as he turned back. He grinned and shook his head. "This isn't goodbye."

The shadows were long by the time the caravan pulled off the road and on to the farm's gravel driveway. Over the decades the landscape changed significantly. New barns were constructed, tree lines removed and fields expanded.

Regardless of the aesthetics it was a place Matt and Christian knew well and where they felt safe. It didn't feel like home, but something much more. They knew no matter what happened or how long the duration, there'd be no place better to weather the storm. As a base of operations, the farm's mountain top location offered geographical advantages.

With the ambulance in the lead, the vehicles rolled slowly past the large white farm house. They parked parallel to the sizeable garden which consumed a large piece of property on the south west side directly behind the house. On the opposite side some feet removed from the vehicles was a small red barn. The old wooden structure housed pigs when the brothers were young, but was now used for storage.

"Mr. Spahl, can you make sure everything gets unpacked?" Matt asked as he exited the ambulance. "Christian and I are going to head up to the house."

"We'll take care of it," Mr. Spahl assured him. "Jeff, Paul, Kurt." He called as he motioned to the vehicles. "Patrick you too. Let's get everything unpacked and staged over there."

The gravel made a distinct crunch under their boots as Matt and Christian approached the house. They were surprised to find Bill on the front porch waiting for them.

"Think he knew we were coming?" Christian asked curiously.

"Always possible," Matt answered. "Is there anything Bill doesn't know?"

Bill was average height and heavy set; yet still more than formidable for a man in his early-80's. His hair had long since gone gray and several patches even turned completely white. His unkept beard was a topic his wife Marge constantly addressed. Their 50-year marriage saw the two of them travel the world together. Age and a decline in Marge's health unfortunately forced limitations on them both.

The property had been in his family for generations and in addition to being a farmer he spent more than three decades as an educator. Despite his responsibilities, he made being a husband, and father to his daughter his number one priority. Now a grandfather, Bill spent much of his time with his granddaughter, Riley. He took great pride as he introduced her to all facets farm life.

Bill looked as if he had just come from the barn. He stood on the front porch in his socks. Mud was caked on his faded blue jeans. The sleeves of his brown and white plaid shirt were rolled up to the middle of his forearms. A silver watch band with dark face encircled his left wrist. His outer shirt was unbuttoned to reveal a sweat-stained white V-neck t-shirt beneath. There was a soft black glasses case in the breast pocket of his shirt which contained his reading glasses.

Bill's hands were tucked into the waistband of his jeans. He let out a deep sigh of relief and a smile stretched across his bearded face when Matt and Christian reached the sidewalk, "Glad you finally made it!" He called. "I was expecting you boys two days ago."

continued in paradise, volume 2...

POST SCRIPT

Now that you have finished PARADISE, Volume 1, you may have questions. Allow me to offer some semblance of an answer.
Who was Jack Tallon that Dr. Singer described in chapter 22? Were Ralph and Tyler able to recover from their injuries? What happened to Matt Chico and his parents? Were they able to make it home and if so, did his son arrive? What happened to Rob and Kevin? What happened to Giovanni and Heather? Were they able to make it home? Was Paul able to return to the hospital and reconnect with Dr. Singer? Did the group find safety on the farm? Did they organize search parties to locate their loved ones who were still unaccounted for? Were they able to get answers about how the outbreak began?
These questions and more will be addressed in, PARADISE, A Zombie Apocalypse Saga, Volume 2.
Until then dear reader, keep the blinds closed, lights low and doors locked.
If the wind carries the ominous moans of the undead, assemble your loved ones and avoid the "Safe Zones"!

ABOUT THE AUTHOR

Matthew M. Stracco's literary works have appeared in The Mind Carpenter Literary Magazine (1993 & 1994), Weird New Jersey Magazine (2001) and the Federal Manager Magazine (Spring & Fall 2019). He currently lives somewhere in the Garden State and is ready to move to a more defendable location should the dead rise.